For Fallon.

Because I said I would.

ACKNOWLEDGMENTS

My family: You guys came together and had gotten behind me on this project. Thank you. You took me by surprise on that one. No offense. Your grace in putting up with all of my doings, even the bad ones, has not gone unnoticed. And thanks for letting me use the family computer that this story was both started and finished on, and for the countless amounts of paper and ink used to print it. I am grateful.

Ric: Thanks, buddy, for the wonderful and thorough editing job on this manuscript. Your criticism was the first step on the long and arduous journey called editing. Thanks for sticking with me.

Grace: For your kindness and support for all my creative efforts. Thank you. I owe you one.

Alan Moore: For teaching me the importance of honesty in the written word. Thank you for inspiring me to write.

Stephen King: For continuing to teach me to write through your work. You showed me that it's okay to have a dark side.

Jesus Christ: Thanks, Lord for being there for me when no one else cared. And thanks for Your Word, upon which this story is based.

FIRST NOTE

I was born and raised in Winnipeg, Canada and have rarely been anywhere else. I've traveled as far south as Chicago and as far north as Flin Flon. I've never been overseas and the farthest I've ever been from my home province of Manitoba was to Penhold, Alberta.

The story that you hold in your hands takes place in two locations: Winnipeg and Toronto. Personally, I have never been to Toronto but I did take the time to learn about the city a little. For both cities, the locations and settings in this book are both real and imaginative. The make-believe settings were created for the pure joy of it and because, simply put, I could. There was something about being in control of an arena that was solely mine and didn't exist anywhere except for on the page that I enjoyed. Those who know each of those cities will be able to pick out those differences.

I hope you smile at the names of places you do recognize, and equally smile at those of my imagining.

Now sit back, put up your feet, and read on.

The darkness stirs. A nightmare occurs. And the Beast is sure to find you.

I hope you enjoy my story.

- APF

"Then I saw another beast, coming out of the earth. He had two horns like a lamb, but he spoke like a dragon."

Revelation 13:11 (NIV)

PROLOGUE

Cold, dark and gray. That seemed to be the standard for cemeteries nowadays. That also seemed to be the standard of life for Harry Thomas, who had been standing at the foot of his wife's grave for nearly two hours now. His wife, Lauren, had been dead for nearly a week. And earlier that evening, he had pledged that he would spend the entire night with her, and keep her company.

Lauren had been the victim of a convenience store robbery. She had been working the later shift, as she usually had, and was cashing out for the evening when a tall man in a black coat entered the store, pulling a sawed-off shotgun out of the dark backpack he had slung over his shoulder. He had made Lauren give him the money that was in the till and as many cigarette cartons as his bag could hold.

Accidentally dropping one of the cartons on the floor, the man had taken her slip of the hand as a sign of stalling, and had opened fire. Lauren had received a bullet just below her heart and had bled to death in the ambulance no more than twenty minutes after.

Now, looking at the tombstone that marked his wife's grave, Harry remembered that haunting night at the St. Boniface Hospital Morgue where he had identified her body. The memory of seeing Lauren, half covered in a gleaming white bed sheet—would stay burned in his mind forever.

The moonlight barely reached the earth through the blanket of heavy clouds that graced the sky. A few drops of rain started to fall, quickly accelerating to a downpour. It was the type of rain that was neither cool nor refreshing, but rather like wet, tiny spikes pricking the skin.

Harry looked up toward the sky and shook his head in disbelief at the dark cloud that was setting in high above him. Of all nights to rain, it had to be this one.

"Damn," Harry said, and glanced down, watching the water splash against the etching of Lauren's name on her tombstone. He decided that he would leave and come back to spend the night with her another time, perhaps when the cosmos would cut him a break and withhold the rain for a night.

Harry pulled the collar of his trench coat up, covering his neck, and splashed toward the cemetery gate. He reached the exit and stood at the border between the world of the dead and the living. He rethought his decision. He felt ashamed, guilty. He had made his wife a promise and it was a promise that he intended—needed—to keep. He *would* spend the night, rain or not.

As if the night had heard his challenge, the rain beat down even harder. Harry was soon soaked to the bone, the rain paying no heed to his tan colored jacket.

Sighing, he turned back toward Lauren's grave. When he reached it, he knelt down and closed his eyes.

"I promised you, hon," he told her. "I'll stay the night even though it seems I'm not wanted here. At least not by Mother Nature, anyway."

He smirked at his poor attempt at humor, and almost hoped for Lauren to respond by saying that he could go back home to where it was dry.

But she didn't.

Harry drew a deep breath and held it, focusing himself. He had to stay. Had to. Not once throughout his marriage to Lauren had he ever gone back on his word, and he wasn't about to start now. It was only the thought of being warm that made the idea of going home seem appealing, but there was nothing there for him to go home to. Nothing but an empty, dark house and a few leftover slices of pizza.

Harry exhaled, feeling more collected. "I'm cold. I'm wet. I just want to find some place dry. You understand that, don't you?" he asked her.

Lauren didn't give any sign that she did.

Harry ran his fingers through his black hair. He trotted deeper into the cemetery hoping to find shelter under one of the trees. After standing beneath a few of them, it seemed that none of them would provide enough cover from the ever-persisting rain.

Harry thought for a moment. There was an alternative—an option other then leaving the cemetery, or possibly finding shelter in a nearby bus stop. A bus shelter would be much more pleasant than what he had in mind. But it was something that he would have to do if he were to avoid catching pneumonia, and still keep his promise.

He hated this moment of indecision but knew that he needed to stay in the cemetery. Needed to be near Lauren.

Harry walked over to the nearest mausoleum, hoping that perhaps its owner had accidentally forgotten to lock the door, or that maybe vandals or occultists had smashed open the lock.

Harry approached the mausoleum door and read the name above the entrance: MANDALAY. He shuddered. Something didn't feel right. He assumed that it was just his knowing that the mausoleum was filled with dead bodies that made him squeamish. Wiping the rain off his face, he swallowed his fear. Harry reached out his shivering hand, closing it around the stone handle, the cold of the handle felt all the way up his arm. He pulled. The door opened.

"Here we go," he said to himself, and entered.

Inside, the coffins were stacked one on top of the other: four in length and five down. Each coffin was encased in a stone holding, each holding labeled by a marble plaque.

Through the dim lighting of the moon that seeped through the cracks in the stone roof, Harry studied the holdings, wondering to whom this large family had once belonged to and if any other of their family members were still alive or not. He also wondered what type of family would feel the need to build a temple for their family members' remains.

Harry shook his coat, ridding himself of the excess rain. He was cold and still drenched to the bone. Goose bumps formed on his skin.

The artwork on the marble plaques was unlike anything Harry had ever seen. The markings weren't elaborate or breathtaking in any way but each had its own captivating design, all displaying beautiful symbols and letters of a language he couldn't understand. The marble looked as if it had been etched in to very carefully, each design possibly meant to convey something about the deceased person.

Harry turned his attention back to the door. He opened it and peered outside, hoping that the rain had let up a bit. It hadn't. It kept beating down just as strong as before. He closed the door and blew on his cold fingers, remembering how his wife used to blow on them after he would come in from shoveling the snow off the driveway. The memory pained his heart. He loved Lauren so much and now everything seemed so empty without her. He didn't know if he would be able to move on and let her rest in peace.

Through the gray gloom that lit the burial house, Harry noticed that, opposite to the coffins, was a picture frame hanging on the wall. He stepped closer to get a better look. The frame was made of dark oak. Glass lay over the frame, protecting the brown tinted piece of paper beneath. Written on it, using similar symbols and designs that adorned the marble plaques, were what appeared to be names. They were in black ink and they fanned downward like a Christmas tree. There were at least twenty names in all. It looked to be a family tree.

Harry touched the glass and traced some of the symbols with his fingertips. The glass was warm.

"Odd," Harry commented. He rubbed his hands together and turned around to have another look at the coffins. His hands stopped moving when he saw that the carvings in the plaques had disappeared, leaving only a smooth, polished surface.

He reached out to touch it. As his hand swam through the air, Harry grew suddenly warm, a swirl of anxiety passing through him.

His vision went black—and then there was nothing.

* * *

Harry woke up lying down on his back in a small, confined space. Both his chest and back were pressed firmly up against something hard. The smell of where he lay was musty, but at the same time surprisingly sweet like the way sugar smells in a cup of hot water. He had a paralyzing epiphany. Was he lying inside a coffin?

"Oh, Lord," he breathed into the darkness around him.

He thought that he might be dreaming all this, yet it felt all too real. The sweet, musty smell was a tangible one—a 'real life' scent, confirming all the more that he was not asleep. He had forgotten Lauren and his promise, his mind focusing only on where he was.

Hands and arms squished by his sides, Harry wriggled his body, trying to free at least one of his arms. They were caught between him and what he assumed to be the lid of the coffin.

Harry pulled his hand upward toward the direction he was facing, turned his palm outward, and felt the hard surface above him. It was smooth, grainy in places, and very thin in others. Hopefully, in this case, *thin* meant *weak*. Harry pressed forward, trying to free himself. Nothing happened. He was trapped.

For several minutes, Harry banged the inside of the coffin lid (which was more like tapping because of the confined space), and shouted for help.

The inside of the coffin grew dreadfully warm, reminding Harry that he had only a limited supply of air. If he didn't try to conserve his air, he would suffocate quickly. Then again, it would probably be better to suffocate sooner, instead of conserving air, prolonging an inevitable death.

Like a child throwing a fit on the floor of a toy store, Harry wriggled and squirmed inside the coffin, banging all sides. Exhausted from his efforts, he pressed upward against the lid in one final effort. He pushed with the palms of his hands and the front of his knees until all the strength was sapped from his muscles. It felt as if another force were pushing from the other side of the lid.

"Let me out!" Harry cried, sucking up another mouthful of the remaining oxygen.

Harry pushed against the lid again. Something pushed back.

"Let me out! I didn't do anything! What do you want?" More air swallowed. More seconds of his remaining life stolen.

Harry started to panic, the words pouring out of his mouth slurring together into gibberish.

"Letmeouthelpcomeonwhatdidldol'llgiveyouanythingI'mgoingtodie!"

He went on spewing out words until he became too overheated to utter another breath. His eyes, heavy now, started to droop. He was completely helpless. All strength went from his body. *This is it! I'm dying! I'm going to die! Lord, save me! Please! I need You!* He could almost see his words dance before his eyes.

Then there was silence. Quiet hummed in his ears.

Harry twitched. He was unconscious, his body jerking from the lack of oxygen. He needed air or soon he would be dead.

His body twitched one final time, violently, causing his back to arch, his chest to shoot upward. The lid of the coffin hinged open. Harry instinctively gasped for air.

He was breathing. He was alive!

After regaining full consciousness, his blurred vision clearing, the humming in his ears quieting—Harry found himself to be in a dimly lit room. The light was yellow and warm. The room was both soothing and comforting, feeling as if a hot blanket was being wrapped around him. His skin prickled like it does when you put on a hot sweater fresh from the dryer. Harry blinked his eyes, feeling disorientated. Reality opened up to him. He recalled everything that had happened—being in the rain looking for shelter, the mausoleum and the artwork on the caskets, his sudden awakening in a coffin, the struggle, then nothing.

He sat up in the coffin. Placing his palms on the casket's edges for support, Harry helped himself to stand. His clothes were still wet. He wasn't in the mausoleum anymore. He was in a room almost twice its size, each wall lined with old leather bound books. The room wasn't dark and cold like the mausoleum, but its opposite: gold with warmth. The walls were made of pale oak, the ceiling made of a darker wood Harry could not name. He was in a library. It didn't make sense.

He looked around for a door, for some sort of way out. Nothing. Not a single opening anywhere. He was trapped again.

Harry was surprised that after everything this evening, he wasn't deathly afraid. Instead, it felt more like a confusing dream that makes perfect sense when experiencing it.

Harry started to walk, trying to keep himself warm. He approached one of the bookshelves. Each red leather volume it contained was dated according to a year and a country. He dared not touch anything. *If I did that*, Harry thought, *I would probably faint and wake up some place else.*

Harry was startled when something cold and invisible grabbed his hand. He couldn't move and he couldn't breathe. Worse, he couldn't find his voice to scream. This couldn't be happening. The cold sensation of another hand grabbing his own paralyzed every part of his body. His pounding heart was the only thing letting him know that he was still alive. In his head he heard himself scream for help.

The cold hand guided his fingers to one of the red leather books and forced him to pull the volume out. ENGLAND 1903, the label on the spine read.

Book in hand, something knocked Harry down to the floor, hitting his head against the wooden boards. His body went limp and a sulphurous air swept through his lungs. He coughed. The muscles in his hands unwillingly tightened around the book's covers. Harry sat himself up, unable to let go of the book. He tried to stand, but an unseen weight kept him down. Giving into the elusive unseen force, he brought his knees to his chest, his head between his legs. The room smelled of dying gas, adding to the scent of the sweat on his skin.

The book became hot. Harry's hand immediately went to release it, but his grip only tightened. Without any will of his own, Harry opened the book to the first page.

A thick drop of sweat fell from his forehead, evaporating on contact when it hit the book's light brown paper. The first page of the book was blank. On the next was a series of shapes and swirls akin to the ones he had seen earlier in the mausoleum. The third page was blank as well except for a small, twisting symbol placed in the exact center of the page. An almost transparent sheet was the fourth and the fifth was written in an old English script. It read: Henry McLure, A Man for Children, Entry No. 03964. He started to involuntarily read. Despite all efforts, he could not look anywhere save for the page in front of him. This is what he read:

Henry McLure was always partial to his next-door neighbor's daughter, Mary-Anne. We watched as Henry, a forty-seven year old man from Dublin, took a liking to the innocent twelve year old. We remember watching him late at night, studying her bedroom window, waiting for her silhouette to grace the worn curtains that hung there. During the first few occasions, we only wanted to familiarize him with her nightly routine, to get him to know her better.

Henry grew to enjoy watching her undress in the moonlight, his imagination replacing her silhouette with clear pictures of her naked body.

Soon, his nightly study overflowed into the day and he would visit Mary-Anne's family, asking for a cup of sugar or to borrow a dustpan, each time hoping that Mary-Anne would be the one to answer the door. She usually did since school was out for the summer and she would spend her days at home helping with chores and preparing meals.

A Stranger Dead

Henry loved it when she answered the door. She wore white slippers, a conservative, patterned dress pulled up tightly around her neck, the silk material resting on her young developing breasts.

One day, after returning from Mary-Anne's home after borrowing the town newsletter, Henry went in to his bedroom and turned off the lights. He then undressed and lay on his bed. Reveling in the darkness and the feel of his body above the cool sheets, he fantasized about making love to Mary-Anne. In his minds eye she would rest on top of him, looking at him with a faultless trust, willing to obey his every command.

We smiled as Henry continued this private activity for several weeks, each time his mind retreating into a sexual paradise with the child. Even when he had nothing to borrow from his neighbors, Henry liked to make an effort to see her. Henry would peek into the backyard and watch her plant flowers—tulips, as we recall. Or see her play with her puppy, Charlie, on the sunny days. Then, as a habit, he would go back to his bedroom and pleasure himself, thinking of Mary-Anne.

Then, in the fall of 1903, Henry stopped visiting his young neighbor. He stopped leaving his house. He even stopped leaving his bedroom except for using the privy and getting the occasional scrap of food to eat. We were pleased with the progress we were making with him. We were pleased that he spent all day lying naked on top of his bed sheets, masturbating to Mary-

Anne's image. He had been one of our most successful projects up to that date.

His hunger for her continued to grow and soon his solitary fun was not enough. On the eve of October 23, 1903, Henry crept quietly into Mary-Anne's backyard and stood by the shudders to her window. He saw that they were slightly open and if he listened carefully, he could hear her breathe, hear her dream.

Through the cracks in the shudders and just beyond the curtains, he was able to see her, see her beautiful chest rise and fall, see her precious body wriggle underneath the sheets.

Seeing Mary-Anne in nocturnal slumber aroused Henry. He gripped his crotch with childish glee, needing to have her.

Back in the library, Harry closed the book, overpowering by sheer will the unseen forces that tried to keep it open. His brow was wet with sweat from the horrible tale that he was reading. The document disgusted him so much that he leaned forward on his knees, bringing up his supper from earlier that evening. The salty, sweet substance poured from his mouth, producing a murky puddle on the floor.

Harry fell over into a fetal position and cried. He was too scared to think, too scared to breathe, and too scared to react. A warm wind swept through the room and Harry faded away into welcoming blackness.

All was dark and he heard nothing.

Harry was dreaming. A deep sleep. The kind where after you wake up your body still feels heavy. He dreamed that he and Lauren were back in Flin Flon where they had rented a cabin every Christmas. The two of them were huddled together in front of a fire, resting in each other's arms, feeling their warm skin pressing together. They had just made love. They sat in front of the fire wrapped in a large, soft quilt made of down, simply reveling in each other's presence.

Harry stroked her hair and she rubbed his leg. They both let out the occasional sigh of comfort. Although, in the dream, it felt perfectly natural to be with Lauren, deep down inside himself, Harry knew that something wasn't right. In the back of his mind he somehow knew that they weren't supposed to be together. Not anymore, anyway.

The dream blurred and Harry was walking in a desert with remnants of old buildings spanning out all around him. Everything his eyes caught site of looked dead, the only hint of color coming from the gold sand beneath his feet.

As he walked into the ruins, he saw the MANDALAY mausoleum. He approached it, feeling an irresistible urge to go inside. Warily, he entered and closed the door behind him. From the doorway, directly in front of him, Lauren lay naked beneath white silk bed sheets, her sleeping chambers regal. She was sitting upright with her hand pressing against the sheet that covered her chest.

She smoothed the crinkled area of bed sheet beside her in a circular motion, urging Harry to come lay beside her.

When Harry approached and pulled back the bed sheet to climb in to bed next to her, he jumped back when he saw the red leather book. The book of ENGLAND 1903.

When Harry turned away from the book, wanting to run, the locale turned to a neighborhood from long ago. Across from him was a window with worn shutters hanging loosely in the frame. They were closed. He was looking at the window to Mary-Anne's bedroom.

Harry saw Henry standing outside the window. He watched as Henry opened the window, pushed the old worn curtains aside, and climbed inside Mary-Anne's bedroom.

Harry's perspective changed and now he was inside Mary Anne's bedroom, with Henry climbing in through the window. Mary-Anne was sleeping in her bed, her hand coming out once from under her blankets, scratching her cheek.

After stepping into the room, Henry took a few moments to watch the child sleep before climbing into the bed next to her. The child awoke with a start.

"Mr. McLure? What are you doing here? Wha—" she started but was quickly hushed when Henry covered her mouth, cutting her off.

He raised a finger to his nose and signaled for her to keep her voice down. He removed his hand and Mary-Anne spoke in a soft whisper. "What are you doing here?"

Henry didn't say a word as his large, rough hand encompassed her small breast. Mary-Anne screamed and in reaction Henry swung his fist into her right temple, knocking her unconscious.

"I'm sorry, my dear," he told her. "I didn't want to harm you."

Henry then heard frantic footsteps hurrying down the hallway outside Mary Anne's bedroom. Henry scooped up Mary-Anne and climbed out the window, carrying her into his own backyard.

In the distance somewhere, Harry could hear Mary-Anne's father shouting for her. Her parents were in her bedroom, having approached the window, searching the night for their daughter.

Harry, who could do nothing but watch the events taking place, found himself whisked away into Henry's backyard as Henry laid Mary-Anne on the ground, carefully, as if she was made of glass. Henry slowly stripped her of her nightgown and folded it up neatly, putting it behind her head as a pillow. Harry tried to run and stop the maniac, but he couldn't move. He tried to shout, but couldn't find the breath.

Harry watched as Henry parted Mary-Anne's legs and went down to taste her. Harry winced in disgust and tried to look away. He couldn't. His eyes were being forced to watch. He had no choice. Henry then moved on top of Mary-Anne and entered her.

Between Henry's rise and fall, Harry could see large speckles of blood on Mary-Anne's naked stomach; her face twitching in subconscious pain as Henry ripped her apart. Harry's chest and stomach ached. The saliva inside his mouth turned acrid. He refused to believe what he was witnessing.

Henry writhed back and forth, his pace quickening. Harry wanted to close his eyes when he heard Henry's orgasmic cry echo in the night. He couldn't. Something kept them open. Harry then heard a squishing then popping sound accompanied by Mary-Anne's unconscious scream. Her parents, somewhere in the background, were shouting something Harry couldn't make out.

Then all was quiet.

Henry lied limp on top of the child. Mary-Anne was still passed out from the pain of having her genitals forced to do something they were not ready to do and from the hard blow to her head that Henry had administered earlier.

Harry wanted to scream in anger and cry out to God. Tears streamed down his face.

* * *

Harry woke up again in the library, his face lying in a pool of vomit and sweat. The dream was over. Thank God.

He was trembling, his vision blurring. A cloud of smoke settled on top of ENGLAND 1903. The stench of sulfur pierced his nose. Harry tried to refrain himself from throwing up but to no avail. His body lurched as he brought up the remaining half-digested food in his stomach. He couldn't remember what it was he had eaten earlier. Nothing mattered save for the scream of the innocent child, echoing in his mind.

After spiting up small amounts of sour, milky liquid, Harry wiped the tears from his eyes and tried to stand.

His legs shook, barely able to hold his own weight. Dizziness raged through his head. He let the spinning clouds of green and blue fade from his vision before walking over to the coffin that he had taken him into the library.

Harry wanted to leave. He would give anything for the chance. He needed to find out *how* to leave. The library didn't seem to have any openings anywhere.

Harry, still shaky, crouched by the coffin. He looked around its borders, trying to see exactly how the coffin was able to get here in the first place. *I should have looked for a way out when I first got here,* he thought. *Instead, I took a look around. Idiot.*

The coffin was pushed up tight against the wall. Harry gripped one of the corners and pulled, hoping to reveal an exit.

"Figures," he said, when all he saw was the oak boards of the wall behind.

Harry fell back and sat with his legs partially crossed, his arms wrapped around his knees.

Several thoughts swarmed his head, everything from this being a dream to something as outlandish as an alien abduction becoming a plausible conclusion.

Sitting motionless, his eyes gazed blankly at the ground ahead of him. "It's going to be all right. I'm going to be okay," he said, trying to reassure himself.

He chanted those words, his mind nullified, his body rocking back and forth in a steady rhythm. *It's going to be all right.* Back. *I'm going to be* okay. Forth. *It's going to be all right.* Back. *I'm going to be okay.* Forth. *It's going to be all right.* Back. *I'm going to be okay.* Over and over.

He was tired. He curled up on the warm floor and fell asleep.

* * *

Harry had been in the library for over a day now. Repeatedly, the cold hand that had touched him and led him to ENGLAND 1903 made him read more of the books in the library as well. Soon the days melted into weeks, the weeks into months, and the months into years. Time slipped away as Harry began living through a series of lonely moments, and of pain. Living through a series of dreams and of nightmares, his mind barely aware of his true surroundings.

He had no need for food or water, or anything else. Whatever supernatural force was holding him captive, sustained him and kept him alive.

PART ONE

THE MEETING

Twenty-five years later…

Chapter One

With the flick of a lighter Gwen Reeves lit another cigarette. She was sitting in the back booth at Fizzler's, a coffee shop located on the top floor of Brentmere College, Winnipeg.

She, like a lot of the students, liked to come here on breaks or spares between classes, grab a booth, and sip coffee while thumbing through the latest chapters assigned that day. Today the topic in her Religious Studies class had been "The Holes in the Human Soul," a chapter in a book titled, *Soul and Heart: A Study of Religion Today.* Its main focus was to explain why people are attracted to different religions, and why they normally migrate to a religion that best suits their needs. This, however, was only one of the courses she was taking. The others, though somewhat similar, dealt with the occult and their practices. She was also taking a course that studied magic and its belief system.

Gwen had enrolled in these courses because she was fascinated with all things supernatural and what rational thinking couldn't explain, and she wished to further her understanding of the worlds that existed beyond her own. She knew she could have taken a more scientific approach to this field, such as a course in temporal theory, quantum dimensions, and the study of black holes—but to her, that defeated the purpose of believing in something that could not be seen.

Besides, what's the point in believing in something if you can prove it? Isn't that the whole point of faith? Gwen thought as she sipped her coffee. She watched the smoke curl off the end of her cigarette. Smoking. A nasty habit she had picked up four years ago and had not been able to quit.

She had been in the coffee shop for nearly an hour and she still had another hour to go before she had her afternoon class at 2:30 P.M.

Gwen was about to take another drag off her cigarette when Marty Bones approached her table.

"Hey, Gwenny, got a minute?" he asked, plopping himself down on the seat across from her.

"Sure," she replied.

Marty pushed Gwen's books, which were piled up on the table, aside. Now he was able to see her better. She looked beautiful today. Her dark hair was tied back tight in a ponytail, fully showing off her hazel eyes. She wore a white sweater and blue jeans.

"Listen," he began, "my parents are going away for all of next week and I was wondering if you wanted to stay with me?" He ran his fingers through his own dark hair as he waited for her response.

Gwen and Marty had been dating for over six months but, unfortunately, for both of them, neither had a place all to their own. Gwen shared an apartment with three other girls, and Marty, at age twenty-eight, still lived with his parents.

When Gwen had first met him she thought that he was too old to be a student. But when they became friends, she quickly learned that he acted as if he was ten years younger, and was sometimes just as naive.

Gwen, herself, was twenty-three. She didn't see being younger than him to be a bad thing, but when he would sometimes sing along with the jukebox at the pool hall using the pool cue for a microphone, she couldn't help but wonder how serious a person she had hooked herself up with.

Then again, I'm serious enough for the two us. That was Gwen's usual thought when she was tempted to tell Marty to smarten up every time he did something that would turn heads.

Gwen sat silently, pretending to consider his offer.

After a moment she smiled, then said, "Absolutely. Of course."

Marty's brown eyes lit up. "Great! Tell you what, I'll meet you outside after your class and then maybe we could grab some dinner. You can tell me which astral deity is stronger and why, and I can tell you about this wicked picture I drew today. We'll meet at the usual spot, okay?" Marty was always beside himself every time he mentioned that he had drawn a new picture.

Secretly, he had never appreciated Gwen's studies because he believed that we were all responsible for our own destinies, and that any thought of a higher power was foolish. Marty was more into his artwork and how he can amaze any person who was looking at it. Marty's main expertise was airbrushing portraits of humans and animals. He had once given Gwen a picture of herself that he made about a month or so after they had started going out. Gwen had been astonished at its realism, the image appearing as if it were a photograph.

"Whatever suits ya," Gwen said.

"Good. I gotta run. I left a painting to dry this morning and I gotta go grab it before Mr. Shamblin locks up."

Marty leaned over the table and gave her a peck on the cheek.

"See ya, cutie," Gwen said, touching him on the shoulder.

"Later. Oh yeah, by the way," Marty paused and started sniffing the air just as dogs do when a scent catches their attention, "something's burning." He eyed her cigarette. "Oh, it's you. Pee-eww!"

Marty smiled and walked out of the coffee shop.

Gwen smiled after him.

As silly as Marty was, she loved him. There was no doubt about that. He had brought out the lighter side in her, one that wasn't so serious and looking at life as a job. Gwen liked, no, *loved* the way he made her feel. Regular daily pressures disappeared when he was around.

Gwen stubbed out her cigarette and pulled her books back out in front of her. She supposed that it wouldn't hurt to do some review for her next class. She opened her book and started to read.

* * *

Gwen sat with her back slouched against the base of a large oak tree on the front lawn of the college's grounds, waiting for Marty to meet her. It was now 4:53 P.M. even though to Gwen it felt much later. Every part of her was tired. She had been up late the night before, unable to sleep. She had slipped in to one of those states where no matter what position you tried lying in, you couldn't get comfortable. All her tossing and turning had kept her awake, her body eventually grabbing its second wind, keeping her up even longer. On top of that, all her classes that day had involved heavy reading and writing.

Sitting comfortably, Gwen had just closed her eyes and begun to feel the soothing comfort of sleep nearing when she sensed someone sit down next to her.

"Hey," Marty said, nudging her shoulder, waking her up.

"Hi," Gwen returned. As soon as she stood up she got a mild head rush, but quickly shook it off.

Marty reached down beside her feet, hoisted her backpack, and swung it over one shoulder. "Man, what do you got in here? Bricks?"

Marty readjusted the strap on his shoulder so that it was sitting more comfortably.

Gwen started walking. Marty followed. "Try three text books and one honkin' huge binder stuffed to the gills," she said. Those who knew that Gwen and Marty were a couple assumed that Gwen was the one in control, what with the way she would sometimes seem to boss him around. But in reality, it was an equal partnership and each of them carried their own weight. That, Gwen had always figured, was why they worked so well together.

The two of them trotted across the long stretch of grass that led from Brentmere College to Main Street. Reaching the bus stop, Marty let down Gwen's bag and straightened up, slowly feeling the blood flow back into his neck and shoulder.

After five or six minutes their bus stopped in front of them, bringing with it the unpleasant smell of exhaust. They both wrinkled their noses at the stench. They paid their fare and looked for a place to sit. The bus was packed, with not a seat in sight. Fortunately for Gwen, a man got up and let her have his seat. Marty frowned at the gentleman's chivalry, and had no choice but to stand in front of her. He gripped the balance bar above his head and handed Gwen her bag, landing it with full force on her lap.

"Ow," she said.

"Whoops," Marty said half-jokingly at his carelessness. Gwen gave him a quick grin.

Across from her she caught a disheveled looking man eyeing her up and down. *Homeless*, she figured. *Probably scrapped together enough money to get off the streets for one afternoon. It's sad.*

Gwen looked up at Marty and tapped his arm, getting his attention. Her eyes went from his to the homeless man, then back to his again. It took him a moment for her meaning to register. Catching on, Marty stepped more directly in front of her, blocking the other man's view.

"Thanks," Gwen murmured. She hated it when people stared at her. Marty was the only exception.

He smiled back at her and audibly exhaled a day's worth of stress. "So where do you want to go to eat?" he asked.

"Doesn't really matter to me, just not burgers again, 'kay?"

"I thought about going someplace nice, y'know, with a bit of atmosphere—but I'm somewhat short on funds right now so I was thinking maybe we can save that sort of thing for next week."

Gwen thought of a substitute. "Why not Bubble Perk? It's nice there and it's cheap."

"Sure," Marty said, looking up at his hand that was awkwardly gripping the bar above him. He hated standing.

The bus ride took the usual twenty minutes to get from the inner city to the suburbs. Gwen and Marty were fortunate enough to get off school before the 5:30 P.M. rush hour.

About a block away from Bubble Perk, they got off the bus, having to double back a block toward the restaurant. They went inside and a waitress greeted them, asking their smoking preference. Marty was just about to say non-smoking when Gwen cut him off. He didn't care too much for cigarette smoke but put up with Gwen's habit anyway.

The waitress seated them in a booth in the middle of the restaurant. They each ordered a coffee. When the waitress left, Marty fumbled with the buckles to his backpack and Gwen lit a long awaited cigarette. She took a long, satisfying drag, breathing the smoke out as if she had just tasted all of life's passions at once.

Finding what he was looking for, Marty produced a large cardboard tube from his bag. He unscrewed its lid. Gwen saw what he was doing and moved her ashtray, making sure that the table was free of ashes. She knew he was about to unveil his latest work and it was important to him that the table was clean.

Marty carefully pulled a rolled up piece of shiny paper out of the cardboard case and set down the tube beside him. He unrolled the paper. Gwen put her cigarette in the ashtray.

"Wow," she said, impressed.

Marty held the picture in front of her. "What do you think?"

"Seriously. Wow. It's very real…it looks like something you would see collected in a fantasy calendar. Very good."

Gwen stared at it, not telling Marty that it was stirring something inside her. His picture showed a dingy gray, rocky terrain in the foreground with an old, leafless oak tree coming out of the ground toward the right. The sky was a swirl of red with black cloud that reflected in a lake of crashing waves below. There were shadows embedded deep in the rocks, giving the painting dimension. Its use of airbrushing gave it a photo realistic quality. Stylistically, in the bottom, right hand corner, it was signed "Marty Bones."

The dark feeling continued to brew inside Gwen. It wasn't the discomfort of anger or sadness. It was a strange, hidden emotion that turned her stomach. A black upsetting anxiety that something dark and evil was going to happen. Her mind drifted toward that feeling but snapped back when Marty spoke.

"You like it?" Marty asked expectantly.

"Of course!" Gwen exclaimed. "Was this the painting that was drying this morning?"

"Yeah. It didn't take too long to dry, either."

The waitress returned with their coffee. Marty started rolling up his artwork.

"Did you make that?" the waitress asked, pointing at his picture. "It's really good."

"Yes and thanks," Marty replied with a smile.

The waitress returned the grin and set the coffee down while Marty finished rolling up the picture and replaced it back in the tube. Gwen retrieved her cigarette from the ashtray.

The waitress pulled out a pen and notepad from a pouch in her apron. "Do you guys know what you want to eat or—"

Marty and Gwen looked at each other then told the waitress that they need more time to decide.

Between flipping through the menu and mentioning the different types of food, Gwen and Marty talked about the week that would follow and what sort of things they would do while she stayed with him. They decided that either on the upcoming Tuesday or Wednesday they would skip school and spend the day in bed, later going out for some Chinese food. They would take in a movie and possibly play a few pranks on some friends. The pranks were Marty's idea but, though mean, Gwen enjoyed the thought of throwing a dozen eggs at Julie Mitchell's house. Julie had always, for some unknown reason, hated Gwen, and the very thought of revenge made Gwen smile. Gwen would go over to Marty's on Saturday night a couple of hours after his parents had left.

She took another puff of her cigarette while Marty flipped through the menu.

"I think I'll go for the super-burger," Marty decided.

"Sounds good," Gwen said. "I'll probably just get a salad or something. I'm pretty tired and I don't feel like eating much."

"You sure?"

She nodded. "Listen, I was wondering if you could do a little something for me."

Marty gave her the *look*, the *look* being something Marty always gave her before they had sex.

"No. Not that," she returned half-smiling.

Marty's jaw dropped, jestfully, of course.

Gwen continued. "No. I was wondering if you could draw a title page for me. We just started Christianity in class today and I would like a title page for its section in my binder. Of course you would probably have to draw a few more title pages for some of the other religions, but don't worry, you'll be well compensated."

She gave him a sly smile and Marty beamed back.

"Sure," he said. "Anything specific you want on it?"

Gwen took another puff of her cigarette. "Not really. I was thinking something dark and moody. We got an outline of the chapters of the Bible we'll be studying, today." Gwen gestured with her hands as she explained this. It was a habit Marty thought attractive. She continued: "The last book in the Bible is the book of Revelation. It deals with the end of the world, stuff like that. I skimmed through a little of it. You would be amazed at all the imagery that it uses. Maybe you could find an idea in there? There are dragons and deserts and creatures coming out of the earth and the sea. It reads like a fantasy novel but I don't think that any of that stuff could ever happen."

"Sounds neat. I'll give it a glimpse and see what I can come up with," he said, smiling.

The waitress returned and they placed their order.

Chapter Two

The room was as black as pitch. There was no shred of light and the floor seemed to be made of rough carpet. Gwen could almost feel the confinement of the room's walls.

She stepped forward slowly, feeling the air around her. The scent of cinnamon poked at her nose. She continued walking forward, her arms outstretched, until she felt cold concrete with her fingertips, avoiding walking into it. She turned around and started walking back the way she had come.

Once she felt as if she was in the middle of the room, she turned right. Again, after a few paces, she felt cold concrete, and stopped to avoid walking into it. She turned a hundred and eighty degrees. Assuming she was facing the other side of the room, she stepped forward again. Her pace slowed. She was nearing something. *Another concrete wall,* she presumed.

Gwen kept moving, hoping to confirm her assumption. Instead of touching concrete, she felt something warm and soft. It was hair. She moved her hands along its matted and coarse strands, following them downward for at least two feet until they ended and there was nothing left but black air underneath. Her hands moved sideways, finding more hair that ran straight across but eventually stopped. She kept feeling the hair in front of her, following its patterns until she could discern a shape.

She withdrew her fingers when she felt the hair change to something smooth and moist. It was skin. She was touching a head.

* * *

Gwen woke up sharply, feeling her heart rapping violently against her ribcage. She shivered as the cold air of her apartment swept over her sweat-soaked skin. It was only a dream. A sigh of relief flushed through her body. She lay there, slowing her breathing, her eyes open until she was fully awake. Gwen knew that if she closed her eyes again, she would fall back asleep and more than likely return to her nightmare. That's what usually happened when she had bad dreams.

Satisfied that she was fully awake, Gwen rose out of bed, pulled her sheets back, and let them air out for a few minutes. She went over to her dresser drawer, switched to a nightgown and went to the kitchen for a glass of water.

She went to the refrigerator and opened it, and expected to see the water pitcher. It wasn't there. The refrigerator was empty. Even the shelves and the freezer were gone. In their place was a black hole of nothingness.

Then the black hole began to change. Gwen stood transfixed at the sight. Swirls of darkness began forming into recognizable shapes and objects, transforming into a long hallway lined with coffins stacked one on top of the other.

Despite being tempted to step forward and take a closer look, completely intrigued by what she saw, Gwen instead stood still, wide-eyed at the impossible spectacle.

One of the coffin lids began to move. At first it rocked gently, as if the coffin were in an unseen cradle. The rocking soon grew into violent quaking, its lid banging open and closed. *BAMM! BAMM! BAMM!* Open. Closed. Open. Closed. *BAMM! BAMM!* Open. Closed.

It stopped. The lid flew open, cracking on its hinges. A swirl of purple mist poured from its opening, swimming towards her. Gwen screamed and slammed the refrigerator door. She collapsed against the wall beside the refrigerator, her limbs fat with hot needles. She cried. Then she woke up—again.

She was in her bed, drenched with sweat. Like before, her heart beat ferociously in her chest. She lied there in the darkness, staring at the ceiling.

This time Gwen didn't change her nightgown and didn't go into the kitchen.

Chapter Three

There was a knock at the door. One loud bang followed by two quick bumps and another loud bang. It was Marty. He was picking Gwen up for school.

From inside Gwen's apartment there was the shuffling sound of locks being undone and the final thud of the dead bolt being released. Gwen opened the door, letting him in, running a brush through her long, wet brown hair. Marty always found her attractive in the morning. He enjoyed the way the long strands of hair curled slightly against her shoulders. Wet hair: not *that* was a turn-on for him.

Gwen went into the bathroom to finish doing her hair. Marty bent down and opened his backpack, searching for his standard cardboard tube that he carried all of his artwork in. He did it as quietly as he could, as it seemed that none of Gwen's three roommates were awake yet. Especially Denise.

He had met her not long ago when he, Gwen, and some of her friends had spent an evening at a bar. It was the first time he had ever had the chance to sit down and talk with her. Denise had mentioned that she was an early riser.

"I got something for you," Marty said in the direction of the bathroom.

He heard some objects clang around and looked up to see Gwen coming toward him, her fingers fumbling as she put her earrings in.

"What's that?" she asked, nodding toward his hands that were immersed deep within his backpack.

"Ta-da!" Marty sang and flipped out the cardboard tube, and handed it to her. "Tell me what you think."

Gwen pulled out a piece of paper from inside the tube and unrolled it. It was her new title page. The page was colored digitally, across the top reading: Christianity. Below the heading a large, detailed red dragon graced the page, its claws coming out toward her with its tail swirling about behind it. The background was a mix of yellow, black, and orange. Below the dragon was a sea of water and flames.

The page was more than what Gwen had expected him to create for her. She had only asked him to make it for her yesterday. She was amazed that it took him so little time to make something so beautiful.

"Thanks so much!" she beamed. She wrapped both arms around him and pecked his lips. Gwen, still holding onto Marty, looked at the picture again. "I love it," she said, "and you." She pecked him again.

Gwen put the title page back in the cardboard tube and grabbed her bag that was already waiting for her at the door. Marty grabbed his backpack as well and opened the door for her. They left for school.

* * *

The large lecture hall was packed full with students. Gwen was sitting in the back corner, doodling in her notebook, and occasionally glancing at the title page Marty had given her.

Her professor, Mr. Parks, was talking about the end of the world and what events the Bible said would take place in the end times. It was Mr. Parks's strategy to gain interest in the Bible by starting at its end and working backwards. In his opinion, the last book in the Bible, the book of Revelation, was the most interesting. It would be easier to grip the students' attention by reading from it first. And he was right. The book of Revelation *was* the most interesting, and had gained Gwen's interest almost immediately.

She listened to Mr. Parks as she doodled in her notebook, taking in all of the professor's words. She jotted down the notes that she deemed necessary.

At the end of the lecture, Mr. Parks challenged each of the students to present him with an essay that summarized these end times, and how each event prophesied to take place would have an impact on the earth when it happened. They were given a little over a week to do it. And this would not be enough time, knowing Mr. Parks. Every time he demanded an essay, he was, in truth, demanding a short novel. Eighteen pages were the minimum and the students were even encouraged to go above and beyond that. Gwen had struggled a month earlier with an essay regarding the appeal of Buddhism. By the time she finished, she had managed to only squeeze out the minimum eighteen pages. Her effort paid off however when she received ninety-three percent as her grade.

Being an organized person, Gwen wrote down how she would undertake this project and what resources and other information she would include in her essay. Her plan was to highlight all the prophecies the Bible stated and then research any similar events that had already occurred throughout history, using them as examples to describe the carryover impact on the world today.

Some of the things, like plagues and wars, would be easy to look up, but the others that blatantly involved the supernatural realm, would be much more difficult.

How was she supposed to compare this "out of world" vision that the apostle John had, anyway? She didn't know of anyone who had experienced a vision or even something close to one.

* * *

It was mid-afternoon and Gwen found herself a nice comfortable spot by the chain-link fence that bordered the rear grounds of Brentmere College. She leaned up against it and fumbled for the package of cigarettes in her front pants pocket. She opened it. Only two cigarettes left.

"Shit," she said. She would have to buy another pack on the way home from school. How she would be able to survive the rest of the day with only two cigarettes left? They had become her life support and without them she was just as well off as a nymphomaniac without sex.

Gwen flipped open a small Bible that was issued her at the beginning of her course. She went to the back of the book, to the book of Revelation, and began highlighting anything that caught her eye.

As she was beginning to get into the thick of it, a shadow cast over her pages. Gwen looked up to see who was there.

No one. The shadow was gone.

She furrowed her brow, took another drag off her cigarette, and went back to work. Already she could tell that this project was going to take a long time. There was far too much information.

Later she would call Marty and tell him that she couldn't get together that night. She had a date with the Centennial Library.

* * *

Far away from Gwen, Marty was twirling a paintbrush in his hand, looking at a blank canvas. His assignment was to create an image that expressed his inner self. He hated cliché motives. Drawing something that was about you was just a poor excuse for those who couldn't draw anything specific if asked to.

Marty brought his palette up by his chest and dabbed it with his paintbrush. He splotched the brush up and across the canvas then took a step back to examine his slowly evolving image.

He painted to the fast paced symphonic music that he heard in his head. When he did this, the other students in the class periodically gave him stern looks as they would always be sitting in front of their easels while he preferred to stand when he painted.

Marty drifted into that place for him where he became totally encompassed in whatever it was he was drawing and, or creating. Marty felt almost as if he were inside the picture. An hour and a half later, while he was adding the finishing touches, the sound of someone shouting something in the hall outside the room snapped him back to reality.

Marty cleaned his tools and put away the old, ratty plaid shirt he wore while painting, and left his work to dry. The painting was beautiful, rich and deep. It was the picture of a woman, her face pale and yearning as if she had been hurting for a millennium.

The light pouring in from the side window complimented his picture and when the light caught it just right, the woman looked like Denise.

* * *

It took Gwen awhile to locate the Centennial Library, as she didn't like driving downtown and got which one-way street turned where, mixed up. But after stopping at a gas station for a pack of smokes and clarifying with the clerk which street ran which way, Gwen had no trouble finding her way there.

Once at the library, Gwen parked her car, smooshed her cigarette out on the dark pavement with her heel, and went inside. The interior of the library was lot nicer than she remembered.

Across the tiled floor ahead of her were a pair of checkouts, each divided by security aisles to prevent shoplifting. Directly beyond those aisles was a high-countered station marked INFORMATION REFERENCE, and an old secretary at that high counter, furiously typing away at a computer. She seemed to be comparing the stack of books beside her to an index of some sort.

Gwen walked through the security aisles, and up to the desk. "Excuse me?" she interrupted.

The secretary looked up.

"I was wondering if you could tell me where I could find some books on Christian dogma?"

Giving her an annoyed glance over her bifocals, the secretary sighed and began typing a few key words into her computer. She scanned the appropriate screen, and then raised a bony finger, pointing toward the sign that read RELIGION just over to Gwen's left, past the computers meant for surfing the Internet.

"Just over there," she squawked, "under the sign that says 'Religion.' You should find what you want." She immediately went back to work.

"Thank you," Gwen said. *Bitch,* she thought, and went over to the couple of aisles that composed the Religion section.

After finding what she was looking for, Gwen settled herself at a desk and spread out the stack of books, opened her bag, and took out her legal pad, pens, and Bible.

Throughout the evening she took notes, photocopied a few references and retreated outside once in a while for a cigarette.

By the time she finished for the evening, she had accumulated eight pages of notes and four photocopies. Not a bad start.

There was, however, one article she found in a five-year-old issue of the *Winnipeg Sun*. The article had described an incident where a man claimed to have had visions regarding the sins of the world and something about its end. The article also went on to explain that these were simply the ravings of a lunatic but, regardless, the story could not be ignored. Other supernatural occurrences were also making the news at the time the article had been written. At Browngate Evangelical Church, a pastor in the midst of praise and worship with his congregation was suddenly struck by lightning from inside the church building. The pastor, thrown backward from his podium that had been cracked in half, miraculously recovered from the fall in only a few minutes and stated that what had happened was a manifestation of God's power in the here and now. Instead of being harmed, he had been filled with love and joy.

There were other articles involving people being miraculously healed, too—incidents where the medical community had no other explanation other than it being a genuine honest-to-God miracle.

The article about the man who claimed to have had some kind of vision had to be explored. It could make on hell of a paper.

Outside, Gwen walked briskly to her vehicle, trying to escape the chill of the night breeze. As her key was finding its way into the lock, Gwen caught a reflection not her own in the driver's seat window. She turned around and, like earlier, where she expected to see the person who cast a shadow over her notebook, no one was there.

Hastily, she got into her car, buckled her seat belt, and started the engine. She wanted to get home as fast as possible and under the safety of her covers. She attributed her imagination playing tricks on her to not getting enough sleep after her nightmare last night.

Traffic on Main Street was heavy, even for eleven-thirty at night. Between changing lanes and stopping at lights, Gwen replayed the reflection she saw on the glass over and over in her head. Reflection or imagination, it bothered her.

An edgy feeling welled up inside her. The same feeling you get after watching a scary movie and you become paranoid that someone is either behind you, or hiding under your bed.

The image she saw in the window, though frightening, was also vaguely familiar, oddly comforting. It was a face, dimly lit, but she could see that the face had been pale, dark, with black holes for where the eye sockets should be. Long strands of black hair had covered most of the face.

Ahead, just near the Disraeli Overpass, there was a lane blocked for construction. Gwen turned on her left-turning signal, and checked the rearview mirror for other cars. When she did, she saw the face again, this time staring at her from the back seat.

Gwen pulled over just before the roadway transformed into an unruly construction site. She slammed on the brakes, her body jutting forward, her chest squealing in pain from the penetrating grip of the seatbelt. She put the car in PARK and threw open her door, stepping out into the cool night.

"FUCK!" she screamed. "WHAT THE HELL!"

Gwen stared up at the night sky. The sky stared back, offering no answers. She lit a cigarette and began pacing back and forth beside her car, massaging her head.

"What the hell was that?" she asked herself, repeatedly.

Cars sped past her, the occasional one blinking its lights at her as if her standing on the side of the road was some sort of sin. One of the drivers had stopped to see if she was all right, but she told him to fuck off and get the hell away from her. Her mind felt like a worn punching bag. Why was she seeing things?

Three cigarettes later, Gwen had finally collected and calmed herself and gotten back in her car. She remained at the side of the road, smoked one last cigarette, and headed for home.

Chapter Four

The sound of water slowly being drained came to a halt. The coffee was ready. Denise poured three cups, adding cream and sugar accordingly, and returned to the table where Jenna and Carlee were sitting. She gave each of them their cup.

It was four days later, a Sunday night. Gwen was staying with Marty, and had no idea that her roommates were hosting this little get together behind her back to discuss her sudden change in behavior.

"I don't get it," Denise started, taking a small sip of her hot coffee, watching as her two friends also tested the temperature of their drinks. "Normally, when Gwen gets a little edgy, I just give her some space and we get along just fine. But after what happened the other day, well, I don't think I can let it go as easily."

Jenna nodded, agreeing.

Denise paused and took another sip of her coffee. On the other side of the table, Carlee was lighting up a cigarette. Carlee was the listener of the quartet. She usually sat back during discussions, only adding her two cents when she saw fit.

"Look at this!" Denise nearly shouted, bringing her fingers to the three thick, faded red scratch lines on her face. "I can't believe she did this!"

"Does it hurt?" Jenna asked.

"Only if I try to smile," Denise said, calming, giving a small smirk.

Yesterday, before Gwen left for Marty's, she and Denise had gotten into an argument regarding Gwen's share of that month's rent. Jenna and Carlee had been out for the evening.

Gwen had come barging into the living room, evidently stressed out, looking for something. Denise had asked Gwen if she could get her share of the rent, because it was due in two days. Denise had wanted to make sure that she had all the money together before Gwen left to stay at Marty's.

Gwen asked if she could give her the money on Monday instead. She hadn't done her banking yet and her branch wouldn't be open until then, when the rent was due. Denise knew Gwen's style and though Gwen was a neat and organized person, she also had a habit of always being late. She also knew that if Gwen and Marty were together, she probably wouldn't see the money until Tuesday or Wednesday. Which, by then, would be too late.

Denise had asked Gwen to write a post-dated check for her to cash on Monday afternoon, giving Gwen the morning to do her banking. Gwen had refused. After much debate and finally arguing face to face, Gwen had raised her hand, bringing her nails sharply across Denise's face, scratching long, red slashes across her cheek and jaw. Denise had fallen to her knees, cradling the torn flesh, and watched as Gwen grabbed her bag and stormed out of the apartment.

That was the major event, which issued this private meeting between the three girls.

There were also other smaller things that had happened in the last few days that had raised question. Gwen's attitude had changed, and she had become much more distant. Not in an extreme and obvious way, but there had been subtle changes in her behavior that her friends were able to notice. Gwen had become easily agitated and paranoid, almost as if she was always expecting something to go wrong. She had been going to bed much later than usual, and her roommates were able hear Gwen talking to herself through the thin walls which separated each of their rooms.

Jenna, who was the first one to notice the change, thought that Gwen had maybe done something that she knew was horribly wrong. Jenna had mentioned something to Carlee about it, but was told to just let Gwen be and that she was probably just having a bad week. But this latest incident had crossed the line. It was time for Carlee, Jenna, and Denise to get together and see if they couldn't figure out what was happening.

"The funny thing is, I'm not mad at her for scratching me. It's just the very thought that she *actually* did it. That's the part that bugs me," Denise said, touching her face again. "What do you guys think of this? Is something happening between her and Marty that we don't know about?"

Jenna looked at Denise. She was staring at the surface of the table.

"It's not Marty, that's for sure," Carlee said, joining the conversation. She exhaled a thick cloud of smoke and leaned forward in her chair. "Why would she be over there now if it was?"

There was another pause and Carlee leaned back again in her chair, taking another drag off her cigarette. All three of them felt like detectives trying to figure out a motive for a murder.

Denise said, "Well, she's obviously got some sort of problem. I know she's at Marty's, but I want to deal with this now. I want to call her and clear this up, but odds are we'll probably just argue."

Jenna blew on her coffee, took a swig, gulping audibly. "Listen, why don't we see how this plays out and see how she acts when she comes home next Saturday? In the mean time we could cool down a little. We're all upset."

The other two nodded.

The three of them changed subjects and finished their coffee. They were finished with Gwen for the evening, even though they all knew they didn't really get anywhere. That was fine with them. Their intentions had been good.

* * *

Soft cushions are always better, Gwen decided.

She was cuddling snugly against Marty underneath a large, soft down quilt. The two of them had just made love on the couch in the front room of Marty's parents' home. The couch doubled as a hide-a-bed, but their eagerness had gotten the better of them, and they couldn't wait the extra two minutes that it took to set the bed up. Comfort had never been an issue for them.

Gwen and Marty hadn't been able to be alone together for almost two weeks, and for both of them, that was a long time. Tonight had been their special reunion and they both thought that sex would be the best way to give each other the old how've-you-been?

They lay on the couch, catching their breath, reveling in each other's love. Gwen recalled the time when her mother had told her that the safest place to be was in a person's arms. She had been right. Gwen had never felt more secure in her life.

Marty kissed the top of Gwen's hair, the scent of her strawberry shampoo flooding his nostrils. It smelled good.

He and Gwen had been together long enough for him to read her face and the pattern of her breathing. Marty knew that something was wrong.

"Is something on your mind, m'dear?" he asked in a stuffy British accent, trying to lighten the mood.

Gwen was silent for a moment, then, "I've been having these dreams." Her tone was quiet, distant. "I don't know why. Every time I go to sleep I see this—bogeyman. At first I couldn't quite see his face or anything else about him, but the more I dream of him, the more of him I see. I don't know him, Marty."

The word "bogeyman" caught Marty's interest. He adjusted his position and sat up a little.

"Probably just a reoccurring nightmare," he told her. "God knows I've had those."

Gwen bit her lip as if trying to focus. "I've also day-dreamed and seen him when I'm awake, too."

Marty continued listening.

"First," she said, "I saw his reflection in my car window. Then I saw him while I was driving, too. I looked in the rearview mirror and saw him sitting in the back seat, staring at me."

Gwen didn't dare tell him about pulling over to the side of the road and having a small fit. Marty was overprotective and he would have thought this a dangerous thing to do. Especially just off Main Street, since nearly all who either lived or ventured on that street were drunk most of the time. He didn't want Gwen running the risk of upsetting the wrong person.

Marty adjusted the quilt and brought Gwen in a little closer, squeezing her tighter as he did.

Gwen took his hand and intertwined his fingers with hers. "I thought that maybe I was imagining things. I haven't slept much. And I hate dreaming of him. I'm always tired. You know that feeling you have when you feel like your watching everything on a screen and you're not sure if you're really awake?"

"Yeah," Marty said.

"Well, that's how I feel. All the time."

"When was the last time this happened?"

"Four days ago."

Marty thought for a moment. "Has it happened since?" He felt Gwen pull away from him. She turned to face him, sitting all her weight on her arm and elbow.

She spoke slowly, her voice almost a whisper. "I was getting out of the shower yesterday," she took a long deep breath through her nose and exhaled slowly, "before I came here, and after I dried off, I wiped the steam from the mirror and started brushing my hair…"

This beautiful image filled Marty's mind. He envisioned her standing in front of her mirror completely naked, her hands moving rhythmically through her gorgeous dark, wet hair. He felt a stiffness starting to form between his legs.

"I wasn't really looking at anything, just brushing my hair, but when I looked back up at the mirror—there he was…standing right behind me."

She stopped speaking for a moment as she relived the experience. "I remember screaming and turning around. And like every other time I think I see him, he was gone. I looked back at the mirror. Carlee knocked at the door and asked if I was okay."

"What did you tell her?" Marty was worried and didn't know what to make of what Gwen was telling him.

"What could I tell her?" Gwen sounded almost surprised at the question. "I said that I was fine and that I had accidentally scared myself. I don't know what's going on."

Gwen eased herself back down, snuggling close against him. They lay there for a few more minutes and allowed the mood to change. Satisfied it had, Marty rolled on top of her, and they coupled again.

* * *

Back at Gwen's apartment things were back to normal. Carlee was in the living room having a cigarette and watching television. Denise was in her bedroom doing a crossword and Jenna was tidying up the kitchen. Their discussion about Gwen was over for the night.

* * *

Gwen was taking a hot bath, something she enjoyed after sex. It was both soothing and relaxing for her. Marty was slouched on *their* sofa watching an improv' comedy on the local network. When he had heard the bath water turn off, he jumped off the couch, slipped on a pair of boxer shorts, and set the hide-a-bed up for them.

He prepared a spot for her and just as he was fluffing the last pillow, Gwen came out of the bathroom. She slipped on her robe and retreated into the front room and hopped onto the bed. She rubbed up against her boyfriend.

"How was the water?" he asked.

"Perrrfect…" she purred.

"Good." He kissed her forehead. She moved upward and kissed him full on the mouth.

They pulled the plush covers over them. A small, dimly lit lamp provided enough light for them to still carry on a conversation without sitting in total darkness.

Marty saw that Gwen was tapping her fingers nervously on his thigh.

"You're still upset, huh?" he asked.

"Not really…yeah, kind of." Gwen got off the bed, walking about eight feet away. She bent down and got something out of her bag and brought it back to the bed. She pulled the covers over herself and held the object tightly against her chest, the same way you would hide a gift from someone before giving it to them.

"What's that?" Marty asked, pointing at her tightly overlapped hands.

Gwen said nothing and readjusted herself so she was facing Marty more squarely. He could tell by her downcast eyes that she was concerned and worried. Worried that whatever she had to show him might be bad news. He could feel the tension of the room fill his stomach. In the dim light he watched as Gwen's eyes went from her hands and met his, then back to her hands again.

"Those dreams I've had," she said, "they scared me. I've had scary dreams before, we all have, but none of them have ever scared me the way these ones do. I became even more scared when I started having them when I was awake. But yesterday, I detoured and dropped by the library to do a follow up on a story I found on Wednesday while researching a project for school. That's why I was late."

Gwen swallowed hard and Marty wondered about the taste she had in her mouth. This whole thing was unusual for him. Normally, their relationship was more happy-go-lucky than anything else, and the sudden dark turn that it was taking was unsettling.

Marty waited a moment then looked at Gwen. She continued her story. "I found something yesterday on an old micro fiche. I almost fell off my chair when I found it. Last Wednesday, I found a news article about a man who had claimed to be having visions of the end of the world. It made me laugh at first, but then I read some other articles about people having other," she lifted her hands and made quotations her fingers, "supernatural experiences."

Marty smiled.

"So anyway, I started believing them and became more and more interested. Yesterday, when I went back to the library, I wanted to see if any of the other newspapers had printed anything else about this guy. It took a few hours, and then in a copy of an old *Free Press*, I found something." Gwen looked at a folded up piece of paper in her hands. "I found another article about him."

"What's his name?" Marty asked.

"Well, here." Gwen handed Marty the folded up article. He unfolded it and furrowed his brow. The paper that he held was a print out of a microfiche dated January 2nd, 1997—a little over five and a half years ago.

He bounced back and forth between the text and the picture, comparing what he read to what he saw. Marty lowered the paper and saw Gwen's eyes starting to tear up.

"That's him," she said, pointing to the man with the dark, long beard and hair.

"Harry Thomas," Marty said, his finger on the man's name scripted in bold beneath the picture.

"Harry Thomas," she repeated, her voice more firm than his.

Marty put down the paper and reached over and hugged her tight. They held each other for a long while.

They still had a lot to talk about.

Chapter Five

Cigarette butts spilled onto the passenger side of the car. Putting out a cigarette in a tall mountain of an ashtray proved to be a stupid thing to do.

"Shit!" Gwen said and punched the dashboard in front of her. She leaned over and cupped her right hand under the ashtray in a futile attempt to prevent any more ashes and butts from spilling over. Frustrated, she furiously shook her hand over the mat on the passenger side, shaking the ashes and butts off. She used her pant leg to wipe off the rest. She made sure that the cigarette she had tried to butt out was indeed that: out. Thankfully, there was no smoke coming from it, meaning that is was.

Gwen gripped the wheel again and continued driving toward Hans Memorial Hospital.

Hans Memorial. A hospital built in 1940 in honor of the late Frederick Hans, a brilliant psychotherapist who dedicated his life to helping those who didn't know any better then to simply exist in the world that they were given, or the ones that they had created for themselves, or both. All those who didn't know their left foot from their right were sent to him. Some of his patients had been able to get a handle on life, and others didn't, or couldn't. But it was that very "couldn't" that Dr. Hans had given special attention to, and it was because of those efforts that the hospital had been built.

Gwen had the newspaper article on the seat beside her. She picked it up and looked at the picture of Harry, long hair and beard and all, being forced into an ambulance. The caption below it read: Harry Thomas being taken to Hans Memorial Hospital for psychiatric therapy.

The article had stated that Harry, a missing person for twenty years, was found lying next to a tombstone in Eagle Park Cemetery. Once he had been identified, it turned out that the tombstone had belonged to his wife, Lauren. An elderly man, who had also been visiting the grave of his deceased wife that day, had found Harry and tried shaking him awake. When he couldn't, he had called 911 and waited for the paramedics to arrive. Four men in white uniforms showed up and were finally able to revive Harry.

"The second we woke him up he jumped on me," one of the paramedics was quoted saying. "He starting hitting me in the face over and over until my partners got him off me and restrained him. He broke my nose. He was babbling incoherently, talking about rape and murder and dark forces. He kept saying that he'd been having visions, all to do with the sins of the world. And he wouldn't keep quiet until we reached the emergency ward at St. Boniface hospital."

It was at St. Boniface that Harry had been identified, proclaimed legally insane, and sentenced to Hans Memorial Hospital for further study and aid.

The article closed off with the paramedic with the broken nose saying: "This may sound strange, but something didn't feel right when we picked him up. I mean, I've seen some weird s—, but, man, this just felt, I don't know, somehow wrong."

Ten minutes passed and Gwen turned on to Hans Memorial Boulevard. Another three minutes and she pulled into the parking lot, searching for an open stall. *You're coming to see me, aren't you, Gwen?* She slammed on the brake, completely caught off guard by the voice that had sprung into her head. She almost hit the car that was easing its way out of a parking space in front of her. She heard the angered honk of its horn as it sped away.

Gwen closed her eyes. "Please oh please," she begged to no one in particular, trying to convince herself that she was dreaming again. She pulled into the parking space, put the car in PARK, and turned off the engine.

Her heart pounded. Nervousness flowed through her stomach, creating knots that would tie, then release, tie then release. She pressed her hands to her face, trying to calm herself.

The night before, she and Marty had stayed up until almost five in the morning talking about her planned visit to Hans Memorial Hospital. Marty insisted that even though she had been going through a series of weird coincidences, it would be better if she would just forget about it and try to move on. He had said that she was probably tired and overworked because of school, and that this was just her mind's way of fighting back at her. Gwen didn't accept that theory. She knew that Marty meant well, and that he was trying to protect her, but she insisted that she would do this. She would go to Hans Memorial Hospital and get some answers.

"What about school?" she recalled Marty asking.

"Fuck it," had been her response. She didn't give a damn about school. Not right now. Her sanity was all that was important, and if Harry did, in fact, exist in Hans Memorial, she would demand to know why the hell he was bothering her, and how the hell it was even possible.

She decided to have a cigarette before going through the hospital doors.

* * *

The two automatic glass doors at the main entrance slid open and Gwen entered the lobby. Slightly off to the left, in front of her, was a small cubicle with a plexi-glass window where the receptionist, a heavyset black woman in a nurse outfit, was sitting. Beside it, in an adjoining cubicle, was a security station seating two security guards. The rest of the lobby was covered in plants. A glass roof was overhead. A few chairs meant for waiting were scattered throughout. The lobby was serene in atmosphere and the presentation spacious.

Obviously an environment meant to encourage tranquility, Gwen thought.

She made her way over to the nurse and waited until the woman looked up from her paperwork. Gwen looked at her name tag: Elsie Fortsmith, Secretarial Nurse. Finally Elsie looked up.

"Can I help you?" she asked, her Jamaican accent thick.

"Umm...I'm looking for somebody," Gwen said, nervous, but at the same time eager to see Harry.

"Doubt if you'd find anybody you'd want here," Elsie said with a smile.

Gwen shuffled through her purse and brought out the newspaper clipping of Harry and placed it in front of Elsie. Elsie scanned the article.

"I'm looking for Harry Thomas," Gwen said. She couldn't believe she was *actually* doing this! Couldn't believe she was *actually* at a psychiatric hospital, a loony bin, looking for a crazy person!

Elsie smiled and tapped a few keys on a keyboard to her left. Gwen could tell that she did it with hesitation, but couldn't figure out why. Then she remembered Harry's violent outburst after the paramedics had found him.

Could Harry be dangerous? Gwen asked herself.

Elsie finished with the computer and returned her attention to Gwen. "Mr. Thomas is on the third floor in the Y-wing. The Y-3 unit"

"Thanks," Gwen stammered and started to walk away.

Elsie shouted through the plexi-glass, "Come back here, dear."

Gwen turned and walked back. "Yes?" she asked.

"I need you to sign in and I need to hold onto your license."

"What for?"

"Is just procedure, dear. Nothin' to be worryin' about."

Gwen liked the way Elsie said "worryin'." It sounded more like *wuuryin*.

Gwen gave Elsie her license, signed in, and left for the elevators.

When the doors opened on the third floor, Gwen didn't immediately come out. She waited, peering out, hesitant to move. The doors began to close. Gwen stopped them and stepped out, approaching the T-junction in front of her. There was sign on the wall saying that the Y-wing was to her left.

She went down a long hallway, following the arrows, and turned right. She saw a few doors on her left. Each door had a letter and number. After she passed Y-1 and Y-2, she stopped, knowing what the next one would be—Y-3, Harry's presumed home. Gwen gripped the doorknob, turned it, and found herself before another receptionist. It was a man, this time. He was short but looked powerful, sporting a buzz cut that made him look almost bald.

"I'm here to see Harry Thomas," Gwen told him.

The man glanced up from a *Wizard* magazine and looked her over from her head down to her waist. He couldn't see her legs from behind his desk.

Gwen could tell by the dance in his eyes what kind of thoughts he was thinking. She hated it when guys did that to her.

"Is he expecting you?" he asked.

"Umm—no."

The man leaned forward on the desk, rocking on his elbows. "Are you family or friend?"

"Well...uh..."

A flash went over the man's eyes. He pulled out a clipboard and made Gwen sign in. She did and watched the short man get up and motion for her to follow him. Butterflies swirled in her stomach like a hurricane. She questioned whether or not this had been such a good idea after all.

The short man led her into what appeared to be the lunchroom, telling her to sit at the small table by the window. He left a moment afterward.

Gwen sat down, put her purse on the floor beside her, and glanced out the window on her right. She could see the parking lot below and a bit of the downtown skyline. She decided it wasn't a bad view, given that she was in a hospital, and assumed that at this kind of hospital, it was very rare that a patient got to see the outside world. Usually they were kept cooped up in a room, waiting to get better. Then she remembered she was in a hospital where people stayed for more than just a few days. *Most likely for the rest of their lives,* she concluded. It was a shame.

Her eyes went down from the window, seeing the ashtray on the table. She was tempted to light a cigarette but decided against it, thinking that it would be rude. She was surprised that smoking was even allowed here. *People need cigarettes whether they're crazy or not,* she figured.

Gwen looked around the lunchroom, taking note of the four tables, each table seating four. It appeared not too many people stayed in Y-3.

The far wall and the wall adjacent to it had cupboards and a sink. The two remaining walls held pictures, which appeared to have been drawn by children. In the middle of one of these walls was a corkboard with different events posted on it; some were notices for arts and crafts and baking, others for therapy sessions and group activities.

At least ten minutes had passed until the short, stocky man reappeared in the lunchroom doorway, his right hand hiding behind the second of the double doors. He stopped, looked at Gwen, this time getting an eyeful.

Gwen shuddered. *Creep,* she thought.

She turned away and looked back out the window, but turned back when she heard more than just one set of footsteps coming toward her. The short man had a blank expression on his face, his eyes leering at her. His right hand, the one hidden behind the door, was holding another man by the sleeve.

Harry, Gwen knew.

Harry wore light blue striped pajamas, no slippers. He dragged his feet when he walked. Gwen could her the sound of his rough skin rubbing against the tile.

She was apprehensive, but secure all the same. It *was* Harry. She knew that for a fact. His black hair was shoulder length, so was his beard. Sprinkles of gray were peppered throughout both. Dark purple circles hung like upside-down umbrellas below his blue eyes, blending into the thin, worn skin of his cheekbones. He looked as if he had been on the losing side of a fight.

The short man pulled out a chair across from Gwen and sat Harry down. He looked Harry in the eye.

"Behave," he said sternly and made his way over to the other side of the room, giving Harry and Gwen a measure of privacy. He wanted to be nearby, in case something happened. When he sat down, his eyes never left the pair, making Gwen even more uncomfortable.

Here she was, face to face with her nightmare. Tears built up in her eyes and began to leak out. She didn't wipe them away. Harry sat there and stared blankly at her. They stayed like that for an indeterminable amount of time until Gwen's rushing thoughts were broken by a whisper in her head. *It's all right, Gwen. I'm not going to hurt you.*

More tears streamed down and she covered her face with her hands. Harry sat motionless. After swallowing hard, Gwen looked back up at him.

"How are you doing this?" she asked, her voice barely audible.

He didn't answer.

"DAMMIT TELL ME!" she screamed.

Suddenly the short man stood up from his table and was about to walk over to them to see what was the matter, but sat back down again when Harry shot him a menacing glare.

Harry's blue eyes went back to Gwen. "I'm sorry, Gwen. I didn't mean to scare you—not at all." His voice was gentle and raspy, soothing and convincing.

Harry's gaze filled with love and compassion. Gwen put her hands on the table in front of her, focusing her attention on them.

"How can I hear you inside my head?" she asked.

Harry was silent. Gwen, frustrated.

"I don't know," he finally replied.

Gwen didn't say anything.

"Gwen," Harry leaned closer, "there's something I have to tell you."

Her tears stopped. Harry had her attention.

"I guess the first thing I should tell you is how I can speak into your mind," Harry stated.

He just said that he didn't know how, Gwen thought. She nodded anyway, giving him permission to speak. She was shocked at how well spoken he was. She had just expected him to mumble his way through this visit only for her to go home disappointed, but relieved that she wouldn't have to go back and see him again.

"I promise I will tell you," he continued, "but there are other things I have to tell you first."

Harry reached into the top left pocket of his pajamas and pulled out a package of duMaurier cigarettes. He lit one then offered his package to Gwen. She accepted the offer. She also used his lighter, noticing that his hands hadn't warmed the metal casing. It was ice cold. She lit her cigarette and returned the lighter to him. Harry slid the ashtray that was on the side of the table between them.

"Gwen, I have been here for five years. You probably already knew that. But there were twenty long years elsewhere before I was put here. How old are you?"

"Tw-twenty-three," she stammered. She didn't want to share anything about herself but right now she didn't care. Answers from Harry were all she wanted.

"I spent almost your entire lifetime in"—he lit his cigarette—"it's hard to describe."

Harry paused, his eyes glazing over. Gwen thought he was going to cry. Instead, Harry adjusted himself in his seat and continued. "My wife died twenty-five years ago. Her name was Lauren. She was killed in a robbery. She worked in one of those little convenience stores. You know the type. One day a man walked in and pointed a gun at her, wanting all the money that was in the cash register. As much as she tried to cooperate, it wasn't enough. He killed her."

Gwen exhaled a cloud of smoke. "I'm sorry."

Harry nodded at the condolence and took a puff of his cigarette. "It was a week later...or was it more...I have trouble remembering that night. Sometimes I can remember it so clearly and other times—My mind, something's wrong with it. That's why I'm in a place like this, right?" Harry cracked a small smile and Gwen returned it uncomfortably. She wasn't sure if it was offensive to laugh at a joke like that.

Harry went on. "For some reason I found myself in one of those," he made square and block shapes with his hands, "houses for the dead. You know, the ones where coffins are stacked up one on top of the other?"

"Mausoleums?" Gwen suggested, filling in the blank. She remembered her nightmare with the stacked coffins in her refrigerator.

"Yeah, mos-el-ul-eums," Harry said, trying to form the word. He took another drag. "It was dark, then light, then dark again. I was exposed to things. Strange things. Things that made me throw up."

He's definitely crazy, Gwen thought, but was amazed at his sincerity, and how he honestly believed that those things had *actually* happened. Gwen was also amazed at how intrigued she was by his story. Something in the back of her mind beckoned her to sit and listen and not be afraid.

"What happened?" she asked.

Harry took a long look at her, and then glanced over at the bald man, then back at Gwen. She followed his eyes the whole time. He leaned closer, the expression on his face telling her that he demanded the truth. The truth about the question he was about to ask.

"Gwen, do you believe in God?" He kept on leaning forward.

Not quite sure what to say, Gwen replied, "I believe that there is a force bigger than all of us, if that's what you mean."

"No. That's not what I mean." He pounded his fist once on the table and sat back. "I mean do you believe in a being so big, so powerful, so unbelievably strong that He could control events, dictate them, tell the future." He said this sternly rather then asked.

Gwen thought for a minute then told him that she didn't believe in such a being. She told him that she believed in an outside force but also that everyone was capable of changing the future and that there was no set plan; events would simply pan out as they came along.

"That's unfortunate," Harry concluded.

She tapped her cigarette in the ashtray. "Why?"

"Because." He stroked his beard, his fingers curved as if a comb, smoothing out the knots. "Just…because."

There was an awkward silence. Gwen broke it. "Harry," she said, taking her turn at leaning closer, "I don't know what you're trying to say to me. Just tell me what happened to you and why you're haunting me."

Gwen was surprised at herself for talking so boldly. She was also surprised that she admitted that he *was* haunting her.

"All right," he agreed calmly. "I was kidnapped. Brought to a place where records were kept. Not the records you listen to. I'm talking about books, pages upon pages. Those kinds of records. The records where all the sins of everyone who has ever lived were kept. Not only that, I saw them. I saw their sins." He looked at the table, the smoke from his cigarette clouding around him. "I saw them."

Harry leaned back in his chair, knowing that Gwen didn't believe him. The truth was Gwen didn't know *what* to say. Part of her decided that he was crazy but somehow she knew otherwise. Something was causing these nightmares, these visions—if that's what they were. She couldn't dismiss his claim, despite how much she wanted to. But Gwen Reeves was a hard person to convince. Harry would have to tell her more—prove more.

"What do you mean, you saw them?" she asked.

Harry stubbed out his cigarette.

Gwen noticed that hers was also burning close to her fingers. She stubbed hers out as well.

Harry thought for a moment then readjusted himself again. "It's impossible to explain, but I'll try. I won't be able to tell you all of it today. Hell, if I were to tell you everything, it would take years. But tonight, I'll tell you as much as I can."

Gwen crossed her legs and listened as Harry began to speak.

Chapter Six

Denise answered the phone shortly after 6:30 P.M. Coming through the line was Marty Bones. He was looking for Gwen.

"Hi, who's this?" came his voice over the receiver.

"Denise," she said.

"Denise, it's Marty. Is Gwen there?"

"No. Isn't she with you?"

"No." Marty sounded disappointed.

"What?" Denise offered. She sat down on the orange easy chair next to the phone.

Marty sighed. "It's just that she left this afternoon to go somewhere and I'm surprised that she's not back yet, is all. I didn't think that she would take this long."

"Where'd she go?" Denise twirled the telephone cord between her fingers.

"Sorry, Denise. I can't tell you. Nothing personal."

"S'okay." There was silence. Denise said, "Do you want to talk?"

"What do you mean?"

"Talk. Y'know? Two people, conversing?" She accented the word "conversing."

"All right," Marty drawled.

And Denise smiled.

* * *

At Hans Memorial, the clock on the wall read seven. Gwen had been there for almost four hours. She could see that the bald man was starting to get tired of supervising the visit.

Harry had just stubbed out his eighth cigarette and for the past two hours had been explaining to Gwen what had happened to him in Eagle Park Cemetery. He told her about his visit to his wife's grave and how he had been determined to spend the night. He told her about the rain and how he found shelter in the coffin house. Harry couldn't remember the word "mausoleum."

Once he began talking about the library, Gwen felt as if time stopped. She had become engrossed in his every word.

"The library was small but monstrous all the same," she recalled him saying. "The books were everywhere. Lining the walls and stacked up high on the floor."

Harry couldn't describe each vision because, frankly, he just couldn't remember them all. If it took twenty years for him to see them all, it would take twenty years for him to tell them all as well. But he did tell Gwen of his first vision, that of Henry McLure. He told Gwen of the perverted rape of Mary-Anne and how he threw up after watching Henry fondle her breasts and drive himself into her. How he threw up after watching Henry's bloody orgasm. Hearing this made Gwen make a sour face, and almost feel like throwing up herself.

"There was another presence in the room," Harry had said, "something that I couldn't see but knew was there. Every so often I would feel this ice cold hand run along my back and trail along my shoulders." Harry did the motion with his hands and arms when he described it.

Gwen had asked him why he hadn't left? Why he didn't get the hell out of there when things started to get dangerous?

"I couldn't," he had said. "I couldn't leave. The room was sealed off, and even when I just *thought* of trying to escape, a sharp pain ran through me. Whatever was there in that room wanted me to stay. I obliged, though now I realize I shouldn't have. I should have killed myself and died right there in the library. Except…there was nothing to kill myself with. Nothing but books. And they were doing enough of a number on me as it was."

Now, at seven o'clock, their conversation was drawing to a close. Visiting hours was only until 8 P.M., stretched a little longer if it was important.

Gwen looked over at the bald man. He had changed his position so that he was sitting on one chair, putting his feet up on another. Gwen felt bad for making him wait there for so long. She also knew that Harry had not had a visitor in years. He told her that he had one son, Carl, and that he had come to the hospital a few days after the newspaper article was printed, announcing that Harry was still alive.

Carl had visited Harry to say good-bye. He had told Harry that he couldn't handle having a father in the nuthouse and, on top of that, having a father that left him alone for twenty years. Carl hadn't understood that his father'd had no other choice. Carl, a baby at the time, had been at Harry's parents the night Harry hadn't come home. Carl had remained with his grandparents ever since and was raised by them.

Despite Harry's pleas, Carl had remained stubborn. He had filed for a parental divorce a week later. A month after that, the divorce was final. He was no longer Harry's son and Harry hadn't heard from him since.

The sad account unsettled Gwen. Her opinion of Carl Thomas was nothing short of an asshole. How could he have abandoned his father like that?

"Harry, were you awake when all this was happening to you?" Gwen asked.

"It's hard to say. I have trouble remembering. I haven't thought of these things in such a long time." He ran his fingers through his hair, sighing unnecessarily loud. "I'm getting tired. I don't remember, Gwen. Probably, but I'm not sure. I just want to go to sleep." Harry's words were losing consistency.

He abruptly got up and walked toward the bald man. The bald man stood and took Harry by the arm. They left the cafeteria. Before leaving herself, Gwen sat at the table for a moment, trying to discern if Harry had really gone and left the room. A minute ago, she and Harry were deep in conversation and then, suddenly, Harry had decided enough was enough and had left her.

He's insane, Gwen thought. She sat for a moment, wondering if the bald man was going to escort her out. After five minutes, she got up and left, not bothering to wait for him to return.

She was upset at Harry for leaving so suddenly. Her mind was so clouded that she forgot that she was staying at Marty's and decided that she would call him when she got to her place. He always cheered her up.

Gwen went down the stairs and almost passed the receptionist area before remembering that she had to sign out. Elsie was still there and still just as oddly moody as before. Gwen signed her name and the time of her departure. Elsie returned Gwen's license to her and Gwen went out to the parking lot.

On the ride home traffic was moving along briskly. Gwen wasn't sure if she wanted to go back to Hans Memorial Hospital again.

Maybe, she considered, and left it at that.

* * *

Gwen came home to an empty apartment. Everyone had gone out for the night and she was alone. She dumped her keys on the bench by the door and threw her jacket over the chair in the front room. She flopped herself on the couch and gazed up at the ceiling.

What a night, she thought. She exhaled a long breath and closed her eyes for a moment, trying to change her mood. The inside of her eyelids were a dark red with swirling shapes of black floating into focus and then back out again. In her mind's eye she saw Harry, the cafeteria, the bald guy, then Harry again.

He just left, she said to herself, not understanding why Harry had up and gone like he did. *Maybe I will go back. We'll see.*

She sat up, feeling a swell of fatigue behind her eyes, and crossed the room to the telephone, settling into the easy-chair beside it. Gwen dialed Marty's number.

After seven rings she was about to hang up when Marty picked up the phone. "Hello?"

"Hey," she greeted him.

"Gwen! Where are you? Are you all right?"

She crossed her legs. "I'm fine. I just got home."

"Home? I thought you were staying over here for the week?" Marty's tone was that of disappointment, even disapproval.

She understood what he meant, but not fully comprehending. Then it hit her.

"Oh, shit!" she cursed, slapping her thigh. Her meeting with Harry had sapped her mind, making her forget about anything or anyone else. "I'm sorry," she said sympathetically, "my head's kind of clouded. I wasn't thinking straight."

There was silence on the other end of the receiver. Gwen could envision Marty staring blankly downward, a signature of hurt written across his face. Her spirits lifted a little when he broke the silence.

"So do you want to come over or…" He trailed off.

Without hesitation, Gwen exclaimed, "Of course!" She could see him smile at the other end. "Really, Marty, I'm sorry. I just had a lousy night, is all."

"It's okay," he said, obviously hiding his hurt.

"I'll be over as soon as I can and I expect that bed to be nice and warm when I get there."

"You got it, babe!"

"All right. See you soon." Gwen giggled quietly into the receiver.

"Love you," she said.

"Love you, too."

They both hung up. Gwen grabbed her jacket and hurried out the door.

* * *

Back at the Hospital, Harry had returned to his room with the bald man gripping his arm the whole walk back. The two of them seldom spoke when they saw each other. On occasion Harry would ask for a glass of water but other than that, they exchanged few words. It was only tonight that Harry spoke to him. Spoke into the bald man's mind, telling him to forget anything he may have overheard between Harry and Gwen. He was also reminded that he hadn't allowed Harry a visitor this evening. For the bald man, Harry and Gwen's meeting had never occurred.

Harry Thomas was considered dangerous to some and his visiting privileges had been taken from him long ago.

When Harry was in his room, he was locked in for eight hours to sleep, his only sight into the rest of the hospital through a small window with a wire screen mesh, built into the door.

Harry had hated being treated like a prisoner but soon began to appreciate the feeling of security that it brought him. He had been used and ravished for twenty long years. It was nice to be someplace safe.

Harry had already brushed his teeth and gotten himself ready for bed before he saw Gwen. Not that there was much to get ready since he wore his pajamas all day long and only changed them once a week, usually when a nurse told him to. And he also didn't mind going to bed with the stale taste of cigarette smoke in his mouth, either.

His room was small but cozy; the walls painted light beige that looked more like a dark yellow at night. A window was built into the wall at the head of the bed, the glass dual pained with bars on the outside running vertical. He didn't mind the bars. He knew they were for his own good. In fact, he was happy to even have a window.

During his first two years as a patient of Hans Memorial, his room didn't have one for fear that he would smash through the glass and bars and try to escape. But after doing his best to behave himself, his psychiatrist, Dr.

Woodrose, offered Harry a room with a window as a reward for his efforts. Dr. Woodrose had also told the staff in Y-3 that Harry could be trusted and that he had no intention of escape. If anything, his patient was starting to enjoy his stay at the hospital.

If, during the first two years, Harry had realized the full potential of his telepathic abilities, he definitely would have sooner forced the hospital staff to give him a room with a window.

In his room, there were no posters on the walls. He couldn't remember any past interests. Harry spent most of his time reading. The hospital had an extensive library of reprints of old 1950's romance novels. Sometimes, when his memory was working right, he would imagine that he and Lauren were the stars of the novels he read. But when it wasn't working right, it didn't really matter to him. He was just happy to be out of the cemetery library and inside someplace safe, reading something he *wanted* to read.

Harry prepped his blankets and pillow, ready to close his eyes. He had already turned the lights off and left the only illumination to a small lamp on his night table. He always slept with that light on and had a fit every time the bulb burnt out. This, of course, forced the nurses and security to put him in the quiet room for a few days. And in the quiet room, there were no lights, which always made matters worse. The quiet room was what the staff at the Hans Memorial called it but to the patients who have had the displeasure of being sent there, it was referred to as the "Darkroom."

Harry got himself comfortable, went under the covers, and enjoyed the warm feeling of the quilts. Ever since emerging from the cemetery, he always took a moment to say a thank you to God for bed sheets. In the library, when he was allowed to sleep, his clothes, soaked with sweat, always made him shiver. There had been no blankets there.

Harry was almost asleep when he heard soft whispers coming from the walls of his room.

He couldn't make out what was being said and when he opened his eyes, he didn't move. There, before him, were horrible faces glowing in the dark.

* * *

The morning sun shone brightly through the cracks in the blinds of Marty Bones's bedroom. It was 6:23 A.M.

Gwen opened her eyes, looked over at Marty who was sleeping with his mouth open beside her, and eased herself out of the bed. Being careful not to disturb him, she put on her housecoat over her nightgown, and went downstairs. For as little sleep as she had, Gwen was feeling refreshed. *Maybe I don't need coffee,* she thought. *Ah, the hell with it,* and she put a pot to brew.

When it was ready she sat in the front room on the same sofa that had been her and Marty's love nest two nights before. Between sips of coffee, she tried to figure out why she felt so good and so awake. Then she realized that it had been her first night without nightmares in a good while. Gwen smiled at the notion.

Her thoughts turned toward Harry. She remembered how Harry didn't answer her question about how he had been able to put thoughts into her head. She would have to go back and ask him. Or, should she? Maybe she should she try to forget that their whole meeting ever happened? But Gwen realized that she didn't have a choice. She had to go back and see Harry. She couldn't explain why. But somewhere, deep down inside, she knew that what was happening between her and Harry was for a reason, and that no matter what the reason, it had to be fulfilled.

* * *

Every Tuesday, Brentmere College seemed to be busier. More students seemed to show up, making each class seem a little more full. For the students, it was an issue of convenience, because they knew that as the week progressed, the greater the tendency was to slack off. Most concluded that if thousands of dollars were to be spent on a course, they might as well put their best foot forward, and learn at a time when they still cared about what they were going to do with the rest of their lives. Others had to go to classes earlier in the week simply because it was the only time their chosen course was available.

This morning, Marty Bones was feeling heavy of spirits. He shuffled his feet as he wandered through the halls to his first art class. He and Gwen had barley spoken a word on the way to school. They had had no previous argument, which ruled out bitterness as the problem. He just hated the fact that Gwen wasn't being as talkative as of late and equally hated the feeling that she was keeping something from him. What had she been up to the other night? How could she forget that she was staying at his place for the week?

Marty would have to ask her about it later. He was late for class.

* * *

Lying in bed, Denise's heart was weighted by the dream she'd just had. It was normal for her to have unusual dreams, but this particular one was a first.

During the night, while her body was hidden beneath her sheets and her head rested gently on a soft pillow, her mind had drifted off someplace else, more specifically, to *someone* else—to Marty.

When Denise was first introduced to Marty, she wasn't at all impressed with Gwen's selection of a boyfriend. Denise personally preferred men in the more well to do class who didn't have the tendency to make a joke every two minutes. But as time went on, the more she approved of him, and the more support she gave their relationship. Marty was as loyal as a puppy dog and from what Gwen had told her, just as cuddly.

In terms of being attracted to him, well, that was never going to happen. Denise had very specific tastes and Marty didn't fall into any of her criteria. Not a chance. He had a tendency to almost bob his head when he walked reminding Denise of Jar Jar Binks. Furthermore, his nose was too long. Denise could just imagine herself going in for a kiss and getting poked in the eye by cartilage and skin. She knew she was being superficial and quick to judge, but that's how she'd always been, and it was too late to change her thinking. She took comfort in believing that she wasn't the only one who was fussy when is came to picking a guy.

What Denise could not figure out was *why* she had the dream she'd just had.

She had been lying in bed for almost ten minutes, wracking her brain for some kind of explanation. She had none. Last night, her brain had for some reason decided to throw Marty into the mix of images, and sounds, and fantasies.

From what she could remember, she was in a park, sitting on a bench. She wasn't looking at anything, save for the excessively long grass at her feet, but what she vividly remembered was the sopping wet clothes that she had been wearing. Denise didn't know how she had gotten wet, but in her dream it seemed normal to be sitting on a bench drenched from head to toe.

From behind her, Marty had appeared and put his arm around her shoulders, offering to dry her off. She had accepted his offer and, in a whirlwind of motion, Marty's hands were moving all over her body, drying her off, the warmth of his touch seeping into her pores, giving her the same kind of tingles she felt when using her hair-dryer.

She remembered looking at Marty afterward, noticing that his face had changed. He was no longer the beak-boy she remembered. Instead, he was very beautiful, like the men on the covers of underwear packages, and *GQ* magazine. Denise couldn't recall how long she had been staring at him before she had woken up.

It was a weird dream, that's all, she concluded, and went back to sleep.

* * *

It was three o'clock in the afternoon and Gwen was sitting at Marty's kitchen table. She had always liked Marty's kitchen. It was large and it resembled one of those cozy country kitchens that you sometimes see on television. She had gone to her class that morning, deciding to give it a shot in spite of her earlier decision of neglecting her classes while she sorted things out with Harry. She had left early when she lost interest. She couldn't will herself to concentrate. She had found Marty after he had finished his art class and told him that she wasn't feeling well, informing him that she was going to go back to his place to rest. That was a lie and Gwen hated lying, especially to Marty, but what choice did she have? What was she supposed to say? She couldn't tell Marty about her meeting with Harry and how Harry wasn't well mentally. Marty would react the same as before and become overprotective, and wouldn't let her go back to see him.

She would simply have to play this thing out day by day and hopefully, soon, some sort of resolution would finally be reached.

She would go see Harry.

Chapter Seven

Elsie was sitting at her desk when Gwen returned to Hans Memorial that Tuesday evening. It was the same routine: sign in, go to the Y-3 unit on the third floor, ask the bald man for Harry, and get escorted to the cafeteria to wait.

As before, Harry was brought in by the arm and seated in front of Gwen, the bald man telling him to behave again.

Gwen was happy that the hospital had a regular routine. It was comforting to know that because of it, nothing should go wrong. Hopefully.

Hello Gwen, was Harry's greeting. He was inside her head again.

"How are you?" she asked, noticing a flush of weariness in his face.

"It's funny that you would ask a question that demanded two answers," he replied.

"What do you mean?" she asked.

Harry's smile was almost smug; a smile Gwen didn't care for. He wondered if she knew that he was referring to both to his physical well being, as well as his mental health. "Let's just say that I'm tired today. I had a little trouble falling asleep last night."

"Are you all right?" Gwen pulled out her cigarettes from her purse.

"Just tired. We'll leave it at that." Harry scratched a flake of dry skin off his nose.

A silence settled. It was broken when Harry slid the ashtray from the side of the table between them. He lit a cigarette. Gwen did the same.

Once a solid cloud of smoke was hovering above them, Harry began what was to be a very long conversation.

"Gwen," he said, her name spoken sternly. "I was in the library for what I learned to be twenty years. While I was in there, I had no recognition of time. None. Better explained, it had the same type of time-sensation that dreams have. What seems like a minute in a dream is actually hours in real life."

Gwen took another puff of her cigarette. Harry's eyebrow suddenly arched. Gwen didn't notice the questioning expression on her own face.

"Let me clarify something for you," he said. "I don't think I mentioned how this library even came into the picture, or did I?"

Gwen shook her head. Harry had briefly mentioned something about a library but hadn't delved into any further detail about it.

"As you recall, I went to visit my wife's—Lauren's—grave." Harry waited for Gwen to nod before he continued. She did. "It started to rain. Eventually, I had found shelter in a coffin house."

Gwen nodded again and crossed her legs, getting more comfortable.

Harry took a stiff puff of his cigarette. "When I was inside the mos...mosalph, um, you know what I mean, something strange happened. I don't remember too much, but I knew that I was looking at something beautiful before I felt shaky—shaky and tired. Everything went black and I woke up in a—" Harry pressed his forehead with the palm of the hand that was holding his cigarette, trying to focus his thoughts. Sometimes remembering specifics was difficult. "A coffin," he finished. "Some place small. I can't recall how I got out of it but when I did, I was in the library. Maybe I wasn't on Earth anymore—who knows who was doing this to me? Aliens, I had thought."

This is a bit much, Gwen thought. *I can't believe I'm sitting here, listening to this. It doesn't make any sense but his sincerity when he speaks—I don't think he's lying. Why am I starting to care about what he has to say?*

"Gwen?" Harry asked, bringing her out of thought.

"Oh, sorry," she said, realizing she had drifted off.

Gwen stubbed out her cigarette and lit a fresh one.

Harry leaned on his elbows, rocking himself forward against the table. "I know this doesn't make sense, but please bear with me. I assure you that it will." He smiled reassuringly before he continued. "Almost immediately after I arrived in the library, the hallucinations started. I was seeing things, and people. Watching people commit the most gut-wrenching things. I hated it but couldn't change it."

Tears pooled in his eyes at the memory. Gwen offered him a tissue from her purse. He accepted without hesitation.

"Do you want to stop?" she asked, a hint of concern in her voice. Seeing people start to cry always caused tears to prick the corners of her own eyes.

Harry dabbed the tissue under his eyes. "No. I just find it hard not to cry when I visit the past. You should see my psychiatrist's office. There's two extra boxes of tissues there just for me." He managed to squeeze out a small smile. Gwen smiled back at Harry's attempt at humor. That was two jokes in as many visits.

He squished the tissue then put it in the front left pocket of his pajama top for future use. Crying would be inevitable.

"As I said yesterday, what I was seeing was all the things that people have done that go against the Word of God. They—"

"Word of God?" Gwen interrupted.

"Yes, the Word of God. I don't know how much you know about Christian dogma, Gwen, but the Word of God, or the Bible, as it is commonly known, is essentially a written blueprint for life. It's God's desire for the human race, all recorded in a book. When I say desire, I mean how God wishes for each of us to live our lives. In it are rules that are designed to protect us rather than hinder us, unlike what most people think. When one of those rules is broken, He calls it a sin, and it was these sins that I saw. All of them. Not one person's left out."

Gwen wrinkled her nose. "What do these sins have to do with me, or you for that matter?"

"Years ago, no one knows when, there was a fallout in Heaven. An angel named Lucifer tried to overthrow God, and literally attempted to become God himself. God of course, being a jealous God, wouldn't stand for it, and kicked Lucifer and his followers out of Heaven into Hell. One third of Heaven was lost that day.

"Making a long story short, ever since then, Lucifer, or the devil, as he is called, has been trying to get his revenge on God by robbing Him of His greatest love: us. Essentially, Lucifer has been trying to get humans to follow him rather than God. Thus, when that human dies, they go to Hell rather than Heaven. I know all this from countless Sundays going to church." Harry was proud of himself for saying all that without getting his words mixed up. He finished by saying, "Now, here is where all this makes sense."

Before continuing, Harry had to stub out his cigarette, which was burning so low the heat from it could be felt on his fingers. He lit a fresh one then went on. "From what I could gather, I was exposed to the sins of the world to understand the extreme severity of the era that was about to come. You see, Gwen, sin has power. It has enough power to literally cut humanity off from God Himself and unless you are redeemed—you are lost." Harry emphasized his last three words.

Gwen's eyes grew large and her heart started to beat hard. She was getting anxious for what Harry was about to reveal.

He leaned closer to her. Gwen looked over to the bald man, who was watching them intently. The bald man gave her a dirty look. He didn't want Gwen to get close to Harry. She returned the scowl and leaned closer to Harry just for spite.

Harry twirled his cigarette between his fingers. "Sins had been accumulating, stored if you will, in that library. Every book within it contained a written account of every single sin committed by mankind. Five years ago, the recordings stopped for a brief period. For how long I don't know, but in that moment"—he paused, squinting his eyes, seriously—"in that moment my hallucinations and visions stopped. I thought that I was being released. Then I saw the books begin to glow, then slowly melt."

Harry could tell that Gwen thought he was sounding far-fetched. He put up his hand as if to caution her but instead said, "Please bear with me. The books melted, like wax on a candle. The liquid, or whatever the hell it was, flowed toward the center of the room, toward a very large book in the center. Within moments a cradle or a cocoon or something like that formed, and through the red-ish, semitransparent liquid, I saw a child. A baby. It was disgusting, all swimming about in a big glob of goo." Harry leaned back in his chair. "After that I was back at my wife's grave."

Gwen, too, sat back, taking a long drag off her cigarette, exhaling a small grimace. Harry grimaced, too, but at the memory. He knew that his story was hard to believe. To convince someone of this was pretty much impossible. Hell, for the past five years he had been trying to convince Dr. Woodrose this had all been real, and had gotten nowhere. He was hoping that somehow Gwen would be able to swallow it all.

After all, there was something different about her.

* * *

It was seven o'clock when Marty Bones got an unsettling feeling in his stomach. It wasn't nausea or butterflies or even anxiety that swirled around in his mid-section. He couldn't quite place it, but he knew something was wrong.

Heart quickening, Marty raced to the telephone and tried to raise Gwen on her cellular. Much to his dismay, she had turned it off. He left a message on her voice-mail for her to call him back as soon as she got his message.

Marty sat down on the plush, leather chair in the living room and waited for the feeling to pass. He prayed that Gwen would be all right.

* * *

At five past eight, Gwen stretched her arms and released some of her restlessness. She had been sitting with Harry for nearly three hours.

During that time, Harry had told her that the sins of the world had fused together, forming a human being. A son of Satan, as he called the child.

Hearing this, Gwen almost announced that she had to get going, but when Harry looked deep into her eyes, she was compelled to stay. When he did this, he had put more than just thoughts into her head. He had put an overwhelming desire to listen to him and to oblige to whatever he would ask of her.

"Please Gwen, I'm not trying to scare you," he had said. "But it is imperative that you listen to me, no matter how impossible all this sounds."

Harry went onto explain that this child created by the world's sins had been foretold in the Word of God and that he would soon reign over the earth, eventually bringing it to its end.

Gwen recalled her school assignment on the end times. She found it more than coincidental that she would receive an assignment like that right before she had met Harry. *Somehow Harry knew about it and used it to bring me to him,* she concluded. *Whoa, slow down, Gwen. You better test the water before jumping in the pool.*

Harry had also finally explained to her how he was able to put those damned thoughts into her head. For twenty years he was exposed to demonic powers and the true power of such suggestion, such controlling words and exploitation. He had said that their ability to force almost irresistible thoughts into a person's head had rubbed off on him, like static off a rug. Somehow, being exposed to them for so long granted him with their ability. Whether this was divinely ordained or not, he didn't know. He said that he pretended that it was so that he didn't feel guilty about using such dark abilities.

Harry had used that power to his advantage when he had discovered it. Approximately a year after he had been sent to Hans Memorial, he had found himself extremely depressed and missing his wife. Tears flowed freely and the searing pain of hurt continuously washed through his chest.

He had begged a nurse for more anti-depressants, but because he had already had his prescribed dose for that day, he had been declined.

Harry had threatened suicide and started thrashing his room apart, tearing it up in a fit of frustration and hurt. He had screamed uncontrollably when he accidentally scrapped the inside of his palm against the corner of his bed, the skin having been torn open in two places.

Two large male nurses accompanied by three security guards were quickly alerted to his room, to try to stop him and give him a sedative. When they arrived, Harry had been throwing his mattress back and forth across the room, spilling and breaking anything that was in its way. Blood was matted in handprints on the mattress. One of the security guards had shouted at him to stop, but Harry told them to all go to hell.

Two of the guards leapt at Harry, tackling him to the floor while one of the nurses prepared the sedative; Valium, a nurse later recalled. Both of Harry's arms had been pinned and the third security guard sat on his legs, trying to keep them from flailing. The nurse with the sedative kneeled down beside Harry's arm, the other nurse preparing a place for the needle to go in.

"This won't hurt as much if you would just stop fighting!" the nurse with the needle had said.

Harry stopped struggling and squeezed his eyes shut, all his emotion rushing to his head.

"I wish you would just leave me alone!" he had shouted at them.

After the needle was administered, the guards and nurses slowly eased their restraint and backed away. Harry, dazed, got up and pressed his back against the wall of his now torn up room. For what seemed like an eternity, the five men looked glassy-eyed at him, a flash coming over their eyes, until one of the nurses asked, "What is it that you need, Harry?"

Harry swallowed hard and as politely as he could he had asked the nurse for some more anti-depressants. The nurse told him that he had already had his prescribed amount for the day and that he couldn't be administered any more until morning. Harry's eyes lit up in fury and he glared at the nurse. From Harry's perspective he could see right into him, and for a brief instant, felt indescribably powerful. He asked for his medication again and the nurse obliged. Shocked, but glad, Harry thanked him and then curled up on his mattress (which was in an odd position on the floor) and went to sleep. When the nurse returned with the anti-depressant, he woke Harry, gave him the pills and a small shot glass of water to wash them down then let Harry return to sleep. To this day, the nurse could still not recall why he had obeyed Harry's command.

Since that incident, Harry had experimented with this feeling of power and eventually discovered that he could control people's thoughts. At first he tried it on small things like medication, then on bigger things like being able to go outside into the courtyard, something that was not allowed for any patients in the Y-3 unit for fear that they might try to escape. He had also thought about using his power to have himself discharged but knew that he would be unable to take care of himself on his own.

He decided to stay at the hospital because he wanted to, not because he had to.

Gwen was amazed when he told her this and tried to put him to the test.

"Try me," she said. "Get me to do something."

Immediately Gwen grabbed a fresh cigarette and lit it.

"Well?" she asked, her face showing that she was waiting.

Harry tapped his finger on the top of his cigarette package. "I wanted you to have another cigarette," he said calmly and then smiled.

Gwen removed the cigarette from her mouth and looked at it with disbelief. She decided to test him again.

"What am I thinking now?" She waited for Harry's answer.

He said nothing.

"I thought—" she began.

"I can't read thoughts, Gwen. I can only insert them," he said, and smiled again.

"Oh."

There was a hint of disappointment in Gwen's voice. She had hoped that he could read her mind. That way, he could get a better idea as to what she was feeling inside. Harry leaned closer to her. Gwen took his cue to do the same. Just before he spoke, the bald man interrupted them.

"You got less than an hour, Harry!" he told him. The bald man didn't need to shout. Harry wasn't *that* far away.

Gwen was thankful that on Tuesday evening's visiting hours were extended by an hour until nine o'clock.

She and Harry leaned close together again.

"This creature, Gwen, was born five years ago. Now he's a child and he's going to grow up quickly. Our time is short. Have you ever read the book of Revelation?"

"Bits and pieces. I skimmed through it. I had to for a school project," she said.

"Do you recall it mentioning that a second beast will come out of Hell and it will follow the first beast? The first beast being the devil?"

Gwen nodded. "The Antichrist."

Harry nodded, approving of her knowledge. Her eyes were fixed on Harry's. He wasn't putting thoughts into her head. She was truly interested in all that he had to say.

"This beast will one day rise to great power," he continued. "He will have a position in the world's government that will force every human being on the planet to obey him and follow his rule. There will be those, Christians, which will resist him because they know he's an agent of evil. But there will be many many more that won't. Those who resist him will be persecuted and captured and even killed. And those who follow him will have a good life. We can't let this happen. We can't let this man or thing or whatever the hell you want to call him do this!"

"We?" Gwen asked sharply.

Harry grinned. "Yes, Gwen—We."

Chapter Eight

Harry Thomas was satisfied with his most recent meeting with Gwen. He had told her everything, or mostly everything, that she needed to know. He was glad of Gwen's ability to take in all that he was saying. Sure, he had opened her mind for her, but she still absorbed all the information much faster than expected. He also remembered that his relationship with Gwen had been preordained and because of that, he had nothing to worry about.

Gwen would finish learning what she needed to know, and then she would execute his plan. It was imperative that she succeeded. Millions—if not, billions—of lives counted on it

Harry looked ahead, avoiding eye contact with the bald man, who was gripping his arm. They walked back to Harry's room (the bald man walking, Harry dragging his feet) and Harry was locked in for the night. He followed the same routine as always: turning off the main lights, and turning on the lamp near his bed. He fluffed his blankets and pillow, and settled in. He lay there thinking about Gwen. There was only one thing left for him to do and he would do it tomorrow when she visited again. After that, Gwen would leave her old life behind forever.

* * *

The lock was sticking a little, but Gwen managed to finally release it and let herself into Marty's front landing. He came out of the kitchen, and when he saw her, he hurried over to her and scooped her up in his arms. He kissed her lips briefly then set her down.

"What's gotten into you?" she asked, her arms still around his waist.

"I was just worried about you, that's all," he told her.

Gwen removed her coat and shoes, and followed Marty back into the kitchen. She sat down at the table while he got them both something to drink.

Each having a cup in hand, Marty sat down on the chair next to her and looked at her with a sigh of relief.

"What?" she asked, while chugging down her glass of fruit punch.

He gazed at her lovingly. "Nothing. I'm just happy you're here."

"Where else would I be?"

Marty looked away, his attention on his cup.

"That's not what I mean. It's just that…that earlier I got, I don't know, a strange feeling, like something was wrong. I'm just happy you're okay." Marty looked at her for a moment, took a sip of his fruit punch, and then asked, "You are okay, aren't you?"

"Of course. Why wouldn't I be?" she replied.

He sighed. "I don't know."

Marty stood up, went over to her, and kissed her.

Before either of them knew it, they were naked, making love on the kitchen floor. Gwen enjoyed Marty's eagerness and how 'into it' he was. After, when the moment had cooled, they went upstairs to Marty's bedroom to finish what they had started in the kitchen.

As the fatigue set in, Marty asked where she had been earlier. She told him the truth: Hans Memorial Hospital to see Harry. Marty was not impressed. Gwen eased the tension by sliding her hand between his legs. Marty wanted to pull her off him, but instead relaxed and let her play. She assured him that she saw Harry for her essay assignment and that Harry had been very insightful into the topic of visions and what it was like to have one. It was a partial truth, anyway.

Marty wasn't sure what to say next, but he took a stab at it. "Is this Harry Thomas guy all he's cracked up to be?"

"What do mean?" Gwen sat up a little.

"I mean is he helping you with your project. Are you getting what you need or—"

"What?" she beckoned him.

"I don't know, it just seems kind of strange that you would go see a guy like that twice."

"Guy like that," Gwen said, repeating Marty's words more sternly.

"Gwen, the guy is in the nuthouse. I just think that maybe it would be a good idea for you not to see him anymore."

"Why?" She propped herself up on a pillow and faced him.

Marty sat up also. Gwen's hand left him. She clasped her fingers together above the sheets. Marty could sense the tension starting to rise between them.

"I don't think a young girl should go to a psychiatric hospital for a school project. Doesn't that seem odd? What's there that can't be learned from a book? It's almost like you're fixated on this guy."

He turned away. She covered herself with the quilt.

"Marty," she said, "I don't like where this is going. What does it matter?" She crossed her arms under her breasts.

They both took a deep breath. They didn't want to fight, especially just after being so intimate.

"It matters because this guy could be dangerous," he said, raising his voice unexpectedly. Gwen's mouth dropped.

He started speaking with his hands. "I know I probably sound overprotective, but think about this: this isn't normal. Far from it. The guy could be a serial killer or something. He was found at his wife's grave for fuck's sakes. As far as we know, he could have killed her. And who knows? Maybe she wasn't the first person, either?"

Gwen frowned, her teeth grinding together. "You're damn right you're sounding overprotective—and don't you dare tell me what to do!"

He turned back to her. "Gwen…"

"Forget it." Gwen got up, bringing the quilt with her, causing Marty to scramble for the sheet that was twisted around his leg. She got herself dressed, glaring at him the whole time, and walked down the stairs.

"What are you doing?" Marty called after her.

"I'm getting some air." She shook her head in disbelief. "I don't believe this."

The building fires that were burning inside of them began to overheat, and the inevitable shouting match came.

Marty followed after her, waddling quickly, trying to keep the bed sheet around his waist to cover himself. "Gwen, get back here! Why the hell is this guy so important! What the fuck is going on!"

"What the fuck is going on! What the fuck is a matter with you! Why the hell are you starting a fight!" Gwen shot back, her throat pinching from the strain of her voice.

Then, they both started screaming.

"I didn't start anything Gwen! I just asked a simple question!" Marty clutched the sheet to his waist, his fists tightening around its bunches.

"Yeah, but then you blew it way out of proportion! What I do is my *own* fucking business!"

"It *is* my business if something looks like it might be dangerous for you!" he snapped back.

Gwen then fired back a remark that startled them both: "GO TO HELL!"

She put her shoes on, grabbed her coat, and stormed out the door. The door slammed so hard behind her that the clasp didn't latch and it bounced back open.

"Shit!" Marty said and turned back toward his bedroom to get dressed.

* * *

The next day Gwen didn't go to school. Coming straight home after leaving Marty's, she had thrown herself onto her bed and cried herself to sleep. At one point throughout the night she had woken up with a splitting headache and the realization that she had been crying while she slept. She slept fitfully and cried some more, then finally fell back to sleep around four o'clock.

In the morning, Marty didn't come to pick her up for school. Gwen didn't care. She didn't want to have anything to do with him. Not now. Maybe not ever, by the way she was feeling.

He didn't understand what was happening between her and Harry. There was no way that he could have understood.

Gwen lay in bed, reveling in her anger towards him. She planned to sleep most of the day away then to get herself ready and go see Harry again.

She ended up sleeping until one-thirty that afternoon. When she woke up, her headache was gone and she was feeling much better. There was an urge to call Marty. She ignored it.

* * *

Marty didn't go to school that day, either. He had laid awake most of the night, thinking about his fight with Gwen and how stupid it really was. But he did feel that he was right. He only wanted to protect her. But like all their other discussions that turned into arguments, it had gotten way out of hand. Marty was finally able to fall asleep around two o'clock that morning. He slept until one o'clock that afternoon.

When he got up, he drowned his sorrows in a bowl of cereal. He watched television until he dozed off.

* * *

Hans Memorial Hospital was a bit busier in the afternoon, Gwen saw, when she glanced at the half-full waiting area in the lobby. Elsie wasn't there when Gwen checked in. A young girl, no more than twenty-four, named Sandy, was in Elsie's place.

Elsie probably doesn't come in until around three or four, Gwen figured.

She went through the preliminaries of signing in then went up to the third floor. Subconsciously, she expected to see the bald man, but instead, she saw that an incredibly cute guy with brown hair had taken his place. His nametag read Carl and beneath his name it said that he was the Head Orderly on Y-3. Gwen admired his well-proportioned physique and assumed that he must workout daily. After a quick, dirty thought, Gwen asked him if she could see Harry.

Carl escorted her to the cafeteria, and Gwen was forced to sit somewhere else instead of the usual window seat. Where she and Harry normally sat was a young, rough looking man sitting with an older woman. Gwen assumed that the young man was the older woman's son. Gwen felt bad for her. It must be hard to know that your child is suffering and there's hardly anything you could do about it.

Five minutes had passed before Harry was escorted into the room. Carl sat him down in front of her and let the two of them be. Gwen was surprised that Carl hadn't told Harry to behave, instead offering him a smile as if he were happy that Harry had a visitor.

Deep, gray circles swelled beneath Harry's eyes. His hair was more of a mess than usual, some of its strands tangled up in his beard. The blue striped pajamas he wore also looked worn and dirty.

"Are you feeling okay?" Gwen asked, concerned.

Harry sighed, a wheeze in his throat. A weight pressed upon Gwen's heart. She was starting to care for Harry, like a close friend. She hated it. It was too strange.

"I'll be fine," Harry said.

They both sat quietly for a short time, each in their own little place of discomfort. Gwen slid the ashtray between them and lit a cigarette. She offered one to Harry. He declined with a wave of his hand.

Again, there was silence. Gwen looked over to where Carl was sitting and noticed a puzzled look on his face.

He's probably wondering why we aren't talking, Gwen thought. She gave him a small grin. He returned one to her. He looked gorgeous when he smiled.

Finally, Harry came to life and drew Gwen's attention towards him. "Gwen, we haven't much time," he said with a cold stare.

"What do you mean?" She ashed her cigarette.

Harry's eyes stared past her, as if speaking to someone behind her shoulder.

"It's hard to explain, and I apologize for being too vague, but I've been warned not to see you anymore."

Gwen wrinkled her brow. "Warned? By who, the doctors?"

"No. Not by them. Like I said, it's hard to explain. I've been having visions again, seeing things that have been telling me to leave you alone. I think I'm going crazy again. I was good for a while, there. No more visions. Now…they're back."

Gwen didn't like what she was hearing. The way Harry was talking disturbed her. She suddenly became very uncomfortable.

She took a stiff puff of her cigarette and exhaled it slowly, trying to relax. "Harry, I don't quite understand. You're starting to scare me."

Harry reached for her hand. She pulled it away. "Gwen, listen to me. There's something I have to tell you."

Carl sat comfortably across the room, slouched in his chair, happy to see Harry finally talk to his guest. For as long as Carl had helped in taking care of Harry, he had never seen him have a visitor before. He knew Harry was lonely, and as much as the nurses tried to befriend him, Harry brushed them off and told them that he'd rather be alone. The only nurse whom Harry would sometimes talk to was Carl. *Harry probably likes me because I have the same name as his son,* Carl figured. Harry didn't know that Carl knew his son's name. The orderly had one time asked Dr. Woodrose what he thought of Harry's taking a shining to him. That's when he learned of Harry's son, Carl.

Just then, an odd and cold feeling came over Carl. His body felt as if a large snake were slithering figure 8's up and down his body. Over and over, the rough skin scratched through his uniform.

His muscles locked. He unwillingly stood up. His legs were uncontrollably forcing him to walk over towards Harry and Gwen. He tried to speak but instead was only able to produce a wet gurgle.

Out of the corner of his eye, Harry saw Carl coming towards them. Harry's body began to twitch violently when he saw what was covering Carl. It was a large red and orange snake with two heads circling over and around his body. Beneath the snake's empty black eyes its lips curled backward, revealing yellow, dripping fangs. Harry grabbed Gwen's hands, forcing her closer to him.

"HARRY!" Gwen shrieked in surprise. Her legs were shaking.

"Gwen, listen," Harry said with grave seriousness, "they're coming for me. Listen closely to what I have to tell you."

"QUIET!" hissed a voice that only Harry was able to hear. He looked over and saw the snake's long leathery tongue lashing out, licking Carl's face. The orderly was only a few feet away. Time was running out.

"Walk away, Harry," the snake said. Harry glared back with determined eyes. He pulled Gwen even closer, feeling her resist. Gwen saw the panic flush into Harry's eyes, as intensely as he could see it in her own.

"Harry you're scaring me! Let go!" Gwen told him, trying to pull her hands away from his tight grip.

Carl stopped at the table. Gwen looked up at the orderly.

"Help me, please," she pleaded. A tear dripped from her eye.

Carl's eyes looked distant. He grinned and extended his hand, grabbing Harry's arm, pulling him upward off his feet. The mother and son near the window stopped their conversation and watched the spectacle.

"BACK OFF!" Harry shouted, using his palms to push Carl to the floor, himself staggering backwards from the force.

Harry grabbed Gwen, both hands on either side of her jaw, and painfully pulled her head toward his. Gwen felt her head smack hard against his skull, a red flash sweeping over her vision. Immediately, she felt as though she was being covered in a warm, gooey liquid. Her skin turned to gooseflesh.

Everything went fuzzy. Her body gave out under her. She collapsed to the floor, not feeling the impact of her body hitting the tiles.

Carl grabbed Harry and delivered a swift punch to his face. Harry shook it off and shrieked at the sight of the two-headed snake. He tried desperately to jerk himself free from Carl's hold. He looked down towards Gwen and watched with sympathy as she began twitching on the floor in a fitful REM sleep.

Harry had given her a dream.

The mother and son by the window were frozen in terror as Carl and Harry struggled. They both breathed a sigh of relief when four security guards, hearing the screams from down the hall, filled the doorway. At the sight of the guards, the snake that covered Carl let out a low growl.

They raced over to the two men fighting, and ripped them apart, with three of the guards rendering Harry unconscious in the process. The fourth security guard checked with Carl to see if he was okay. Carl nodded. The security guard told him that a couple of nurses have also been alerted to the situation.

The snake slithered away from Carl. It had failed. Sliding across the floor, it faded into nothingness. Carl felt the intense grip on his body release the moment the snake disappeared. The orderly wobbled over to a chair and sat down.

Seeing that Carl was seated, the guard went over to Gwen. She was curled up in a fetal position on the floor.

"Miss? Can you hear me?" the guard pleaded with her, his voice loud.

Gwen didn't respond.

The guard was about to ask again when a nurse came from behind him and put a hand on his shoulder.

"It'll be all right," he said. "I'll take it from here."

The guard made his way to the mother and son duo, calming them down while the nurses got to work.

The nurses laid Harry's limp body down on a bed on wheels, taking him to the infirmary. A nurse attended to his cuts.

Carl, escorted by the same three security guards that had tackled Harry, was led into a separate room where he would have his wounds tended to. He didn't really know what had happened, but was pleased to find that his voice had returned. He tried explaining to the guards all that had happened. They didn't believe him.

Gwen was taken on another bed on wheels to the emergency room, where she was to be treated for shock. A muscle relaxant was introduced into her system. Soon her body finally stopped twitching.

She had fallen into a deep, coma-like sleep.

* * *

Marty had been brooding all day long. He couldn't believe that he and Gwen had had a fight. Sure, throughout their relationship there had been a few bumps and grinds, but this was the first one that really got him hurting inside. The first that made his stomach feel as if it were filled with sand.

In between television shows he thought about phoning her to try and reconcile. He was confident that she was at home hurting, too, but his pride got in the way. He still felt completely justified in all his actions. He was looking out for her, that's all. He didn't call.

It was a little after four o'clock when he finally put his foot down and got his ass in gear. In spite of what he had felt earlier, he picked up the phone and dialed Gwen's number, secretly hoping that either she wouldn't answer or wasn't home. On the third ring Denise greeted Marty.

"Hi," Marty said back to her. He was glad that she answered instead of Gwen. This way, he'd be able to collect his thoughts and maybe vent on Denise for a little while first.

"Hi, Marty," she said, almost enthusiastically. "What's up?"

"Not much, just calling for Gwen. Has she told you anything?" He bit his lip in anticipation.

"No. Was she supposed to? She was still sleeping when I left for the day and she was gone when I got home about ten minutes ago. She didn't spend the night at your place?" Denise sounded concerned. Marty liked it.

"No," he said, his voice small.

"Why? What's wrong?"

"Well, we kind of had a fight and I was sort of hoping to talk to her, maybe try to work it out."

There was a pause before Denise asked, "Is there anything I can do?"

Marty pondered the question for a moment. An interesting thought crept into his mind. "In fact, there is," he told her. "Do you want to come over?"

There was silence on the other end of the receiver. Marty wondered if he had said something wrong. He was about to say something else as a recovery, but Denise spoke up and eased the tension.

"I'd be delighted," she said.

Chapter Nine

The air was thick with warm mist, shaded a soft purple. It smelled like stale peanuts. Gwen wasn't sure where she was, but she felt comfortable, familiar, as if she had been to this place one time before. The pale purply haze clouded most of her vision. Through the fog, Gwen strained to see where she was.

Her mouth fell open as she took in her surroundings. She was in a library.

The library.

The fog began to fade. The library was almost exactly like she had imagined it when Harry had described it to her. The walls were lined with heavy, oak bookshelves containing large, red leather bound volumes of text; each labeled with a place and date. The room grew warm with dim, yellow light. The smell of stale peanuts remained.

Gwen looked around some more and saw, in the corner, a coffin with its lid hinged open. She stepped closer to get a better look. Gwen presumed that this was the same coffin that had transported Harry to this place so long ago. A layer of dust had settled inside its plush lining, adding to the musty smell it emitted.

Moving on, Gwen approached one of the bookshelves. She looked through the names and labels on each of them, trying to find one particular volume. Her uneasiness left her. She was comfortable.

She found what she was looking for: ENGLAND 1903.

She had searched for this particular book because it was the only book that Harry had happened to mention. Gwen reached out with her hand, trembling, wanting to touch its leather spine, but pulled back recalling that a cold hand had forced Harry to do the same thing.

She breathed out audibly, relieved, proud of herself for not taking an unnecessary risk. Gwen stepped away from the bookshelf and turned around, scanning the rest of the room. She saw a dried up puddle of pale yellow chunky mush on the floor. She gagged when she realized what it was: Harry's throw up.

Without warning, the floor began to shake violently and Gwen felt her feet sweep out from under her. She fell backwards, landing hard on her tailbone. There was a small rumbling. She knew that she had better cover her head. The books that were on the shelf flew off their ledges and showered all around her, some of the books knocking her palms hard against her skull. Their impact caused an echo inside her head, its awful ring remaining.

When the showering of leather and paper stopped, Gwen stood up, brushed herself off, and surveyed the room.

Before she had a chance to ascertain what had happened, another minor quake hit and again she was tossed backward, bruising her tailbone a second time. She let out a grunt of pain.

In the middle of the room, a large and translucent red, gelatinous blob began flooding in through the cracks in the floor. Soon the blob grew to a foot in diameter. Gwen could see what was inside it: a baby. She gasped and almost threw up in the same spot Harry had at the sight of the child swimming about the blob in that sea of red, sticky goo.

Something moved beside Gwen's leg. She looked down. A large book slid in the direction of the baby and its encompassing fetus.

The room filled with the sound of shuffled movement. Gwen watched as all the books turned to face the fetus, each bowing toward to it in worship.

Gwen screamed into the filthy, dry air. Someone, or something, else present broke her sound, shushing her. Gwen jumped to her feet and began to tear, completely afraid. Her heart felt as though it would jump out of her mouth, her stomach feeling as if a whole nest of bats were invading it.

Gwen bent over, preparing herself to throw up. The wave passed.

The fetus pulsed, the baby inside curling itself up then extending out its limbs repeatedly.

Gwen jumped when she felt something cold slide into her hand. She looked down and saw that she was holding a smooth, shiny, silver revolver.

It was then that everything became clear. Gwen knew what she had to do.

* * *

Slowly, everything flowed from black to a blur of colors, then finally to the sharp image of a television set. Gwen squinted her eyes, focusing, trying to discern where she was. At first she expected to be in the *library* but instead found herself in a hospital room. The brightness of the white walls made her cover her eyes.

There was pressure on her left forearm and when she looked at it, she saw that she was hooked up to an intravenous unit, some sort of drug being pumped into her. She closed her eyes again, letting the discovery of her new surroundings settle. She started to slip back into a stupor, but was pulled out by a soothing voice. She opened her eyes, focused, and saw a doctor looming over her, one hand holding a stethoscope, in the other a clipboard.

"Hello, Gwen," he said. "I'm Doctor Avery."

"W-what happened?" Gwen groaned, her throat dry. She was thirsty. Curls of hair lay flat and damp against her forehead.

Dr. Avery paused a moment, then answered her question. "You passed out in the Y-3 unit cafeteria while visiting a patient of ours. Do you remember visiting anyone, Gwen?"

"Harry Thomas," she replied, her voice a whisper. She was extremely tired and was having a hard time trying to keep herself awake.

"Harry Thomas," Dr. Avery repeated. "That's right. Do you remember what happened during your visit?"

Gwen swallowed, feeling as if a stone went down her throat. She did her best to recollect the events prior to her sudden collapse. "We...we were sitting at a table in the cafeteria talking, then"—Gwen saw a quick flash of Harry grabbing her wrists—"He grabbed me. HE GRABBED ME!"

She sprung up, her eyes wide. Dr. Avery put his hands on her shoulders, trying to calm her. He finally persuaded her to lie back down again.

"It's okay, Gwen. It's okay," he assured her.

"What...happened to Harry?" she asked.

Dr. Avery brought his clipboard up so it rested on an angle against his chest. He pulled a pen out of his coat pocket. "Don't worry about him. He's been tended to. I must sincerely apologize for his behavior and I'm sorry that Carl didn't act sooner."

"Carl?" she asked.

"The nurse who was supervising your visit with Harry Thomas," Dr. Avery said.

Gwen nodded, and asked if she would be all right and how much time she would have to spend in the hospital. Dr. Avery told her that he wanted to run a few more tests to determine what had happened, why she collapsed. Pen in hand, he scribbled something on his clipboard as he made her state her name, address, and phone number. He compared the information to the driver's license that was found in her purse. Gwen told him her information just fine. He smiled, content that there wasn't any memory loss.

What Dr. Avery didn't know was that the tests were not going to find anything wrong with Gwen. Her sudden collapse had nothing to do with herself, or even Harry for that matter.

Strange forces were at work in the lives of Gwen Reeves and Harry Thomas. Forces that neither one would be able to see, nor hear.

PART TWO

THE CHILD

Chapter Ten

Five year old Calvin Mandalay stood on his driveway in a decorous Toronto suburb, gripping his basketball, holding it high above his head as he prepared to make his next shot.

Like most boys his age, Calvin enjoyed basketball and every night for the past week and a half, he had come outside after dinner and shot baskets until his mother had told him to come inside for his bath before bedtime.

Even though he was only a little over three feet tall, Calvin was talented when it came to playing the game. He had gotten his mother and his Uncle Ken to mount a basketball hoop (complete with net and backboard) onto the no longer working garage door about three feet above Calvin's head. His uncle was proud of him and kept telling Calvin that he was a natural at the game. Calvin didn't quite understand what that meant, other than it had meant something good. And coming from Uncle Ken, that had made it extra special.

Calvin was growing up fast in a single parent home, his mother working shift work as a cashier at a nearby supermarket. Uncle Ken would come over at least three times a week to help her around the house, and take care of Calvin when she was not around. Ken didn't have any kids of his own, so he paid extra special attention to his nephew every time he came for a visit. Calvin looked up to him as a father. And Ken treated Calvin as if the boy was his own son.

Here, above his brow, Calvin saw the red rim of the basketball hoop just below the blur of the orange and black treaded ball before of his eyes. He bent his knees and pushed upward with all of his might, launching the ball skyward. It twirled as it sailed through the air, spiraling, finding its way through the red and blue net that hung loosely from the rim. The ball landed hard on the ground and bounced back down the graveled driveway to him.

The preparation for his next shot was interrupted when he heard his mother, Victoria, calling him. "Calvin, honey, time to come in."

He glanced over at her. She was half hanging out of the doorway, wearing jeans and a pink knit shirt.

"Can I shoot it jus' one more, Mom?" he asked.

"Just once and then you have to come in and take your bath," she instructed him with her index finger.

Calvin quickly returned his attention to the hoop, gripped the ball, and positioned it high above his head. Another hoist upward and the ball sailed, meeting its target.

There was no doubt; Uncle Ken had been right. He *was* a natural.

* * *

After a hot bath and much debate with his mother over whether or not *Soft Bubbles Shampoo For Kids* would sting his eyes, Calvin Mandalay was tucked into bed. His mother saw how tired and cranky Calvin was, and assumed that he had been tuckered out from shooting baskets in the cool night air.

Like most nights, when Calvin was put to bed promptly at half past eight, Victoria made herself a cup of tea and sat in the front room, this time always being her first official *sit* for the day.

Being a single mother had taken its toll on the thirty-six year old woman. Her hair was prematurely graying, the smooth skin under her eyes forming tight little wrinkles. The receipt of early gray hairs didn't bother her that much, a problem easily cured by monthly visits to a hair salon, where she would have her hair dyed a dark brown with a tint of red. The gradual decline in her appearance would get her down from time to time, though to be expected, when you had to divide your time between full time hours and full time childcare.

Despite the physical drawbacks of being a mother, Victoria wouldn't trade a moment spent with Calvin for anything in the world. He was a blessing to her and he had come along at the right time in her life, a time when she had needed him the most.

It was almost six years ago, in late October, when Victoria Mandalay had lost her husband to the seduction of a much younger woman. Eighteen years old, if she recalled. Victoria had been suspicious of an affair for quite awhile, but when her husband, David, had come right out and confessed it, Victoria felt she had no choice but to send him packing.

It was a year of intense depression before realizing that she needed something else in her life, something to possibly lift her spirits. It wasn't until one night, after more than her share of drinks at a pool hall just down the road, that Victoria happened upon an elderly woman at a bus shelter. Like her, the elderly woman had been waiting in the cold for the city transit system to take her home. Before Victoria knew it, she was blurting out all of her life's disappointments at the old woman, rambling on and on about David's affair with the eighteen year old girl.

The older woman, Victoria couldn't remember her name, other than it had started with an S, had somehow gotten onto the topic of children and the joy that they bring. Victoria remembered laughing at such a silly thought, but by the time she had gotten home that evening, she had the name and number of an adoption agency in her coat pocket. After six months of debate, Victoria gave in and went down to Love and Leaves, the child adoption agency recommended by the older woman, and applied for a child.

It had taken a month of preliminary interviews, but the board at Love and Leaves decided that Victoria was a suitable applicant and that an official adoption interview would be arranged.

At one of the earlier interviews, Victoria was surprised at the types of questions they had asked her: how long had she been a Canadian citizen; her sexual preference; even her religious background. Answering these seemingly useless questions had been worth it because six months later she was allowed to bring home a baby boy. She was surprised at how quickly she was allowed to have the child, but never gave it a second thought, as she knew so little of these matters. She named him Calvin after her father and gave him the middle name of William after her brother.

She was never informed of how baby Calvin was brought to Love and Leaves or how the boy was found by an elderly gentleman, in a basket deep inside a cemetery on a loosely trodden path in a city a province away.

Victoria Mandalay could never know that. Never.

* * *

The dreams of Calvin Mandalay were no different than that of any other five year old. He dreamt of superheroes, mostly adventures fighting by the side of his hero, The Cosmic Kid; of some of the things that had happened the previous day; and, of course, being an all-star basketball player, the only five year old allowed to play in the NBA.

But tonight was different.

Calvin was sleeping in the bedroom across from his mother's, when he was abruptly awakened by a whisper in his bedroom. *Run, Calvin, run,* was the call.

First thinking that he was hearing things, Calvin dismissed the soft whispering. But when the voice whispered to him a second time, Calvin sprang out of bed, burst through his mother's bedroom door and dove into bed beside her.

Awakening with a start, Victoria looked over to where her son was snuggling furiously under her arm.

"What's wrong?" she asked, clearing her throat of the taste of sleep. Calvin didn't say anything, instead burying himself deeper beneath her arm.

Victoria readjusted herself so that she was able to look at him. Calvin huddled in a little ball beside her, his eyes squeezed shut as if he didn't want to see anything.

"Calvin, honey, are you okay?" she asked again, gently.

He didn't respond, pretending to be asleep. Victoria knew that when Calvin decided not to speak, it was his way of showing her that he was upset. Comforting her son, she wrapped her arm around him and with the other, pulled the covers over him and herself. She rubbed his shoulder and neck to calm him down.

She would ask him about what happened in the morning.

* * *

"Hey there, kiddo!" was Calvin's greeting from Uncle Ken the following morning.

The boy's uncle sat on the chair closest to the window in the kitchen while his mother sipped her coffee. She turned her attention to her son.

Calvin walked sluggishly into the room and slid slowly into the chair opposite Victoria.

"Good morning," she said with a smile, glancing up at the messy pile of dirty blonde hair that Calvin had on top of his head.

"So, how's the game going?" Uncle Ken asked. "Dream of hoops and nets last night?"

Calvin gave him a smile and shook his head, shaking the residual sleep out of his system.

"Here, let me get you something," Victoria said, rising from her chair toward the cupboard where the cereal was kept.

"No school today?" Uncle Ken asked.

"I don't start 'til twelve, 'member?" Calvin said, poking fun at the fact that Uncle Ken always seemed to forget that he was only five years old, and that kindergarten class didn't start until the day was half done.

"Silly me," Uncle Ken replied, mocking himself. He knew that his nephew didn't start until noon but enjoyed playing the part of Mr. Forgetfulness.

Victoria returned to the table and placed a bowl of flakes in front of Calvin. He grabbed the handle of the oversized spoon with his small hand and dug in, spilling milk as he lifted the cereal to his mouth.

"So, did you sleep good, Calvin?" she asked.

"Sure he did," contributed Uncle Ken.

"Well, he must have. He slept with me on the big bed." Victoria had a smile on her face, a sight that pleased Ken. She didn't smile often but when she did, the room seemed to almost practically light up.

Calvin placed the spoon back in his cereal bowl, causing more milk to slosh out of the sides. "I guess," he said.

"You sure?"

"Um…yep."

"Okay," Victoria agreed, knowing full well that it wasn't the truth. She didn't see any point in dragging on about it any further. She knew Calvin had had a bad dream but also knew that if he wanted to keep it to himself, then she would have to respect that.

Uncle Ken turned his attention to the boy. He had to restrain himself from laughing at the sight of his nephew who had flake pieces and milk running down his chin.

"When you finish up with that we'll go outside and play, all right?"

Calvin smiled wide and almost lost the cereal that was in his mouth onto the table. "Okay," he said, and continued to eat.

Chapter Eleven

Gwen Reeves arrived at the Toronto City Centre Airport, queasy from the flight. She had never been a fan of flying. The very thought of rising thousands of feet above the ground always brought a wave of nausea to her stomach.

Once retrieving her bags from the luggage pick-up centre, Gwen walked outside and caught a courtesy bus to another depot where she waited another fifteen minutes before catching the next Airport Ferry. When onboard, she walked over to the side of the boat and leaned against the railing, watching the white, crested waves crash down beneath her.

If she had been asked a week ago where she would have thought her life was headed, she would have responded, "Where everyone else's life winds up…the usual: a career, a family, a pet…"

Now, she was in Toronto, searching for a child she had never met, solely on a feeling of conviction pressed upon her from a power that was supposedly higher than her own.

Of course, she had every reason to believe that the child *did* exist. All that had happened to her over the past the week plugged that theory.

A large part of Gwen was upset with Harry for putting her up to this, part of her in wonder and a part confused. She still wasn't able to understand why Harry had picked her out of the hundreds of thousands of women in Winnipeg—or why she had to undergo so many strange experiences to get her to where she was now. But at the same time, Gwen was secretly honored that she had just been given the chance to literally *save the world.*

Her purpose in Toronto was simple: kill a child who would one day grow up to become the Antichrist. A child who would one day lead billions of people away from God. But was it God who bestowed this honor upon her?

She didn't know.

All she knew was that a man in Hans Memorial Hospital, who had once had the acid trip of a lifetime, showed her that this was something she had to do. Something she had to do because *he* could not. He was trapped in a world of confusion and there wouldn't be a snowball's chance in Hell for him to escape that disoriented world and commit this murder. Even if Harry had opted to free himself from his confines, he couldn't have left the province. The hospital had all, if any, identification on him, something that is needed when applying for an airplane ticket. He could have tried hitchhiking cross-country, but for the amount of time that it would have taken, he couldn't have survived on his own. He was dependent on the hospital to supply him for *all* his needs and if he were somehow separated from that, he would die. *But what about his mind control?* Gwen wondered. *Ah—who knows why the hell a crazy person does the things they do.*

When Gwen had originally recovered from her collapse in the cafeteria, she had spent a lot of time by herself, reliving the visions of her recent encounters. It was during this time alone that everything had become clear about what had to be done.

Why it was her that had been specifically chosen to kill the boy? She didn't know. She would leave that to God.

If He was real, that was.

* * *

His eyes stung with sweat and the stagnant air of the Darkroom, the only light seeping in from the small window in the door.

Harry Thomas had been in here for long time—at least a few days now—ever since he had been accused of attacking Gwen in the cafeteria. But he hadn't attacked her. It had been the opposite. He had to tell Gwen what she was destined to do and who she would be dealing with when the time came to do it.

For Harry, trying to reflect back on his time in the library, or even remembering some of his time in the hospital, there was a difficulty between distinguishing the past and the present, the present and the future. Even discerning what was real and what wasn't real was hard. Harry spent most of his time in a dreamlike state, an unknown moment between consciousness and sleep. Every so often—now, more frequently—the numb sensation in his mind would ease and he would attain some form of coherence.

It had never been made clear to Harry who or what was behind this showcase of evil, and he didn't know who, or what, was haunting him now; who had made haunting faces glow on his bedroom wall; who had whispered to him. He did, however, know what had to be done about the child that had been born in the library five years ago. Or, was it three years? Or two? It didn't matter. Its death was the only solution.

Maybe it was God who gave me this vision, Harry thought. *Maybe I'm somehow special. Yeah. I like that. I'm special.*

He sat crouched in the corner of the Darkroom, wearing nothing but his thin pajama bottoms. He had been too hot with his shirt on.

His theory about God being behind his visions did make sense. Perfect sense. Someone had to witness the seriousness of what was to come. Someone had to realize that this Antichrist would offer the illusion of wealth and prosperity to any and all who followed him, and then drag them down to Hell when Christ returned. What took Harry a while to figure out was why hadn't he been allowed to be the one to kill the child? But, when he reasoned out an answer, it made sense: he couldn't kill him. Not like this, anyway, locked up in a mental institution, completely caged away from the rest of the world.

Was it the will of God for him to be locked up?

Maybe. Then again, maybe not.

God would never allow that to happen to me now, would He? Maybe that's why I found Gwen? Harry thought. *Maybe God helped me find her because I'm locked up in here? Yes, that's it! I remembered her name when I came out of the library! Gwen! Gwen! Gwen!*

Harry lied down on the cold floor. He curled himself up to keep warm, using his shirt as a pillow.

* * *

Earlier that afternoon, Gwen had checked into the Hillcrest Motel, West of the Toronto City Centre Airport. When she arrived, she was surprised to learn that a room had already been reserved in her name. Assuming it was

Harry who had made the arrangements (how? She didn't know), she signed in and made her way to her room. Inside, she dropped her bags on the floor and flopped on the bed. There she fell asleep, and dreamed of nothing.

She woke up three hours later to the strange sensation that someone else was in the bed with her. She rolled over to look, and bolted out of the bed when she saw the other side of the double bed partially sunken in, as if someone were sleeping there. Gwen stood frozen against the wall alongside the bed, staring at the mattress, her breathing coming to a crawl. Then, as if knowing it was being watched, the bed returned to its normal state, its surface growing smooth except for the tussled sheets where Gwen had lain.

* * *

Four hours later, Gwen was sitting naked at the edge of the bathtub, her head bowed, goose bumps forming on her flesh from the soothing, hot water.

She had spent the better part of the evening watching television from the chair beside her bed. She was too shaken up to lie back down on it, even though she was slowly convincing herself that the indent she saw on the bed was somehow part of a dream, or a waking hallucination. Lord knows she's had plenty of those.

When the tub had filled, Gwen eased herself in, and closed her eyes once she became comfortable, one knee bent, and the other straight. She needed this. Needed something to relax her. The harrowing last few days was beginning to take its toll. A fatigue seemed to be constantly looming over her and she was having trouble concentrating.

A feeling came over her. An odd feeling. A feeling most people search their whole lives for. She felt purpose. A reason for existing. The reason that she was born.

Gwen had a hard time explaining this feeling to herself. The only way she could explain it so that she would be able to understand it was that, throughout the course of her life, she had felt more or less like she was trudging her way through it rather than experiencing it. Now, because of Harry, because of all the oddities that had happened, she felt as though she was living.

She felt real. And it felt great!

* * *

Harry awoke to a loud thumping sound, its pulse echoing throughout the room. He sat up abruptly and searched the darkness for the cause. Through the small glass window on the door he was able to see someone peering in on him. He couldn't quite place the face, but whoever it was did look familiar. It wasn't a nurse or any of his forgotten family or friends. But it was someone he knew…or had known. A sudden chill swept over him when he finally realized whom he was seeing.

It was a Watcher. And he was being watched.

* * *

"Thanks for coming," Marty's greeted Denise as he opened the door for her.

An hour earlier he had invited her over to talk. He had called her, panicking, wondering where Gwen was and why she hadn't been to school. Marty had already cooled down from the fight that he and Gwen had, and he was ready to talk to her. But every time he had telephoned, or had looked for her at school—she wasn't there. After several days or so of thinking he had just missed her when looking for her, he decided to call Denise to see if she knew where Gwen was.

Denise told him that Gwen had suddenly packed up her bags and left without word or warning. The only reason Denise knew that Gwen had gone on a trip was that the duffel bag that she and Gwen shared was missing.

In his foyer, Marty took Denise's coat and hung it up while she wandered into the living room. His parents were still out of town so they had the house to themselves. He offered her something to drink. She declined. She was eager to talk about Gwen. They sat down on the couch at opposite ends and looked at each other, uncertain where to start.

After an awkward pause, Marty broke the ice and got the conversation rolling.

"So?" he asked, beckoning her with his hands, then slapped his palms down on his knees.

Denise shrugged. "I'm not sure where to start, really. Things just started getting funny with Gwen and now…she's gone."

Marty leaned forward, forearms on his thighs. "She didn't move out or anything, did she?"

"Oh, no. We would have talked about that first, even if for some reason she felt that we weren't getting along. I have to give her a little more credit than that," she said.

Denise thought of the fight she and Gwen had. She touched her fingertips to where Gwen had scratched her. The wound had healed, fortunately not leaving a scar. Denise finished by saying, "But something's up with her. Definitely."

Marty's brow knit together. He was tired of thinking. "I know. It's hard to put into words, isn't it?"

"Yeah." Denise took a breath then, with a look of concern in her eyes, said, "I guess the main issue is, how are *you* doing?"

Marty paused before answering the question. His mind flashed back to the argument that he and Gwen had before she left.

"All right…I guess," he said, knowing full well that it wasn't the truth. He was feeling horrible and he missed Gwen. He missed the way things used to be: simple.

He continued, feeling the sudden urge to vent. "I just don't understand how she would let herself get all mixed up with some guy she's never met before. A guy in a loony bin, no less!"

Denise backed away as Marty quickly changed into a more aggressive posture. He didn't notice her change in position and continued talking. "I just thought that she was smarter than that. The truth is, Denise, I don't know how to deal with this. It's like a whirlwind. I mean one minute she and I are having sex and the next thing I know, we're fighting about some nutcase in the funhouse. What the fuck is that?"

Marty paused, frustrated. Denise didn't know what to say to him. The only thing she could think of was to tell him what she was thinking. "I don't know if this means anything to you, Marty, but I'll be there for you if you need me. I have a pretty good idea how you feel and I'm personally mad at Gwen myself, but at the same time, I'm worried about her. Who knows what's going on with her right now? She could be dead for all we know. Okay, maybe not dead, but real confused. Real messed up."

The two of them stared at each other.

* * *

The cigarette burned slowly tonight. Gwen felt as if she had been smoking her before bed cigarette for hours, but in reality, it had only been a few minutes. She was tired and at a point of complete mental numbness.

She wasn't sure what was real and what wasn't. The irrational was becoming rational and she felt herself just going through the motions of life instead of actually living it. And it was that feeling of going through the motions that had turned her stomach upside down. Earlier, she had felt more alive than ever. Then she plummeted; shit hitting the fan. She shook her head, confused.

Dark circles had formed under her eyes and she was terrified to go to sleep. She had been reliving the moment when she saw that humanlike shape embedded in the mattress. Whatever was haunting her was very real, and it wasn't Harry anymore.

It was something worse.

Gwen sat in her chair, smoking her endless cigarette, and waited for the night to pass.

* * *

Marty and Denise talked for two hours about Gwen. Neither of them seemed to reach any conclusion as to what to do, but they both felt good knowing that they each had someone to talk to.

Until tonight, they had never really spent the time to get to know each other. The only communications they ever had were nods of recognition, or the occasional "Hi." There was that first chat at the bar and that one talk over the phone, but that was it. Today, however, they were talkative. Both had a lot to say and both had a lot of feelings to share. They both cared about Gwen and both loved her in their own way. They only hated the way she was acting and were both concerned for her and what she was doing. Denise told Marty that Jenna and Carlee were also hurting from Gwen's abrupt departure and were as equally mad.

"Friends don't fuck each other over," was what Jenna had told Denise.

When Denise left his house that night, Marty found himself crawling into his bed thinking about her. He had enjoyed talking to her and it had felt good to finally get some of his stress off his chest.

He also decided that Denise was beautiful, but quickly dismissed that thought when a sharp mental image of Gwen crept into his mind. Was Gwen okay? He hoped so. He would talk to Denise about it tomorrow.

Chapter Twelve

At three o'clock in the afternoon the next day, Calvin Mandalay took a much-needed swig of water from the tap in the kitchen. In between gulps, he caught his breath and then refilled his glass for more. As he guzzled his second cup, Ken walked in and accidentally startled him.

"Whoa, slow down there, Stretch," Ken said, putting a hand to Calvin's back.

The boy pulled the glass away from his mouth and smiled. He liked being called "Stretch" even though he wasn't very tall for his age. "Stretch" was Uncle Ken's way of telling him that he supported his love for basketball and that he loved him.

"Sink a couple of good ones?" Ken asked.

"Uh-huh," Calvin replied, returning the glass to his mouth, its rim clacking against his teeth.

Ken sat down at the table. Finished with his water, Calvin sat down and joined him.

"You know, if you practice everyday, you're going to wow the crowds in high school. Plus," Ken said and leaned closer to Calvin, giving him a little wink, "you'll get all the girls, too."

Calvin grimaced at his remark. Girls were disgusting. He remained silent for a minute, a look of tension in his eyes.

"Something wrong, Calvin?" Ken asked, noticing the knit of his nephew's brow.

Calvin squirmed a little. "I had a bad dream last night."

Ken leaned back in his chair and looked at his nephew understandingly. "Oh," he said. "Do you want to talk about it?"

"No," Calvin said and looked back to the counter where he had left his cup.

Because Ken loved his nephew, he wanted to help him in anyway that he could. He knew that nightmares for young boys, certain ones, anyway, could haunt them for the rest of their lives. Not only that, but he saw that whatever Calvin dreamt was bothering him and that talking about it would be the first step in preventing dreaming about it again.

Ken came closer to Calvin and spoke as if he were letting him in on one of life's little secrets. "You know, they say that if you don't talk about a nightmare after you have one, you could dream about it again."

Calvin immediately sat up straight, a look of worry filling his eyes. "That wouldn't be good."

"No, it wouldn't."

Silence fell between them; the same kind of silence that arises when a parent is about to tell their child about the birds and the bees.

"I remember," Ken began, "when I was a kid, I once had a bad dream, too. In the dream, I was in my house and was standing in my bedroom. Suddenly, this bald man with blue skin came out from under my bed. At first it all made sense to me, all part of the dream y'know, but when I looked at him, I noticed that he had a nose like Gonzo. I got scared and went to go find my mom, your grandmother."

Calvin, sitting straight up in his seat, hung onto every word.

Ken continued: "I opened the basement door and my mother was standing there in the dark, blow-drying her hair. I told her that I had a Porky-hymer in my room. Porky-hymers were what these long nosed people were called. For some reason I knew that. She turned around and at first I thought she was going to come upstairs to help me."

Hope flashed over Calvin's face. He was rooting for a happy ending to the dream. Ken furrowed his brow, signaling to Calvin that there was no happy ending to this little tale.

"She turned around and much to my surprise," Ken went on, "she had a long nose, too. I couldn't believe it! My own mother! The same kind of monster I wanted her to help me get away from. Then I woke up. I never told anyone about that dream and every so often after that, about once a month, I still dream that the Porky-hymers are coming to get me."

Calvin shuddered at the story. Ken knew that he shouldn't have told his nephew about the nightmare, but he felt somehow obligated to let Calvin know that a person should confront their inner demons instead of burying them deep down.

"That's weird," was Calvin's only response.

"Yes, it is," Ken agreed. "But do you see what I'm saying? You should tell me about your dream. That way, you might not dream about it ever again."

That seemed like a good idea to Calvin.

"Let me get a glass of juice first, 'kay? I'm still thirsty," the boy said.

"You just drank a ton of water!" Ken said. "Then again, we wouldn't want you dry out and turn into a prune now would we?"

* * *

In the Darkroom, Harry sat in the corner, shivering. The Watcher had come to check on him, come to make sure that he was detained and couldn't start raving about what was to come.

As if aching from a sudden hunger pain, Harry jumped up to the room's door and began banging and shouting profusely. He pressed his face up against the glass of the tiny window, his breath fogging his face in and out of view.

He needed a cigarette.

* * *

Calvin returned to the table with his glass of juice not knowing where to start. He didn't like the thought of anything scary happening to him, and now, after Ken's story, he grew queasy, wondering if he could keep his juice down. Calvin glanced up. His uncle was staring back at him, his salt and pepper beard shimmering slightly in the kitchen light. He thought that Ken was showing too much interest in what he had to say.

Calvin tried to recall the nightmare, but had a hard time remembering all of what had taken place in it. All he knew was that it had made him feel weird and wiggly all day.

"Well?" Ken asked, urging Calvin to spill his guts.

"I don't know," Calvin said. "I can't 'member it too well."

"Try to. You'll feel a whole lot better if you try," Ken assured him.

"Okay, um..." Suddenly, recollections of the dream flooded Calvin's memory, making him feel as though he were experiencing it all over again. The boy looked up at his uncle, his young eyes begging, asking permission to refrain from telling his dream. Ken waited patiently. Calvin gave into the silence and spoke. "I was sitting under a tree in the backyard. I think it was raining. It was dark, too."

"Were you scared because it was dark?" Ken asked.

"No...But I didn't like the rain. It was too cold and wet. And when I was under the tree, I felt something really, really cold on my back."

"Did you turn around to see what it was?"

Calvin's eyes cast down to his lap. "No. I got up and ran for the house. Then I woke up."

Ken folded his arms, resting them on his slowly developing potbelly. "I see. Gave you the willies, huh?"

"Yeah, but that wasn't the scary part," Calvin said, emphasizing the word "scary."

"No?"

"When...when I woke up...I heard a voice." Calvin's eyes rose and met his Uncle's.

"What kind of voice?" Ken adjusted his posture, awkwardly entertained by what his nephew was sharing with him. When he heard about other people's dreams, he became like a kid again: couldn't wait to skip to the ending to find out what happened next.

Calvin took a sip of his juice and fell silent.

"So, what did it say?" Ken encouraged him.

The five year old drew in a deep breath, his lower lip quivering. "It told me to run."

* * *

He had been sleeping with his body sprawled out in the middle of the room for the past four hours. When he awoke, he had a dull ache at the back of his head from resting on the hard, concrete floor.

Harry sat up and shook the cobwebs out. He still wasn't used to sleeping in total darkness. The last time he had closed his eyes in a pitch-black room had been long ago, sleeping in the same bed as Lauren.

When he had slept in the library, the room never lost its odd golden glow. In his room at the hospital, he had his night-light. But, in the Darkroom, he had nothing, save for the tiny amount of light that came in from the window on the door.

Thankful he hadn't just had a nightmare, Harry got up, and began pacing back and forth, being careful not to bump into the walls of the tiny room. He had hoped that his eyes would have adjusted to the dark, using the little light available to help him see.

His mind raced from being completely blank into a swarm of thoughts concerning what had happened before he had fallen asleep: he had gotten mad, wanting a cigarette. The nurses had ignored his cries. Harry had forgotten his mind control then. Now he wished he had remembered. He would be smoking right now if he had. He had needed a cigarette. He had been upset.

He had—seen the Watcher.

Harry hadn't been sure if a Watcher even truly existed until now. The image of the man firing his dark eyes through the small window in the door kept playing over and over in Harry's head. The Watcher had been old and had grinned at Harry, baring a set of overly white, straight teeth.

In essence, the Watcher was very similar to Harry, yet different all the same. The Watcher knew of the Antichrist and who, and where, the child was. He also knew about Harry and what had happened to him twenty-five years ago. He had the ability to put thoughts into people's minds, too.

The only significant difference between he and Harry was that he was free to roam the outside world whereas Harry was not.

Harry knew the Watcher would go after Gwen and try to stop her from killing the child. When he thought of her, his heart sank, realizing that he missed her. Even after having spent only a short amount of time with her, over the course of a few evenings, Harry felt like he had known Gwen much longer. Maybe he had? Wasn't Gwen's name presented to him while he was in the library? He couldn't remember.

A nurse walked by the door, startling Harry when she looked in. The nurse gave him a forced smile then continued on her way.

Harry's thoughts were about to return to Gwen when he abruptly realized that he still wanted his cigarette. In a fit of frustration, Harry jumped at the door and began banging his fists against its flank. The thumping echoed throughout the Darkroom.

He ran in circles about the room, yelping, hoping that a nurse would see him.

* * *

Coat hooks. Stupid yellow coat hooks! Calvin frowned as he gazed furiously upward at the always-mocking coat hook that looked down upon him. He was standing on his tiptoes-toes.

Standing on his toes had never been a problem before, but after stubbing his left big toe last week while running down the stairs at home, hanging his bloody coat up had become a chore for him.

After rising up, his toe aching, Calvin hung up his jacket then made his way to his favorite after-recess spot in his classroom. There was a painting table in the far corner of the room that he liked to sit beside, alone, relaxing his legs after all the running he had done during his break. Calvin sat down on the rough, carpeted floor, and looked around the room. He laughed quietly to himself at Mary and how her pants were so tight that they seemed to go all the way up her butt. With a smile, Calvin drew his eyes to the window. An old man was carefully walking down the sidewalk across the street. Calvin liked the big, gray over coat that the old man was wearing. It looked so warm and comfy.

Even at five years old, Calvin wondered what it would be like to be an old man and to walk so slowly. Calvin figured that old peoples' batteries had worn out and that was why they always seemed to take so long at everything. But he didn't have to worry about his batteries. No sir. His batteries were still fresh!

The old man's slow steps came to a halt. He glanced at the kindergarten window where Calvin was sitting. Calvin turned away, but when he looked back, the old man gave him a wink.

That's...weird, Calvin thought.

The old man walked away.

Chapter Thirteen

Gwen Reeves stubbed out her cigarette on the front steps of St. Catherine's cathedral and entered, feeling uneasy. She hadn't been inside a church in a long time. The last time she had attended was five years ago when going to a friend's funeral. It was then that she had lost her faith and stopped believing.

Her friend, Sue-Ellen, had been battling with cancer ever since she was fifteen years old. Throughout the entire time of her struggle, Gwen had prayed for Sue-Ellen, pleading with God for her healing. For a period of about three months, her prayers seemed to have been having an affect. Sue-Ellen was feeling much better. Then, without warning, the cancer fought back, this time so strong that it had stolen Sue-Ellen's life. Since that day Gwen had not been able to forgive God for that. It was His fault. However, deep down, beneath the hostility toward her Creator, Gwen knew that she still believed. But to this day, she wouldn't admit it.

Now, Gwen found herself back in a church, staring at the well-crafted stain glass windows around her, a slight headache coming on from the incense that was burning. She never understood why the Catholics burned the stuff. It did nothing but smell bad.

She walked through the front foyer and into the main dormitory. Far in front of her an elderly man was lighting a candle in front of a statue of the Virgin Mary.

Probably for his dead wife, Gwen thought. She wondered if Harry had lit a candle for Lauren after she had died.

Gwen and the old man were the only people in the church.

She scanned the pews and the walls, and found what she was looking for. Off to her right, a row of three dark oak chambers stood proudly, the chambers being meant for confession. To her they looked more like the outhouses you would find in a Western except that there were no half-moons gracing the doors.

Confident that a priest would be inside one of them, Gwen drew a deep breath through her nose and exhaled through her mouth, trying to calm her anxiety. She stood in front of one of the confessionals for several minutes before going in. She hoped there would be a priest inside. She also hoped that there wouldn't be.

She opened the long, thin door, removed her coat, and settled down on the red, velvet kneeler. Almost immediately she heard the sound of wood sliding on wood. Barely visible through the black metal grate in front of her, she could see a priest, his face partially hidden in the dim lighting. Out of his presumed expectancy of it, she crossed herself: forehead, chest, left, right shoulders.

"Tell me your sins, my child," the priest said, his tone stern.

Gwen knew the routine. "Forgive me, Father, for I have sinned. It has been five years since my last confession."

Gwen had no idea how she was even going to bring up what she had come here to say. She searched for the words, finding none. There was a burst of tears; a week of anguishes pouring out.

The priest, Father Vernoff, was caught off guard. He offered a futile attempt at sympathy. "Shhh, my child. There is nothing you could have done that the Lord would not forgive you for."

Gwen continued crying.

"It's all right," Father Vernoff soothed. "What's your name?"

Gwen swallowed hard, sniffled, and then told him her name.

"Gwen, don't worry. Take you time. You can tell me whenever you're ready. I assure you that as far as the East is from the West, so far hath the Lord removed our transgressions from us."

"It's not that, I..." Gwen choked. She cleared her throat. "I don't have anything to confess...it's...I need help."

The priest furrowed his brow. *If you're not here to confess—then why are you wasting my time?*

He asked, "Then what is the problem, Gwen?"

Gwen pulled a tissue from her purse and dabbed at her eyes. She calmed herself down a little.

"What do you know about the end days, Father?"

"What do you mean?"

"The end of the world? The book of Revelation? The Antichrist?"

"I know that there are certain events that have to take place before Jesus Christ Himself will come again."

"What about the Antichrist? Who is he really?" Gwen scrunched the tissue in her fist.

"Well," he began. Gwen could tell that this would be a long and drawn out speech, but she would endure it. She needed to find out who it was that she was sent here to kill.

Father Vernoff went on. "The Antichrist is said, according to the book of Revelation, to come upon the earth towards the end of the world. Once here, he will sit high on a throne of evil and rule over mankind. Think of him like the President of the world. When he comes into power, he will brand all mankind with the Mark of the Beast. Essentially this Mark will enable you to purchase items and trade with others. If you don't have it, however, you will probably starve to death out on a street somewhere. He will have global rule and he will know what all people do. The Mark is his power over them."

What Father Vernoff just told her did ring a bell. Gwen had read about it when she began preparing her essay for school. School? That seemed like such a long time ago. Seemed so far away.

"The Antichrist will one day share the same fate as the devil himself," Father Vernoff said. "In fact, he will be the messiah to all occultists and satanic groups, or even a messiah to those who are not believers in our Lord Jesus. According to the book of Revelation, he will reign in power for a total of seven years. Three and a half of those years are called the Tribulation, and the remaining three and a half, the Great Tribulation. Once those seven years have ended, the sky will split open and Christ, along with His Heavenly hosts, will pour down from the heavens and end the Antichrist's terrible reign on the Earth, destroying his platform against God." The priest turned a look at Gwen. His mouth snarled. "He will be a man of evil, the seed of Satan. Why do you ask about this?"

If you only knew, Gwen hollered to herself. She had thought long and hard about coming to a church and asking for help, asking for information. Should she tell the priest about everything? Should she just take this little nugget of information and leave? Should she simply make up some sins to say so that she wasn't wasting the priest's time? Without thinking, her mouth opened. "I'm here to kill the Antichrist."

There was an uncomfortable silence. Gwen couldn't believe she had just said what she did.

"Pardon me?" Father Vernoff asked.

Gwen repeated herself, this time a little more slowly. "I'm here to kill the Antichrist." She said it again! What was wrong with her!

"I see," the priest said, almost mocking her.

Gwen knew that his reaction would either be that she was out of her mind, or that she was here to make fun of the Catholic faith just for kicks. Gwen could only hope that he didn't close the small sliding door on her. He didn't. Instead, he only repeated what he had said: "I see."

Gwen stirred forward on her kneeler and leaned closer to her side of the metal grate. "I'm not trying to cause any trouble," she said. "But it's true, as crazy as it may sound. If you will give me a moment to explain myself, then maybe you will help me."

Father Vernoff leaned closer to his side of the metal grate, as well. "I have no time for games, young lady. There are other people you can talk to about this, you know." It was obvious what he was hinting at.

"If you're referring to shrinks, thanks, but I'd rather not. I'm not crazy! Please let me explain!" Gwen recoiled at the sudden rise of her voice.

"I'm sorry," Father Vernoff said and began to slide the miniature wooden door closed.

"Please!" Gwen shouted, stopping the priest in mid-slide. "If you were any man of God, you would have at least a small amount of concern for me and would hear me out. If you think I'm crazy, that's fine. But at least set an example of what a good Catholic is supposed to be. Closed ears were the reason I abandoned your faith."

Father Vernoff fell silent. What Gwen had said wounded him, as did any slighting against the Catholic Church. He slid the wooden door back open. "All right then, go ahead." He was obviously impatient.

"Thank you," Gwen said calmly.

She gathered her thoughts as best she could and began to tell the priest everything from the beginning, starting with the dreams about Harry. She could tell by the way that Father Vernoff was fidgeting that he was uncomfortable with listening to her. She continued anyway, hoping that he would change his mind and force himself to be more interested.

Father Vernoff thought that the dreams she had about Harry were only nightmares, nothing more. But when Gwen told him that she had *actually* met Harry in real life, he almost jumped through the roof of the confessional booth. It was at that moment that his mindset changed and he began to take her seriously. She continued onward about her school assignment regarding the book of Revelation and how she thought it amazingly coincidental that she received that assignment at the same time she was destined to meet Harry. She explained her meetings with Harry and how he had at first scared her with his shaggy appearance and how, strangely enough, she had felt a sudden calm when she was around him.

She asked the priest if God was behind all of this. Father Vernoff didn't have an answer at the ready. He told Gwen that she should finish her story before he would come to any conclusions.

When Gwen proffered more detail about her meetings with Harry, Father Vernoff questioned her credibility, and again begun to assume that she was making everything up. He definitely did not believe her when she revealed that Harry was able to put thoughts inside her head, urging her to listen to him, and how Harry had also given her dreams and visions of him, too.

After almost twenty-five minutes of explaining, Gwen had finally reached the story's climax and began to talk about how Harry had gone deep into her mind, depositing images and sounds of the birth of the Antichrist. She also mentioned that when Harry had done this, his unexpected change in behavior caused the nurses in the room to assume that he was attacking her.

The detail in her description of the formation of the world's sins sent a chill down Father Vernoff's spine. The vivid imagery he saw in his imagination turned his stomach.

Gwen also told him about her time in the hospital, her trip to Toronto, especially the incident in the motel room where she saw her bed shift under the weight of an invisible human being.

When all was said and done, Gwen finished by asking him a simple question. A question that she had been wondering about for the past two days: was *what* she had been charged with the right thing to do?

Father Vernoff couldn't answer. He was still trying to absorb all that she had told him. He could feel deep down in his spirit that there was authenticity in what she had said, but he couldn't bring himself to admit it. He uttered a quick prayer, hoping for an immediate response.

None came.

For Gwen, it felt so very good to get everything off her chest.

Father Vernoff on the other hand, felt a weight form on his heart. Something in the back of his mind provoked him to say something. He half believed her. Sort of. Over the years, being involved with the Catholic faith, he had seen a lot of hoaxes of amazing spiritual circumstance, and an equal number of miracles; things that could not be explained in the natural realm. He was a firm believer in the Word of God and all that it said and taught. However, he was not a firm believer in those that came to him with things of supernatural importance. He was skeptical about those types of things and he knew it, but it was also that quality that made him a good priest. He was gifted in the discerning of the supernatural, what was real and what wasn't. Or at least what he thought was real and what wasn't. But as for Gwen's story, he could not arrive at a conclusion. Gwen's tale had sounded farfetched, yet somehow he couldn't help feel that it had all made sense, despite none of it being specifically mentioned in the Bible. No sort of prophecy had been made about a woman, or anyone for that matter, who would come and try to kill the Antichrist in an effort to prevent his reign of terror.

"Gwen," he said, looking over to her. He could see the hope swelling in her tear-glazed eyes. "I'm not quite sure what it is that you want me to say, so I'll tell you what I feel. By feel, I mean what I was sensing when you told me everything that was bothering you." His heart hurt as he spoke to her. "I cannot encourage you, by any means, to go ahead and kill somebody in spite of who they might be. The Bible is very clear in the book of Exodus that a man shall not kill."

"But—" Gwen began, quickly being cut off.

"Please, let me finish," Father Vernoff said, a small raise of his hand. "Now, it is true for me to say that your quest is a noble one. Ridding the world of the Antichrist, who wouldn't call that noble? But what concerns me the most is on whose grounds you would be doing this. Certainly not God's. Do you not think He would have even allowed the Antichrist to be born, knowing that He would make one of His children kill? I don't think so. He doesn't work like that. But at the same time, your story is quite convincing." Father Vernoff paused. "But, unfortunately, I am a spiritual skeptic, and I must say that, with no offense intended, that this is more than likely a fabrication of your imagination."

"But what about the dreams? My meeting with Harry? What can you say about that?" Gwen shot back. More tears filled her eyes, her heart sinking with disappointment.

"I don't have an explanation for those specific events, Gwen. I really don't." *Other than you might be making this all up and that you know enough about Catholicism to have a convincing case,* Father Vernoff added to himself.

"So what should I do?" Gwen asked.

"Do you have any friends or family you can talk to? Anyone else, besides a, as you put it, shrink, that you can go to for advice?"

"No. Not really. I have a boyfriend, but I already tried to talk to him about this. Well, part of it, anyway. It didn't work out." Gwen remembered the tissue in her fist. She opened her hand, smoothed the tissue, and then wiped her eyes again.

Father Vernoff had never dealt with anyone he thought was mentally unwell in all his years as a priest and, right now, he was uncertain as to what to do. He only wanted this conversation to be over with. Father Vernoff again silently said a quick prayer, asking for help. He couldn't hear, or feel, a response, but down in his gut he felt a plausible solution reveal itself. It was a bit cliché, but appeared it would work. He was going to lie, committing a sin on Holy ground. This blushed his heart with shame.

"Gwen, this is something obviously serious. What I can suggest for you to do is this: do what you think is right. Do what you think others would feel is right. I cannot stop you from killing anyone. All I can do is advise against it. I am left with no choice but to ask you to ask God for help. As well, consider the possibility of seeing a doctor. I am willing to bet that if you asked, you'll get the answer you're looking for from at least one of them. Sorry I couldn't have been more help."

Father Vernoff slid the wooden door closed, leaving Gwen alone on her side of the confession booth. She took a moment to think about what he had said, smoothed the wrinkles in her pants, and then exited the booth. When she got out, she noticed that the old man was still in front of the statue of the Virgin Mary. He turned around, stared at her, and flashed her a brief smile, his straight, white teeth standing out against his thin lips. Gwen returned the grin and walked towards the door.

What a waste of time, she thought as she picked up her pace. *No wonder I stopped coming to church!*

Once Gwen had left, the old man walked over to the confession booth and went in. Father Vernoff heard someone on the other side of the wooden door and thought that maybe Gwen had returned. This gave him second thoughts about sliding open the door. But, Gwen or not, he had a job to do. He slid it open, and was relieved to see an elderly man kneeling down in front of him.

"Tell me your sins, my son," Father Vernoff said.

The old man put his hand near his breast pocket and said, "Forgive me, Father, for I am about to sin."

* * *

Outside, Gwen had just turned onto the sidewalk when a sound as loud as a firecracker came from inside the church, echoing in the still air.

* * *

It was just after four o'clock in the morning when Calvin had awakened to a sharp sting in his groin. Quickly, he got out of his bed and went to the bathroom. After relieving himself, he got back into his bed and glanced around his room before trying to get back to sleep.

Lying on his back, Calvin watched the deep red and blue shapes forming in the darkness above him and allowed his imagination to go to work.

What will I dream next, he wondered. He had been having a good dream before he woke up to go pee. He had been on someone else's driveway, shooting baskets, scoring every time. Then, from out of nowhere, someone appeared beside him and asked if he could play, too. Calvin was never able to see this person's face, but that was okay. This new person was such a great basketball player! The game had become so much more alive and real.

Just before Calvin closed his eyes, he looked over at the bedroom window. The old man he saw earlier that day was staring back at him through the glass.

Chapter Fourteen

The Internet's great, Marty acknowledged. He curled a smile as he surfed the World Wide Web.

Marty enjoyed this time alone and felt fortunate that his parents decided to extend their vacation for another week.

He had made his usual stops on the 'Net: the news, movie rumors, art updates, and his e-mail. After that, he flipped the screen to a search engine, and hesitated before typing.

Is this cheating on Gwen, he asked himself. He was tempted to search for a couple of adult-themed web sites; something to satisfy himself and relieve the tension that was building up until Gwen got home.

That is, if she ever came home.

* * *

Why am I so cold? Victoria Mandalay asked herself when she woke up early the following morning. This was one thing that she hated. She'd rather be too hot than too cold. For the first little while after her husband had left her, she would often wake up in the middle of the night, drenched in sweat, shivering. She would get too hot under her quilt, begin to sweat, the cool air of the room attacking her skin. It had gone on for a couple of years until, one night, it had suddenly stopped. Thank God. She couldn't remember how many times there had been when she never even had the time to shower before work, forcing her to go through rest of her day not smelling as best she could.

It was strange that she was cold this morning.

Victoria got out of bed and went across the hall to check on Calvin. He was sleeping soundly, covered in a mountain of blankets, his pillows scrunched up around his head. She paused in the doorway for a moment and thought about how lucky she was to have him.

Despite all the things that had gone wrong in her life, and all the times that love seemed so far away, she knew that she could always count on her little boy to be there for her. Always.

Around seven o'clock, she went downstairs and made herself a cup of coffee. Between sips, she browsed a Sears catalogue, hoping to find a sale of some sort. Of course there was none.

Victoria hunched over her mug, stirring the coffee slowly with a teaspoon, while staring blankly at the black spaghetti strapped nightgown in the catalogue. She was tired, but too restless to sleep. *Why does life have to always be so fucking hard?* she wondered. Things had never seemed to come back to a normal state of happiness since her husband had left her. David had been her whole world.

She had been quite fortunate though, when it came to the whole procedure of meeting someone, dating, getting engaged, and then finally marrying. David had been her first and only boyfriend. She hadn't even casually dated anyone else before him. She had never had to go through the torture of heartbreak like most women did. And when her friends used to come crying to her over their latest lost love, she always told them that it couldn't really be all that bad, and that, in time, the pain would go away. It wasn't until after Victoria had gotten hurt that she realized what she had told her friends wasn't true. The hurt *does not* get better in time. It only gets worse.

But at least she had Calvin. Deciding to adopt him was the best decision she had ever made. She needed the companionship, the fun, and the love. Lately though, Calvin seemed more quiet than usual. It had always been Victoria's natural tendency to worry about him, but was she worrying about him too much? She thought not. She was his mother and he was her responsibility. Maybe she'd talk to him later and he could tell her what, if anything, was bothering him.

Roughly a quarter past seven, Calvin came down the stairs to the kitchen. His mother hadn't noticed him enter. She was too focused on her coffee and the nightgown in the catalogue.

He sat down across from her. Victoria came out of her trance.

"Good morning," she said.

"Morning," Calvin said, his eyes tired.

Victoria closed the catalogue and set it aside. "Did you sleep good?"

Calvin shrugged his answer then allowed his head to fall sleepily in his hands.

"Not enough sleep?" she tried again.

"No, jus' tired," he muttered into his hands.

"I see." *Something is definitely bothering him,* Victoria thought. "Do you want breakfast now or do you want to wait awhile?"

He shrugged his answer again.

"I'll get you some cereal," she said.

She got up, prepared him a bowl and set it down in front of him. His head rose, eyes squinting. He lazily picked up the spoon and dug in.

Victoria was unsettled by how quiet he was. Usually he was much more chipper in the morning. She decided that this would be a good time to see what was bothering him.

"You look sad, Calvin. Did something bad happen?"

"No," he said, inhaling a spoonful of flakes.

She leaned her head on her hand, resting her elbow on the table. "Really? You sound like a grumpy bear."

He didn't smile as she expected him to. Calling him "grumpy bear" always seemed to crack a smile on his face, especially if he was making an effort at being serious. Calvin could never keep a straight face. Never. He was too happy a child.

Victoria didn't know what else to say. She had never been good at filling the sympathetic mother role. She took a long sip of her coffee and a moment to think.

Before she could open her lips, Calvin asked, "Are old people bad?" He wiped a drop of milk off his chin.

The question took Victoria by surprise. Not that it was a strange question, but only because it had popped up right out of the blue.

"I don't know," she said. "What do you think? Your grandmother isn't bad and she's really nice to you." She counted the following off on her fingers. "Just look at all the quarters she gives you, the chocolate bars, the toys."

Again, Victoria thought he would smile. He didn't.

"I mean the ones you see on the street," Calvin said. He furrowed his brow, upset that she didn't understand him the first time.

"Why do you want to know?" she asked.

"Jus' wondering."

Victoria watched as he took another heaping scoop of cereal. "Some of them can be, I suppose," she said. "I don't necessarily mean that they're bad, but that some of them might not be any fun to hang around with."

She took another sip of her coffee, emptying her mug. Victoria was satisfied with her answer. "Why do you want to know?"

Calvin put down his spoon. "I saw an old man yesterday at school. He was sorta scary!"

She sat up straight, posture perfect, and leaned forward so quick that Calvin jumped. "At school? Do you know what he was doing there?"

"He wasn't at the school, Mom, jus' outside it. I didn't like the way he looked at me." Calvin made a twisted face like the one he made after the first time he had sucked on a lemon.

"How did he look at you?" Victoria was even more worried now. The last thing she needed was some old pervert eyeing her son.

"He winked at me," Calvin said.

"He was just being friendly," she said, trying to put him at ease. She wished someone would say the same thing to her.

"Was he really?" Quietly, he added, "He scared me."

"Did you tell your teacher?"

"No. I got up and went over to where Sonny was banging two trucks together." He ate another spoonful of flakes, milk dripping onto his chin.

"Oh," she said.

The conversation seemed to have ended.

Calvin got up, saying that he had to go pee and that he couldn't finish his cereal. Victoria remained at the table, wondering about the old man and if Calvin had told her the entire story.

After he went to the bathroom, Calvin reached up over the sink to wash his hands. Instead of turning on the faucet he found himself looking at the mirror, studying his reflection. He was confused by what he saw.

His boyish features had diminished. He looked older. Not like an old man or a grown up adult, but older still. The lines on his face were more defined and his skin didn't look as rosy. Bristles of hair stood up at the back of his neck. Being so young, growing up into an adult seemed like so far away, but at that moment, growing up felt all too close.

It scared him.

* * *

Marty Bones was just coming out of the bathroom when the doorbell rang. He scrambled down the stairs, barely zipped up, and opened the door. Denise was standing on his front steps.

"Hi... What are you doing here?" he asked.

"I was in the area so I thought I'd stop by," she replied.

Denise's hair was wet, hanging about chin length. Marty caught himself thinking something he shouldn't. He loved wet hair.

It took Marty a moment to realize that he was still standing in the doorway and Denise was still outside.

"Sorry," he said, "come in."

"Thanks. I didn't scare you, did I?" Her body brushed against his as she entered.

Marty ran his fingers through his hair. "Me? How?"

"By suddenly dropping by like this," she said, unbuttoning her coat.

"You kidding? No. Actually, I could use the company." Marty took her coat. As he was hanging it up, he couldn't help himself but smell the collar. It had the scent of Vanillaberry perfume. It smelled great.

They went down the stairs to where he had been on the computer browsing the Internet earlier. Fortunately for him, it was turned off. Denise didn't appreciate dirty web sites. Gwen had told him that once. Plus, if she found out that earlier Marty was looking at them, she might have been inclined to tell Gwen and Gwen didn't care for them, either. Denise had a bit of a big mouth, and if something bothered her, or more importantly, if she knew something would bother a friend, she would definitely not keep it quiet. It was one of her many quirks that had cost her a few boyfriends in the past. They had not liked the fact that she didn't keep something that was supposed to be between her and someone else a secret. One time, one of Denise's past boyfriends had made a sexual joke about Jenna and the bathroom plunger. They had broken up two days later.

Estranged to him, Marty felt nervous. Rarely did he feel that way. He had been around Denise before and felt fine. But right now, he was alone with her, and for the past couple of weeks, ever since Gwen had been acting differently and left soon after, he couldn't help but feel drawn toward Denise. Marty didn't know Denise all that well, but what he did know was extremely appealing. He also found her very attractive. She had a certain sensuality about her that made him feel a small tingle between his legs, putting his thoughts and feelings into overdrive. He knew full well that what he was feeling was wrong, but as he watched her sit down on the couch next to the stairwell, it somehow felt right.

The past couple of weeks with Gwen had been horrendous. First, she began acting differently. Second, she started hanging out with a mental patient in a psych-ward. Third, she had refused any and all help he had offered her. And, finally, she had taken off without even saying good-bye, leaving him not knowing where she was, if she was all right, and worried sick.

Although all of this had hurt him, he was also kind of glad that she was gone. After all, she had hurt him and he sure as hell was going to hurt her back, even though Gwen didn't know it.

Denise was sitting with her legs curled up under her while Marty stood on the bottom step, lost in thought.

"Is something wrong?" she asked.

Marty realized how quiet and awkward he was being. "No. I'm just kind of confused as to what's happening with Gwen. I still haven't heard from her and I'm getting worried. We had a fight just before she left and I guess I'm still a little upset over it. I wish I could talk to her, to straighten things out, but I don't even know where she's gone. I'm actually getting sick of thinking about it."

"I know what you mean." Denise patted the sofa cushion beside her, signaling for him to sit down. "Personally, I think we should just let Gwen be and deal with all of this when she comes back."

"You mean *if* she comes back, right?" Marty said.

"She'll come back. She has you here and I know that she wouldn't just leave you behind."

"But she did."

Marty sat down beside Denise. She adjusted herself to accommodate him. Was it Marty's imagination or did she just move a little closer?

"How's the art thing coming?" Denise asked.

"Not bad. We're starting to do oils in school. I'm really enjoying it. It's just that I'm finding it hard to concentrate. The other day, I had everything ready, all set to go, but nothing came out."

"Artist's block?" She curled a finger around a lock of her dark hair.

"If there is such a thing," Marty said with a smirk.

Denise ran her hands back through her hair, squeezing it into a ponytail, then let the ponytail fall. There was a certain sensuality about the way she did that, and Marty felt himself yet again thinking about things he should not.

Denise's eyes rose to meet his. "What?"

"Nothing," Marty said, clearing the lump of cotton in his throat.

Denise raised an eyebrow, and then smiled at the foolish idea that had come to her.

"Do you feel like painting?" she asked.

"Well, yeah, it's what I do…Wait…What do you mean? Right now?"

"Yes. Now." Her eyes seemed to smile.

"Sure, I guess. Except I don't have much for paint." He scratched the back of his head. "Do you want me to paint you something or—"

Denise slid herself closer to him. "I was thinking more along the lines of painting something together."

"Okay," Marty said. He could feel his pulse in his wrists. "Um…Why?"

"Well," Denise began, playing with her hair, "to be honest, I like you Marty, and not in that friendly way." His eyes widened. She was getting *too* forward for comfort. "I know I don't know you too well, but I'd really, really like us to become friends—and maybe more."

Denise looked ashamed after she had said this. She knew it was unfair of her to say that to the boyfriend of her best friend. Marty could see that she felt bad.

"Sorry," she said, and shifted back a little toward her corner of the couch.

"It's okay." He put a hand on her shoulder.

She smiled at him. For a long moment they both stared at each other, lost in hypnosis before snapping out of it. They both grinned shyly.

Marty led her down to the basement where, in its corner, he had a blank canvass already set up for his next painting session. To its right was a table with a couple of trays of paint, a jar full of brushes, and a jar of water for rinsing the brushes. A small can of paint thinner sat on the floor neatly beside the table.

Marty turned on the overhead light with Denise following right behind him. He grabbed a brush, gave it to her, and took a paintbrush off the easel tray for himself.

"So what do you want to paint?" he asked.

Denise walked around him. She began doing what she was saying. "Why don't I dab this in some color, then close my eyes and—"

Splat! The brush hit the canvass. Her eyes were closed, her hand moving freely from side to side, up and down, odd lines of red slashing in all directions.

She opened her eyes and laughed at her creation. "Looks like something my niece would do," she said.

"Don't worry," Marty said and pushed Denise aside slightly, "here." He sank his brush in the tray of paint—black this time—and began filling in some of the gaps that Denise's random lines had made.

"Good," she said, leaning back on one leg. "Good."

"Why, thank you. Care to take a turn?" Marty said in his phony British accent.

A Stranger Dead

She dipped the brush in another color—yellow, this time—and outlined the lines she had previously made.

They both laughed. This was fun. Marty decided that Denise should come and visit him more often.

PART THREE

THE POWERS THAT BE

Chapter Fifteen

Harry's time in the Darkroom had come to an end, and he was released back to his regular room. At first, a few of the nurses had some reservations about it, but quickly changed their minds when they saw Harry had been keeping quiet for the past couple of days. He was also allowed to finally smoke again. Being allowed to smoke made Harry very happy.

Once back in his room, Harry sat on the edge of his bed and stared at the floor. It was clean. The nurse had tidied his room while he was away.

He worried about Gwen and what the Watcher might do to her if he found her.

Harry patted his breast pocket, forgetting that the nurses still had his cigarettes. His disappointment quickly lifted when he remembered that he had a fresh pack in the top drawer of his nightstand. He opened it, grabbed the package, and sifted out a cigarette.

He looked down at the cigarette, relishing in the stark whiteness of its rolling paper, the rich tan of its filter.

"I know I was always say this to you guys every time I open up a new pack but, damn, it's good to have you around. Not having you for twenty years was hell. Thanks for always being there for me," he said.

He then imagined what he always thought the cigarettes might say in reply: "Anytime, Harry. Anytime. We love you as much as you love us."

He brought the cigarette to his nose and deeply inhaled the smooth, raisiny scent—much better than the sweat stained, acrid smell of the Darkroom—then jumped when a nurse with the last name of Robinson banged on his door and opened it.

"No smoking in your room, Harry!" Robinson shouted.

Harry pulled the cigarette away from his nose and looked straight into the nurse's eyes.

His voice became smooth but stern. "Is that what you think I was doing, you twit? Do honestly believe I'd break one of your bloody rules after spending a week of hell in your Darkroom? You really are a simple person, aren't you?"

Robinson, taken aback by Harry's mocking, said, "Take it into the cafeteria if you need to smoke."

Robinson turned to close the door.

Harry called after him. "Of course, and by the way, don't let the door hit you on the way out."

Robinson gave him a frown and closed the door, slamming his thumb in between the door and the frame.

He screamed and Harry laughed.

* * *

With the flick of her lighter, Gwen lit her fourth cigarette. She was in her motel room and had just finished watching a rerun of *M.A.S.H.*

They'll never take that show off the air, Gwen thought with a smile. She puffed on her cigarette in a worried frenzy. This morning, she had gone outside, walking, getting some fresh air. She had passed by a newsstand. One of the headlines had read: PRIEST SLAIN BY GHOST!

She had stopped, picked up the newspaper, and read further. She learned that the dead priest had been serving at St. Catherine's Cathedral and was killed the same day that she had visited there. The killer was never caught. Was it a coincidence? Maybe. Then again, maybe not.

Gwen thought about the old man that she had seen lighting a candle. *Could he be the killer? No, couldn't be. He was just an innocent widower saying prayers for his dead wife.*

She took another puff of her cigarette. Slowly, a sound welled up, coming from her bathroom. It was the sound of water running.

"What the—"

She got up to take a look. She clicked the light switch to ON, not knowing what she'd find. She almost choked when she saw a body floating in the bathtub. It was a boy. The steaming water around him was oily, stained a pinkish color.

Gwen screamed. Suddenly, she found herself kneeling at the edge of the tub, staring at the body.

Her first thought was to run. She tried—but couldn't move. Her knees were glued to the floor. She reached for the faucets, trying to turn the water off. No matter which way they turned, the water continued to flow, growing hotter and hotter, starting to boil. To her astonishment it didn't overflow, but instead the water remained at the same level, swishing back and forth over the boy's body. His skin was turning from peach to a pale gray, the blue of his veins starting to show through his thin skin.

A stinging stream of tears welled up in her eyes, trickling down her cheeks. She squeezed her eyes shut.

"Why are you crying?" a voice asked.

Gwen's eyes shot open. The dead boy was only mere inches away from her face. She could barely breathe. His eyes were bloodshot, as if he had been crying for days.

"Why are you crying?" the boy asked again.

"I-I don't know," Gwen stammered.

The boy laid his palms on the tub's rim, lifted himself slightly out of the water, and leaned toward her. "Don't you like me?"

Any stability that had kept Gwen erect on her knees disappeared. The boy snatched her by the wrists, keeping her from falling over. He repeated his question.

"No, I don't," Gwen replied, the stench of the boy's breath twisting her stomach into a knot.

The boy smiled. His teeth were the same pinkish color as the bath water. "I don't like you, either. I hate you, Gwen! I hate you!"

"Why?" she was compelled to ask. The salty taste of her tears was on her lips.

"Because you won't go away!" he answered, almost growling. "I'll never be King unless you go away. I will make you go away!"

The water boiled more intensely. Dark strings of sticky blood began to leak out of the tiles in the wall bordering the bathtub.

The boy reached his hands forward and caressed Gwen's breasts, squeezing them hard. "Marty will die, too! I don't like him, either!"

Gwen wanted to run—leave the motel. Wanted to run and go screaming down the street outside, hoping that someone would help her. "P-please go away..." she begged.

"No, NO NEVER!" The red in the child's eyes grew darker until they were black. His voice changed from that of a child into a deep, garbled mess. "Come here, Gwen." He pulled her forward with strength that could not be his own.

He kissed her, his tongue sliding all the way down her throat and into her stomach. A searing pain emerged in Gwen's abdomen. She fainted.

She awoke when she felt the cherry of her cigarette burning her fingertips. She quickly stubbed it out and slumped in her chair.

She thought she heard the boy laughing from the bathroom.

* * *

The Grass Root. A seedy dive, also known as the "Classy Ass." It was a haven to the less fortunate and the hopeless in North Toronto. It was a place where those who had little money could still go out and buy a beer for a couple of bucks. There were cracks in the artificial wood wall paneling. Poorly powered yellow lights lit the room, a thick cloud of smoke, which always hung in the room whether the bar was open or not, hovered loosely in the air. The smell of unwashed skin could almost be tasted if you breathed in deep enough.

The most famous attraction at the "Classy Ass" was the cougars—the poor forty to fifty year old women who would come there night after night looking for a night of hot-lovin' with someone who was much younger than themselves. Their stories were all the same—men their age didn't cut it any more. The old rods of steel had turned to rubber. But here, the meat was fresh. Well, almost. The average age attendance at the Grass Root was twenty-five to thirty-five year olds, men with disheveled faces, down on their luck and at the bottom of the barrel. Sometimes, if the pickings were slim, the forty to fifties of the cougar crowd picked them up and make them feel worth something for three to ten minutes.

Sitting in the middle of the bar was the Watcher, an elderly man who called himself Sherman Gray. He sat hunched over an ashtray, thick smoke billowing out the end of a chubby cigar, a half empty glass of beer next to the ashtray. His brow wrinkled to almost a frown, where, above its lines, he wore a black fedora, hiding what little hair he had left. He was a little too dressed up for a slum like this one, but a faded white button-down shirt, a loose tie, and suspenders holding up a pair brown slacks had always been his favorite outfit.

From behind him, he felt a poke on the shoulder. He looked up to see what he presumed to be a forty or so year old woman looking down at him.

"Hey, ol' timer, mind if I sit?" she asked.

He looked up from his ashtray, eyeing the remains of her once shapely figure. The black, half-beaten dress she was wearing wasn't appealing or complimenting, but Sherman saw past that. He could feel the lust welling up inside her and working its way down to her crotch.

"No, not at all," he replied with a half-cocked grin.

"Good. My fuckin' feet are killing me. Been walking all over all night, y'know?" She sat down, crossed her legs, hiding what was under the much too-short hemline of her dress.

"No, I don't," he said.

"What?" she said, not catching on. The blue glow of shadow around her eyes sullied her expression.

Sherman took a heavy puff of his cigar. "Nothing."

"How did you manage to keep this table all to yerself? This place is packed tighter than an Asian hooker."

The old man smiled through the cloud of smoke. "There are only certain people I choose to sit with."

She flashed him a half-grin and began grooving her head back and forth to the music. Creedence Clearwater Revival was playing "Down On The Corner" through a set of scratchy speakers. She turned back to him and noticed that his head had dipped back down toward the table.

"Haven't seen you around here," she said, leaning a little bit closer. "Ya new in town?"

Sherman looked up and tilted his fedora slightly to the side. "Sort of."

She played with the pink scrunchie in her phony blonde hair, arching her back, purposely pushing her sagging breasts forward. "Aren't you a little old to be hanging around a place like this, drinking beer all alone?"

"I don't know," he said, "aren't *you* a little old?"

She scowled at his remark then stuck out her hand across the table. "My name's Gelinda. Gelinda Strong."

Sherman took her hand gently in his and curled up the corner of his lip. Gelinda thought she felt a small, warm shock go through her hand.

"Sherman. Sherman Gray," he said.

"Nice to meet you, Mr. Gray. Would y'like to buy me a drink?"

He released her hand. "No, I wouldn't."

"Really? Are you sure about that?" she asked in a sleek voice. She got up and walked around to the other side of the table and put her hands around his collar. She began rubbing his neck seductively. Sherman could feel the tremors in her hand. She was an alcoholic.

He turned to face her, looking into her eyes. Gelinda felt as though a cloud had been veiled over her vision, her mind turning blank.

"Yes, I am sure," he said. "Why don't you go to the bar and fetch me a beer? Then, when you've brought it back to me, go entice a friend and bring her over so that the three of us can talk."

A flash across her eyes, she turned silently and went over to the bar. Sherman brought his cigar to his lips and adjusted his hat so that it was sitting straight again.

Out of the corner of his eye he could see Gelinda pull up the hem of her dress and retrieve a wrinkled fiver out of her overstretched panty hose. She was mildly attractive for her age, but definitely did not dress the part. Sherman knew that Gelinda wasn't a bar favorite. On more than one occasion she had stirred trouble with the bartenders. She always seemed to be begging them to start running a tab for her, and, after every refusal, she would reach down into her stockings, and produce the funds needed. She was desperate. Sherman's type.

She returned with the beer, set it neatly in front of him, and watched as he poured it into his now empty glass.

After he took his first sip she wandered off back into the crowd.

The song on the jukebox changed and it was the Dire Straits' turn at bat. "Money for Nothing" rang loudly. When Gelinda returned she had a slightly younger woman, probably forty-one, hanging onto her arm. Her name was Cathy Geddes. The two girls had met each other only moments before, but Cathy felt an odd magnetism towards Gelinda that she couldn't quite place. When Gelinda had told her about Sherman, Cathy immediately fell into a trance and walked over with her.

"Sherman, I'd like you to meet Cathy," Gelinda said.

"How do you do," he offered and took Cathy by her hand. She felt a similar warm spark tickle her, the same as Gelinda had. Her striped black and purple dress didn't become her. Not to mention her short, wildly spiked hair.

The two girls sat down at the table with him and watched in awe as he stubbed out his cigar and produced a fresh one from his inner breast pocket. When he lit it, the girls became even more enthralled in their growing passion for him, even though he looked well over seventy years old. If they knew how old he really was, they wouldn't have believed him.

"Would you like to fuck us, Mr. Gray?" Gelinda asked.

The two girls brought their heads closer to each other, trying to look cute. Instead of a couple of cute smiles, Sherman saw two mouths full of yellow teeth and poor gums.

"No," he told them and took another swig of his beer.

The girls looked at him, astonished. Sherman inhaled another lung full of the cigar and blew the smoke toward them. The room filled with the smell of sulfur.

"I want you to kill each other," he said with a seducing smile and tense eyes.

"Of course," Cathy said. "Let's go outside."

The girls got up and led Sherman into an alley behind the bar. There, the shadows were thick and the noise of the city was loud. Sherman pulled out two handkerchiefs, one red and one blue. Submitting to him, the girls allowed themselves to be gagged. Secondly, he handed each of them a small pocketknife. He sat on the ground in front of them, not feeling the cold pavement on his behind.

No one heard the girl's stifled cries as they each took turns slashing each other. The constant honking of car horns from the nearby traffic masked Sherman's laughter.

* * *

Gwen had fallen asleep again in her chair, this time waking to an even more startling sensation than that of a burning finger.

Somebody was in the room with her.

She tried to dismiss the feeling and go back to sleep but before she could, a cold voice spoke into the darkness of the room.

"Do you understand, Gwen?" the voice asked. "Do you finally understand?"

Gwen sat up in her chair and looked around the room. She didn't see anybody. She considered turning the light on, but if it was her imagination that was speaking to her, then running to the light switch seemed futile. But if it *wasn't* her imagination—

"Do you understand, Gwen?" the voice repeated.

A rock formed in her stomach. For a brief moment she thought that the child from her dream had left his tongue inside her.

"The child will rape you, and the world, unless you do something Gwen! You must do something to stop this! You *will* do something!"

Gwen called out into the darkness, asking who was there, but only silence responded.

She lit a cigarette, and held the smoke in her lungs for a moment before fully exhaling. The cloud she breathed out seemed to pause in mid-air before settling into obscurity.

"Do you understand, Gwen?" the voice asked again.

Yes, Gwen said to herself. *Yes, I understand perfectly. I understand that I've gone nuts and that I'm hearing voices.*

She took another drag off her cigarette and this time, when she exhaled, the cloud of smoke took on the appearance of a face. Harry's face.

"Do you understand?" Harry the cloud asked. "Dammit, answer me, Gwen! Do you finally understand!" His voice was that of a lion.

"Go away! Go the fuck away!" Gwen screamed and fell forward off her chair. The cigarette flew from her fingertips and crashed against the carpet, sparking itself out.

When she stood up, the smoke cloud had disappeared. Through teary eyes, Gwen searched for her fallen cigarette. She was relieved when she saw that it wasn't still lit.

Her heart ached from pounding so hard.

"I understand," she finally said and flopped backward on her bed.

Fatigued from the encounter, she fell asleep and didn't wake up for the rest of the night.

Chapter Sixteen

Relaying information to Gwen was growing more difficult each day. At first it had been easy to go into her dreams and submit thoughts to her. Now, communicating with Gwen over such a long distance was tiring. Each time Harry had tried to establish contact, he felt as though his brain was hitting a brick wall. Transmitting his thoughts over such a great distance was like trying to push a strand of hair through Styrofoam—damn near impossible. He had only been able to succeed in the transmissions when he focused himself, concentrating on his thoughts and feelings—with those acts in themselves becoming all the harder to do, as well. His mind was more like a spilled pot of spaghetti than a coherent organ of intellect.

Harry sat cross-legged on the floor of his room, back pressed against the bedpost, his head leaning against the mattress. He once again tried to reach Gwen. He couldn't. Had his demon abilities left him? Had he even communicated with Gwen in the first place? He didn't know. Harry could only hope that the last thought he had transmitted to her still rang in her head, and, most importantly, that she would listen to it.

Coming out of the Darkroom had been liberating—almost. There was no more darkness or the stenches of sweat and gas, but here, in the confinement of his room, Harry was more crowded than ever. What was closing in on him? Why was it so hard to breathe? Too many cigarettes? Harry was sick to his stomach and his head ached with confusion. He didn't want to call Dr. Woodrose and ask for help. He didn't want a nurse. He didn't want to rest.

Why me, he thought. *Why me? Of all the people on this fucking planet!*

His wife had been murdered, his child abandoned him, his doctors didn't believe anything he told them, and now he had sent a young woman out into danger. He might as well have signed her death sentence or offered her a seat in the electric chair. Maybe even a noose and a high beam so she could hang herself. But regardless of any risk involved, it had to be done. Was it fair? Too many questions.

"God!" he cried and buried his head between his knees. "Help me!"

As if in answer, there was a knock at the door. Harry heard the latch unlock. He looked up to see his visitor and instead of finding a nurse as he had expected, he saw an old man.

Sherman Gray.

Harry sat speechless as Sherman closed the door behind him, somehow locking it from the inside. He walked over, quicker than any old man, and sat on the bed next to Harry.

They sat in silence for several minutes, Harry quaking with fear.

Sherman adjusted himself and began to speak.

"Hello, Harry," he said softly, his voice a smooth whisper, "I know what you've done."

Panicked, Harry sprung up and lunged for the door.

"Help me!" he screamed. His fists pounded on the door, the thuds echoing in his room. From down the hall, Nurse Robinson heard him and came to his room to investigate.

Robinson unlocked the door from the outside and opened it, then stumbled back as Harry flew into his arms.

"Help me please!" he begged, his weight pulling down on the nurse.

"What happened, Harry?" Robinson asked, concerned.

"He did!" Harry exclaimed and pointed to Sherman who was still sitting on the bed.

Robinson didn't see anybody. "Who, Harry? Who?"

"Him, you fool!" Harry barked. He was still pointing towards the bed.

Robinson walked into the room and circled around. "There's no one here," he said.

Harry ran back into the room, grabbed Robinson by the hand, and stood him directly in front of Sherman.

"He's right here. Can't you see? There's an old man right here on my fucking bed!"

Robinson, astonished at how genuinely terrified Harry seemed, thought about how he could calm him down. He took a step forward and sat on the bed in the same space that Sherman occupied.

"See, it's just me, Harry. No one's here," he said.

Sherman was now standing beside Harry, whispering into his ear. "He can't see me, Harry. I just want to talk. Tell him to leave."

"Go to hell…" Harry muttered.

"What?" Robinson asked.

"Get me outta here. Please!"

"I can't, Harry. You're confined to quarters except for meals and smoking privileges."

"Then I really need to smoke!" Harry shot back.

"Nice try, Harry," Robinson said.

Harry grabbed the nurse by the shoulders and yelled, "GET ME THE HELL OUTTA HERE!"

Robinson broke Harry's hold and stood up. "Calm down, Harry. Calm down. There's no one in here but you and me."

Harry decided to execute his mind control over him. Sherman noticed and immediately reached Robinson's mind before Harry did. *Harry stays here. Harry stays here. Harry stays here.*

Harry could feel what Sherman was doing. There was no way he could fight him. Sherman was telepathically stronger. There was only one thing to do. He ran out the door.

Get him! Sherman's voice rang inside Robinson's head. The nurse bolted after Harry, yelling to the other nurses not to let Harry leave Y-3.

Harry ran, trying to find a way off the floor. He could hear the nurses closing in on him. He skidded to a halt before running into a pair of locked doors. Harry grabbed the handles and shook them violently, the doors rattling in their hinges. Locked. He turned around. Robinson, accompanied by three others, was running towards him. Harry darted straight for them, tackling Robinson, bringing him to the ground. The other nurses jumped on top of them, trying to get Harry off their colleague like football players piling up over a ball.

Harry kicked and screamed as he was pulled off the nurse. Once standing, there was a prick in the back of his arm. He knew that feeling all too well: sedative.

Harry was hauled back to his room and tossed onto his bed. Three nurses stood at his door, Robinson behind them, dusting himself off.

"Go to sleep, Harry," Robinson told him.

Harry cried, his voice barely audible. "Help me. Take me away."

The door to his room closed, and he was alone. That was, until, he felt the weight of his mattress shift. Sherman was sitting next to him.

"Go away," Harry mumbled into the mattress. He tried to move but his body was too sluggish from the sedative. Even if he did manage to get up, where would he go? Not past Sherman. And if somehow he had managed that, a whole herd of nurses would stop him again and force more drugs into his system, making escape impossible.

"No," Sherman said, "I will not go away." His voice was that of a dictator.

"Why?"

"Because I have to tell you something."

Harry squeezed his eyes shut. "I don't want to hear it."

"Of course not. You know the truth just as I do, but, unfortunately for you, no one other than yourself can see it. Well, almost no one."

His head hurt, his muscles sapped of strength. "What do you want?"

Sherman raised his voice but did not yell. "Call off Gwen."

"No."

"Then I will."

Harry wanted to shout but could only slur his words. "Leaferalome…"

"I can't, Harry. You know that's impossible for me." Sherman lied down next to Harry, positioned himself on his stomach, and leaned on his elbows, his fingers clasped together.

Harry wanted to strangle him, wanted to get away from Sherman's oily smell. His body had fallen asleep. His mind was falling away, too. "Ithashto…bbe…done…" Harry mumbled, his glassy stare peering up at Sherman.

"It was foretold that the Antichrist would come," Sherman told him. "Who are you to change that?"

Harry fell silent.

"Exactly," Sherman replied.

"I…hab an…expernce…" Harry said, his lips barely moving.

"We've all had experiences, Harry. Yours was an accident. Nothing more. No purpose."

"No acsdent…always…a purpuss…" Harry paused, then, "wait…whaddayamean…acsdent?"

"It's hard to explain, really. But let's just say that there are other forces at work her other than the Nazarene and his fallen angel. Someone who doesn't subscribe to the black and white of our existence but stays in the gray, messing with both sides. No one knows his, hers, or its name, or where they come from. All are without clue. We have only one small shred of information: the letters 'V' and 'M.' We don't know what that means, but that doesn't concern you, anyway, Harry. I'm sure both Heaven and Hell will figure out who this third party is in due time."

"Wha..." Harry could hardly be heard.

"I've said enough," Sherman said, "but the question remains, who are you sided with, Harry? Black, white, or gray?"

Harry focused himself. He spoke more clearly. "Does it matter? The child must not live."

"He will live, you will see. He serves my master whether he knows it or not." Sherman got off the bed.

"Yer no all that...powerful...are you?" Harry asked, recognizing that maybe Sherman couldn't stop Gwen. His voice came back a little stronger now.

"I can do whatever befits my purpose," the old man replied and produced a newspaper clipping from inside his tattered blazer. He unfolded it and showed Harry the headline: TWO GIRLS SLAIN IN SLASH FIGHT!

Harry's eyes widened. "You did this?"

"I did. And I can do far worse. They were two and Gwen is but only one. Imagine, Harry, imagine." The newspaper was folded and was replaced back inside his coat.

Again Harry fell silent. What was he supposed to say now?

"If you wish for another demonstration," Sherman continued, "that can be arranged. Gwen is right where I want her. Alone. Away from Marty. Away from friends. Especially away from you. I arranged for Gwen to stay at a motel far from the boy. Plus, a minor effort on my part had been made to scare her away but—"

"She is too strong," Harry added, cutting him off.

"Maybe."

Sherman stood, straightened his coat and tipped his hat, leaving Harry alone to the darkness. Harry lay there on his bed, feeling the air turn cool around him, an acrid smell surfacing. He also sensed the sharp presence of something sinister lurking in the shadows of his room.

He could only pray that Gwen was all right and that Sherman would leave her alone.

Chapter Seventeen

If you told Calvin Mandalay that somebody was hunting him, he wouldn't follow you. If you told him that he would die, he would not understand. The very idea of death was too far off and unheard of. It didn't exist and it never will.

Tonight, Uncle Ken decided to teach Calvin a card game. Since the boy was learning to count in school, WAR seemed to be a good choice. Ken had fixed the deck, with all the face and ace cards omitted. He didn't want to confuse Calvin by explaining the values of the different faces and what the A on the ace card was worth. Just simple numbers. Nothing fancy.

He explained the rules of the game and Calvin caught on quickly, although sometimes Calvin confused the six with the nine.

Ken studied his nephew, glad that he was managing given his mother's circumstance. He figured it must be hard for a child growing up in a home where his only parent couldn't deal with the responsibilities of everyday life and relied on an uncle to act as the father figure.

Ken didn't have any children of his own, so sometimes relating to Calvin was more difficult, and sometimes he didn't know how to care for him. But, he did know that if life didn't steer in a more positive direction for Calvin, the poor boy would be condemned to grow up an unhappy child.

Ken dealt the cards and the game got underway. If Ken had been playing the game with someone his own age, there wouldn't have been much talking, but since Calvin was so young, Ken knew that flipping over cards in silence would become boring.

"So, how are your friends doing?" Ken asked, watching Calvin compare the numbers on the cards.

"I don't know," Calvin shrugged. He beat out Ken's 3 with a 10. Calvin smiled, victorious.

"Hey, you got me," Ken observed. "What do you mean you don't know?"

They kept playing.

"I don't know, good, I guess," Calvin shrugged again.

"Do you see them much?" Ken fidgeted with the cards in his hands.

"Only at school. Mom won't drive me anywhere."

Ken frowned, disappointed in Victoria for being more reclusive as of late. He assumed that she was so depressed that she didn't feel like doing anything, or going anywhere—even driving her son to a friend's house.

"That's too bad," Ken said sympathetically.

"It doesn't matter. I like being inside. I jus' wish—" Calvin stopped speaking and compared his 6 to Ken's 9, then acknowledged that nine was more than six.

"You just wish—" Ken prompted.

"I don't know. I can't 'member. Most of my friends are acting weird, anyway."

"Really?"

"They're acting like I'm a monster. Yesserday, I was eating a banana and Jake looked at me like I got fangs."

Ken couldn't help but smile. "Maybe Jake doesn't like bananas," he told him, rather than suggested.

"He eats them alla time," Calvin said in defense. The boy readjusted himself in his chair and straightened the growing stack of cards in his hands. He was beating his uncle.

Ken, even if he wanted to, couldn't let Calvin win. WAR was a game of chance, pure and simple. It could not be rigged.

"Sometimes friends act differently with each other, Calvin. I remember when I was younger it sometimes felt like my friends were acting weird, too. I remember thinking that one of them thought I had two heads."

Calvin giggled at the thought of his uncle having two heads. Ken was glad the joke brought on a smile.

"Sometimes I wish they would just go away. Sometimes I wish I could be all by myself, jus' like Mom is," Calvin told him.

Ken's heart sank at hearing this. He was not liking the way Calvin was starting to view things: more pessimistically. Ken flipped out his next card, laying down an 8.

"Y'know, Calvin, there's this one little boy I see at church all the time. Maybe if you came with me one Sunday you could meet him."

Calvin looked at him blankly then laid down an 8 as well.

It was WAR.

"Uh-oh," Ken said.

"What now?" Calvin asked.

"What happens next is we both lay down three cards faced down on the table. Then after that, we flip over another card. If my card is higher than yours, I keep all the cards that we laid down, and if it isn't, then you keep all the cards." Calvin nodded, understanding. "You ready?"

"Yep." The boy huddled around his hand of cards, hiding behind them as if this really was a war and his uncle would attack him.

Ken laid down three cards, the fourth being a 3. He was glad the card was so low. He really wanted Calvin to win at his first game of WAR.

"Three," Calvin acknowledged and fumbled his cards, also laying down three. His fourth card was a 2.

Calvin had lost.

"Here," Calvin said and pushed the cards towards his uncle.

"Sorry," Ken said, taking the cards in his hands.

"It's okay."

"Like I was saying, you should come with me one Sunday and meet this boy. His mother told me he likes climbing trees just like you do. Sometimes he pretends that he can fly and jumps off the lower branches."

The game continued.

"I don't know. I don't like new people. They always look funny," Calvin said.

"C'mon, it would be fun. When we first get there we sing some songs, then we listen to a man talk about God for a while."

"Issat what you do at church? Learn about God?"

"Yeah. Hasn't your mom ever taken you before?"

"Mom says God's not nice."

Ken sighed. He didn't want to force the issue of coming to church on Calvin, but he really wanted him to start hearing good things about life. From the way Calvin had been talking, he could tell that his mother's negative influences had rubbed off on him. Negative things about life, love, friends.

Back in the game, Ken beat Calvin again.

"I'll tell you what, if you want to go with me, you can. Okay?" Ken said.

Calvin laid down a 6 and looked up at Ken with a frown. "We'll see," the boy said.

Ken also laid down a 6.

"War again," Calvin said and laid down three cards. He prepped the fourth in the hopes of beating out his uncle. He laid it down. It was another 6.

"Three six's in a row, eh?" Ken said.

"Isn't it always!" Calvin shot back.

Now what did he mean by that?

Ken played his next card but it was only a 3.

"You got me," Ken told him.

"I know. You shouldn't mess with triple six," Calvin said in a voice that didn't seem to be his own. He swiped his cards off the table and formed them in a neat pile before him.

"What do you mean?" his uncle asked.

"About what?" Calvin asked, puzzled. His voice had seemed to return to normal.

"Not messing with triple six."

"What?"

"You just told me that you shouldn't mess with triple six."

Calvin brought his cards up to his eyes, studying them. "No, I didn't."

"Yes, you did."

"When?"

"Just now."

"No, I didn't!" Calvin said sternly. He gave Ken a stare that made his uncle uneasy.

What's wrong with him? Ken asked himself before starting the next round.

Chapter Eighteen

Gwen Reeves had been milling about her motel room like a zombie all morning. Her thoughts were fragmented, convoluted, and scattered amongst a sea of confusion and chaos. She was no longer acknowledging the events that surrounded her. Her mind had given way after her last real nightmare, not Harry's visit. When she had first awakened from it, she could still feel the boy's tongue swimming inside her stomach. A few short moments later she was leaning over the side of her chair, throwing up.

Then she had cried.

Gwen still couldn't understand why she had been given this task and its overwhelming responsibility. She couldn't fathom the forces at work or why she had been forced to meet a hairy man in an asylum. Her head was heavy, as if someone had filled it with sand, and her vision being that of an observer looking through plated glass. She had hit her breaking point.

Now, alone in her room, she paced back and forth, Harry's voice echoing in her mind: *Kill him. Kill him. Kill the child, the monster. Kill him!*

Gwen gave into the voice. Yes, she would kill the child. And, later on, when she could think a little more clearly, she would decide how she would do it.

* * *

It was afternoon and Gwen sat at the table in her motel room, sucking heavily on a cigarette. Her eyes fixed blankly on the slowly filling ashtray, her fingertips tapping the smooth, oak-finished table.

By now the voice of Harry had subsided and she was able to think more clearly. There was an overwhelming need to carry out his request to kill the boy. She had to. She had to finally end this nightmare and get back to a normal life. Get back home. Get back to Marty.

Gwen combed her fingers through her hair, disgusted at the oil and sweat that was saturating her scalp. So many thoughts ran through her head, only one of which that kept coming forward: how could the murder be done?

Gwen had never killed anyone before. Now she had to analyze each way she could go about doing it, and, more importantly, how to get it done without getting caught. The first thought that came to her mind was to take a bus downtown, somehow buy a gun, and follow through with the traditional method of murder. This notion was quickly dismissed when she realized that the police could easily match the bullet to the model of gun and trace it back to its owner. And she didn't know where to begin looking for an underground connection to purchase a weapon, anyway.

Taking a drag off her cigarette, Gwen thought of the many ways to kill the boy, frowning with disappointment at how few options there were that would be untraceable.

Gwen finished her cigarette and lit another one after taking a sip of Baja Rosa from the room's liquor cabinet.

The method she would choose had to be fast, effective and relatively painless for the victim. Gwen didn't want the child to suffer, no matter what kind of monster he might grow up to become.

She would have to plan her attack and go through every possibility of what would take place before, during, and after the event.

She could leave no room for error.

The very thought of going to prison made her shudder. Then another consideration occurred to her, if God was somehow involved in all of this, why didn't He kill the boy instead of her? Why didn't He get Harry to do it?

Then she remembered.

It was too much for one person to both understand the boy's significance and to carry out the execution. There had to be two. One who would experience the truth of the circumstance, and the other to learn of that experience and carry out its desired purpose.

It wasn't fair. That much was clear. But who was Gwen to argue with almighty God, anyway? Somewhere, deep down inside, she knew that if God were really behind this entire mess, then He would see her through until its end.

* * *

Two hours later, Gwen had conjured up a vague idea as to how the murder would be done. It would just take a little planning.

* * *

Marty Bones sat in front of his computer late that night. It was part of his routine to check his e-mail before going to bed. As he typed in his password he thought of Gwen and hoped that maybe she had written to him. Marty was pretty sure that wherever Gwen was, she had access to a computer. He really needed her right now. He didn't know if he would be able to trust himself with Denise.

The e-mail window began to load, but the only messages that came through were various updates from different news groups; artsy stuff mostly. Marty didn't bother to read any of them and deleted them from the disk cache.

His spirits about his relationship with Gwen were at an all time low. Earlier in the day, he had found himself getting mad at her for taking off so abruptly. Even though he felt his feelings were justified, he did his best to remain optimistic and put faith in the fact that Gwen knew what she was doing no matter how outrageous the whole circumstance might seem.

Marty turned off the computer and sat in the darkness. His heart was torn in two. He was completely in love with Gwen. But, on the other hand, her sudden change in attitude and her actions had not made sense. Deep down in the pit of his stomach, he had a haunting feeling that his fight with Gwen had something to do with her disappearance. Marty wished he could turn back the clock and start things over again with her. Anything would be better then being without Gwen.

At the same time, he was feeling an unexpected attraction towards Denise. He couldn't explain it, but knew that it was more than just simple lust.

Marty hated moments like these. Moments where he didn't know what to do and wished more than anything that all existence would stand still so he could receive a break from all the confusion and uncertainty.

Gwen had always been the last person he had thought of before going to sleep at night and the first when he would awake the next morning. Surely he could trust himself to be faithful in her absence?

But he couldn't. And he knew it.

Denise had been over earlier, and she and Marty had hung out, watched a movie, and munched on some corn chips. They had sat on opposite ends of the couch in the rec. room and, more often than not, Marty felt himself tempted to sit closer to her and put his arm around her. It hurt him to know that he thought about cheating on Gwen, but made himself feel better when he told himself that he was just being honest about his developing feelings towards Denise. The problem was he didn't know what price he was willing to pay for her. He would have to give Gwen time, but as to how much, he didn't know.

Marty decided he would wait a week then he would think about things again. Until then he would do his best to keep his contact with Denise to a minimum and hope that Gwen would try to reach him before the week ran out.

* * *

The image of the Antichrist stood prominently in Gwen's mind. The information that Harry had deposited in her was growing clearer with each passing moment. It was as if there were a magnetic pull between her and the boy. Gwen *knew* where in the city the boy lived. She decided that come morning she would rent a car, drive out to where he lived, and have a look around. She would examine his surroundings and plan a method of execution and escape.

Given her knowledge on murder and available resources, Gwen had decided that she would poison the child. And, hopefully, for the boy's sake, it wouldn't be too painful. When she thought about the boy's age and size, it was concluded that a simple drug overdose would do the trick. She would worry about administering the drug at the appropriate time.

Gwen even thought of where she would obtain a drug potent enough to do such damage. As in all cities, if you were to be at the right place at the right time, a drug transaction could easily occur.

Before she could think any further about her plan, the outdated phone in her motel room rang. Wondering if it was Marty, she picked up the receiver.

"H-hello?"

"Hello, Gwen," came a smooth voice on the other end of the line, taking Gwen a moment to recognize it.

Her heart sank. It wasn't Marty. It was Harry.

"Hello," Gwen said more calmly.

"I hope that I didn't alarm you."

"No, not at all."

"Good."

"How did you get to a phone? I thought patients in your ward couldn't use telephones."

"Yes, that's true, or, at least, that's the general rule, anyway. I simply persuaded a nurse to let me use one. Tricks of the mind, y'know. The nurses are quite foolish and weak minded. I have at least learned that much by now."

"Yes, I suppose you have," Gwen replied, thinking about Harry's ability to creep into a person's mind and control what they think and feel. She lit a cigarette.

"You know the thing I asked you to do for me?" Harry continued.

"Yes."

"There's been a change in plans." Harry's voice shook.

Gwen furrowed her brow. "In which way?"

"Come back home, Gwen. Just forget about this whole ordeal. Don't come and see me, either. It's best to just pretend that none of this had ever happened so we could both get on with our lives."

Gwen sensed that something was wrong. Her stomach turned upside-down, a sharp pain pricking her heart. As a reflex to her reaction, the same voice that had driven her nearly insane earlier had returned and echoed in her head: *Kill him. Kill him. Kill the child, the monster. Kill him!* The stanza repeated over and over. Gwen knew that turning her back on her responsibility would be the wrong thing to do.

"Gwen? Are you still there?" came Harry's voice anxiously.

"Yes," Gwen nearly whispered.

"Please stop this. I was wrong."

"Why?"

"Like I said, I was wrong. You shouldn't have listened to me. I'm in the nuthouse for crying out loud! I can't be all that credible!"

Gwen looked off elsewhere in her room. "But the dreams, the visions?"

"Nevermind those," Harry told her. "Last night something happened to me and I—I dreamed of someone else. Whoever it was had told me to call you back home to Winnipeg. I'm just making good on that. Gwen, please…please forget it all. I made a mistake."

There was a time of silence. Gwen could hear Harry's unsteady breathing. The knot in her stomach twisted even more and tears poked at the corners of her eyes. It was too late. Her mind had already been made up.

"I'm sorry, Harry. It has to be done."

She hung up the phone, staring at the burning amber of her cigarette. *Why would Harry change his mind after all the fuss he had made over this?* she wondered.

Gwen walked over to the window and opened it slightly, letting fresh air into the humid room. Her stomach was still sick and her heart still hurt. She asked herself if she felt this way because she actually *did* want to kill the boy. For every second that passed, killing the child had become all the more right.

It had to be done. That's what she had told Harry.

She sat in her chair, smoking. Maybe in the morning she would feel better and things would be much more clear.

* * *

In the room next to Gwen's, Sherman Gray sat on the edge of the bed near the telephone that was on the night table. Gwen hadn't listened. Next time he would have to be more persuasive.

Chapter Nineteen

Calvin Mandalay had been playing basketball by himself all recess. He preferred it this way, as he had never been a big fan of running around aimlessly with the other kids. Sure, he enjoyed the competition of other people, but for him, there was something special about standing alone in front of the basketball hoop, trying to sink as many baskets as possible.

At home when he played, it allowed him time to think, as far as a child's thinking goes, and it gave him the chance to get away from his mother when he heard her crying in her bedroom.

He worried for her and although he didn't understand her problems, he knew that something bad deep down inside her was getting the best of her. After all, a person shouldn't be sad all the time now, should they? Maybe when he was older he would know how to ask her why she was always so sad.

Calvin had heard her talk about her husband once in a while to Uncle Ken, so he assumed that maybe it was this husband that was causing her so much grief.

He also secretly wondered if it maybe was himself.

His mother had always been good to him despite the fact that he was adopted, but sometimes Calvin couldn't help questioning if his being around was doing her any good. He hated thinking about that. Every time he did a small spike of hurt went through his heart.

He decided he wouldn't think about that now. Right now, sinking the ball was all that was important.

Calvin stood in front of the net with the ball poised above his head and, before taking his shot, took a quick look around to see if anybody was watching. To his right a small group of girls that looked a grade older than him sat in a circle, giggling, the girl seated in the middle occasionally looking up at him. On his left were a few boys his age who would laugh and point at the girls while one of them would run across the basketball court to the group and shout "Tim loves Sandra!" then run back. Calvin shook is head in disapproval. Why would a boy love a girl, anyway? Girls were disgusting.

He returned his attention to the hoop and aimed his shot. A perfect swish. Calvin retrieved the ball and set himself up for another shot. This time the ball bounced twice on the rim before going in. He heard one of the girls to his right clap her hands and give him a holler. He flashed her a grin and got ready again. Just as he released the ball the third time, he heard one of the girls squeal and saw that the boy who kept relaying the message that Tim loved Sandra had tripped and fallen in the middle of the girl's circle, landing on top of most of them. His shot was disrupted and the ball slammed against the backboard, bouncing off to the far side of the court. Calvin went to retrieve it and found himself face to face with an old man who was holding his ball. It took Calvin a moment to realize that it was the same old man that he had seen through his classroom window.

"You're pretty good," the old man said, handing him the ball.

"Thanks," Calvin replied and returned to the basketball court.

The old man followed and stood a few feet behind him. Calvin shuddered at his presence, but was soon calmed. He didn't mind having the older man there anymore. There was something comforting about this elderly gentleman, something reassuring. Calvin prepped his next shot and got it in.

"Amazing," the old man said.

"What?"

"I was watching you from over there," the old man told him, pointing to the wire-meshed fence that bordered the school ground. "I was impressed that you got it in every time."

"Not every time," Calvin said, trying to discredit the compliment. The only compliments he ever took to heart were the ones from his mother and Uncle Ken. Compliments from other people never seemed sincere.

"Your last shot didn't count," the old man told him as-a-matter-of-factly. "That boy distracted you."

The old man nodded toward the boy who had fallen on top of the girl's group.

"Still," Calvin said sternly.

"Trying to be the best, eh?"

"Yep."

Calvin shot the ball against the backboard, rebounding it into the net.

"Can I take a shot?" the old man asked.

Calvin gave him a wry smile and handed him the ball. The old man positioned himself where Calvin had been standing and poised the ball on his fingertips. With a light flick of his wrist he sent the ball soaring high into the air, scoring a perfect basket.

"Wow!" Calvin exclaimed. "How'd you do that?"

A Stranger Dead

The ball seemed to magnetically return to the old man's hands. He prepared himself to shoot again.

"Just a little trick I've been toying with for the past little while," the old man returned. "By the way, my name is Sherman."

"I'm Calvin," he told him, his eyes remaining on the basketball Sherman held in his wrinkled hands.

"I know."

Calvin didn't know what he meant by that, but didn't care. The old guy could really shoot!

Calvin was also surprised at how relaxed he felt around him. Normally he didn't care too much about meeting strangers. It had always seemed that they were trying to crowd in on him and get to know him too quickly.

Sherman poised the ball and repeated his magic shot. Again, a perfect swish.

"Would you like to try?" Sherman asked.

"Sure," Calvin said and stepped up beside Sherman.

Sherman handed him the ball and stood behind him, stooping a little so that his head was beside Calvin's. He reached around the boy and positioned the ball on Calvin's fingertips, helping him angle his shot just right.

"Okay, it's really simple," Sherman began. "I know you don't think balancing the ball on your fingertips while trying to shoot is a good idea but you have to learn to trust yourself, the ball, and the net. The ball knows where it needs to go. The net knows what needs to come towards it. And you know what you have to do. The three of you are friends; best pals. All friends help each other. And you, the ball, and the net are no exceptions to that rule. Just relax, Calvin. Your friends will help you, okay?"

"Okay," Calvin agreed. Sherman sounded like a smart man.

Sherman made sure the ball was steady on the boy's fingertips then told Calvin to shoot. The ball sprang up from his small fingers, only to roll off them and dribble a few feet away.

"I can't do it," Calvin said hopelessly.

"Let's try again," Sherman encouraged, and retrieved the ball.

Once again he propped the ball up on Calvin's fingers and aimed the ball at the net for him. "Now remember, *you* are in control, Calvin. Not the ball. You. You are the big and strong friend in the group. Close your eyes and imagine the ball flying off of your fingertips and landing perfectly in the hoop."

Calvin closed his eyes and watched in his mind's eye as the ball sailed through the air and went through its target. He opened them and felt a sudden comfort and confidence in his abilities.

With slight hesitation, Calvin released the ball forward. It flew through the air gracefully and it seemed inevitable that it was only going to hit the rim and bounce to the ground. Then, without warning, the ball changed its course and rose slightly, allowing it to fall flawlessly down through the net. In all his life Calvin Mandalay had never smiled so big.

"Very good," Sherman said and patted him on the shoulder.

Calvin turned and looked up at the old man. "I didn't think it was going to make it in."

"You may have not thought it would go in, but you *knew* it would go in."

"You're right," Calvin said and thought once again about the vision he had about scoring the basket.

As Sherman went to retrieve the ball, the recess bell rang and the entire schoolyard became alive with children scrambling towards the school's entrances. Sherman walked over to Calvin and handed the ball back to him.

"You should practice that shot," Sherman told him.

"I will," Calvin said, taking the ball and starting to walk toward the school. He looked down at the ball and never in his whole basketball career did the ball feel so righteously placed in his hands.

"Do you play here everyday, Calvin?" Sherman called after him.

Calvin turned around and shielded his eyes from the sun that was glaring brightly behind Sherman.

"Usually. Depends," he replied.

"Maybe I'll see you tomorrow."

"Bye."

"Bye," Sherman said and stuffed his hands in his pockets.

Most of the kids had already gone inside. Calvin picked up his pace so he wouldn't be late. Before entering the school entrance, he turned around once more, facing the basketball court, hoping to get one last look at Sherman.

The sun shone brightly in his eyes. Sherman was gone.

* * *

It was late afternoon and Victoria Mandalay was in her kitchen washing dishes. She had been too tired the evening before to do anything about them.

Alone in her kitchen, she watched the suds float over her hands, the small bubbles from the soap floating into the air. It was times like these that she thought of David.

There was a time when after dinner they would wash the dishes together. She would wash and he would dry. David had never been one for touching dirty dishes. Sometimes, while she was washing, he would come up behind her, wrap his arms around her waist, and kiss her softly on the neck. Victoria would do her best to stay focused on the task at hand, but always found herself succumbing to the pleasure he would bring upon her. She would turn around and kiss him back passionately, forgetting the dishes.

The two of them would then shed their rubber gloves and ease themselves to the tiled floor where they would make love.

Victoria missed those days. Those were the days where life was all about love and she had a purpose. A meaning.

Standing over her kitchen sink, she noticed that she had stopped scrubbing the oven rack and was already reaching for a paper towel. She was crying again.

She hated herself for not getting over David. Hated herself for allowing him to rule over her life from six years in the past.

Victoria had talked about it with other single mothers and women who had been in much worse situations than hers, but no matter what the story, hers always seemed to hurt the most and be the most tragic.

Her circumstance wasn't about physical abuse or name-calling or a husband turning into an alcoholic or a criminal. Hers was about betrayal. The one person in the world that she had put all her faith and trusts in had let her down. Victoria had forgiven David for the affair but he still chose not to come back to her, instead running away into the arms of some young vixen.

The fact that her husband ran away with someone younger wasn't what bothered her, either. Victoria knew what she was capable of offering in a relationship and many times her husband had complimented her on it. But, evidently, it hadn't been enough. *That* was what bothered her. That she didn't succeed in her marriage. That *she* wasn't enough.

The only message of hope that kept her going was that she seemed to be enough for Calvin. Victoria knew that sometimes she would get too caught up in her own depression and end up neglecting him, but she also knew that Calvin understood some of the difficulties of life and that she sometimes didn't feel too well. She was also thankful that Ken was there whenever she needed him. He had been a blessing to their family and she took comfort in the fact that Calvin also loved him. Victoria could only imagine the life Calvin would have led if she hadn't taken him from the Love and Leaves adoption agency. Bouncing from foster home to foster home was no life for a child. Especially one as bright and talented as Calvin was. He seemed to catch on to everything so quickly.

Victoria dabbed at her eyes with the paper towel, then set it on the counter beside her and resumed her dish washing.

Tonight, after Calvin came home from school, they would do something special together. She would make it up to him for not spending much time with him as of late.

* * *

When Calvin came home from school that day Victoria offered to take him to Dickey's for the evening. Dickey's was one of those places that for an excessive fee a person could eat all the pizza they wanted and receive one hundred game tokens for the arcades.

Calvin immediately jumped at the offer and no more than five minutes after setting his bag down at the front door he and Victoria were in the car, already driving down their back lane.

The drive there was like all the other rides that they took together. Victoria had the radio station tuned to something Classical with Calvin spending his time looking out the windows and making comments about the various buildings in the city. He couldn't understand why people were always downtown and why most of them wore suits. He also couldn't understand why some people were sleeping on the street. Victoria explained to him that the street was their home because they didn't have enough money for a place to live. Calvin then wondered how much a patch of sidewalk would cost.

"I met someone at school today," Calvin told his mother.

At first it didn't seem as if she had heard him, her eyes hypnotized by the road ahead of her.

"So I—"

"I heard you," Victoria nearly snapped.

Calvin stopped speaking for a moment before continuing. "He was watching me play basketball."

"Who?"

"He said his name was Sherman."

Victoria was still distracted by the road. She wanted to give more attention to Calvin but driving always seemed to allow her mind to focus on something other than her ex-husband.

Calvin continued. "Me and him played together. He showed me a new basketball trick."

"What kind of trick?"

"I don't know. It's kind of a special way to make the ball go into the net. It's good."

"Is he a new student at school?" she asked.

"No. I don't think the school would allow him to come. He's too old."

She shot a glance his way. "Too old?"

"Yeah, he's even older than you, Mom."

Victoria's eyes narrowed. She had heard stories of older men coming into school grounds and doing disgusting things to children. Even kidnapping them.

"Did you tell your teacher?" Victoria asked, her thoughts making her even more worried. The last thing she needed was for her son to befriend a stranger. And the fact that it was an *older* stranger, made her all the more concerned. She decided she would notify Calvin's teacher as soon as she was able.

"No, I didn't," Calvin told her.

"Okay, look, it's not good for you to hang around with people who aren't your own age, Calvin," she said as calmly as she could. "Sometimes people who are a lot older than you may seem nice at first, but they could end up being really dangerous."

"Sherman was nice to me, Mom," Calvin said, defending the old man.

"He might have seemed nice but he could really be mean. If you see him again, I don't want you to talk to him, okay?" she told him. "I want you to tell a teacher right away. I also want you to tell me."

"Okay," Calvin agreed, disappointed.

Victoria's tone became lower and firmer. "I mean it, Calvin. He's dangerous."

She gave Calvin the *look*. The *look* was something she gave him when she meant business or when he was in trouble. Calvin hated it. It intimidated him and made him angry at the same time.

"Fine," Calvin said, and looked out the window.

"Promise me."

"I said fine." Calvin folded his arms, scowled at her, the slumped in his seat.

The rest of the evening went along just fine, the miracle of children being that they could be mad one minute and happy the next. Calvin ate more than his share of pizza while his mother sat in a booth and watched him as he ran from one arcade game to another. Victoria was glad to see him having so much fun. Sometimes she worried that he spent too much time outside on their driveway playing basketball by himself. It was good to see him interacting with other kids once in a while. Calvin came by their table occasionally to tell his mom which monster he had just pulverized in the game "Monsters and Men." Each time Victoria gave him a smile and encouraged him to go play some more.

All though neither of them mentioned it, they were both thinking about Sherman, wondering what kind of person he was. Calvin hoped that Sherman would show up at school the next day and teach him another shot.

Victoria was thinking the opposite.

She prayed that her son would never see the old man again. It was upsetting how Calvin seemed so enthusiastic about meeting him. She tried not to think about it. Tomorrow she would call his teacher.

Chapter Twenty

Gwen had rented a car from the cheapest dealership she could find. It had also been the nearest dealership to her motel. After she had gotten up that morning, and smoked her morning cigarette, she had grabbed the Yellow Pages and called around trying to find the best deal. When she found what she needed, she caught a bus and got herself a car. The vehicle was nothing spectacular, but it was a car nonetheless. On a morning like this, anything would do. Even a black, 1999 Saturn.

The traffic was dense this morning and it seemed that every time she changed lanes, someone either ended up giving her the finger or honking their horn. The breeze that blew through the window ruffled her blue sweater and calmed her frustration.

While she was driving Gwen thought about Marty. After thinking about him the night before—*really* thinking about him—for the first time since she had left home, all her feelings for him had flooded back in one wild rush. She missed him and felt bad for leaving so suddenly and not telling him where she was going. Gwen hoped that Marty didn't think her abruptly leaving was because of the argument they had had.

In the past when they had fought, they wouldn't speak to each other for a few days, but soon one of them would stop acting like a child and call the other to apologize, even if it wasn't really their fault. The reconciliation would always be followed up by make-up sex. The best sex Gwen had ever known. Sometimes she wished they would fight all the time just so she could always experience that kind of passion with him.

Poor Marty. Gwen felt sorry for him. A part of her wanted to turn the car around, go home, and revel in the pleasure of make-up sex, while another part of her couldn't care less about such a thing. Determination to accomplish the task she had been charged with was ruling over all emotion.

The child had to die.

Gwen smiled to herself then consulted the map she had neatly placed on the passenger seat. She took the next off-ramp and headed toward Willowdale.

* * *

Rainygravel Road was pleasant. The street was built out of smooth, dark cement that was without potholes or misplaced ribbons of tar. Trees traveled skyward on each side of the road, forming a canopy of leaves and branches above it. The sun pierced through the holes in the canopy in sharp streaks of light, bouncing off the cars that were parked next to the curb.

Gwen wasn't at all astonished that she had made it to the right neighborhood as quickly as she did. She had no way of proving it, but an eerie yet comfortable pain had built up in her stomach, pulling her in the right direction, like a magnet would a paper clip.

She had turned onto Rainygravel Road from Finch Avenue and was now roughly halfway down the street. The magnetic feeling in her gut grew stronger. Gwen wondered which of the old-fashioned houses belonged to the boy. The closer she got to her target the more she found her body reacting. Beads of sweat formed along her brow. Her heart rate quickened. With each passing moment she felt more and more like she was falling apart.

For a brief moment she debated turning around and going back to the hotel to rest, but a voice that suddenly boomed in her head put a stop to that.

Here.

Gwen hit the breaks, her body lurching forward against the seat belt. When she straightened herself, she looked up and watched in disorientation as a squirrel crossed the road. The magnetic pull still persisted until she looked to the house on her right.

Then it stopped. She was there.

The house wasn't what Gwen had imagined. She had been expecting something straight out of a horror movie. Something with shattered windows, a dead lawn, and trees without branches sprouting up from patches of mud in vertical disarray. The house would be poorly painted and the eaves trough would be hanging from the roof by a few loose nails.

What she found here on Rainygravel Road was the opposite. The house was beautiful. Small, but beautiful. It was made out of old, white paneling that looked as if it had been well kept throughout the decades. The numbers 642 hung loosely just above the front door. It had two levels and a front porch with flowerpots along its edge. In front of it was a long sidewalk running the length of the road with bright, green grass on either side.

Straining from her position, Gwen rolled down her window and peaked as much as she could around the corners of the house. She could see that there was a back alley, presumably with a small, detached garage and driveway that belonged to the house.

Gwen searched the windows for activity and was disappointed when she saw none. Satisfied with her discovery, she put the car in gear and turned right at the next stop sign then took another immediate right turn after that.

The back alley was typical: a simple street with old garages and miniature driveways on either side. She drove down the back lane looking for number 642. When she found it, she took note of all of its appearances: a garage with a basketball net and a gravel-paved driveway, a contrary to the street in front of the house, and a small wire-framed fence. Gwen also took notice of the back door and smiled to herself at its simplicity. There was only one door instead of your average combination of a heavier door with a lighter screen door attached to it.

No motion sensitive lights, either, she saw. *Perfect.*

Gwen sped up and went around to take another pass at the house. This time when she drove past it she saw a woman who looked almost twice her age smoking a cigarette on the front steps.

Probably his mother, Gwen assumed. *I hope she didn't see me parked out in front of the house. Maybe that's why she came outside?*

Gwen didn't stop this time and drove right by. She would come back later.

* * *

"Would you like to talk about the other day, Harry?" Dr. Woodrose asked.

The two of them were in a small visiting office one floor above Harry's room.

Harry sat across from Dr. Woodrose, shrugging his shoulders in response to the question. The doctor had been taking care of him ever since he had been admitted to Hans Memorial Hospital. Dr. Woodrose was used to getting nothing but silence from this particular patient. There were only a few documented occasions where Harry did the opposite and wouldn't stop talking.

"Harry?" Dr. Woodrose prompted, looking over the rims of his all-too-square reading glasses.

"Not really," Harry murmured. Inside his head, Harry laughed at how the doctor looked. Dr. Woodrose had on a woolly, brown suit, and a shirt so crisp that it seemed to be saturated with starch. An unusual combination of comfort and unease. His tie was horrible, a shiny gold with blotches of green spattered on it.

Dr. Woodrose tapped his pen on his clipboard. "I think we should talk about it, Harry."

Harry didn't say anything.

"Nurse Robinson is very upset that you knocked him down. He would like an apology," Dr. Woodrose said in a way that made Harry's skin curl. He hated the way his doctor and nurses sometimes baby-talked to him. This was a prime example.

Sighing, Harry said, "He didn't believe me. He didn't believe someone was in my room."

"Nurse Robinson said you saw an old man in your room. Is this true?"

For the past few weeks Harry's mind had been clouded. During most of that time he had difficulty distinguishing between reality and the world he lived in inside his head. Right now he wasn't sure if he should answer yes or no to the doctor's question. The situation itself was already so big it was hard to move. By answering yes, he might make things worse. Dr. Woodrose might ask too many questions about Sherman Gray and why he had visited. That would then lead to Gwen, and Gwen would lead to the child, and the child would lead back to his time in the library, and the library would lead back to his wife—it would keep going back, probably to the beginning of time, knowing Dr. Woodrose.

Then again, if Harry said no, Dr. Woodrose might think that he was hallucinating again.

"What really happened, Harry?" Dr. Woodrose asked, interrupting Harry's thought process.

"Nothing," Harry rasped.

"Well, surely something must have happened to get you as spooked as you were and to knock a nurse down and try to escape."

Harry kept his eyes on his feet. "It was nothing."

The doctor crossed his legs and put his clipboard down on the floor beside him. After a moment, he removed his glasses, folded them, and placed them neatly beside his clipboard. He leaned forward slightly.

"Look, Harry, I don't want to have to recommend isolation for you again. I know how that makes you feel and that you do not like it in there." Dr. Woodrose explained this like a father would his son. "I understand that it probably seems like I don't believe you about what you saw. I'm just trying to help you, Harry, that's all. What really bothered you yesterday?"

Harry bowed his head. Dr. Woodrose could tell it was going to be a long session.

* * *

It was getting darker when Gwen drove by the house again. The street lamps had turned themselves on, shining brightly in the early evening light.

When Gwen slowed in front of the house, she rolled down her window and lit a cigarette. She didn't want the car tainted with the smell of smoke when she returned it to the dealership. The air that rushed through the open window was refreshing. It cooled the sweat that was forming on her forehead and neck. Amidst the gusts of wind, she could hear something bounce against the pavement over and over again.

A basketball.

Gwen leaned forward in her seat but couldn't see anything. Suddenly that warm discomfort returned to her stomach. She winced from its effect.

She knew she had found him.

Without hesitation she drove to the back lane. The car drove at an appropriate pace—not too slow, not too fast. Gwen didn't want to speed past the kid and somehow scare him when she drove by him. She had to keep him from being aware of her.

Out her window, she could still hear the thumping of the basketball and a louder thump when it hit the backboard or the rim.

Gwen drove by the back lot of house 642 and sure enough, the child was there.

Calvin prepped himself for a shot and got it in. He had been practicing the same maneuver that Sherman had taught him and seemed to be catching on quickly. The ball bounced off the backboard and landed in the net then tumbled along the gravel toward his feet. When he picked it up, he stopped suddenly, and watched the black Saturn as it drove by.

He scowled. A welt of hatred brewed deep inside him.

Chapter Twenty-One

It was all falling into place. The key to destroying Gwen was to destroy her heart; the only thing she had ever listened to before Harry and his "suggestions." Sherman knew this, and earlier that morning he had made a very special phone call. One that would change the course of Gwen's life forever.

* * *

Marty Bones stood outside the door to Gwen's apartment. He was exhausted. His body felt as though it was filled with lead, and the corners of his eyes stung with the redness of endless hours of crying.

Last night Marty had barely slept, and when he did, he dreamed of Gwen, of their fight, and of their love. Now, his emotions had drained him and an odd sense of apathy had become his only feeling. He had given up on their relationship. Nothing mattered.

He needed someone to talk to. Earlier, after gulping down two cups of coffee and checking his e-mail hoping again that Gwen had written, he had tried calling Denise. She hadn't answered. The phone rang over a dozen times before he hung up.

Marty decided that he might as well just go over to her apartment, use his spare key, and wait until Denise got home. He knew that seeing her was like walking into the lion's den, himself being the prey. He didn't care. All he wanted now was a shoulder to cry on and someone to put their arms around him, telling him that everything was going to be okay.

He was happy that Gwen lived so close to him. That meant that Denise was close to him, too.

With a sigh and a mournful shake of the head, Marty unlocked the door and went in. The apartment was empty and quiet.

Good, Marty thought. He stepped further in and removed his shoes and jacket. He flopped himself down on the couch in the front room, staring up blankly at the stuccoed ceiling.

A warm blanket of sleep was almost upon him when he was quickly drawn out of his daze by a clinking sound coming from the bathroom. Marty sat up alertly and looked in its direction.

The bathroom door opened and Denise came out wearing a robe with a towel wrapped around her head. The moment she saw Marty she yelped in surprise and nearly fell over, her hand clasping her heart in fright.

"Are you all right?" Marty asked, going over to her.

"Dammit! You scared me," she said and shakily tried to stand.

"Sorry. I tried calling but no one answered," he said.

"I was in the shower," Denise said with another sigh of terror. "Fuck, you scared me!" And slapped him playfully on the shoulder.

"Sorry. I was just going to let myself in and wait 'til someone got home."

Denise continued catching her breath and broke free from Marty's helping hands.

"Where is everyone?" he asked.

"Jenna's working and Carlee's at school, where you're supposed to be, by the way," she scolded him.

"Not today. I'm a little out of sorts."

"Damn right you are. Fuckin' walking in here like some cat burglar. Sorry. My heart's still pounding." She held her chest again.

Denise noticed how red and puffy Marty's eyes were. He looked as if he had been walking against a harsh wind for hours.

"Are you all right?" she asked.

Marty looked off elsewhere into the apartment. "Not really."

Denise removed the towel from her head and furiously dried her hair with it. Marty liked how beautiful her hair looked when it was wet. He watched almost obsessively as she dried it.

"Do you need to talk?" she asked.

His eyes snapped back to hers. "Do you got a minute?"

"Yeah, it's my day off. Just give me a sec to change."

"Sure," he said, wandering back into the living room while Denise went to her bedroom to change from her robe into something less awkward.

A few minutes later she came out wearing a white T-shirt and gray sweat pants, minus a pair of socks. There were two couches in the apartment and she sat on the one opposite to him.

"How much sleep did you get last night? You look tired," Denise said, taking note of the gray circles under Marty's eyes. His face was pale save for his cheeks that were flushed red from crying.

"Not much. This whole thing with Gwen is taking its toll on me," he told her. "I haven't been able to go to school and all I seem to do is sleep all day. I just don't feel like doing anything anymore."

She brought her legs up, curling them under her bottom. "It's that rough, huh?"

"Yeah," he breathed. "Fuck! I hate this! It's like, why do things have to be this way? We were getting along just fine and then she gets all wrapped up in that guy from the nuthouse. We never really fought until then. Only little tiffs."

Marty leaned forward on the cushion and put his head between his legs.

Denise asked, "Gwen hasn't tried to get a hold of you has she?"

"No. I keeping hoping she'll call or write, or something. It would be nice to know where she is, and if she's okay or not." He pinched the bridge of his nose and fought back the tears. Denise got up from her couch, crossed the room and sat beside him. She hesitated if she should put her arm around him, and then decided it best that Marty have some space and just take comfort in the fact that someone was nearby.

"Marty, I know Gwen," she said, "and despite all the shit that's gone down, I can guarantee you that she's thinking about you. You mean too much to her for her to throw you away."

Hearing this caused Marty to finally burst, and he began to cry. Denise gave in and put her arm around him. He leaned on her shoulder trying to catch his tears in his hands so he wouldn't get her all wet. They sat still for several minutes both waiting for this moment of anguish to pass.

When the outflow of tears eased, Marty straightened himself a little and wiped his eyes and nose, slimy snot leaking onto his fingers.

"Eww," he said, sounding almost feminine. He never liked slimy things. Even as a kid he made a conscious effort to keep his hands clean.

"Wait here," Denise said and got up, going to the bathroom to retrieve some toilet paper.

When she returned, she handed him a wad of tissue to wipe his hands.

"Thanks," he said.

She sat down beside him and rubbed his back. Her touch was soothing.

"Thanks," he repeated. "I'm sorry if you feel like I'm beating this thing with Gwen to death. It's just that it hurts. You don't do that to someone—get up and leave. Especially when you say that you love them."

Denise didn't know what to say. She ran her hand down his back then back up, focusing on his neck. All though she couldn't admit it to herself, she enjoyed the way the muscles around his neck felt: taut and firm.

"Have you talked to your parents about this?" she asked.

"No. They're not home yet. They ran into some friends while they were away and decided to extend their vacation. Again. Even if they were here, I couldn't talk to them about it. They never understood what I saw in Gwen. There are certain things about her that they never approved of. They'd probably be happy that she and I aren't seeing each other right now."

"Sorry I asked," Denise said, almost sarcastically but with a hint of an apology.

Marty smirked. "During the day it isn't so bad. I can either paint or watch TV, but at night, that's when it's the hardest. All alone in a dark house. Sometimes it feels like I'm in a fucking asylum."

"Here," Denise said, and extended her arms to offer him a hug. Marty embraced her and held her tight. She did the same, both of them squeezing their eyes shut as they did.

Just then an odd, soothing sensation come over Denise. She was filled with lust and desire. Her heart skipped a beat and she squeezed Marty harder. He returned the gesture. She could tell that holding her was making him feel better. Was it misplaced affection? Maybe, but Denise was a lonely girl despite the fact that she could have had any guy she wanted. And misplaced affection or not, feeling needed was all that was important to her.

Marty sniffled, causing his shoulder to jerk up and down slightly. Denise lifted her head, and in a whirlwind of uncontrolled desire brought her face closer to his so that both their noses were touching. They kept their embrace and looked into each other's eyes. Marty's were glazed over and red, but beneath them Denise could see that he cared for her. It might not have been in the context that she hoped for, but he did like her. More than a friend.

A lot more than a friend.

Their noses brushed together and in another swoon of uncontrolled desire Denise brought her mouth to his. At first it resembled a kiss a mother might give her son, but that didn't last for long. Before either of them knew it, they were kissing every spot of each other's neck, hungry like starving wolves, every so often their lips fully embracing.

Marty was quite aware as to what he was doing, but despite all his efforts, he couldn't pull himself away from her.

He needed her as much as he needed Gwen.

He needed to feel loved.

Denise lowered herself to lie on her back as Marty playfully teased and kissed her neck. She was hearing the most beautiful voice in her head—and in her heart: *Take him. Give him what you've always wanted to. He will not resist. He needs this. Use him. Listen to me.*

In automatic obedience, Denise wrapped her legs around him and began moving herself against him in seductive rhythm. Ten minutes later she and Marty were in the thralls of passion, each movement a symbol of desire and each word a longing whisper.

Unbeknownst to either of them, in the corner of the room, Sherman Gray watched their coupling in approval.

* * *

Marty stood in front of the mirror in the bathroom, splashing his face with frigid water, trying to calm himself down. The cold water felt good on his hot cheeks. Denise was in the bedroom waiting for him to return. Marty didn't know if he should go back to her.

He saw some of Gwen's things scattered on top of the linoleum that bordered the sink. Her red toothbrush caught his eye. Red. Gwen's favorite color. He lifted it, stared at it, and then put it in his mouth, hoping to taste the familiar taste of her mouth. Instead, it tasted like stale toothpaste.

Gwen, his mind echoed. He squeezed the toothbrush and rubbed his thumb along its bristles then set it back down on the countertop. With a sigh he looked back up at the mirror and gazed at himself, watching the droplets of water trickle down his face, avoiding looking into his own eyes.

Marty could not face himself after what he had just allowed himself to do. Without any hesitation or moment of judgment, he had cheated on Gwen.

Some of the guys at school would have given him a pat on the back for two-timing his girlfriend. Marty didn't deserve a pat on the back. He deserved a kick between the legs. Maybe that would stop him from going back to Denise? The thought brought on a grin.

He turned the water off and stood behind the closed bathroom door for several minutes before reentering the bedroom. Denise was propped up against her pillow with her legs covered and small breasts exposed. Her hair was still damp from her shower. Marty found her dark curls irresistible. He didn't know the source of his fetish, but he enjoyed it anyway.

She reached out to him in need. Marty stood frozen, his stomach filled with molasses, a slowly stiffening manhood pressing tightly against the towel around his waist. He felt as though he was living up to a stereotype. The one where all a guy wants is to get it on with anything that has a hole.

But for Marty this wasn't about that. Far from it. For him it was about feeling wanted. Feeling needed. Filling that void in his heart that was once filled with the most satisfying of all feelings. Feeling loved.

Just a hug. That's all, Marty told himself and leaned over the bed to embrace Denise. He lost his balance and fell on top of her.

"Sorry," he said, shocked that he had fallen.

"It's okay," she whispered and brought herself even closer to him.

Denise was warm and Marty enjoyed the way her skin pressed tight against his. After settling into each other's arms, Denise asked, "Do you hate me?"

Images of Gwen flashed before Marty's eyes, as did pictures of him making love to Denise.

"No," he said, "why would I?"

Her eyes filled with innocence. "I just don't want to break you and Gwen up."

A little late for that, he thought. His mouth went dry. "Yeah, well, it seemed like we had broken up when she left."

Denise adjusted herself so that Marty was more on top of her. "Do you really think that?"

Marty looked into her eyes. "I don't know. It hurts, but I don't want to think about that right now."

She kissed him on the cheek, then on the lips. That warm feeling that was almost tangible earlier swept over her again. Denise drifted from the consciousness of *actual occurrence* into a place where her actions were controlled by a deep longing inside her.

Marty was about to roll over onto the other side of the bed when Denise pulled him inward and placed her lips against his.

He didn't resist. He couldn't...He didn't care anymore. It was time for him to feel good and to hell with everybody else!

The two of them slipped into the waiting arms of passion as Denise gave herself to him. He didn't care if he was making the same mistake twice.

As before, Sherman Gray watched them from the corner of the room.

He smiled. He had succeeded. It was done.

Chapter Twenty-Two

The dream had been all too real.

When Gwen woke up, she found herself sorry that Marty wasn't with her. She just had a nightmare where he was in a trouble he could not avoid.

Gwen missed him.

She hesitated calling him, fearing what kind of conversation they might have. She did not need another argument with him. But there was another way to get a hold of him, and she would do it later when she went out.

Right now, she just wanted to go back to sleep. Hopefully, she wouldn't have another bad dream.

* * *

Like all the other bars that were in the more well to do downtown Toronto area, Velvet Hands bore a certain elegance—one that would make you feel rich even if it wasn't so.

Gwen had entered Velvet Hands in the early evening in the hopes of closing a drug deal before the night was over. She entered through the revolving doors and fell surprised when the doorman told her that her coat had to be checked. She reluctantly complied, not happy in case she had to leave suddenly, only to find herself stuck waiting in line for other people to retrieve their coats. Her black leather coat had cost her one hundred and ninety-eight dollars and some odd cents after taxes. Not the best of quality but expensive nonetheless. It would be a shame to end up having to leave it behind.

Gwen entered the club and walked toward the polished oak wrap-around bar with a matching elegant glass and bottle holder above it. Even for six-thirty in the evening, Gwen noticed that it was unusually busy. People usually didn't cram into clubs like this one until closer to eight o'clock and sometimes even that was too early.

Gwen sat down on a hard-backed stool at the bar and watched as a gentleman with a close-trimmed haircut served drinks. Gwen glanced around and thought it fantastic that Velvet Hands had not two but three levels. To her left was a marble-tiled dance floor with a strobe light flashing full spin, to her right an artistic wall lined with booths and tables.

She grabbed the ashtray on the countertop in front of her, and the pack of matches within. She had forgotten her lighter back at the motel room.

When she finished lighting her cigarette, she looked up and saw that the bartender was waiting to get her something to drink.

"What can I get for you?" he shouted with a thick English accent over the music.

Gwen paused for a moment to discern what he had said.

"A Caesar," she shouted back, "and make it spicy."

The bartender nodded and grabbed a glass from behind the counter. He threw it up in the air behind his back, catching it with the opposite hand in front of him. He prepped and mixed the drink in a fancy fashion, garnishing it with lime and celery. Gwen was impressed. The bars that Marty normally took her to were nothing special. They never prepared her drink at those places with such a show.

The bartender grinned, and set the drink down in front of her. She paid him for it, tipping him a Loonie. Seeming to not be grateful for the tip, he quickly left her so he could serve an already drunk man at the far corner of the bar.

Gwen sat listening to the music while alternating between her cigarette and stick of celery. Her mind drifted towards Marty for the umpteenth time that day. After the dream she had had the night before, she had spent the entire day thinking of him, his image constantly popping in and out of her head.

Most of the images were from her nightmare, keeping her unsettled. In the dream, she was back home in Winnipeg, in the Faculty of Art at Brentmere. Marty was with her and she was watching him paint one of his pictures. It was like old times: laughing at stupid jokes, kissing, playfully teasing each other, all while he painted. Nothing but fun. The dream began in the art room, filled with other students. But the more and more in depth Marty got into his painting, the fewer the other students, until, finally, she and Marty were alone. Out of the two of them, Gwen had been the only one who had noticed the other students vanishing. It did seem natural, though, for people to suddenly disappear.

When Marty was finished his painting, he had allowed her to inspect it. It was a picture of an old, worn bridge over a blood-red river with black trees on either bank. The picture was morbid, something Marty would never draw. Despite the sinister nature of the picture, it was still very beautiful, and when Gwen looked at it, she was drawn to it. Just as she was about to tell Marty her thoughts, he, too, was gone. She looked around the classroom and found him in the far corner of the room with his back against her. A gleaming white lab coat had replaced his paint smock. He had it spread wide open as if he were concealing something on the other side of it. When Gwen approached him, to see what was behind the lab coat, she gasped in horror when she saw a faceless, naked woman kneeling before him, profusely bobbing her head back and forth between his legs.

Marty looked at her and said, "See, Gwen? Look what you made me do."

Gwen had awoken then and had begun to miss him.

And, boy, did she miss him.

Her senses re-focused themselves back to the bar in front of her and the loud music that seemed to come from all sides. She twirled the cherry of her cigarette along the rim of the ashtray. That afternoon, she had e-mailed Marty, using a computer at the city library. The plan was to return to the library tomorrow to see if he had written back.

She hoped that he would.

* * *

One hour and three Caesars later, Gwen finally found who she had come here for: someone who looked like they could sell her something illegal. She was thankful that she had, too, because three times in the past thirty minutes, the drunken guy from the end of the bar had asked her to dance. On all three occasions Gwen had given the bartender a glance that read: can you help me out, here? But, being smug, like all bartenders tend to be, he simply smiled and watched in amusement as Gwen tried to stop the drunk from putting his hands all over her, while the intoxicated fellow tried to impress her with innuendos.

A man dressed in a black suit with black shirt and tie, and matching long black hair tied back in a ponytail, had stepped up to the bar beside Gwen. He gave her a nod and a smile, winking at her from behind the perfect circle frames of his glasses. The bartender handed him his drink: a Mudslide. The man in black ignored the bar stool in front of him, instead opting to lean his back against the bar railing and study the people that surrounded him.

Gwen wondered if what she was thinking was even accurate. He certainly looked like someone who would push illegal substances, but how would she go about approaching him, never mind making a purchase? She had never even tried drugs let alone bought them.

The man in black shifted his gaze briefly to her, then back toward the dance floor where he watched a tastefully dressed brunette dance seductively by herself. Gwen thought about hitting on him, hoping that he would offer her something that she could use on Calvin, but found herself too timid to even try. As consolation to her indecisiveness, she lit another cigarette and ordered a Mudslide as well, hoping that he might take notice that they were both drinking the same drink. She knew the approach was pathetic, but she didn't know what else to do.

When she received her drink, she nudged the man in black with her elbow. He turned to her.

"Good stuff, eh?" she said with a smile. *Fuck, I sound stupid!*

"What?" he said, not hearing her voice over the music.

Gwen leaned closer. "Good stuff, isn't it?" She raised her drink so that he could see it.

"Yeah," he agreed, and then walked over to the other side of the bar.

That was rude, Gwen thought and stood, shocked that he would abruptly walk away for no reason. She dragged on her cigarette. If she didn't do something quick, she would blow any chance of getting something to kill the boy. Adding further to her distress, the man in black lingered at the bar for only a few more moments before moving toward the brunette on the dance floor. Instead of talking to her as Gwen had expected, he merely eyed her as he walked past and disappeared into the crowd.

Gwen slammed back the rest of her Mudslide, stubbed out her cigarette, and tried to follow him. Since she had entered Velvet Hands, the crowd had doubled in size. It suddenly seemed that almost every man in the place was dressed entirely in black. But, fortunately, very few had long hair.

Gwen twisted her way between the tables and people milling about, looking for him. He couldn't be seen.

Satisfied she had checked the first floor thoroughly, Gwen climbed the stairway leading up to the second floor and searched the same way she had the first, with again no results.

The third floor, she had found out through speaking with a bouncer, was for those with an invitation. Gwen wasn't allowed to roam through it. As she was shooed away, she did her best to peer around behind the bouncer to see if she could see the man she was looking for. She couldn't.

Gwen walked down the stairway to the second level, still searching for him. She leaned over the edge of the balcony that overlooked the main bar and the dance floor and scanned the people below.

Then she saw him.

The man in black was back at the bar, leaning over the countertop, speaking with the bartender. Gwen bolted down the stairs, almost running into a couple that were kissing at the bottom. From the stairwell, Gwen could see that the man in black had left his conversation with the bartender. Fighting against her frustration, Gwen took a frantic look all around her. She saw him again. Thank God. He was walking out the main entrance. She started to follow him outside, but remembered that she had checked her coat. *Shit!* she thought. *Ah, to hell with it. I'll get it later.*

Gwen followed him outside, pausing on the steps as she watched him stand at the street corner lighting up a cigarette. She went up to him.

"Do you got a light?" Gwen asked, producing her own package of cigarettes.

"Sure," he said and handed her his lighter. He thought it interesting that the same girl who had spoken to him inside the bar was talking to him again. Gwen wasn't his type, but he found himself willing to give her a chance anyway.

Gwen lit her cigarette and noticed that, across the street, a kid who could be no older than seventeen with thick, bottle-capped glasses was staring at her from a bus shelter.

"Thanks," Gwen told him and handed him back his lighter.

So far so good, she thought. *I might as well go for it. It's now or never.*

"I'm pretty stressed out," she told him. "Do you know of anything that could help me?"

"Excuse me?" he asked, not paying attention to what she had just said.

"Do you know where I can get something to take this edge off?"

"What?"

Do I have to spell it out for you? Gwen thought. "I'm looking for some stuff I can't get over-the-counter. Do you know where I can get some, or, do you have any?" She choked on the question. The man in black obviously had no clue as to what she meant. He didn't reply.

Gwen looked around and saw that the kid from the bus stop had crossed to her side of the street.

Just then, the man in black spoke. "If you think I'm dealing' you're mistaken." He took a drag off his cigarette. "Sorry I can't help you out." He stepped away from her.

"Sorry," she said, ashamed.

He turned back. "Don't worry about it. I get it a lot. Anyway, see you around." He dropped his cigarette, smothered it out with a polished shoe, and walked away, purposely avoiding any further conversation with her.

Gwen stood staring after him not believing what had just happened. She felt incredibly stupid. She didn't know what she should do next.

Gwen could feel herself starting to panic. She felt like she had just blown the whole mission that Harry had charged her with. It was a reflex feeling, but an intense feeling nonetheless. Gwen had never been partial to accepting failure.

From behind her a voice spoke. "I can help you."

Gwen turned around and saw the kid with the thick glasses.

"What do you mean?" she asked, not wanting to talk to anybody just then.

"I know what you wanted from that guy. I can help." He smiled. His teeth were crooked. Dots of acne peppered his face. "I have connections, and can get you whatever it is you're looking for."

This is too freaky! Gwen told herself. *Then again, it's probably just a coincidence that this kid was out the same night I was looking to buy.* An aching feeling grew in her gut, telling her that this kid couldn't be trusted. Somehow she just knew. She decided not to risk it. She didn't want any more trouble than her trip had already wrought.

"Sorry," she told him, "you're a little young."

"Not much younger than you, I'm sure. Final offer. Take it or leave it." He pushed his glasses up his nose.

Gwen gave it a second thought and despite the awkward feeling that replaced the panic, she decided to take another shot at obtaining what she needed. She figured it was all or nothing…danger or not.

"Okay," Gwen agreed. "How do you want to do this?"

"Come back to my place. I'll make a phone call and you'll get your stuff within a couple of hours."

Gwen did not like the idea of going home with a complete stranger but, then again, before she had met Marty, it had started to become a bad habit for her. There had never been sex when she had gone home with a guy she dated, but there definitely had been some heavy fooling around.

It's okay, Gwen. A voice rang in her head. It sounded like Harry, but Gwen wasn't sure. Harry had been acting strange as of late. He had tried to tell her to leave the kid alone and come back home.

She listened to her heart and decided to continue and pursue her mission. If Harry didn't want her to do it for him, then she would do it for herself and all those that it might affect. From what she knew of Calvin, he would grow up to be too dangerous a person. It was up to her to prevent that.

The kid with the glasses tugged on her sleeve. She told him to wait a minute while she ran back into the bar to retrieve her coat. She emerged from the entrance a few minutes later and accompanied him across the street back to the bus shelter.

"My name's Robin, by the way," he told her.

"Diane," Gwen replied. *No use giving him my real name.*

"You're very beautiful, Diane."

She glared at him. "Let's just get this over with."

Chapter Twenty-Three

Victoria Mandalay had come home from work and went about her usual routine: deposit her purse and shoes at the door, say hello to Calvin, go to the bathroom, then hit the answering machine. When she checked her messages, she was surprised to find a message from Calvin's teacher, Mrs. Fuller, asking her to call back when she had the chance. It was too late to phone now but tomorrow it would definitely be on the priority list. Victoria was going to call Mrs. Fuller today regarding Sherman, but the supermarket had been busy and she didn't even get a break to have her lunch.

Outside, Calvin was playing basketball. Victoria could hear the melodic thumping of the ball hitting the backboard and bouncing off the pavement. She entered the kitchen, poured herself a glass of orange juice from the refrigerator, and watched him through the window above the sink. Calvin jumped around on the driveway, hurling the ball at the net, his mouth moving as if he was talking to someone.

Victoria assumed that he was providing the sports commentary for his movements. She didn't know that he was really talking to someone much more real than an imagined audience.

"How's that one?" Calvin asked Sherman. The old man was leaning up against the garage door near the basketball net.

"Good. You are learning quickly, Calvin," he replied.

Calvin took another shot.

"I really like playing with you, Sherman. You're really nice. I told my mom about you."

Sherman raised an eyebrow at this. "You told your mother?"

"Yeah. She said I shouldn't talk to strangers, but you're not a stranger right, Sherman?"

Deep inside himself Sherman Gray snarled. He didn't want Victoria knowing about him. She might mention something to Ken and with Ken being a Christian that could cause difficulties. Best not to meddle with people who side with the enemy.

"Of course not, m'boy," Sherman smiled, "you and I are great friends. After all, we love basketball, don't we?"

Calvin beamed back, eyes squinting. "Yep!"

"How's school going, Calvin?"

Calvin returned to his spot in front of the net. "Easy."

"That's good. You're realizing your abilities. You know, Calvin, I could help make things even easier for you at school."

The boy's eyes lit up. "Really? How?"

Sherman grinned. "Well, I could talk to Mrs. Fuller and ask her to make things much more fun for you. I know how hard school can sometimes be. Even *I* went to school a long, long time ago."

It must have been a really long time ago, Calvin thought. *You're super old.*

"Okay," the boy said. "How'd you know my teacher's name?"

"You told me, remember?"

Calvin couldn't recall mentioning his teacher's name to Sherman but believed the old man anyway. He knew that Sherman wouldn't lie to him.

"I can also help you, Calvin," Sherman said. "Did you know the better you get at basketball, the smarter you become?" He always took great joy in the gullibility of children. He could tell them anything and they would believe him.

"Is that true?" Calvin asked.

"Yes, Calvin. I wouldn't lie to you."

"I know that, Sherman," the boy said with confidence. "I know that."

Peering out the kitchen window, Victoria smiled. She always enjoyed watching Calvin play. Every time he smiled she felt good about herself. Often she would wonder how happy a child Calvin really was. She sometimes felt guilty that she couldn't always be there for him when her own emotions governed her life. She was glad that Ken always picked up the slack and took care of Calvin when she wasn't feeling too well. Ken was a good man. He always had been. At the time when she had separated with David, he had held her hand every step of the way.

Ken should be married, she reflected, *and not babysitting me.*

Ken, for his age, was a good-looking man. His peppery-black hair wasn't thinning, and the only thing that really revealed his age were the creases permanently etched in his face from his ever-present smile. If Ken wanted to, he could have his pick of any woman he wanted. But instead, he chose to help family. Of that Victoria would always be grateful. She loved her brother. A lot.

Victoria finished her juice and went out the back door to join Calvin.

"Hey, kiddo!" Victoria greeted.

Calvin shifted his gaze from Sherman to his mother. Using the boy's distraction as an opportunity, Sherman left them alone.

"Hi, Mom," Calvin replied and took another hard shot at the net.

"You out here playing by yourself?"

"Um"—Calvin thought about Sherman and remembered that his mom didn't want him talking to him. Calvin noticed Sherman had left—"yep. Just me. No one else."

"Who were you talking to?" she asked.

"Nobody, Mom. Just me. I say things out loud when I'm outside. You know that."

Victoria gave him a smile. Calvin took another shot and the ball bounced off the backboard. Victoria quickly jumped in front of the ball, catching it before it rolled down the driveway. Calvin was glad that she wanted to play, and he was more than willing to accommodate her.

For a whole hour the two of them played on the driveway, working up a decent appetite for dinner. Calvin was disappointed to hear that Uncle Ken wouldn't be joining them for supper that evening. Ken had to work late but had told Victoria that he would stop by the house later on if he had the chance.

* * *

Denise had fulfilled him. Of that Marty was sure. The deep, yearning void in his heart caused by Gwen's sudden absence had vanished. For the first time in weeks Marty felt content. Denise was lying beside him, snuggled up close beneath his arms.

Marty had gone to school that morning then came back to the apartment to see Denise again. After the previous night, he had found himself hungering for the joy she had given him, for another night interspersed with sleeping and lovemaking. He had found what he was looking for: someone who would always be there for him.

When they had awoken that morning, they made a conscious effort to be extra quiet, lest Jenna and Carlee catch them. They had shared a shower then dressed for the day. When the coast was clear of all roommates, they left the apartment and had breakfast at a diner down the road.

"Are you all right with all this?" Marty recalled Denise asking. He sat across from her in a booth, bundled up in a wool sweater she had given him. Winnipeg mornings were always cold.

"Of course," he had replied.

Denise was beautiful that morning. She wore an autumn jacket with a thick, blue sweatshirt underneath, and a pair of old, faded jeans. While eating breakfast, Marty had forgotten Gwen and all the pain she had caused him. Yet, secretly, his heart was torn in two between her and Denise. But, as they ate breakfast at the diner, his heart made its choice. He wanted to be with Denise.

She had invited him over again that evening after school knowing that Carlee would be working and Jenna would be at a friend's place.

After having returned from his classes that morning, he hadn't even had a chance to walk through the doorway before Denise jumped all over him in a flurry of hands and kisses. Before either one had realized what had happened, they were both on the floor, lying naked together on top of their clothing. Denise looked at him and laughed. He joined her in her lilt. It was down right hilarious. They felt like a couple of kids in high school who could hardly wait to see each other just so that they could get it on.

"That's funny," Denise commented on the moment.

"For sure," Marty said. "That was great!"

"Oooh, yeah!"

They laughed again.

"Shall we try for round two?" he suggested.

"Ding-ding," she whistled, and rolled on top of him.

* * *

Marty was alone in Gwen's apartment. There was no light in the living room except for a stream of moonlight piercing its way through the cracks in the shades. Everything appeared as if he were roaming around inside a black and white photograph.

Marty rolled back the sheets and got up from the sofa that he had been lying on. He looked around the apartment. It was quiet. Wearing nothing but boxer shorts, he went to each room, trying to see who else was in the apartment with him. He knew that he wasn't supposed to be alone.

Every room—the bedrooms, the kitchen, the bathroom—was empty. The only place he hadn't checked yet was the linen closet near the doorway. For a brief instant he thought that Denise, Gwen, Jenna, and Carlee, was hiding in it and that they were about to jump out at him in surprise.

Marty's hand hovered over the handle to the closet, a flutter of hesitation rushing through his stomach. He grabbed the handle, pulled, and saw nothing but the black pitch of darkness. Instinctively, he flicked on the light switch for the closet. He screamed.

It was Gwen.

She was hanging by a thin rope from the ceiling of the closet. Carved into both of her cheeks was an upside-down cross and, in the middle of her forehead, an equally deep cut pentagram. She wore a white flannel shirt that was caked with blood. She wore black pants that were ripped around her womanhood and buttocks. Her shoes and one sock were missing.

Marty covered his mouth, holding his gagging stomach in check. He nearly threw up, but managed to keep it down. When he felt he had composed himself enough, he squeezed his eyes closed then opened them, slowly raising his head to see Gwen again.

She was in the same position, still dead, but something was different. Her white shirt had become black and the black pants white. Marty caught onto the change of attire immediately. A familiar voice rose up behind him: "Do you mind that I changed her shirt?"

Marty spun around. Coming out of the now lit up kitchen was Denise, wearing an apron with an embroidered picture of Gwen displayed on it. Marty knit his brow together, not having fully understood what Denise had meant. Then, as if the haze of confusion was removed from his thoughts, all became clear. He remembered that Denise was supposed to change Gwen's shirt after they had killed her. Marty wanted Gwen to wear a black one instead of white. They had earlier bought the black and white outfit for Gwen, but were unhappy when they accidentally bought a white shirt instead of a black one. It had been too late for them to return the outfit for a new one, so they had to wait until Gwen came over. After they had killed her, Denise used one of her own black shirts and a pair of her white pants. Marty didn't know why they didn't use Denise's clothes in the first place, other than they didn't want to get them dirty with blood. Regardless, it somehow all made sense.

Marty looked at her with an appreciating smile. "Thanks, Kitten."

"That's what I'm here for. Do you like my new apron?" she asked, showing him the embroidered picture of Gwen on it.

"Yes, of course. Very nice," he replied and came over to embrace her.

Her warm body pressed tightly against his. He assumed that she was so warm because she had just been baking in the kitchen.

Denise leaned her head closer to his, licked his ear, and whispered, "I'm Gwen."

Marty woke up with a start. The damp, dark bangs of his hair pressed tightly against his forehead. It was a nightmare. Nothing more. He peered to his left and saw Denise sleeping cozily beside him. They were in her bed, the door to the bedroom closing out the rest of the world.

Queasiness set in his stomach. He rolled out of bed and looked out the window. Moisture formed on the glass in puffs as he breathed upon it. The night outside looked calm and cool. Below, surrounding the almost empty parking lot to the apartment building was a boarder of dark green, blotched here and there with brown leaves that had withered slowly from the surrounding trees. Pale moonlight shone on everything.

Everything was at peace, except for the steady thumping of Marty's heart.

Chapter Twenty-Four

"Forget it!" Gwen shouted at them.

"Look, if you want this shit you're gonna hafta fuck us!" Robin shouted back. Standing beside him was the courier who brought the drugs, more than an adequate amount of heroin.

"No thanks," Gwen said, and headed towards the door.

The courier grabbed her and threw her to the floor. She crashed down hard and fell on top of her purse that she had kept by her the whole evening. Gwen had not seen this coming. During the bus ride to the apartment, Robin had seemed harmless. Even during the hour and a half wait after ordering the heroin, he had been very nice to her. Robin had been helpful in getting Gwen a drug strong enough to make an impact. He even warned her that if she took too much of it, that it could be fatal. It was just what Gwen was looking for.

While they were waiting for the goods to arrive, they watched television and Robin made her popcorn and offered her a drink. But when the courier arrived, he transformed from a hospitable host into a hungry rapist.

Gwen, who was now cradling the shoulder that she hurt when she hit the floor, looked up at Robin. Robin could see the disappointment in her eyes. He had betrayed her. No matter. He was already too numb to take pity on her. His own life had done that to him.

Gwen wasn't scared of Robin. It was the courier that frightened her. She had a can of pepper spray in her purse, and it would probably help her escape, but the glare from the courier kept her on the floor. He was older, a lot older, at least sixty years older.

"How about I just pay you now and leave?" Gwen offered, still holding her shoulder. "I have enough. I'll even give you extra." She wasn't sure if she had the courage to stand up and try to make a break for it.

"Sorry, Diane. No can do. Money isn't the issue here. Me and the delivery guy are lonely, and it's not often a hot dame like you shows up askin' for a favor. Most of our customers look more like, well, him," Robin told her, gesturing toward the courier. "Ain't that right, Mr. Gray?"

Mr. Gray nodded.

Gwen opened her purse and felt a wad of Kleenex and her wallet within. Next to them was the small can of pepper spray.

"Let me just pay you," she said, almost pleading.

"Sorry," Robin said. He motioned for Mr. Gray to pick her up off the floor.

Mr. Gray moved forward and, as he was reaching down to her, Gwen whipped out the can of pepper spray, shooting him directly in the eyes. Mr. Gray fell silent instead of screaming as the stinging liquid pierced him. He let out a loud demonic laugh. The pepper spray hadn't worked.

Robin came down to her, eye level, and grabbed the can of pepper spray from her hand, tossing it aside.

"Pin her!" he ordered Mr. Gray.

Mr. Gray held Gwen's arms above her head and pinned her legs with his knees. She wrestled against his assault. It was no good. He was too strong.

Robin unbuckled his pants and slid them down. Mr. Gray gave Gwen a hard slap to the side of her face, dazing her. Robin maneuvered himself so he sat on her legs while Mr. Gray changed positions so that he could continue keeping her arms down.

"That's my bitch!" Robin snarled.

Gwen could hear Mr. Gray growl, approving of the assault.

"Oh, God!" she gasped, her throat wheezing in panic. Tears flowed as fear began to cripple her.

"God's not listening," Mr. Gray rasped.

Robin fiddled with the buckle of Gwen's jeans, sliding them down her legs. Gwen thrust her hips side to side, trying to shake him off. Mr. Gray slapped her again. She stopped struggling. After her pants were off, Robin removed her panties. She felt ashamed and vulnerable. Her mind slowly drifted away from understanding what was happening to her, her body giving into shock.

Robin parted her legs and positioned himself to enter her. Gwen stared at him with wide eyes, terrified as to what would come next. Robin stared back, his dark eyes searing into hers. Her body went rigid. Mr. Gray looked down at her. Gwen could see the hatred for her that burned in his eyes. She didn't know what she possibly could have done to this old man to bring about this torture.

As Robin was adjusting himself, Gwen managed to shake one of her legs free, and before Robin could pin them again, she shot her knee upward, her force full, slamming her kneecap between his legs.

Robin screamed, and fell over onto his side. The commotion distracted Mr. Gray, giving Gwen a chance to wriggle out of his grasp. She leapt up, darting toward the door. Already she could feel the two men starting to follow. She ran out of the apartment, sprinting down the hallway, and banged on the doors of any tenant who would open them. No one did. She headed for the stairwell, desperately trying to escape. Her head hurt. She forgot that she was still naked below her waist. "Come on!" she could hear Robin shout above the clamoring of footfalls.

Gwen jumped down the staggered flights of stairs in groups of six steps, gaining more distance between herself and her pursuers. She burst through the stairway door and into the lobby. No one was in sight. She looked over her shoulder to see how close Robin and Mr. Gray were. She couldn't see them but heard the echoed banging of their footfalls as they bounded down the stairwell. Gwen bolted across the lobby for the front entrance. She was stopped at the doors by—

—Mr. Gray.

"How?" Gwen started to say, and was abruptly silenced when Mr. Gray grabbed her and covered her mouth with a handkerchief. It was soaked in Ether.

Robin shot through the stairwell door, still trying to finish buckling up his pants.

"Bring her back upstairs," he told Mr. Gray. His eyes were wild. "Her time with us is far from over."

They were the last words Gwen heard before her vision blurred and everything went black.

Chapter Twenty-Five

Tonight was going to be a long night spent with a wet pillow, Harry knew. He lay scrunched up in a ball on his mattress, clutching his sheets, burrowing his face in his pillow. When he had settled in for the night he was hit with an unexpected wave of grief—mostly grief over Lauren, his wife of a lifetime past.

All that was happening: Gwen, the boy, Sherman, even himself—all of it—circled around her death so long ago. If Lauren had not died, Harry would not have been in the cemetery that night, and Gwen would not be in Toronto trying to kill a child.

He felt guilty. He felt alone.

With a loud wail he poured out his anguish into his pillow and bed sheets, and cried for several hours, watching as images of Lauren, Gwen, and scenes from his twenty-five years of mental suffering flashed before him. The pain in his heart intensified with each passing moment. He gripped his chest, worrying he was having a heart attack. The pain of all his sufferings hurt so much. It was hard to breathe. All he could utter were choked sobs. His pulse raced. Sweat covered his skin.

Harry knew that he could ask a nurse for help, but the idea of bringing yet another soul into his world of darkness and despair repelled him. So instead, he remained buried in his sheets, trying to keep himself warm, safe, and calm. His pillow felt the same as it did after going to bed with a head full of wet hair after a shower: most uncomfortable, and cold.

If Lauren were alive, she would cradle him and whisper reassurances to him as she rocked him back and forth like a baby. She had done this once for him…after his father had passed away. That was two short years before she would be dead. Two short years before that horrific night in the cemetery. Yes, there were so many things that she used to do for him. So many things that had made him feel loved. So many assurances that he would never be alone. And Harry knew it could never be that way again. Sometimes, when he thought of her, he would catch himself getting mad at her for leaving him. He would be angry with God for allowing that son of a bitch robber to shoot his wife. *Poor Lauren…Poor me,* Harry thought. *Why did we have to be victims?*

If he was so desperately needed to witness the birth of the Antichrist, had there not been another way for him to be in the cemetery that night? Could whoever was behind this have placed him there under different circumstances?

None of it made sense, and Harry knew that it never would. Three years after being committed to Hans Memorial Hospital he had finally accepted that. But, now, he needed answers. Everything that he thought might take place was actually happening. It was all real and he was paying the price for it.

For years Harry had wondered how he could dispose of the Antichrist. Then, one day, while sitting in the cafeteria, gazing out through the window at the pouring rain, he thought of it. Perhaps it had been the rain that had clued him in. If he was to be a victim, why not someone else, too?

There had been a name that had come with him when emerging out of twenty years of Hell in the library: Jane? Jesse? Gerry? Gene? Gwen? Yes! Gwen! He would find her. He had to. When the name had first come to him, he hadn't fully understood what sort of supernatural powers would arise when he eventually called her. He knew that it wasn't fair of him to place this burden on another. But he wasn't going to be the only victim. No sir. If he were destined to feel a lifetime of pain—so would someone else. That's when he had decided he would call Gwen to him. Gwen. The name that came with him from the library.

Many times since he had met Gwen, he had asked himself if she would be able to withstand it. Withstand the burden. Or, would she end up like him, alone, helpless, and broken?

Harry sat up in his bed and threw back his sheets. A strong flash of anger consumed his entire being. He glared up at his ceiling, pointing his finger skyward.

"Fuck You! How can You have done this to me? Do You hear me? Fuck You!" It was time for God to hear what was on his mind. "Who else could be responsible for this? It's all You, do You understand me? It's all You! Fuck You! I hate You! And I'm taking Gwen through the pain with me! Fuck You, You selfish prick! Fuck You!"

Harry jumped out of bed, still screaming, profanities flying from his lips along with his spittle. He fell to his knees, his fists pounding on the hard floor in a tantrum.

As expected, there was a knock on his door. Nurse Robinson, the same nurse he had tackled earlier, entered his room.

"Harry? Are you all right?" he asked gently.

Harry was surprised that it was he who had entered the room. He thought that nurse Robinson wouldn't come within two feet of him after what had happened.

"Harry?" Robinson repeated gently.

Harry didn't respond, instead sitting on his knees, covering his eyes to stop his tears.

It was evident that Robinson should summon Dr. Woodrose. Thankfully, the good doctor was on call tonight. Some of the other psychiatrists on the ward didn't know how to handle Harry.

Robinson knelt down beside Harry and placed a hand on his shoulder. He could feel Harry wretch and shudder under his touch. "Harry? What's the matter? Do you want to talk?"

Harry remained silent. Robinson patted his shoulder reassuringly. "I'll tell you what, Harry, I'll be right back with Dr. Woodrose and we'll get things all fixed up for you, all right? Just hang on a minute."

Robinson got up and exited the room, leaving Harry to drown in his own misery. While the nurse was away, a musty scent filled the air. Harry glanced up and peered around. Nothing unusual could be seen.

The air continued to change, becoming the putrid scent of sulfur mixed with gasoline.

A strange voice blared into his mind. *Don't worry, Harry. We'll get you fixed up right away. Ha ha ha!*

"Who are you?" Harry asked in blinded rage. He stood up in defensive posture.

The sulfur and gasoline stench in the air depleted. All was quiet.

"Dammit, who are you!" Harry demanded.

No response. The voice was gone.

A moment later, nurse Robinson reappeared in the doorway, accompanied by Dr. Woodrose.

"It's all right, nurse Robinson. Thanks," Dr. Woodrose told him. Robinson left the doctor alone with his patient.

Harry stood in the middle of his room, a blank expression on his face. Dr. Woodrose kept his eye on Harry as he ebbed back toward the doorway. He turned on the lights. Harry didn't blink when they came on.

"What's the trouble, Harry?" he asked.

Harry remained still and didn't move. He didn't hear Dr. Woodrose's question.

"Very well, then." Dr. Woodrose pulled a chair out from under Harry's small desk. Relying on his psychological training, he allowed several minutes of silence, hoping that his patient would buckle under the expectation of speech and blurt out whatever it was that was bothering him.

With Harry, that technique rarely worked, but, nevertheless, he had to give it a try.

Harry remained standing, his posture rigid. His glare was still fixated on the door to his room.

Dr. Woodrose tapped his pen against his clipboard, waiting patiently. Finally, Harry turned his head toward the doctor. Dr. Woodrose saw the pain and anguish in Harry's trembling gaze.

"I can't finish it," Harry told him.

"Finish what, Harry?" Dr. Woodrose responded, knowing that whatever had been bothering Harry for the past few weeks was about to come tumbling out.

"He will win, you know. Despite all efforts, in the end, he will win. My whole life was used for this. My whole life was meant to understand the severity of the situation. But, in the end, it will all count for nothing. He will win and I will lose."

Harry moved over to his bed, sat down, and grabbed his pillow. He played with the corners of the pillowcase with his fingers. Dr. Woodrose adjusted his chair so he was facing him. He thought about asking Harry whom it was that he was referring to, but thought it best that he just let Harry share with him a little bit at a time. That way, hopefully, he would receive the whole story and would better understand what needed to be done to get Harry out of this slump.

Still, Dr. Woodrose did have to hand it to Harry, despite what the other doctors and nurses thought about his patient. Apart from all the grief and torment in his life, Harry kept on pressing through, kept on trying to survive no matter what. Even during the sessions that took place after Harry had spent some time in the Darkroom, the poor guy always seemed to have an air of determination about him. Dr. Woodrose rarely saw this type of perseverance in any of his other patients. For that he commended Harry. Indeed there was something special about this man.

"Lately, I've been sick with guilt," Harry began, his voice a whisper. "I've sent a girl into a battle she cannot hope to survive. It should have been me from the start. I lied to her. Told her that this mission took two—one to experience the evil and one to eradicate it. I spent a lot of time searching for her, thinking about her, from here, lying on this bed and letting my mind wander into the darkness and out into the world, asking demonic forces for help." He smoothed the wrinkles of the bed sheet beside his leg. "I am the villain here. I am wrong. She is innocent. Just another one of God's creatures dragged down a dark path. For that I should be punished. I want her to suffer too, yet…" He didn't finish.

Dr. Woodrose jotted down all Harry was saying. To him it wasn't making much sense. He had heard this story from Harry before, yet he hadn't mentioned the girl. It was sad. Whatever fantasy world Harry was talking about, he had somehow confused it with reality. And, now, whatever tension was in that fantasy world was taking its toll on him.

Harry slouched, his back nearly forming an impossible curve. Dr. Woodrose decided that Harry had finished speaking and, deciding to play along with what he felt were Harry's delusions, asked, "It seems, to me, you don't feel justified asking this girl for help. If it's all right, can you tell me her name?"

Harry looked at him with deep eyes.

"Gwen," he said.

Dr. Woodrose pushed his glasses up the bridge of his nose. "How do you know her, Harry?"

"It's complicated, but her name has been ringing in my head ever since I was brought here. After being committed, I began thinking about what I could remember about my life before the cemetery. I remembered Lauren first. Then my son, Carl, and," Harry paused a moment, then, "a girl named Gwen. I didn't know where her name came from, but for a whole year while I was here, I kept hearing her name in my head, over and over again. Then her name was accompanied by an image and, shortly after, a specific place. It was where she was. Or, where I would find her, or something."

"Did you try to find her?"

Harry looked at him vacantly. "Were you not listening to anything I just said, or were you doodling teddy bears on that damn notepad of yours? For the *second* time, I found her."

"Sorry if I offended you," Dr. Woodrose apologized. "Here." He set his notepad down on the floor beside his chair. "You have my full attention. How did you find her?"

"You won't believe me, but…I used my powers. Used my ability to go into people's heads. Slowly but surely I was able to transmit my thoughts throughout the city and get her to respond."

"You're saying she's from here? In Winnipeg?"

Harry rolled his eyes. "Are you playing dumb with me, Doc?"

"No, I'm just making sure I understand everything you're saying. Please, go on."

"You don't believe me. You never did. But, no matter, my powers are diminishing now. Maybe because this crusade will be over soon? I don't know." Harry fell back so he was sitting slouched in the corner where his bed met the wall.

"Did this young lady—Gwen—hear your instructions in her head, or did she come here and visit you?"

Harry became annoyed. Dr. Woodrose should have known the answer to that question. Dr. Woodrose had access to his chart *and* his visitation files. He should have known that Gwen was Harry's first and only visitor, apart from Carl.

"Because of your question, Doc, I have decided to stop sharing with you. You obviously don't know much of what's going on. I'm ashamed to have you as my doctor," Harry told him.

"Surely, Harry, you don't mean that," Dr. Woodrose stated.

He realized as soon as he had said that that Harry was telling him the truth. Even though Harry was one of his favorite patients, his interest in him was superficial. The hard truth was that he wasn't really *interested* in any of his patients. He was only interested in their ailments and the tales of their problems. He had never been interested in the individuals themselves.

Dr. Woodrose bowed his head, ashamed. Harry noticed.

"All I'm going to say is," Harry began, "that I can't go on knowing that Gwen will die because of something I did. I've had enough loss in my life already and to lose one more thing in it, well, I know it is something I couldn't deal with. Hell, I can't even deal with this shit, now. Good-bye,

Doc. You're help was most unnecessary. Your efforts to help me don't count for much. Never did. You can leave at any time."

After an edgy moment, Dr. Woodrose nodded, his face red. He picked up his notepad and walked towards the door. With a slow turn, he looked back at Harry. His patient remained slouched against the mixture of pillows and sheets at the corner of the bed. Harry kept his eyes forward, ignoring him. Dr. Woodrose reached for the door handle, but was stopped when Harry spoke one last time.

"Don't ever come back here again," Harry told him, his voice soft but firm.

Dr. Woodrose looked at him, emptily, feeling grief stricken by how he had offended Harry. As hard as it was to admit, Harry was right. In the morning Dr. Woodrose would try to find a more suitable psychiatrist for him. In the meantime, he could only pray that Harry would be safe throughout the night and that he wouldn't try to harm himself or get himself thrown back in the Darkroom.

Dwelling on that final thought, Dr. Woodrose nodded in understanding and left the room.

Harry was alone with his pillows.

* * *

Harry had finally fallen asleep three hours later then awoke at the sound of a soft whispering that seemed to emanate from all around him.

He recognized the voice. It was Sherman.

Surprising to himself, Harry felt calm. Instead of fear, soothing warmth encompassed him. It was the warmth of finality, a sense that despite whatever tactic Sherman was going to use against him, it wouldn't matter before the night was over.

How are you sleeping, Harry? Feeling good after your little chat with Dr. Woodrose? Sherman spoke from the darkness.

Harry hadn't turned his lamp on that night. He didn't care anymore if he slept in darkness or not.

"Get away from me, demon!" he commanded and rolled over onto his side, signaling to Sherman that he had nothing to say.

Oh, sure, roll over and hide. Very well. I don't have much to say, either, Harry. I just wanted to be here when it happened.

"What?" Harry asked, breaking his private oath to stay quiet.

Sherman didn't respond.

"What?" Harry asked again only to receive the same reply as before—nothing.

Furiously, Harry kicked back his sheets and jumped to the middle of his room.

"What!" he screamed into the blackness surrounding him.

As if an answer, the atmosphere of the room grew extremely quiet. Harry couldn't even hear himself breathing, nor could he hear anything happening on the outside of his room. The silence hummed in his ears.

In the void of no sound, Harry was grasped by an unseen hand and thrown beside his desk on the other side of the room. Then, like in the library so long ago, an unseen force took control of Harry's hand, forcing it to open the desk drawer and retrieve a pen.

"Stop it, Sherman!" Harry yelled. His voice didn't echo in the darkness.

Fine, he thought, *let's end this now. I got nothing more to lose.*

Harry fought against the invisible hand that was forcing him to grip the pen. He tried using his other hand to free the pen from the other's grasp. Harry knew what was about to happen. Every effort that he made grew more and more feeble, the muscles in both his hands fatiguing after every attempt. Harry's left hand dropped to his side, thumping against the floor. He was unable to move it. The hand that held the pen came slamming down into his left wrist.

"AGGH!" he yelped as he felt the dull, plastic point puncture his flesh. "DAMMIT, SHERMAN!"

As if to coincide with the blast of pain that ignited inside his wrist like fire, the lights to his room flashed on. The lights then flickered in time with his heartbeat: on then off, on then off.

His right hand, still holding the pen, tore through his flesh, ripping a gash from his wrist up to his elbow. Streams of dark, red blood spurted up and out, squirting Harry in the face and vandalizing the floor and desk around him.

On then off, the lights went. On then off.

"Sherman, no," Harry choked. His forearm only hurt for a moment, quickly becoming numb from the pain. Harry closed his eyes. He knew his torture was far from over.

His right hand pulled the pen out of his arm and brought the pen up to his neck, its dull tip pointing straight at him. As much as Harry had once thought about suicide, about ending the pain, he didn't want to die. Not now. Not like this.

Good-bye, Harry. I should have done this from the start. I gave you a sporting chance to leave Gwen alone but instead you continued to fight. I'll see you on the other side, Sherman's voice said, each syllable drawn out slowly and coated with hate.

Harry's frantic heartbeat slowed to a crawl. The lights in the room flickered more slowly, as well. The warm red-black blood that had gushed from his open wound was slowing to an ooze. He was at the final moment before death.

A hot pain suddenly flared up in his throat. Something was stuck there, something that didn't belong. Materializing before his eyes, Harry saw Lauren, Carl, and Gwen—the only three people he had ever cared about. They blurred together in a tornado of images, each person coming vividly into view in turn. Within the moment of an instant and forever, the images were sucked backward into a dark cloud, carrying Sherman's face with it. A victorious grin snaked across the old man's lips before all vanished and nothing was left save for his bedroom, the pulse of the light so slow that it was dark longer than it was light.

Then the sound of the hospital returned and Harry knew what had happened. The pen had impaled his neck. Its dull point touched the back of his throat.

Harry's body crumpled backward and he lay gazing at the ceiling, the warmth of blood flowing down the sides of his neck, down his chest, pooling at his sides.

"Forgive me…" was all Harry managed to say.

His vision blurred. The lights pulsed on again.

Then all was dark.

PART FOUR

CHANGES

Chapter Twenty-Six

Sleeping on her back was the only semi-comfortable position. She knew this when—after managing to get herself back to her motel room and falling onto her bed—lying on her side only made the pain between her legs even worse. She didn't dare to lie on her stomach, either. The aching bruises on her inner thighs and abdomen were already starting to show in faded blotches of purple and deep red.

Gwen stared at the ceiling, her thoughts in complete disarray save for one undeniable feeling: abandonment. She needed Marty. *I hope he got the e-mail,* she thought. *I should have called him. I didn't because I thought that hearing his voice would have hurt and reminded me of our fight. I'd give anything for a fight with him if it meant that I could just hear his voice. I'm so confused. I'm so sorry, Marty. I'm so sorry. Help me, please!*

She sniffled, slowly rubbing the bruises between her legs.

The thought of calling a hospital crossed her mind, but she was too weak to even make an attempt. Instead, she had come home, wrapped herself in her blankets, and hoped that a full night's sleep would help her. She would tackle the trauma of being assaulted and raped tomorrow. The violation of her body hadn't fully registered yet. She was beginning to deny it even happened.

That night, Gwen fell asleep easily, fatigue overwhelming her entire body. She dreamed, her face wincing every time her legs moved as she slept. Only once did she awake with a racing heart. In her dream, she had just relived the horrific experience of Robin and Mr. Gray taking turns on her. Their faces had distorted with each grunt of pleasure, their perverted and sadistic eyes peering into her soul.

She had been beaten. Taken. Broken.

The guarantee of success in her Holy mission appeared to be impossible.

* * *

Keeping to personal tradition, Marty Bones checked his e-mail before retiring to bed. The usual messages scrolled into his mailbox: artist newsgroup updates, goofy e-mails from friends, and all the spam mail that came with a public e-mail account. A violent jolt slapped him in the chest when he saw the message at the bottom of the list: sillycat@zaam.com. It was Gwen's e-mail address. She had written!

With a swift click of the mouse, Marty opened up the message, the computer seeming not fast enough to get to the next screen.

"Come on," he moaned, begging the computer to hurry up.

Once the message was displayed, he read the following:

Marty,

As much as it feels good writing to you, it also feels kinda strange. I feel bad about our fight. I just want to let you know that I'm okay. Don't know how much longer I'll be away for, though. I'm not mad at you, Marty.

I'll probably write to you before I come back home. Shouldn't be too long. We'll see. We'll talk more when I get back.

Write back if ya want!

Love,

Gwen

PS. I'm thinking about you!!

Marty sighed and slumped in his chair. His heart sagged into his stomach. He reread the e-mail four times before closing the window and staring at his mailbox. He wanted to write Gwen back but couldn't. Not after cheating on her. Maybe not ever.

* * *

The morning came as usual into Gwen's motel room, every object in the room turning a shade of blue-gray from the morning light pouring in through the half open blinds. Her sheets, normally white, were a light gray, and when measured up against her skin, not much paler.

When Gwen first awoke she had forgotten the previous night's torture, but her memory soon returned the moment she tried to get out of bed. In an attempt to swing her left leg over the side of the bed, she felt a sharp pain cut through her thigh all the way through to her stomach. Her first reaction was *the cramps.* The bruises instilled on her skin proved otherwise.

"Ow…" Gwen shakily whispered to herself as she slowly maneuvered herself out of bed. Her head hurt. Her cheeks hurt from being slapped. Her neck hurt. There wasn't a single part on her body that didn't ache.

Walking awkwardly, she waddled over the bathroom to conduct the morning business. Her body was stiff. Everything from the waist downward cried in pain.

Gwen needed a cigarette and a full bottle of whatever was left over in the liquor cabinet. The severity of what had happened to her had yet to fully set in. All her feelings, thoughts, sensations, her entire being—was muted.

Sitting near the windowsill, wrapped in her blanket, Gwen stared blankly at the table in front of her. Her mind was on the verge of collapse. She hadn't even bothered dressing for the day. How could she? Every tiny movement hurt.

As the morning turned to afternoon, she soon discovered that her groin wasn't the only thing that was bruised. Her breasts were as well. They sat prominently on her chest like they always did, but instead of the normal shade of golden-beige that they usually were, they looked like miniature purple and blue blotched balloons. Her deep pink nipples had turned a dark violet. They pounded with pain, hurting almost worse than it did between her legs.

If Gwen were to appear to Marty as she did then, he probably wouldn't recognize her. Her face was ghostly pale with dark, red rings stationed around her eyes. Tiny wrinkles had formed at the corners of her lips. Her hands trembled in her lap. Her once shining, deep brown hair seemed to take on a taint of gray in the pale streaks of afternoon sunlight that came in from the window. A cigarette dangled from her pallid, pink lips, the cigarette nearly burnt entirely to its end. The Gwen Reeves that lived in that lonesome motel room in Toronto bared little resemblance to the once radiant Gwen Reeves that had come out of Winnipeg.

As she sat, one sore hand massaging her aching neck, Gwen came to understand why her time in Toronto was becoming so increasingly difficult. The answer was so simple that she was surprised that she hadn't figured it out earlier.

Someone or something was out to stop her. Something wanted to prevent her from killing the child. *But why hadn't they, or it, simply killed me right off the hop to get me out of the way? Why provide the constant fear and torture?* Gwen thought. *There was so many times where they or it could have killed me. What's stopping them? What would happen if they did?* She didn't know the answer, but she knew that there was someone who would. Gwen could only hope that she would be able to get him on the phone.

Stiffly, she got up and wrapped herself more snugly in her blanket then went to the phone on the nightstand. Her hand paused above the receiver then curled back into a fist, hesitating. She sat on the edge of her bed, wincing as a spike of pain poked her bottom.

"Harry wanted me to call this whole thing off," she said aloud.

Gwen sat for a moment, her mind going blank. A constant ache between her legs urged her to phone Harry anyway. Even if he didn't want her to kill the Antichrist, he might as well give her some damn answers! And sympathy! Sympathy for her because of all the shit that had happened to her out here! He owed her at least that much.

Gwen picked up the receiver and grabbed the phone book out from the drawer of the nightstand. She looked up the phone number for the Toronto information operator then asked the tele-service representative for the phone number to Hans Memorial Hospital in Winnipeg, Manitoba. The operator complied and gave Gwen the number. After writing it down, she hung up on the operator, forgetting to thank her for the information.

She dialed Hans Memorial Hospital. The pace of her heart picked up once the line started to ring.

There was a click and a clean voice came on the line with a "Hello?"

"Can you transfer me over to the Psych-centre, please?" Gwen asked, trying to be as polite as possible. Her face scrunched as lightning struck between her legs.

"Hold please," said the sterile voice.

The line went silent for a moment before a steady, monotonous tone began to pulse.

Gwen remained on hold for several minutes, leaving her to wonder if whatever evil was stalking her somehow knew that she was making this call. The thought vanished when someone finally picked up.

"Hans Memorial Psychological Care Centre. How can I help you?"

Gwen recognized the smooth, thick voice immediately. It was Elsie Fortsmith. Gwen tried opening her mouth to speak but only a small gasp of air squeaked out.

"Hello?" Elsie asked through the phone line, wondering if someone was there.

Gwen cleared her throat. "Um, yes. There is a patient of yours I wish to speak with."

"Patient's name, please?"

"Harry Thomas."

The line went quiet for a moment, forcing Gwen to think that she had somehow struck a nerve with Elsie. There was nothing except for the breathing of the black woman. Elsie obviously knew it was Gwen who was calling. Gwen had been the only person to come and talk to Harry in five years aside from his son.

"Hello?" Gwen called out, hoping that Elsie was still there. She needed her to be there.

"You're the girl from a couple of weeks back, right?" Elsie asked, as if she were a cop interrogating a known felon.

"Yes, ma'am." *I don't have time for this,* Gwen thought. *Ouch, my...*

"Were you made aware that Harry Thomas is not allowed to use the telephones?"

"No," Gwen lied. Harry had, in fact, informed her that, for him, telephones were off-limits. Yet, a few days back, he had managed to call her, telling her to return home and let the child be. "I really need to speak with him. It's an emergency."

"What's so pressing, my dear, that a psych-patient would be able to help you with?"

Why is she giving me the run-around, Gwen asked herself. She carefully laid herself down on the bed. The pain between her legs subsided a little. Gwen wasn't sure if she would be able to sit back up again.

"It's personal. I need to speak with Harry. Now!" Gwen demanded. *You nosy bitch! Just patch me the fuck through!*

"I'm afraid that's not possible. Mr. Thomas has had an accident and is in critical condition in the Intensive Care Unit. Do you wish for me to leave a message?"

"Yeah, buh-bye," Gwen said loudly then hung up, landing the receiver hard into its cradle. She felt the shock of it all the way up her arm.

Staring at the ceiling, she thought of Harry. With eyes closed, she attempted to contact him with her mind. She knew that Harry wasn't a mind reader, but it was the only thing she could think to do at the moment.

Harry? Harry? Can you hear me? She waited a moment, imagining Harry's reply. Of course there was none. She couldn't focus. She was too sore. Gwen tried once more then gave up. She decided that Harry hadn't had an accident. What happened to him had somehow been caused by the same evil that had hurt her. Gwen could only pray that it wasn't fatal.

She needed a miracle.

* * *

Sitting next to her in bed wasn't what bothered him. In fact, he really enjoyed Denise's company despite the hot, feverish guilt that raided his heart and mind.

Marty Bones stretched out his limbs then pulled Denise closer to him. His first reaction to Gwen contacting him was that he would never sleep with Denise again. Reading her e-mail message re-ignited all his passion for Gwen. For the rest of that afternoon, he hadn't given Denise a second thought. That was, until, she had called earlier that evening.

"Do you want to come over?" she had asked him, obviously insinuating *why* she wanted to see him.

Marty had hesitated at first, but soon agreed when he felt a lonesome ache in his groin. During the whole drive to her place he hated himself for what he was about to do. He knew he should have told her that Gwen had written him and that it would not be a good idea for him to come by and see her. What he should have done was left a message on Denise's answering machine, breaking their affair off, as soon as his feelings for Gwen had reemerged. But he didn't. He was an asshole.

The moment he saw Denise, Marty quickly forgot Gwen and only wanted to make love and be in the safety of a woman's arms. He was confused, this he knew. And it bothered him. Never before had he been torn between two women. Even when Gwen was in the city, he never looked at another girl in a way that he shouldn't have. It was only when Gwen had left that his loyalty and morals had left, too. He couldn't understand it and he didn't think that he ever would.

Marty found himself relying on the hopes that his behavior would change if Gwen ever returned. He would deal with the consequences of his betrayal to her then. Right now, he was happy and he supposed that was all that really mattered.

Beside him Denise was catching her breath after a quick, and intense, round of sex. She lay with her head on his chest, Marty stroking her hair. She was happy that she was with him. Before, she thought of him as too odd and eccentric. Now she was sleeping with him!

Inside her heart she was experiencing the soothing sensation of gladness that comes before you're about to fall in love with someone. How that feeling got there, she didn't know, but she took that feeling as authentic. After all, she had given her flower to Marty when long ago she had promised herself that she would wait until marriage before receiving a man's touch.

The only clue Denise could give herself was a dream she had a week prior to Gwen's sudden disappearance. It was the first time she had ever dreamed about Marty, the second having been when things started getting strange with Gwen. In the dream, she was sitting on the front lawn in front of an old house that looked as if it was out of one of those movies about the civil war. The house was painted light blue with white trim. A shining, oak porch wrapped around its front. The front lawn was long and green and seemed to span for miles in all directions. The land around was completely flat except for one tree that stood proudly to the right of the house.

Sitting on a blanket on the front lawn, Denise wore a red T-shirt and blue jeans and no shoes. She was relaxing, eyes closed, enjoying the brightness of the mid-day sun, when a shadow loomed over her, blocking the sun's rays. When she opened her eyes she saw Marty standing above her, a paintbrush in his hand, dripping thick, blood red paint. He sat down beside her and began to hold her, stroking her shoulders and kissing the top of her head. Denise had found herself completely giving in to the moment and not caring about what Marty was doing to her. She even allowed him to paint her entire body red while his hands explored her. She then clasped herself to him, needing his touch. There was, however, one thing about that dream that struck Denise as strangely out of place, besides her sudden intimate interaction with Marty. Out of the corner of her eye, off in the distance, she had seen an old man watching them. Treating the old man as part of her dream, she had ignored him, beckoning Marty to continue pleasuring her.

Even now, as Denise lay beside Marty, she felt the strange, cool sensation of wet paint being spread over her body. She prayed silently to whoever may be listening that these constant encounters of bliss with Marty would never end.

From outside the bedroom window Sherman Gray nodded as if hearing her prayer.

Chapter Twenty-Seven

"You're kidding!" Victoria Mandalay said, her tone coated with surprise. "Yep, that's what I told her."

She glanced over at Calvin and Uncle Ken. It was Sunday morning and they were sitting at the kitchen table. Calvin decided to take Uncle Ken up on his offer about going to church with him that morning. Ken had come over and joined Calvin and his mother for an early breakfast before leaving for the morning service. Victoria had been invited to join them, but she declined, complaining of a headache, yet still insisting on preparing a delicious breakfast for Ken and her son.

"Way to go!" Uncle Ken congratulated Calvin, adding his smile to the one that beamed from Victoria's face.

On Friday, after she had gotten home from work, Victoria received another message on her answering machine from Calvin's teacher, Mrs.

Fuller. It was regarding Calvin's recent behavior at school. Pressed with worry, she called the teacher back hoping that she was still at the school. Mrs. Fuller had fortunately stayed late, going over the paintings that her kids had done that day. Mrs. Fuller was extremely happy to report a sudden acceleration in Calvin's learning skills. Mrs. Fuller relayed an example, stating that earlier in the week, Calvin had been learning his basic counting skills, and simple addition with numbers. She told Victoria that Calvin had caught on immediately and soon was processing addition questions at a grade two level. He was also able to count all the way up to one thousand.

Victoria was excited, yet also ashamed that she thought Mrs. Fuller had called because Calvin had been causing trouble. After some of the things Calvin had told her about his relationships with his friends, she had feared the worst. The only thing that Mrs. Fuller said that worried her was that sometimes Calvin would go to a corner in the playroom and talk to someone who wasn't there. But Victoria was reassured that it was common for children Calvin's age to have an imaginary friend.

At the breakfast table, Calvin blushed as both his mother and uncle looked at him with approving grins. Throughout the remainder of the meal, the three of them talked about how Calvin was doing at school and what the plans would be after church was finished that day. Uncle Ken told them that he had some errands to run that afternoon, but would join them for dinner, as the tradition was. Calvin beamed at the thought of his uncle coming over. Something super-silly always happened when Uncle Ken ate with them. Just last week, Ken had made a snowman out of his mashed potatoes then pretended that his corn-on-the-cob was a missile. He had blown the potato-man to smithereens. Absolutely brilliant!

Calvin chuckled at the recollection and continued to eat his breakfast.

* * *

Sitting in the passenger seat of the big, brown beast that Uncle Ken called his *trucker*, Calvin thought about the dream he had the night before. He couldn't remember what it had been about, but he knew that Sherman had been in it and that Sherman had told him not to go to church with Uncle Ken that morning. *Was Sherman, right?* Calvin asked himself. He looked over at Uncle Ken who was happy that his nephew had come along.

Maybe a message of hope is what Calvin needs, Ken thought. *Maybe next week he'll want to come with me again and he could ask Victoria to join us? She needs this more than anyone right now. Here's hoping.* He crossed his fingers.

Calvin followed Uncle Ken up the massive stone steps and through the heavy gray doors of St. Christopher's Cathedral. Just before the door closed behind him, Calvin turned, looking back to see how high the steps had brought him. Sherman was standing at the bottom, his lips drawn taut, his eyes hard. Calvin hoped that he wasn't in any trouble with the old man. The boy looked back into the church and saw that Uncle Ken had already gone in and apparently hadn't noticed him stopping at the door.

"Do you want to come in?" Calvin asked Sherman.

Sherman tried to come closer, but retreated back, wincing uncomfortably.

"I best not, Calvin," the old man told him. "I'm not welcome here." He paused. "Neither are you."

Calvin turned and went in anyway, despite his friend's continuing protests. He would work it out with the old man later.

Sherman watched as the boy disappeared into the enemy's temple, and then turned his gaze toward Ken's *trucker*. Something needed to be done about that boy's all-too-caring uncle.

Upon entering the vast Cathedral, Calvin felt strangely out of place. He had never been in a church before. He was standing in the lobby. Everybody greeted him with a smile.

He caught sight of Uncle Ken and moved toward him. As he crossed from the main foyer into the sanctuary, Calvin took note that the people walking in front of him had dipped their fingers into a little stone bowl that looked like a birdbath. They did something with their hands where they touched themselves in different places. To Calvin, they looked like robots that only did it because they had to. Feeling that he should, too, he dipped his hand into the birdbath, feeling the warm water on his fingers. Before he could mimic what he saw everybody doing, the water on his fingertips began to burn, causing him to quickly wipe them on his jacket. *How could people touch that stuff?* he wondered. *It's too hot!*

Frowning, he searched again for his uncle. Calvin found Ken sitting in a pew a few rows in front of him. The boy went over and sat beside him.

"Where'd you go?" Uncle Ken asked.

"I just thought I saw something, but it was nothing."

Uncle Ken nodded.

The boy shifted his gaze upward and all around himself. The room was large and warmly dim. The walls around him were a golden color and every window was decorated with images of saints and Bible characters on colorful, stained glass. In front of them was a large altar with three gray, white, and red, marble steps leading up to it. To the right of the steps was a podium with a thick, heavy Bible placed neatly at its center. To the left was a large, freestanding crucifix made of silver. Behind all of this was an even more enormous crucifix suspended on the wall behind the altar so that the entire congregation could see the Lord Jesus crucified. Calvin didn't like the idea of a man nailed to a cross. He didn't see the point.

The chapel was oddly quiet. Calvin had noticed this after he had felt the Holy water burn his fingertips. It was as if he had entered a room full of mutes. The only noise that could be heard came from the foyer where friends and door-greeters gathered to bless each other and talk about church and the get-togethers that would follow afterward.

Sitting in front of Calvin and Uncle Ken was a row of elderly people whose smell seemed to seep back over into Calvin's pew, flowing up into his nostrils. He grimaced and thought it strange that these people would be allowed into a church smelling so bad. The smell couldn't have been an old person thing. Sherman was old but he didn't smell like a mix between spices and rotten eggs.

The boy leaned over to his uncle then cupped his hand over his mouth to conceal his whisper, pointing to the row of egg-stinkers.

"Those people smell," he said, grimacing.

Ken leaned toward him and put his finger to his nose.

"Shhh…" Ken hushed.

A man wearing a long bed sheet came out onto what Calvin thought was a stage, but was really the altar, and made a motion with his hands for everyone to rise. Like Dr. Frankenstein commanding his experimental creature, everybody stood. An organ began to play. It sounded awful and it seemed to echo everywhere. The tones of the organ were soon joined with equally awful singing. Uncle Ken pulled out a songbook and chimed in. Calvin stood and glanced around, his heart beating rapidly the whole time.

The service, according to Uncle Ken, was only supposed to be an hour long, but to Calvin Mandalay, it felt as though he had been sitting silently in his pew his whole life. After some hymns were sung and a few prayers uttered, Father Osato stepped up to his podium and opened his Bible. Father Osato, an older man with short, white spiked hair and thick, square-rimmed glasses that sat on top of a bulbous red nose, wore the traditional priest attire of robe and sash with a black shirt underneath that had a white square placed in the exact center of the collar.

The priest gripped both sides of the podium and looked across the congregation, flashing everybody a glance that read: *Quiet, now, quiet…you don't want me to tell you to shut up, now, do you?*

With a stubby finger he pushed his glasses further up his nose and smacked his lips twice, their sound amplified by the mini-microphone he wore around his neck, and stared at his Bible.

"What's he doing?" Calvin whispered to Uncle Ken.

"He's going to read," Ken whispered back.

Calvin slouched further in his seat and folded his arms across his chest.

"Where's the—" Calvin began with the intention of asking his uncle about the boy he was supposed to be introduced to, but before he could finish, Father Osato's voice boomed through the speakers that hung loosely by thin chains from the roof.

"The Word of the Lord," Father Osato told everyone.

"Thanks be to God," everybody chanted at once, all making a thumps-up and using their thumb to cross their forehead, lips, and heart.

Calvin furrowed his brow then let slip a small smile that Uncle Ken quickly silenced with a sharp glance.

Father Osato once again pushed his glasses up his nose. He began to read. "In John 14:6, Jesus says, 'I am the way and the truth and the life. No one comes to the Father except through me.' Now, what does that mean? And most importantly, what does that mean to you? Here, let me illustrate—"

As Father Osato began explaining that all men and women carry sin in their lives that separates man from God, Calvin saw a flash of black in the corner of his eye. He peered around Uncle Ken to see what it was. There was nothing there except for a row of heavy-set women all wearing dresses that looked as if they had been made from bright curtains and magic carpets. Ken again told Calvin to sit still, assuring him that the service would be over soon. Calvin hoped his uncle was right.

"Another verse which elaborates on what I have just shared," Father Osato's monotonous tone droned on, "is Romans 3:23 which states, 'For all have sinned and fall short of the glory of God.' You see, folks, it isn't this world which keeps us from God, but the sins that each of us commits."

The last time Calvin could remember he had felt angry was when he was playing basketball on his driveway and a black car had driven past him. That same anger had returned now tenfold. And both times this had happened, he hadn't been able to explain why.

His cheeks flushed bright red, a surge of violent energy wrapping itself around his heart. Calvin clenched his fists. With his fingertips he could feel the sweat building up on the inside of his palms. His breathing quickened. There was another flash of black out of the corner of his eye. This time he didn't even bother looking to where it had come from.

Then, as if he was on a roller coaster and riding upward slowly, building toward a flood of vengeful anger, Calvin jumped up onto his seat and screamed, giving Father Osato the middle finger with both hands as he did.

Startled by his nephew's sudden unexplained outburst, Ken grabbed Calvin by the arm and pulled him down close. Everyone in the room was looking at them, including Father Osato who stood behind his podium, his mouth agape, completely speechless.

"What are you doing!" Ken demanded, staring into Calvin's hard-set eyes.

"Get off me, stranger!" Calvin shouted back and pushed him away.

The boy jumped into the aisle and marched straight towards the priest. Uncle Ken moved to go after him. Calvin shot him another sharp glance, snapping out his index finger. "Sit down, stranger! You do not own me!"

Ken obeyed the boy but not out of fear. He inexplicably felt obliged to obey. It was as if the boy was controlling him.

"Young man, I suggest you sit down lest I ask your parents to take you home," Father Osato said with a firm voice and equally firm eyes.

"I think not, Father. I will leave, but you must listen to what I have to say," Calvin said, his verbal ability increasing to that of a well-spoken adult.

Before he could protest, Father Osato locked eyes with the child and fell under their hypnotic power. The priest stood with a firm jaw that refused to open despite all efforts and prayers. The thought of taking the child back to the parents himself crossed his mind, but he was afraid of any scrutinizing the parents might give him for touching their child. He had no choice but to listen.

"Thank you. Thank you all for your cooperation," Calvin said to the entire congregation. He pointed at Father Osato. "It's a shame you put your faith into what this man is saying. He just said that this Savior," the boy pointed to the large crucifix on the wall, "said that no one comes to the Father except through Him. Hmmm…interesting, isn't it? Why would this magical, loving God create us then allow us to fall short of His glory? Oh, I know. Love, right? Well, that would be wrong. It isn't love when you tell somebody to love you and if they choose not to, punish them for it. I don't know about the rest of you, but even at my age, five, by the way," Calvin opened all his fingers and showed them to everybody, "I have common sense. Let's see, on one hand you have the forced choice to love a God who allows all kinds of shit to happen—" Everyone in the room gasped as the child had dared to curse in a church. The boy allowed a dramatic pause before continuing. "And in the other hand you've got eternal damnation, Hell, pain, suffering, whatever. Um, gee, which am I going to choose? Is that love ladies and gentleman? Wouldn't anyone here wish to have the freedom to make the choices that *they* want to make, rather than be forced to make a so-called right choice? And, if they didn't make that choice, they'd get fucking whipped?" Again everyone gasped at the profanity.

"If God was so loving, He would love you despite what you do and not force you into anything. I just thought this was something worth thinking about when you go over to your neighbors' house this afternoon and share with them what you learned in church. Oh, by the way, while you're visiting later, eat a piece of cake for me. That way it would be one piece less for each of you," Calvin pointed to the row of women wearing the dresses made from curtains, "and you wouldn't be so damn fat!"

The boy walked down the altar steps while speechless parishioners followed him with their eyes. Calvin stopped his stride then turned around.

"Forgot one thing," he said and walked up to the crucifix near the altar. He looked at it and for a brief instant everyone thought he was going to seek forgiveness. Their hopes were shattered by a most disgusting sound. Calvin spat at the icon and pushed it over, causing a loud *THUD!* to echo throughout the room. The boy turned and left the chapel, then the foyer, and went outside.

Like taking a rubber band off a deck of cards, the tension and unexplained urge to stay and listen to the boy lifted, and a sigh of relief was exhaled by almost everyone. The muscles on Father Osato's face loosened. He was able to speak again. He surveyed the room and saw all was seated in wide-eyed astonishment. People were already murmuring about the event amongst themselves.

"Ladies and gentlemen, my sincerest apologizes," Father Osato said, trying to bring about a less awkward atmosphere. "If there is anyone here who was unsettled because of what has just transpired, you are free to leave."

The whole room began to stir and many people began gathering their jackets, including Ken who turned red with shame and bolted out of his pew to chase after his nephew.

Ken burst through the front doors and searched the lawn, the parking lot, and the houses that ran alongside the church for any sign of Calvin.

The boy was gone. The only human being in sight was an old man standing across the street from the church. He tipped his hat at Ken, and walked away.

Chapter Twenty-Eight

On a small rise at Fetterman Park, Calvin Mandalay lay on the soft grass, staring blankly at the hazy, gray sky above him. Every so often he would roll over on to his side, inadvertently rubbing his red shirt against the lawn, causing a streak of green to scar the fabric.

It felt to Calvin as though a blender was buzzing inside his brain. The most prominent thing that he could remember was him humming and hawing about how boring Father Osato was…then the sudden surge of anger. As for the specific details as to what happened afterward, Calvin didn't know. His mind wouldn't allow him to recall and understand what had happened. That was, until, he had entered Fetterman Park and collapsed on the grass.

It felt as though he were looking at a jigsaw puzzle with only the border of the image completed, the border representing himself. What was happening on the inside of him was just as jumbled as a pile of scattered puzzle pieces, fragmenting the order of *what* was supposed to go *where*.

Judging by his shortness of breath, Calvin determined that it must have taken him a good fifteen or twenty minutes to run to the park; by the way his limbs felt heavy against the ground, he figured he had been lying there for at least an additional twenty minutes if not more.

After a deep breath, Calvin sat up and crossed his legs. He looked at the empty playground at the bottom of the hill and sighed, feeling as if he would never have the chance to play there again. The world seemed oddly quiescent this Sunday morning; the grass taking on a slight blue hue from the cloudy sky, the street barren except for a bird on the sidewalk, looking for a meal. It reminded Calvin of a cowboy town where everyone goes into hiding as soon as an outlaw strolls in. The only thing missing was a lone tumbleweed rolling idly down a dusty street.

His loneliness abated at the sense of a comforting presence. Calvin didn't even have to turn around to see who was standing behind him. He already knew. It was Sherman Gray. The old man squatted beside the boy and placed a hand on Calvin's shoulder.

"Hello, boy," he said.

"Hello, old man," Calvin returned.

Sherman eased himself down and sat beside Calvin, stretching his legs out in front of him. "Where's your uncle?"

"Probably back at church," Calvin said. "I did something bad, I think, Sherman."

"At church?"

"Uh-huh. I know I should say I'm sorry but I don't want to get lost trying to get there," Calvin said. He undid his shoelace and did it back up again. Anything to keep his mind from thinking about how guilty he felt. He still didn't know exactly what it was he had done.

Sherman pulled his hat forward then pushed it back up again, removing the sweat that had built upon his forehead.

"Did you just come from church?" Calvin asked.

"Yes, I did. I was standing outside as people were leaving and I heard them say what had happened. I figured this is where you'd come. Don't know how I knew, though." Even though he did. He was bonded to the boy. Calvin was *his* responsibility.

Calvin turned an attentive eye toward Sherman. "You know what happened?"

"Yes, I do."

"What did I do, Sherman? What did I do that makes me feel real bad? What?" The boy's voice showed the first signs of tears.

Sherman gazed off to somewhere in front of him.

"I don't think I should, Calvin. It's not that you did anything wrong, but I know that it didn't please your uncle."

Calvin looked up at him, eyes glazed. "How does that not make it wrong?"

"What makes your uncle always right?" Sherman countered.

Calvin didn't answer. The two of them sat silently, letting the mood settle.

Sherman is right, Calvin thought. *What does make Uncle Ken always right? I'm sure he's right sometimes, but not always. He can't be. He's a normal person, right?*

The old man changed his position so he was sitting like the boy.

"Are you going to stay here or go home?" Sherman asked.

"I don't know," Calvin shrugged.

Sherman gave him a smile. "I'll stay here with you as long as you want, but I *do* know you should get home before it gets dark."

"Guess so. Uncle Ken is probably already looking for me."

"Don't worry. He won't find you here," Sherman said.

* * *

Swiftly down the streets by the church, Ken drove, his eyes frantically searching in every direction for his nephew. What had happened earlier in the church had nearly made him sick. He needed to find Calvin and discover what had caused that outburst.

Ken had been searching the neighborhood for almost an hour, covering everything within a ten mile radius of St. Christopher's. He even went past Fetterman Park to see if Calvin was there. The boy wasn't.

His truck sputtered. It wasn't long before it finally died and Ken had to call a tow.

* * *

Shielding themselves from the view of any onlookers, Sherman rendered both himself and Calvin invisible. There was something of grave importance he had to disclose to the boy. Calvin didn't know that they were now unseen.

"I know you're frightened, Calvin," Sherman began, making sure his voice was as soothing as possible. "There are things that have been happening to you that you don't understand. The good part is that it's okay to be confused. It's okay to sometimes sit and wonder what's going on. You're even allowed to cry sometimes, too."

Calvin looked at Sherman with hopeful eyes. For the first time since his outburst the guilt started to alleviate.

Sherman continued. "I remember a long time ago when I started doing things I didn't understand. Sometimes I would get so mad at my dad that I would say and do things that would hurt him."

"What did he do?" the boy asked, trying to get an idea as to what his mother might do to him when he got home.

"Well, I was disciplined, that's for sure. I was kicked out of his house. But don't worry, Calvin, you're mother won't do that to you. My dad was a little—different. I want you to know that I understand how you feel and if you let me, I can help you feel better."

"Thanks, Sherman."

The old man nodded his head. "Calvin, I want you to do something for me. Close your eyes and relax your shoulders. Don't worry, I won't hurt you."

The boy hesitated at first, then obeyed. He slouched his posture, and warily closed his eyes. It felt good to finally slow himself down and try to relax.

Sherman placed both his hands on the Calvin's shoulders then began to massage around the base of the boy's neck. Calvin let out a small moan at the pleasure the relaxing massage induced. He winced when a violent prick of pain poked at the base of his neck.

Calvin collapsed in Sherman's arms. The old man laid the boy down on the grass. Placing his thumb and forefinger over Calvin's eyes, Sherman began chanting. The words were audible, but the old man's mouth never moved. He was depositing a seed of darkness in the boy that would remain inside the child for all time.

* * *

Drifting into a dreamy state, Calvin felt the grass beneath him melt away, being replaced by something hard and cool. An exotic waterfall appeared before him. He looked around, finding himself inside a stony cave. The rocks around him were a light brown in color and remarkably smooth, giving the impression that he was inside a cave made of large gumballs. The lighting was dim, caused only by a stream of sunlight seeping through an indecipherable crack somewhere high up above. The tranquil sound of rushing water echoed off the tiny cavern walls. Inside his chest, Calvin could feel the rumble of the water as it flowed into a stream below.

Being careful not to lose his footing on the unsteady ground, Calvin stepped down a short rocky trail that led to the water. At the bottom of the trail, he kneeled by the stream and gazed at his reflection in the clear, blue water. He watched as his features distorted in its rippling waves, his head taking on odd formations. All memories of having been with Sherman in Fetterman Park were forgotten. It was as though he had always lived in this secret place, with himself as his only company. Every so often he would hear a voice speak throughout the cavern, disclosing to him special words that made him feel more powerful, more dominant.

Using his small hand as a cup, he scooped some water out of the stream and took a slow, satisfying drink. His slurping was interrupted when the Voice spoke from all around him. *Drink the water, Calvin. With each calming sip you take, you will learn more. You will grow. You will get what you need.* This was how the Voice always began its parlance.

The boy finished the remaining water in his hand and scooped up some more to drink. The cool water washed down his throat, through his stomach and settled deep within his intestines, each sensation accompanied by a warm, fuzzy feeling in his heart and mind.

Forgive me, my dear child, for keeping you in the dark for so long. I assure you that you are not alone. I will always be there for you. You are my son. Always remember that. I love you. You are mine.

Calvin took one last gulp of the refreshing water and backed himself away from the stream. He leaned against one of the bulbous rocks behind him and closed his eyes, knowing that the Voice would speak more, and that he should pay careful attention to everything that was about to be said to him.

Smile with joy, my son. Today is the day where I shall open your eyes and allow you to walk away from the confusion you feel. You are special, Calvin. This you know. What you don't know is that I have placed these abilities in you. To further my generosity, I have arranged for Sherman to come into your life. He will be your teacher. My spokesman. Take to heart all that he shows you, every word that escapes his lips. He is my gift to you. He is my gift to you because I love you.

Memories of Sherman flooded Calvin's mind. He smiled at the thought of his dearest friend. A deep and profound loyalty to Sherman grew within him. No longer was the old man viewed as a mere friend who taught him some remarkable tricks. Instead, he was a mentor, a father, and a much older brother. Calvin's heart surged with affection for him, and the acknowledgment that he had fallen in love with the old man.

You must trust Sherman with all that you are, Calvin. He is your link to me. Without him, you will be without me. Do you understand this?

Calvin nodded.

Very well. I love you my child. Always remember that. Now, I must go.

The boy shuddered as the Voice's presence left him. When he opened his eyes, the cavern grew still, quiet. The water stopped running. There was a pressure on his shoulders and at the base of his neck. Even though his eyes were open and he could see all that was around him, the lids of his eyes still felt as if they were closed. Calvin squeezed his eyes shut and opened them quickly, trying to shake the feeling. The darkness of the inside of his eyelids was replaced by the gray-blue of the sky that hovered over Fetterman Park. He sat up on the grass and looked around.

Sherman was gone.

* * *

She hadn't touched a drink in over six months. Six months and four days to be exact. Victoria was now starting to backslide into her old habit, indulging herself in a drink, a "grown-up drink," as she would tell Calvin.

In a shaking hand, Victoria's held a glass of orange juice with a healthy addition of vodka. A good old fashioned Screwdriver, her only salvation. There was nothing like a brisk buzz to get the day going and to help put you to sleep at night.

She had started the daily ritual of a drink in the morning and a drink at night after David had left her. Soon, the habit escalated uncontrollably and alcohol ultimately became her beverage of choice.

Fortunately, it was Ken who had snapped her back to reality, helping her get the habit under control. He proposed that she enter Alcoholics Anonymous, but Victoria would have none of that. She was sick and tired of the group scene. Several of the emotional disorder and support groups that she had attended while trying to get over David had proved ineffective, and in turn had affirmed her decision to abstain from all future external aid.

Reminiscing, Victoria loomed over her glass, gripping it with both hands like a dedicated drinker should. Beside her a cigarette was smoldering away in the ashtray, the smoke curling upward past her face. She needed her salvation. As she took another satisfying swig, Victoria heard the front door open and close, accompanied by someone taking off their shoes. She would recognize the sound of those shoes hitting the tiled floor anywhere. It was Calvin. He was home!

Instinctively, she got up and hurried toward the front door. Calvin had just barely taken off his second shoe when Victoria rushed up to him and wrapped him up in her arms, squeezing him uncomfortably tight. He didn't return the hug.

Tears of relief swelled in her eyes. "Where have you been? Do you have any idea how you wandering away made me and your uncle feel?" She was still panicking, still strenuously worried about where Calvin had taken off to.

"Sorry," Calvin said, his tone flat.

Victoria gave him a final strong squeeze then backed herself away from him, her glazed eyes looking into his.

"I suppose we should have a little talk," she told him. The race of her heart finally began to slow.

Calvin bowed his head, ashamed. He knew that going somewhere without telling anybody was wrong. Victoria knew that he was feeling bad about it. The whole incident at St. Christopher's had made her a nervous wreck, her lower lip still quivering from the shock of the news. Victoria decided to wait until Ken returned before they would talk. At that moment, she really didn't know what to say to her son. I'm glad you're okay? I love you? Or—

"I want you to go to your room and wait until Uncle Ken arrives, okay?" she told him sternly. "We'll talk about it then."

"But, Mom…" Calvin whined, his cheeks paling.

"No buts, Calvin. Let's go." She pointed her index finger in the direction of his bedroom.

Calvin let go a harrumph and marched down the hall. When he rounded the corner leading to his room, and was out of sight, Victoria heard him mutter something under his breath about Uncle Ken. She stormed after him.

"What did you say?" she demanded.

"Nothing. I just said I didn't want to talk to Uncle Ken," Calvin replied, trying to keep things calm. He learned a lesson in serenity from the Voice that afternoon. Also, the effects from Sherman's incredibly relaxing massage hadn't yet worn off.

Victoria's eyes narrowed. She bit her lower lip the same way she always did when she got really upset with him. "You bet you're going to talk to him. It's the least you could do after what you pulled." She paused, upset at herself for getting so angry. "I'm—I'm sorry. I shouldn't raise my voice. I'm just glad you're okay."

The boy's face turned to stone, changing to a furious red. He did an about-face toward his room and stomped off.

A half hour later, Victoria heard a gentle knock at the front door. It was Ken. He greeted her with a hug and by the strong squeeze that she returned, Ken knew that this whole ordeal had rinsed her of all composure. She was exhausted.

"He's in his room," she said, pulling away from him.

"Will you be all right?" he asked.

Victoria's eyes were red and swollen. Tears burned her cheeks.

"I'll be fine," she said, folding her arms across her chest and heading toward the kitchen. She had an appealing orange juice and vodka waiting for her there.

Ken went to Calvin's room and tapped on the door, doing his absolute best not to appear as a threat to the boy. Despite his anger and frustration, Ken's worry for Calvin overruled both.

Inside his bedroom, Calvin gazed up at the white, stuccoed ceiling, watching the bumps on the roof change shape into various objects and faces powered by his imagination. When he heard the knock on the door his heart rate quickened. He knew that getting a good talking-to was soon to follow.

"Come in," Calvin said through the closed door.

Ken walked in. Calvin sat up on his bed.

"Hi, Calvin," his uncle said calmly.

"Hi," was the boy's response. He bowed his head, unable to look his uncle straight in the eye. Ken came over and sat beside him.

"So?" Ken prompted.

"So," Calvin replied. His legs were shaking now.

His uncle noticed. "Your legs cold?"

"Naw. Just nervous."

"Yeah, well, you should be. I'm not going to yell at you Calvin, or anything like that, but what you did at church today embarrassed me. A lot. I can't believe you did such a thing. I have to wonder, do you even know *why* you did it?"

"I couldn't help it," Calvin said quietly.

Ken arched an eyebrow. "What do you mean you couldn't help it?"

The boy looked at the wall behind him then turned to finally face his uncle like a man. "I don't know. I just couldn't help it. For some reason I hated what the priest said. It bothered me and then…" Calvin didn't finish.

The two shared a heart-wrenching moment at the memory.

"I am not impressed," Ken told him, his eyes hard. "Do you have any idea what this has done to your mother? First, you make a fool out of me in front of the entire congregation and, on top of that, you run off, leaving your mother and I worrying about you for an entire afternoon."

"I was fine," Calvin refuted softly.

"That's not the point. Frankly, I would like to know where you went."

Calvin averted his eyes to his still shaking legs. "Fetterman Park."

"And what did you do there?"

"I don't know, just thought about things, I guess." There was no chance in the entire world that he would tell Uncle Ken that Sherman had been with him. He would never hear the end of it if he did. Yet, worse, he would lose the old man as his best friend hands down. He would be grounded for life.

"So, you already thought about this?" Ken asked.

"I'm not dumb, Uncle Ken. I know what I did was wrong."

"Yes. It was wrong." Ken's presence was menacing, an absolute polar opposite to what Calvin was used to from him.

Calvin stood up and faced his uncle. The boy could feel the Voice strengthening him. He felt powerful. Fearless. Ken lost his authority.

"I'm not talking about it anymore," Calvin told him.

Ken grabbed Calvin's hand and tried to pull him back down to the bed. "Yes, you are!" he reprimanded.

Calvin yanked his hand out of his uncle's grip and flashed him a disgusted look. He didn't need this. Neither of them did. The Voice encouraged the boy's anger.

Victoria was in the kitchen, finishing off her Screwdriver, when she heard Calvin stomping down the hall towards her. She set her glass down. Her son marched up to her so that his face was only mere inches from hers.

"Tell Uncle Ken to leave me alone, Mom," Calvin said, his fists clenched.

"What—" she began then looked past Calvin to Ken who was already right behind her son. "What's going on? What happened?"

Ken loomed over Calvin. "You're son is being disrespectful and rude. I was trying to talk to him about his outburst at church today and he started talking back to me."

"Calvin?" she said, looking into her son's eyes. A hint of worry showed in her complexion.

The boy swung around and faced Ken, pointing, and raised his voice. "I told him I don't want to talk about it. I know what I did was wrong, but he won't let it go."

Victoria placed her forefingers on her temples, letting out a small sigh. Ken knew that she wasn't prepared to handle this. He saw the empty glass of orange juice on the table. He could smell the alcohol. Ken turned and addressed the boy, pushing his own authority to its maximum.

"Do you see what I mean?" He gestured to Victoria. "Look at how upset your mother is getting, Calvin. Come on, let's go back to your room so we can talk."

From the corner of Calvin's eye he could see Sherman standing in the corner of the kitchen. The boy allowed a few tears trickle down his cheek before tightening his jaw. He glared at Ken and took a step toward him. "You are not my dad! I didn't make her cry!"

A hot sting shot through Ken's heart as his nephew said the one thing to him that he had hoped he never would. Calvin stomped off out of the kitchen. Ken stood motionless for a moment before putting a comforting hand on Victoria's shoulder. She touched it with her fingers.

Ken left the kitchen to go after Calvin. Around the corner of the hall, he saw that Calvin's door was partially open. When he peered through the small crack in the doorway, he saw Calvin with his face buried deep in his pillow, muttering something between sobs.

He abruptly decided to just let Calvin be for now. It would be best to tackle the issue when everyone was calm. He turned away from the door.

Out of the corner of his eye, he could have sworn he saw someone sitting beside the boy.

Chapter Twenty-Nine

"How is he?" Dr. Woodrose asked, eyes pointing sharply through his thick, square-rimmed glasses. He was standing in the observation room of the Intensive Care Unit at Hans Memorial.

The physician on call in the ICU, Dr. Connelly, raised his eyebrows and released a heavy sigh. "See for yourself."

With a chubby hand, Dr. Connelly pulled back a curtain revealing a two-way mirror that looked into the private room that Harry Thomas was in. The doctor pulled his squat physique to the side, allowing his colleague to peak through the glass. Dr. Woodrose took a step forward and placed a hand on his chin.

Through the glass he saw his patient lying unconscious upon a bed, slightly propped up, tubes entering every orifice. Beside Harry a heart monitor beeped steadily, and beside that, an artificial lung machine exhaled a soft wheeze with every pump. Harry had an intravenous unit plugged into his left arm, feeding his body with morphine to kill the pain.

After having spoken with Harry the other night, Dr. Woodrose had left the Y-3 Unit and had a coffee in the cafeteria to ponder the new self-realization regarding his approach to caring for patients. Once the second cup had been drunk and through the fog of a fatigued mind, he concluded that he would return to Harry's room and apologize. This time, he would make the effort to listen to whatever it was that was weighing Harry down.

Dr. Woodrose had left the cafeteria and returned to Harry's room, tapped lightly on his door, hoping that Harry would still be awake. When no answer came, he thought he would go in to make sure that his patient was sleeping peacefully. Upon opening the door, a jolt of terror fired through him when he saw Harry slumped on the floor, his clothes saturated with blood, a pen protruding from deep in his neck.

This moment of paralyzing shock caused Dr. Woodrose to delay in checking to see if Harry was alive. He wasn't certain how much time had passed while he stood looking down on Harry's body, absorbing the sight and wondering what had happened. Eventually he had snapped out of it and hurried to Harry's side to check for a pulse. It had been faint but Harry was still alive. Thank God. Examining further, he also noticed that Harry's wrist had been slashed open, almost all the way up to the elbow.

Adrenaline coursing through his system, Dr. Woodrose sprang for Harry's bed and found the emergency buzzer next to the pillow. He pressed it repeatedly then went back to attending Harry. Within seconds, four nurses stormed into the room. Two of them went directly for Harry's body while the other two left to seek outside aid. Dr. Woodrose was then separated from his patient while the nurses worked to stop the bleeding. They had whisked Harry away to the emergency room for immediate surgery.

That night, Dr. Woodrose had driven home with a heavy heart. He stopped off at a bar on the way and drank himself silly. Each sip he took was a subtle prayer that Harry would be all right.

Now, as he stood solemnly in the observation room, Dr. Woodrose watched with blank expression as the green line blipped across the heart monitor.

"Has he regained consciousness?" he asked Dr. Connelly.

"He's only come out of it once, briefly as we were hooking the intravenous up to him. That was late last night. Hopefully, within the next day or so, he should be somewhat coherent," Dr. Connelly told him. "We've been feeding him blood, trying to keep him alive. Thank God for donors."

Dr. Connelly could feel the strain that his coworker was going through.

Dr. Woodrose looked at him hopefully. "Can I go in?"

"Sure."

The pair walked out of the observation room and rounded a quick corner that led to where Harry lay. Dr. Connelly allowed Dr. Woodrose to enter, then left him alone. Dr. Woodrose approached Harry's heavily breathing body and removed his glasses. He looked Harry over from head to toe, a habitual reflex he had when analyzing a person or situation.

Dr. Woodrose leaned on the small, metal railing that bordered Harry's bed.

"Don't know if you can hear me, Harry," he said. "I don't know why your situation bothers me so much. I've had other patients in here, but you…you have somehow managed to change the way I practice my craft. What you said the other night, about me being insensitive, well, it made me think. And you were right. I am insensitive. Too cold and calculating." The doctor's voice cracked on that last word.

He realized that was what his profession had been until Harry: a *craft*. No more, no less. Harry's present circumstance had changed that. Psychiatry was no long a *craft* but a way of *life*. A way of giving.

"I just want to say thank you, Harry. I hope that you can come out of this so you can forgive me for being unfair to you these past years. I would still like to care for you, if you'd let me. Can you hear me?" He leaned closer, his head hovering just above Harry's. "Do you hear me? I want to take care of you."

Harry exhaled a wet wheeze.

Taking one final glance over his patient, Dr. Woodrose turned, and left the room.

For Harry Thomas, his doctor's words did not take hold. He was a slave to darkness, having only subtle consciousness. He was aware that he was alive, but as to where he was or even who or *what* he was, he didn't know. Memories of his past were gone, as well as all apprehensions for his future. The ability to reason was no longer present.

Harry was simply existing.

* * *

Wonderful! It was the only way to describe it.

Gwen Reeves had spent almost an entire week in bed resting her body, mind, and spirit. By the time she awoke that Friday morning, despite the stiffness that came from spending so much time in bed, she felt as if she could take on the world—never mind a small child.

The bruises above her middle had started to fade and the formerly unyielding muscles between her legs were beginning to loosen. She wasn't completely sure as to the extent of the internal damage, but she didn't care. She was just happy that she was feeling a hell of a lot better than she had a little less than a week ago.

Celebrating this newfound strength, Gwen popped out of bed and walked briskly to the bathroom to relieve a bladder that had been working hard for sixteen hours to hold everything in. Even while sitting on the toilet bowl she began to laugh, hearing the gush of yellow liquid hit the pool of water beneath her. Today was a good day and the heavy toil of her entire venture to Toronto seemed smaller.

Back in the main area of her motel room, Gwen dove for her package of cigarettes. Holding it, she stared at the pack like a child discovering a new toy. To her surprise, she didn't crave the contents anymore. She placed the box back down on the table and started to get dressed. It was an unusual sensation to get dressed without first smoking a cigarette.

"Soon so very soon, I'll be home..." Gwen sang to herself.

Her mind set was such that for the few minutes that it took her to put her clothes on, she almost forgot why she was in Toronto to begin with. When she remembered, a shudder flew up and down her spine.

It's too late to turn back now. After all, I feel better. I should just do this and get it over with, she told herself. Saying those words made her feel better. *Marty. My Marty. I should call him. Why not? I can do it.*

Before spending the week resting, she had moved the phone over to the table, turning off the ringer. Gwen did not want any disturbances while she slept. Surprisingly, the motel management hadn't come banging on her door asking for a week's worth of stay.

On the chair next to the table, Gwen sat down and crossed her legs. She gave her cigarettes another glance. A subtle craving for them stirred, but nothing that she couldn't simply dismiss.

She picked up the phone and dialed Marty's number. After a few rings someone answered.

"Hello?" a female voice came through.

"Uh—hello," Gwen returned. There was a pause before she realized that the voice on the other end was Marty's mother. Evidently, they were back from their vacation. "Oh, hi. Sorry about that. Forgot when you guys were coming home. It's Gwen. Is Marty there?"

"Hi, Gwen. Actually, no, he isn't. We just got home a few nights ago and there was a note on the kitchen table saying that he was going to spend a few days at your place. Why? Isn't he there?"

The hard smack of an invisible hand hit Gwen in the chest. What was Mrs. Bones talking about? Gwen swallowed a lump in her throat. Her hands started to shake.

"Um…no, he's not or at least I don't know why he would be there. I've been out of town the past little while," she said.

"That's odd. Maybe I should give him a call," Mrs. Bones returned.

"No, it's all right. I'll do it. I just don't know why he's there. Thanks, Mrs. Bones. Hope your vacation went well," Gwen said, puzzled.

"It did. Thanks, Gwen," Mrs. Bones replied.

"Sure, bye," Gwen said and hung up the receiver.

Right now the cigarettes looked even more appealing.

What the hell is Marty doing at my place? Gwen asked herself. A part of her thought that maybe Marty was in some kind of trouble and he had gone to her apartment for help. Another part of her wondered that maybe after reading her e-mail, he decided he would stay at her place until she got back. She also wondered why he would burden Jenna, Denise, and Carlee by staying there. It would be awkward for them. For Marty, too. Then again, he was a good houseguest. Whatever the reason, she had to find out.

Dialing her phone number felt distant. Her apartment seemed like a life she had left long ago. It didn't even feel like home anymore.

Life in Winnipeg was so simple. So clean. So pure. But in Toronto, she had grown used to the darker lifestyle that was instilled on her. In fact, Gwen found herself enjoying it.

The phone rang several times before someone answered. Gwen recognized the voice immediately. It was Denise.

"Hi, Denise. It's Gwen," she spoke softly, trying to hide her confusion.

"Gwen? Holy shit!" Denise exclaimed.

Gwen had to pull the receiver away from her ear because her friend had reacted so loudly.

"Yes, it's me. Is Marty there?" Gwen asked.

Denise didn't answer.

"Hello?"

"What do you mean?" Denise asked, obviously taken off guard.

"I tried calling Marty and his mom said that he was over at my place."

There was a pause, then, "Um…no."

Gwen knew Denise was lying. What was she trying to hide?

"Seriously, Denise, is he there?"

"I said—" And before Denise could finish, Gwen heard a male voice mumble something in the background.

"Who's that?" Gwen said mockingly. She knew full well who *that* was. Marty.

"Nobody. A friend of Jenna's." Denise's voice wavered.

The male voice spoke up again somewhere in the background.

Gwen decided to continue to play dumb. "Seriously, Denise. Is Marty there?"

The male voice asked who it was. Denise didn't answer him, but Gwen could tell that Denise had mouthed the name "Gwen" to her guest.

She heard the male voice say, "Shit!"

Just then, Marty came on the line. "Hello," he said timidly.

"Hi," Gwen returned, upset over whatever secret Denise and Marty were keeping from her.

Instinctively, she already knew what it was, but her heart wouldn't let her believe it. She shuddered beneath the fear of losing him—losing him to a friend.

"Gwen, I…" he started.

"Are you sleeping with her?" Gwen interrupted, not realizing what she said until after she had said it.

On the other end, Marty was taken aback by the boldness of Gwen's voice.

"Of course not," Marty said softly. Love filled his tone and sorrow cracked his voice.

For a brief instant Gwen believed him, but one thing that she had learned over the past few weeks was not to trust anybody. Nothing was ever what it seemed.

Gwen's voice broke, becoming thick with disappointment and false hope. "Marty, tell me the truth. If you are sleeping with Denise, I need to know."

The phone line fell silent, the mood growing somber. A blanket of tears hovered on Marty's breath.

"Yes," he said.

Gwen closed her eyes, a tear spilling down her cheek.

She hung up the phone.

Two provinces away, Marty Bones kept the receiver to his ear until he heard the dial tone. He knew it was over.

Without hesitation, Gwen reached for her cigarettes and frantically pulled one out and lit it.

You can't trust anyone, she thought. *Not even Marty. My Marty.*

She would sit in that chair for an hour then throw on her jacket and drive to the city.

She needed a gun.

* * *

Marty, tell me the truth. If you are sleeping with Denise, I need to know. Marty, tell me the truth. If you are sleeping with Denise, I need to know. Marty, tell me the truth. Gwen's words kept echoing in his mind. When Gwen had hung up on him, Marty had held the receiver tightly to his ear until he heard nothing but the steady drone of the dial tone.

Denise, who sat on the orange chair next to the phone, looked at him with heavy eyes. She turned her head away from him and stared out the window.

Hanging up the phone, Marty looked at her then glanced at the door. He knew that Denise wanted him to leave. He knew that Gwen would want him to leave, too.

Denise, Gwen, himself—all of them—they would figure this out later.

Right now he needed to think.

Chapter Thirty

Ken awoke to the shrill ring of the telephone. It was almost two in the morning and he had been asleep. Lazily, he reached from the bed and picked up the receiver.

"Hello?" he said, drowsiness in his voice.

The line was quiet, but Ken could hear thick, labored breathing come from the other end. Only on one other occasion had he ever received a phone call like this. He knew immediately who it was: Victoria—his sister.

"Vic, what's wrong? What's happened?" he asked soothingly.

Before she could answer, he covered up the receiver so he could speedily hack up late night phlegm without having her hear him do so.

"It's Calvin," she said. "Could you come over? I know it's late but—" She sounded pressing.

"Is he all right?"

"I don't know. I..." She was crying, worried.

He joined her in her concern. "Okay. Give me twenty minutes or so."

"Thanks, Ken," she said then hung up.

He set the phone down in the cradle and fell back onto his pillow, rubbing the sleep from his eyes. He hoped everything was all right.

* * *

When Ken arrived at Victoria's place, she welcomed him with a hug, her eyes worn with tears. She urged him to keep his voice down because Calvin had finally fallen asleep. Keeping that in mind, Ken was led into the kitchen.

Not used to drinking coffee so late at night, Ken opted for tea with a dash of milk, no sugar. Victoria chose coffee for herself. As she was preparing it, Ken noticed that she was trying to hide that she was adding something to her cup from a bottle. From where Ken was sitting it looked like what he was sure was Irish Cream.

A creamer nonetheless, he thought with a wry grin.

"Thanks again. I really appreciate you coming over. I'm sorry that it's so late," she said as she seated herself and set the hot drinks down in front of them.

"It's all right. Tell me what happened," Ken replied.

Victoria wrapped her hands around her mug, feeling its warmth tingle all the way up her arms. "When the sitter dropped Calvin home from school, he went to his room saying that he was tired and that he wanted to lie down. But, after, oh, I don't know, a half hour or so, I heard him singing to himself. Normally he doesn't do that unless he hears a song at school that he can't get out of his head, but as I listened to the words," she paused and sipped her coffee, obviously looking disgusted at the memory, "I knew he *couldn't* have learned that song at school."

Ken furrowed his brow. "What did he say?"

"I don't think I should repeat it."

"I see," he said, then, "I would like to understand, Victoria." He reached out a hand and curled it around hers.

She took another sip from her coffee and another recoil in disgust. "You will find the words offensive, I assure you. Are you sure?"

He nodded. Victoria glanced in the direction of Calvin's bedroom then back at the table. She took a moment to remember all that Calvin had hummed.

She sang, "Mary had a little son, little son, little son. Mary had a little son that drained me of my fun. Everywhere from there I went, there I went, there I went. Everywhere from there I went, blood leaked out my gun."

She closed her eyes as if to absorb the moment.

Discomfort surfaced within Ken. He didn't like Victoria's "song" and was ashamed that his nephew would sing such a thing. He wasn't able to let anything out save for a heavy sigh in response.

"I know," she agreed with his sigh and watched as Ken took a sip from his tea. "I went to his bedroom to tell him that what he was singing was wrong, but when I opened the door, I found him fast asleep. I tried waking him, but you know Calvin, he sleeps like a rock. I couldn't wake him up so I left the room thinking I, for whatever reason, was hearing things. And on my way back here, I heard him singing again. Immediately, I ran to his room, but found the same thing. He was sleeping. I was scared. No, scared is not the right word. Unsettled. Either I was finally losing my mind and hearing things or..." She paused. "...That something was wrong with Calvin."

Ken took her in with concerned eyes. He didn't know what to believe because either one of Victoria's suggestions could be right. Especially the suggestion that something was going on with Calvin. His behavior at church still troubled Ken. He could still vividly remember every detail of his nephew's unexplained outburst.

Victoria continued her story. "I went over to the front room and sat on the couch, thinking about all the strange stuff Calvin has been doing. I thought that maybe if I called his doctor, maybe he could explain why

Calvin was behaving this way. I also thought that Dr. Carol might say I was imagining things and would want me to make an appointment with my therapist. When I finally got a hold of Dr. Carol, he said he wasn't sure what to make of it and that he would have to see Calvin himself. He said that it *is* common for kids Calvin's age to say unusual things, usually stuff they've heard in the playground and whatnot, but when I told him what Calvin had said, well, like you, he was speechless. I made an appointment for Monday afternoon. Maybe Dr. Carol could say something to him, or at least offer an explanation."

Exhausted from all she had said, Victoria produced her package of cigarettes from the pocket of her yellow bathrobe, and lit one up. Ken could see the stress in her posture and eyes. There was no way that Victoria could keep this up much longer. She had never been good at dealing with stressful circumstances, and since the divorce, handling stress had become so difficult that she would usually break down crying before finding a solution to the problem.

"I think that's a good idea," Ken said, referring to Calvin's visit to the doctor. "But what about you, Vic? How are *you* feeling? I can only imagine what you're going through right now."

She placed her head on her hand, leaning on it, taking heavy drags off her cigarette. "I don't know how I feel, and that's just me being honest. I know my breaking point and all I can say is that it's not far off." She watched her cigarette burn. "I hate living this way."

Ken remained quiet, allowing Victoria to bare her heart.

"It's just that—that ever since David left, I can't seem to do *anything*. You've heard all this before but I can't help it. I thought having Calvin in my life might do me some good and it has, don't get me wrong, but I just never expected this. Feeling so empty. Sometimes—actually, *most* times—suicidal." Her cigarette wasn't done but she stubbed it out anyway and lit another. "Maybe I should just stick to the hope that Calvin's going through a phase or that maybe he heard something and he's repeating it, or maybe that he's copying some other kid's behavior. What if Dr. Carol finds something truly wrong with him, Ken? What if Calvin has a mental illness of some sort? It would all be my fault. I-I'm such a terrible mother to him. It would all be my fault!"

She choked back her tears, trying to be strong, and gazed off to somewhere in the kitchen.

"Shh, Victoria, don't say that," Ken said. He steered the conversation in a more positive direction. It would be easier on her. "You're a great mother. Calvin loves you, Vic. I do, too."

She looked back to him. "Great mother, huh? Yeah, right. What if Calvin has picked up on my behavior and this is *his* way of showing it?"

She burst into sobs. Ken reached across the table and set a comforting hand on her shoulder. She handed him her cigarette, which he took, and stubbed out in the ashtray. For several minutes she cried.

Victoria felt heavy, as if someone was tugging on her innards and pulling them down to her feet. All she could think about was the day when David had come home and confessed to having an affair, and told her he was leaving her. All Victoria saw right now was images of her life alone.

Then she saw images of Calvin. His smile. Him holding his basketball. Him and her holding each other as mother and son, the late nights where they had watched Disney movies together. The memories were too much. Victoria started to shake. Ken came around to the other side of the table and held her. His embrace didn't make the pain go away. .

It was all her fault.

The two of them sat at the kitchen table absorbing the silence, Ken allowing Victoria to settle down. She was grateful to him for being there. His presence was what she needed. Hope seemed to emanate from him. A certain *peace* that she felt only when he was around.

It took almost twenty minutes before she had stopped crying. Victoria sat, tired, with tear-burned eyes, puffing a cigarette. She was sipping her third cup of coffee spiked with Irish Cream. Ken was only on his second cup of tea.

The silence was broken by the lilt of a child singing. Immediately Victoria shot Ken a glance. Heart pace quickening, he put a reassuring hand on her shoulder, got up from the table, and went to Calvin's room. For a five year old, Calvin had a delightful singing voice, but his choice in lyrics was not.

Mary had a little son, little son, little son. Mary had a little son that drained me of my fun. Everywhere from there I went, there I went, there I went. Everywhere from there I went, blood leaked out my gun.

Without knocking on the door, Ken quietly entered Calvin's room, hoping to catch him in the act of singing. Just like Victoria had, Ken found Calvin fast asleep.

Ken knelt beside Calvin's bed and gently shook him. "Calvin?"

The child didn't move.

Ken got up to leave. Before he reached the door he heard the boy calling him.

"Uncle Ken, what are you doing?"

Ken turned around. "I heard singing coming from your room. Did you hear anything?"

The boy shook his head.

"Go back to sleep, Calvin," he told him, and then closed the door. Remaining outside the room, Ken stood with his ear to the door, waiting for Calvin to resume his singing. His nephew's behavior troubled him.

For several minutes, Calvin had remained quiet. Ken stepped back from the door, about to return to Victoria. Then it began again: *Mary had a little son, little son, little son. Mary had a little son that drained me of my fun. Everywhere from—*

Ken threw open the door and found Calvin lying on his back, sleeping, his small lips mouthing the rest of the verse:—*there I went, there I went, there I went. Everywhere from there I went, blood leaked out my gun.*

The boy was fast asleep again. Ken, partly proud that he had caught Calvin singing, debated whether or not he should wake him again. He felt that something was very wrong. He couldn't place it, but somewhere in the room, something lingered in the air that did not belong there. Something elusive and foreboding. There was only one thing that he could do.

Again, he knelt beside Calvin and placed a large hand on the boy's forehead. "Father, watch over him. Help us find out what is happening here, and I ask Your protection over Calvin tonight. In Jesus's Name, I pray. Amen."

Ken returned to the kitchen, his posture heavy. It appeared that Victoria hadn't moved since he had left. She still wore the same blank expression on her face, her coffee mug seeming not to have been touched, the same amount of coffee remaining in her cup. The only difference was that her cigarette had burned to the filter.

Sitting down on the chair next to her, Ken looked her straight in the eyes. "Victoria, I caught Calvin singing."

For a moment it didn't register but her eyes fluttered when the words had sunk in. "You did, huh?"

"Yes."

"Did you talk to him?" she asked, her eyes still not moving from the table in front of her.

"Yes, I did. And I strongly recommend that you keep that appointment with his doctor Monday," he told her.

Already Ken could see worried crinkles forming above her brow. He wasn't sure how to say what needed to be said next, but he had no choice. He'd rather comfort Victoria now instead of later, should Calvin be diagnosed with an illness of some sort. Ken drew in a thick breath and breathed out, focusing his eyes on hers, trying to appear reassuring.

"I don't think Calvin knows that he's singing. He said he didn't hear anything when I told him I had heard singing coming from his room. It's one thing to mumble in your sleep, but to form the same coherent melody over and over again, well, I'm not sure what would cause that." He thought about suggesting the possibility of supernatural powers at play, but decided against it. Victoria was not a believer in spiritual warfare, let alone a demonic presence manifesting itself in the natural world.

Ken waited a moment and allowed his words to hit her heart. He hated upsetting her, but right now he didn't have much of a choice. He himself had been worried about Calvin's well being. Some of the things the boy had told him made him concerned. *Especially that day that Calvin and I had played WAR,* he thought. *Calvin spoke of three sixes in a row and how that's the way things always are.*

Once the mood settled some and it was agreed that Ken would accompany Victoria and Calvin to Dr. Carol's office, Victoria walked Ken to the front door and thanked him for coming over.

"Are you sure you don't want me to stay the night?" he offered.

"I'm sure. I don't want to be rude or anything, but I think I just need to go to bed and deal with this tomorrow. Thanks again for coming over. Be sure to get some sleep, okay?" she said half convincingly.

Ken shrugged, then hugged Victoria good-bye. "All right. Take care. I'll call you in the morning."

"Sure," she said, and closed the door.

As he was putting his keys into the ignition, Ken saw a dark flutter in his rearview mirror. When he turned around, he didn't see anything.

He peered out the rear window of his truck and saw an old man walking down Rainygravel Road.

Chapter Thirty-One

This place should be sanitized, Ken thought. He was sitting in the waiting room of the children's ward in St. Peter's Hospital. Scrunching his nose at the smell, he looked over at Calvin. The boy shifted in the seat beside him, obviously smelling it, too. Even though children were the only ones looked after in this section of St.Peter's, the waiting room still smelled like that of the elderly. The smell made Calvin uncomfortable, reminding him of the group of old people that had sat in front of him that horrible morning at church.

The only older person he knew that didn't smell bad was Sherman.

Ken and Calvin were waiting for Victoria to come out of Dr. Carol's office and alert Calvin to his turn at seeing the doctor. Victoria, no doubt because she was Calvin's mother, had been invited into the doctor's office first, despite Ken's insistence that Dr. Carol should see the three of them at once. The good doctor, Victor Carol, said that it was best to hear what was happening from each person separately. He said that that way, from his experience, a more coherent picture of the situation could be formed, instead of he meeting with everybody at once, where, in the heat of discussion, they would inevitably begin to feed information off each other, distorting the true issue at hand.

Across the waiting room was a carpeted play corner meant to keep the children busy while the parents waited for a nurse to call out their son or daughter's name.

"Would you like to go over there and play?" Ken asked Calvin, pointing at the play corner with his index finger.

Calvin looked at the play corner and saw that only one other little boy was playing there with a toy dirt-digger. Calvin didn't like being with too many children at once, but since there would be only two of them in that little corner, he decided to go over. Besides, anything would beat the boredom of waiting with Uncle Ken while smelling the rotten egg odor of old people.

"Sure," Calvin said quietly.

He walked across the tiled floor and crossed into the carpeted area, Ken watching all the while. Calvin walked past the other child who was perhaps two or three years old. The little tike watched with blue eyes and dirty cheeks as Calvin headed straight for the construction blocks.

Keeping to himself, Calvin started to build. Every few minutes, Calvin would look up at the kid and furrow his brow, each time knowing that the other little boy was constantly watching him. When Calvin finished his structure he looked up at the kid again.

"What?" Calvin asked, slightly annoyed.

"'Ou're s'ary," the little boy said and abruptly left the playroom.

Calvin, hurt by what the child had said, peered out into the waiting room, watching as the little tike ran up to his mom, hugging her leg. Calvin hated that stupid kid. That kid should rot in—

Calvin, his thoughts changing suddenly, shifted his gaze to his brand new creation. With the limited pieces that he had, he managed to build a building of some sort, one that kind of reminded him of a building he had passed on the ride over to the hospital.

Just then Ken came over. "What do you got there?"

"I don't know. A building." Calvin showed him the building, smiling.

"It looks good and it didn't take you that long, either."

"No, I guess not," Calvin said, his chin resting on an uplifted knee. He thought about telling Uncle Ken about what the other kid had told him, but decided against it. It wasn't his uncle's business and he had gotten used to kids referring to him as *scary* or as a *monster*.

Before Ken could sit down on the carpeted floor beside him, Victoria appeared, placing a hand on Ken's shoulder.

"It's your turn," she said. Ken nodded and got up to leave.

"Calvin, do you want to stay here or do you want to sit over there with mommy?" Victoria pointed back to where he and Ken had originally sat.

Calvin shrugged and poked at the corners of his newly built monument.

He wants to be alone, Victoria knew.

"I'll be just over there if you need me, okay?" she told him and left.

Alone, the boy watched as she found a red cushioned seat. She sat down and dabbed at her eyes with a Kleenex. Calvin couldn't help but feel that he had made her cry.

Feeling guilty, Calvin went over to sit with her. He climbed up on the chair beside her then leaned his head on her arm. Victoria stroked his hair gently, bringing him comfort. She could tell that he was upset about being here. She started to tear.

"Why are you crying, Mom?" he asked.

Letting out a sniffle, Victoria said, "Mom's just worried about you, hon."

"Do people cry when they're worried?"

"Sometimes," she said. "Sometimes."

"Does Dr. Carol think I'm a bad boy?" he asked earnestly.

She patted his head more reassuringly. "No, of course not. He's worried about you, too. He's known you for a long time and wants to make sure that you're okay."

Victoria tickled his chest. Calvin giggled. "He's going to take out his special heart-listener and listen to what your heart is saying. Then he's going to take a miniature flashlight and look inside those little ears of yours." Calvin laughed. Victoria laughed, too. "Then he's going to look inside your eyes with his mini-flashlight and see if he can see Donald Duck living inside your head."

He giggled again. It was something that Dr. Carol did that always made Calvin laugh. Ever since his first visit to the doctor's office, Dr. Carol always claimed that he could see Donald Duck living inside his head when he looked into his eyes with the miniature flashlight.

"Is there something wrong with me, Mom?" he asked uneasily. *There is something wrong with me,* he knew.

"Of course not, Calvin. Of course not. We're here to see if Dr. Carol can tell us why you're feeling what you feel, and maybe what we can do to help you." She was trying as best she could to make him feel better.

Calvin squeezed himself against her, soothed by the squeeze she gave him in return. He closed his eyes. He was scared because soon it would be his turn to see Dr. Carol. He didn't like how both his mother and uncle were worried about him. He thought he was doing just fine—except for that little outburst at the church, but he was doing everything that he could to forget about that—and that everyone was overreacting. Maybe Dr. Carol would say that he was A-Okay, showing everyone that they were all wrong about him?

His little heart picked up speed. He wished that Sherman were there with him.

Ken came back. "Okay, Slugger, your turn."

Calvin got an extra squeeze from his mother before he got off the chair. He turned back to look at both of them. "Can't you guys come with me?"

With longing eyes, Victoria looked at him, knowing the answer was that neither Ken nor she could. Ken caught her expression. He extended his hand to Calvin.

"How 'bout I'll walk you to his door, okay? I told Dr. Carol that if you wanted us to be there that he should let us in. Dr. Carol just wants to talk to you first and do a checkup. Okay?"

Disappointed, Calvin took his uncle's hand. "Sure."

Victoria watched her brother take her son past the nurse's desk and turn the corner to where the doctor's office was. Her stomach twisted. She knew that Calvin could feel the tension both she and Ken were feeling. She hoped it wouldn't hurt him in any way.

Dr. Carol greeted Calvin and Ken at the door to his office.

"Howdy, Calvin. How are you?" the doctor asked over-enthusiastically. He shoved his hand in Calvin's face for him to shake.

Calvin scoffed on the inside. Here was another adult who treated him like a baby. The boy took the hand and shook it, giving Dr. Carol a wry smile.

"Come on in, Calvin. Thanks, Ken," he said with a wink. He closed the door and helped Calvin get up onto the examining table.

"It's been a long time since I've seen you, Calvin. How've you been feeling?" Dr. Carol asked, fastening a blood pressure band around Calvin's arm.

His blood pressure checked out okay. Dr. Carol asked the boy to remove his shirt.

"Fine," Calvin said, pulling his T-shirt over his head. He got tangled in it, Dr. Carol having to help him take it off.

Within five minutes the doctor had given Calvin a complete physical. Everything checked out normal. As Calvin put his shirt back on, Dr. Carol settled down in a chair across from him. Calvin noticed that the doctor didn't mention anything about seeing Donald Duck inside his head.

"Why do you want to see me?" the boy asked.

"Well, your mom called me on Friday saying that she was worried about you," he explained. "Do you know why that might be?"

Calvin bowed his head, his legs swinging back and forth off the edge of the examining table. "Everybody has been acting weird around me. They think something's wrong with me."

"Do you know why they've been acting...weird...around you?"

"What did Mom tell you?" Calvin asked back, vulnerable, frightened.

"Well," Dr. Carol leaned forward in his chair, "they told me that you've been getting upset a lot over the past little while. It's okay, Calvin. It's okay to get upset. I'm just wondering if you can remember a time where you got upset, and your mom or your uncle might have been worried."

Calvin glared at him. What did Dr. Carol want?

The doctor continued. "Let me ask you something, have you ever hit yourself or anybody else when you were angry?"

"No!" Calvin shot back, thinking that it had been a dumb question. Why would he hit himself anyway? Maybe he'd hit that kid that told him he was scary, but not himself. No sir. That was just stupid.

"What about making a big mess when you lost your temper?" Dr. Carol gave him a knowing glance.

Calvin shifted in his seat, the thin paper on the examining table scrunching and crumpling beneath him.

He flashed back to the horrific episode at Uncle Ken's church. Ever since it had happened, Calvin was only able to remember bits and pieces of the events that had taken place. There was something about the way Dr. Carol poised the question that jogged his memory. The boy remembered feeling powerful when he stood up on the pew and how that power grew when he yelled at the priest. He remembered standing up high, like he ruled over everyone, and there was nothing that anyone could do to stop him. He also remembered giving a speech of some sort that had climaxed with him spitting on a big letter T.

Calvin's face flushed red. Dr. Carol knew that he had struck a chord with the boy.

"Was there a time, Calvin?" the doctor urged.

Calvin shrugged. "Just once."

Over the next couple of minutes Calvin told Dr. Carol about what had happened, as best he could. Happy that the boy was starting to open up a little, Dr. Carol asked if there was anything else he had supposedly done but had a hard time remembering. Calvin, at ease with the questioning, told his doctor that Uncle Ken had said something to him about how he had said something weird when they had played WAR. The boy also mentioned that both his mother and uncle thought they heard him singing songs.

The other night, when Ken had been over, Calvin had awoken to his mother's crying. Quietly, with an ear to his bedroom door, he listened as they spoke about him in the kitchen. It made him sick to his stomach. He was hurt. Why would his mother talk about him when he wasn't around? Calvin didn't recall singing anything, but because his mother had said he did, he couldn't help feel that he might have sung something without realizing it. Mom was usually right when it came to identifying that he had done something he shouldn't have.

Calvin stopped talking and watched as Dr. Carol scrawled something down in his notebook.

The doctor looked up and placed his pen down on the desk beside him. "Does it make you feel bad that your mom and uncle think these things about you?"

"Yeah," Calvin said softly. He wanted to cry.

Dr. Carol, judging by Calvin's grimace, could see that Calvin didn't want to answer any more questions. He didn't want to end up interrogating the poor kid. He decided that he would ask one more question then that would be it.

"Calvin, do you know a guy named Sherman?"

The boy's pulse froze. How did the doctor know about Sherman? *Oh no,* Calvin panicked, *what did Mom tell him about Sherman? I thought Mom forgot about him.*

"Y-yes, sir," the boy stuttered out. Every time he was forced to tell the truth, he always stuttered his words. He would also speak more politely than normal.

"Okay," the doctor agreed, noticing the sudden tension coming from the boy.

"Why?" Calvin asked, now worried more than ever.

"No reason. Your mother just said you met someone with that name. I just wanted to see if it was true."

"You didn't believe her?" Calvin refuted.

The doctor smirked when the boy tried to turn the tables on him. He was clever for a little one. "I believed her. I just wanted to be sure, that's all."

"You didn't believe her?" Calvin repeated, frowning.

"I believed her, Calvin. We'll just leave it at that."

The boy rolled his eyes. Inside his head he heard Sherman's soothing voice calm him, urging him to stop fighting with the doctor. *We wouldn't want Dr. Carol thinking I was causing any problems now, would we, Calvin?*

"No," Calvin said, agreeing with Sherman.

"Excuse me?" Dr. Carol asked.

"Nothing."

After saying good-bye to Dr. Carol, Calvin slowly walked back into the waiting room. When he approached his mother and uncle, he didn't say anything, grabbed his coat, and put it on.

"So, how'd it go?" Uncle Ken asked.

"Fine," Calvin muttered and started walking towards the exit.

"Ken," Victoria said, her heart sinking, "I hope we did the right thing today."

Upset that she had somehow hurt Calvin's feelings, Victoria looked toward Ken, who had already started to follow Calvin. Ken glanced back and gave her a small smile.

Instead of catching up with them, she returned to Dr. Carol's office to see if he had an opinion that might help the situation.

She tapped the frame of the doorway before she entered. Dr. Carol was sitting at his desk, looking over Calvin's file.

"Dr. Carol?" she said, gaining his attention. He looked up.

"Victoria, please, have a seat," he said, gesturing to the extra chair that sat beside his desk.

Victoria sat down. She didn't have to say anything to prompt him to speak.

"Victoria, let me first tell you that you have nothing to be worried about. I'm sure you already presumed this, but Calvin is just going through a normal stage right now. He hears things all day from the kids at school, the teachers, television—it's a long list. Basically, he's just trying to expand his thoughts and words, but somehow feels that others are rejecting him, thus making it hard for him to do so."

Victoria almost interrupted by saying that she had never rejected her son, but she didn't.

Dr. Carol went on. "What I'm saying is that this will probably blow over in a couple of weeks and he'll find his niche in his life as a child." He paused and gave her a reassuring smile. "He'll be fine."

Victoria nodded, accepting the doctor's opinion. It had made sense, but, still, something about it didn't sit right. She couldn't place it, but something told her that Calvin was going through more than just a simple phase.

Chapter Thirty-Two

Lying in bed that afternoon, Marty Bones felt as if all that was wrong with the world was pressing against his heart. He had skipped school that day and tried his best to escape a painful reality by sleeping as much of it away as possible. It was no use. His body wouldn't allow him to sleep another wink. The pain that dug deep in his heart kept him awake. His only comfort came from believing wholeheartedly in Gwen's love for him and that, together, somehow, they would manage to work through this. They had to. He loved her.

"How could I have been so stupid?" Marty demanded to himself, self-hate wrenching his stomach. His feelings for Denise had subsided the instant he heard Gwen's voice on the phone, and at that moment, he knew that *she* knew that he had cheated on her. He was also aware that Denise was upset with him, too. Whatever it was that had drawn him to her had disappeared. All of it.

Gwen was his girlfriend. Not Denise.

Girlfriend. Hmmph, can I even call Gwen that, now? **Marty** wondered. *It would be something of a break if I knew what she was feeling or if she will even bother to come home. I'm such a fuck!*

He rolled over onto his side, his eyes catching sight of the picture of him and Gwen that he kept by his bed. He stared at it, taking in every facet of her, remembering how much he loved every part of her, both inside and out. Squeezing his eyes shut, Marty clenched his pillow. He would never be able to be with her again.

It would take a miracle, he thought.

* * *

Watching television had never been such a chore, but it was the only thing that she could do to try to escape what had happened between her and Marty.

Denise had escaped to her bedroom and spent the entire afternoon safely hiding in her bed. With remote in hand, she flipped aimlessly through the channels, hoping that she would find something that would catch her interest. All that was on were soap operas and meaningless game shows with adults playing games that a two year old child could easily conquer.

Denise glanced to the empty pillow to her right, recalling when Marty had slept there beside her.

I don't know what the hell I was thinking. He had a girlfriend for fuck's sake! she said to herself. *When Gwen comes home I'll have no choice but to move out. Hell, she won't even want to be my friend after what I did. Shit—*

"—I didn't even like him!" she blurted aloud.

Denise punched the bunched up blanket between her legs, slouched her position, and turned the television off. In the next room she could hear Jenna and Carlee talking. The two of them thought she was in her bedroom because she had a headache. They were still in the dark as to what had happened between her and Marty.

Jenna would throw a fit if she found out, Denise thought. As for what Carlee might think about the whole situation, she didn't know. Carlee had had her fair share of guys in her lifetime. Even two-timed one, if Denise recalled correctly.

She wished she could talk to Marty. No, he didn't want to hear hide nor hair of her. He must be furious.

I'm just gonna have to wait it out, she told herself, and closed her eyes.

* * *

Gwen spent that morning lying in bed, dwelling on her problems. It was something that she and Marty had in common: when things got bad—hide under your covers and hope to God the storm passes you by.

Around noon, Gwen got out of bed and lay in the bathtub for a whole hour. The hot water soothed her sore muscles, feeling wonderful against her skin. She consciously tried to relax her body, but she was antsy. Today was the day when she would make good on the mission Harry had charged her with.

Harry had been with her, hiding, in the back of her mind ever since she had arrived in Toronto. Suddenly his presence was noticeably missing. *Is he all right?* Gwen asked herself repeatedly. She hoped that all was well back at Hans Memorial Hospital. A part of her even looked forward to going back there and reporting to Harry that she had succeeded in killing the boy. *Then again, he might get mad. I still don't know why Harry wanted to call this whole thing off. Still, it has to be done.*

A knot formed in her stomach when she realized the truth in that thought. It *did* have to be done. Gwen couldn't believe that she was looking forward to killing the child.

What has happened to me? she wondered. *I'm—I'm—*She wanted to say that she was a killer but could not speak, or think, the words.

After all that had happened: the bizarre meeting with Harry, the nightmares, the desperate struggle to survive as she prepared to kill the boy, her torture at the hands of Robin and Mr. Gray—after all of it—her perception on reality, and herself, had changed.

She was no longer just a simple girl from Winnipeg who did only what was necessary to get through life. Now, Gwen had an incredible sense of meaning and purpose and any doubt that she had about her place in the world had vanished. Completely.

Gwen got out of the tub and dried herself off. She looked into the mirror and stared at the face looking back at her. Damp, brown hair flowed gently down the sides of her face, curling in little wisps on her shoulders. Her once bright hazel eyes had the life sucked out of them. They seemed somehow darker, more distant. Even her once soft pursed lips had become worn and thin.

She had become a warrior indeed. Damaged but strong. Determined and merciless.

* * *

Surfing through the Yellow Pages, Gwen had managed to find exactly what she was looking for—Uncle Bob's Smokin' Barrels, a gun shop on the other side of the city. From the description of the store in the ad, Gwen knew that good ol' Uncle Bob would have the type of gun she was looking for.

What type of gun am I looking for, anyway,? she thought, smirking. *Something simple, but effective.*

She would leave for Uncle Bob's shortly.

* * *

Gwen took the Saturn out along the Don Valley Parkway then merged with the speeding traffic. The combination of the smooth ride of the car and the rays of sunlight streaming through the windows relaxed her. It was as if she were freeing herself from the weight of the motel room, and the weight of her past, the further she drove north.

Instinctively, she turned on the radio. Driving for Gwen Reeves had never been complete unless music echoed throughout the car. Rarely would she prefer absolute silence. Quiet times were reserved for when she had to think and indulge herself in personal reflection.

The speakers blared with rock and roll, the steady beat of the drums and clashing of the cymbals adding to her *freedom* sensation. Hearing the song reminded her of the time she had driven with Marty to Beausejour for ice cream and all that was on the radio was classic rock. She changed the channel. It was country music. *No thanks,* Gwen thought. She changed the channel again and enjoyed a few songs that rang with the heavy, thump-

thump-thumping, beat of dance music. Then came "With Or Without You" from U2. Despite her desire to change the station, she didn't. This song was special to her. It had played in the background the first time she and Marty had ever slow danced together.

Without warning, tears started to stream down her face. The horrific realization surfaced that, when she got home, she and Marty might not be dating anymore. That thought hadn't struck her until now. Gwen pictured Denise, and Marty having sex together. Gwen could see the pleasure in his eyes as he took her, Denise all the while emitting a seductive smile while she betrayed Gwen.

Gwen's heart sank. She wiped the tears from her eyes. She pulled the Saturn over on the shoulder of the highway and turned the radio off. Bowing her head, Gwen let herself cry and suffer in silence as the other cars on the Parkway sped past her.

Why, Marty? Why? How could you? she asked over and over again. The tears streamed forth stronger now. And as if watching a film, Gwen could see all that had happened over the past few weeks. She could see herself sitting in school getting an assignment from Mr. Parks; her meeting with Harry; her fight with Marty; her plane ride to Toronto. She remembered the nightmare about the child in the bathtub and the time she staked-out the boy's house. She watched as the old man and Robin took turns on her. There was the awesome pain between her legs, the bruises, her swollen cheek. Marty's voice saying, "Of course not," then "Yes," when she had asked if he was having an affair with Denise.

Gwen cried. Hard. She had been wrong when she thought she could handle this task. Wrong about being ready to kill the boy. All was far worse. Far more demanding. Far more impossible. The toll of tragedy and the pain of betrayal—by Harry, by Marty, by Denise, by Robin, by the old man—set in full strength, her mind and body trembling under its weight. Then, as if the complete opposite of blessed relief—

—her spirit broke.

Her heart broke.

Her mind broke.

All was nothing, and nothing was everything.

For a solid hour on the side of the road, a solid hour of relived memories and regrets, Gwen let the pain take her, have its way with her, finally…destroy her.

For such a long time she had somehow managed to suppress these horrible experiences but she could only deny what she felt for so long before breaking. Her pain, her loss, the violation of her body, and the sacrifice of herself for taking on such a foolish pursuit—all of it came pouring out. She could do nothing but grieve.

* * *

A good while later, somewhat composed, Gwen took her package of cigarettes off the dashboard and got out of the car. She leaned against its exterior and smoked two cigarettes, doing her best not to cry, trying to stay strong.

"Fuck you, Harry," she told him sternly, as if he were there. "Fuck you! Fuck you! Fuck you!" It was *his* fault. All of it. Fucking crazy bastard!

She took another drag off her cigarette, recalling the last time she was forced to pull her car over to the side of the road. It had been that night when she had seen that gothic vision of Harry sitting in the back seat of her car.

"Fuck you, Harry," she repeated numbly, and dropped her cigarette butt on the pavement.

Gwen got back in the car and waited for the traffic to clear. She wanted to go home but she knew that she couldn't. Not yet, anyway. *It all Harry's fault,* Gwen decided. *It's all Harry's fault!*

She pulled back into traffic and found comfort in the fact that by tomorrow night this would finally be over. She would finally be able to go home.

Chapter Thirty-Three

Without breaking pulse, the heart monitor stationed beside the bed of Harry Thomas kept beeping. All the doctors that had been assigned to Harry's recovery were amazed that he was still alive after what had happened to him.

The arterial damage to both his neck and arm was severe. Harry, when first conscious, was told that the pen from his neck had been successfully removed, and that his arm had been stitched up. He was also informed that he was scheduled for another operation tomorrow afternoon. He was also advised that there was permanent damage to his neck and arm, but as to the extent of the damage, it was still too early to tell. Reassuring him, the hospital staff, especially Dr. Connelly, said that they would help him through therapy once he was healthy enough to move around and had some of his strength recovered.

It was early evening and Harry had roused from a day of fitful sleeping. Remembering that Dr. Connelly had told him every time he awoke he was to page a nurse with the beeper that was clipped to the thin white blanket that covered him, Harry reached for the device and pressed the red button on its top. After pressing it, he waited. A nurse would be along shortly.

While he waited his thoughts drifted toward Gwen. Guilt and fear pricked at his mind. Because of what Sherman had done to him, Harry knew that it would be nothing compared to what Sherman would do to Gwen if, and when, she decided to kill the child. Sherman would not let her succeed. All of Hell's money was on Calvin Mandalay.

That is why Sherman is here, Harry concluded. *He is here to protect and train the boy for his task. Satan was clever on this one. I wonder if he knew about me and that I would contact Gwen?*

A strained wheeze exited his lungs. Harry scrunched his nose under the uncomfortable feeling of the tubes in his nostrils. *If I survive this, then maybe I'll be able to move on. I will have finally lived out my purpose.*

Just then, the curtain that surrounded his bed whisked open and an older man in a white nurse's uniform appeared. The nurse closed the curtain. Harry swallowed hard, coughing on his saliva when he saw who it was: Sherman Gray.

"Hello, Mr. Thomas," Sherman said, a dark smile curling up the corners of his lips.

Harry hacked up the phlegm in his throat, then said, "Get out of here."

"Sorry, old friend," Sherman said, "I cannot do that. Not just yet."

Harry reached again for the beeper on his blanket, grabbed it, and frantically pressed the little red button.

"Don't bother," Sherman said and tugged at the beeper's cord that ran alongside Harry's bed. Harry looked at the cord and noticed that it had been severed. "They can't hear you."

Sherman pulled up a chair, meant for the examining nurse, to Harry's bed and sat down on it. In a futile effort, Harry tried to hit him. Instead, his right arm just jostled slightly on the mattress. He couldn't move. He was too tired. Simply moving to grab the beeper had fatigued him.

"What do you want?" Harry asked, still angry that his arm hadn't worked. The other was no good to him, either.

"Not much, really. Actually, I'm surprised that you're alive. I thought being impaled in the neck by a ballpoint pen would have been fatal." Sherman paused. "I suppose our mysterious third party had somehow managed to keep you alive, despite my efforts. They didn't do a very good job, though, did they? Makes you wonder sometimes, doesn't it, Harry? Make you wonder why the forces of darkness and the forces of light haven't yet combined their power to snuff out this third individual or individuals?" Sherman crossed his legs. "Anyway, I also came to tell you what's been happening several hundred kilometers away. Care to hear? Good. Gwen is hurt, dear Harry, very hurt. A friend of mine had the pleasure of raping her."

Harry's eyes winced shut at hearing this.

Sherman leaned closer to Harry and whispered into his ear, "Me, too."

Harry's eyes shot open. He was crying. Poor Gwen. She was helpless. So was he.

"Leave her alone," Harry managed to say.

"You know I can't do that, Harry. That's why I'm here, to see to it that Gwen doesn't harm our little Calvin in any way. Oh, how I despise you for embarking her on this little quest. Did you honestly think that she could win? It's been foretold, Harry. The child will live. You above all should know the consequences of tampering with prophecy."

"It has to be done." Harry's voice was hard, clear.

"I've heard that before," Sherman said and got up from his chair.

"When this is over, God will have words with you," Harry told him with tired, yet stiff, eyes.

"Let me ask you something, Harry," Sherman paused and steepled his fingers under his chin. "If the big G upstairs were aware of what was transpiring, do you honestly think He would sit there on His ass and do nothing about it? Would He allow murder? Would He have allowed you to suffer?" The old man allowed another pause. "No. He wouldn't have. Think on that a spell and tell me what your answer is. On second thought, don't."

Harry wheezed again, the air whistling through the tubes in his nose. His strength was diminishing. *Sherman was right. God wasn't behind this. It is over and Gwen is as good as dead. Whatever third party Sherman is talking about has to be real. Is real. Isn't real. Real.*

Sherman set a hand on Harry's shoulder. "Good-bye, Harry. I've enjoyed our little chats, but my Master himself has finally allowed me to kill Gwen. I was surprised that he hadn't sooner. At first he just wanted me to scare her away but this ever elusive third individual is making things much more difficult for me. So much more difficult. Gwen persisted through my attacks. Persisted in this little crusade you've entrusted her with. She is broken, Harry—yet, not fully. That's my opinion, anyway. Though, Gwen thinks she is. Broken, I mean. You did a bang-up job with her. Congratulations, old boy." Sherman gave Harry a mock congratulatory smack on the shoulder.

Harry grunted with the pain of its impact.

Sherman went on. "But, no matter, it's all in the past. However, I must say that you were a most worthy adversary, dear Harry. But, in every battle there is the victor and the yielded. And, unfortunately for you, you are the latter, Harry."

The old man gave Harry a sympathetic yet knowing smile. He walked over to the oxygen machine and turned it off. Harry could feel the air stop flowing into his lungs. Each breath through his nose became painful and stung with every exertion. Tears glazed over his eyes. The steady beeping of the pulse monitor accelerated, responding to Harry's heart starting to panic. His body grew warm, sweat clinging his hospital gown to his skin.

Drawing a struggling breath, Harry said, "Heed this, Sherman. You will not succeed. Gwen is stronger than you could possibly imagine."

The old man shoved one hand in his pocket. He shook his head, disappointed that Harry did not understand him.

"I'm sorry to hear that, Harry. You've obviously given in to your delusions. But don't worry, what I'm about to do to you won't hurt for long." He produced a small needle from his pocket. "Do you know what this is? It's a pain killer called Demerol. They give it to cancer patients to help ease their suffering. The right dosage is perfectly fine and efficient, lasting for quite awhile. However, the wrong dosage is fatal. I have over nine hundred milligrams of Demerol here. At least take comfort in the fact that you will not be feeling any pain. Or," Sherman shrugged, "at least after a few minutes you won't be."

Sherman plugged the needle into the intravenous unit and pushed the syringe butt with his thumb. Through the corner of his eye Harry watched as the Demerol merged with the morphine the hospital was already giving him. Once the syringe was empty, Sherman replaced the needle in his pocket and adjusted the dosage on the intravenous unit to its maximum.

He placed his palm on Harry's forehead. Harry put forth a futile struggle underneath his touch. Already Harry felt himself growing incredibly sleepy and still.

"Rest in peace, Harry," Sherman said, and left the room.

There was a buzzing in Harry's ears, a pricking fuzziness inside his head. Then all was quiet.

He closed his eyes and thought of Lauren. "It is finished," he said. "Gwen, what is mine is yours."

The last thing Harry heard was the acceleration of beeps coming from the heart monitor.

He didn't hear it flat-line.

PART FIVE

THE DEFILEMENT OF A PROPHECY

Chapter Thirty-Four

His image burned in her mind as she turned down Rainygravel Road. Gwen Reeves sat behind the steering wheel of the Saturn, her fingers tapping nervously at the edge of the wheel.

She had spent her entire day thinking about Marty. After she had bought a gun, a Cougar Magnum revolver, from ol' Bob, she did her best to keep her mind occupied until nightfall. When night arrived, Gwen figured, she would be too focused on the task at hand to give Marty a second thought. Instead, she had found herself flopped on the bed in her motel room, flipping aimlessly through the television stations, trying to find something that would catch her attention. Gwen had even tried reading the paper, but found no desire to read about the latest war effort in Afghanistan.

She slipped on a pair of black, thin-sulate gloves that she bought prior to picking up the gun. Good ol' Bob had thought it strange for her to buy a gun with a pair of gloves on, but he had seen stranger things in his sixteen year history as a gun shop owner. At first he had been reluctant to sell Gwen the gun, but when she offered him a fistful of cash as reward for his obedience, good ol' Bob, being the sleaze that he is, was too tempted by Gwen's offer to refuse the sale.

After donning the gloves, she had sat at her table, rotating the gun around with her fingertips, and thought of Marty. At one point she had gotten so mad at him that she closed her eyes and fantasized walking straight into his house, gun in hand, and slowly killing him. First she shot him in his arms and legs so he couldn't move. Then she fired another round into his lower stomach. Blood bubbling out of his mouth, Gwen squatted over him, forcing him to swallow the gun down his throat. She had smiled when she thought of it, and then recoiled in disgust at her callousness.

Boy, I'm more fucked up than I thought! Gwen concurred with herself.

When nightfall came, she placed the gun in the front pouch of the black hoody she wore, matching her black jeans and black scrunchie that she had used to tie her hair back. The purpose of her dark wardrobe was to avoid being seen as much as possible. Gloves on, she walked to the car, and headed straight for Calvin's house.

Let's put this to rest so we can all go home, Gwen thought. *Home. Don't know how much of a home it'll be once I get back there. If I ever get back there...*

That was when she had started thinking about Marty, wondering what she would be doing right now if she hadn't met Harry. She and Marty would probably be on the sofa either in her apartment or at Marty's place, enjoying a rented movie, every so often ignoring the television so they could pay more attention to each other.

Gwen didn't know if they would ever have a movie night again.

* * *

Rainygravel Road was quiet. It was 9 P.M. The streets were damp from the light rainfall earlier that evening. The reflection of the street lamps off the pavement reminded Gwen of a nighttime picture she had seen of old Victorian London. It was taken in 1888, soon after the Ripper-canon. She had seen it in her high school history class. She didn't know why she recalled the picture.

Finding house number 642 hadn't taken her long, either. Gwen drove past it carefully, taking note that the lights were turned off in the upstairs.

Perhaps they're not home, she thought, *or maybe they're just downstairs? Hopefully not home. That would be a break. No,* she asserted herself. *This ends tonight!*

Taking the Saturn to the end of the street, Gwen turned left, deciding to park one street over. Walking back, she lit a cigarette and thought to herself that if something went wrong tonight this might be the last cigarette she would ever smoke. As a free woman, anyway.

"Damn, I hope not," Gwen said to herself. Going to jail for murder was an unpleasant thought.

A few minutes later she was at the front lawn of the boy's home. She crept up to the house across the damp grass as quietly as she could, turning her head from side to side to see if anyone was watching her. From what Gwen could tell, the coast was clear. Unfortunately, in the faded moonlight, the windows of the homes on the other side of the street were hard to see, so she couldn't be completely sure no one was watching her. She would have to take comfort in the fact that since barely any lights were on in the other homes, that most of the people who lived on Rainygravel Road were either in bed early tonight, or somewhere else in the house where she wouldn't be visible to them.

Walking alongside the right side of the house, Gwen could hear voices through the walls. *Thank God for old construction,* she thought. She made sure she remained extra quiet so that whoever was speaking inside the house could not hear her.

Gwen crouched beneath a window. Fortunately, the blinds were partially drawn. This would make it easier for peeking in. She rose herself on her tiptoes and looked inside. A light was on. Gwen could see Victoria in her bedroom reading a Danielle Steel paperback. She took notice of the mother's worn and swollen eyes, but didn't give it any significant thought. The door to Victoria's bedroom was closed.

Good, Gwen thought, and moved on toward the back of the house.

The back wall of 642 Rainygravel Road had four windows. Two along the bottom and two higher up, the top two not high enough to indicate that the home had a second floor. The house was only a bi-level with a main living area, kitchen and two bedrooms. The lower level was the rec. room and a guest room. There was a bathroom on both levels. Gwen assumed that Calvin and his mother had their rooms on the upper level. A back door sat in the center of the rear of the house, a crude sidewalk running from it down to a graveled driveway and garage.

He can't be far off, Gwen thought as she peaked through one of the higher windows. She made sure to keep her feet out of view from the lower ones. The window she was currently looking into was the kitchen. She had to strain her neck upward to see inside. A light was on, but no one was in the room. The kitchen was small and Gwen saw an ashtray on the kitchen table. For a brief instant she felt like having a cigarette.

She moved herself over to the next window and was peering into another un-lit room. In the subtle moonlight Gwen could make out some of the objects in what appeared to be a bedroom. There were toys, posters of cartoon characters, a messy bed, a full garbage can, and anything else you might find in a child's bedroom. She now knew that this was where the boy slept.

Only two more to go, she told herself and went to the window on her lower left.

A light suddenly came on from inside, shining brightly into the backyard. Gwen made a careful effort not to allow her shadow to be cast into the room below. She had to pretend like she didn't exist. This whole seek-and-find was becoming a thrilling adventure. The window that was lit looked down into the rec. room. Below, she saw Calvin. Immediately, her heart pounded in her chest, its beat climbing up her veins into her neck.

Gwen felt the gun in her hoody. When she touched it there was a jolt at her fingers, the same as that when you stick your finger into an electrical socket. It didn't hurt, but it didn't feel good, either. Gwen was overwhelmed with the realization that she was *actually* going to kill someone, and that this entire mess would finally be over with. Finally.

Through the window, she cast her gaze upon the child, finding it slightly amusing that this innocent little boy would one day grow up to be the beast prophesied to come and rule over the earth.

Down in the rec. room, Calvin sat on a beanbag cushion two feet in front of the television. In his hands he held a video game controller and on the screen, Gwen could see, was one of those shooting games where you have to solve a maze while coming across various monsters and beasts along the way.

How ironic, Gwen thought.

She decided the best and easiest way to accomplish the task at hand would be to poise the gun at the glass, aim the barrel of the revolver at Calvin's head, fire off a shot, and run like hell. Hopefully, she wouldn't miss and it would only take the one shot to kill him. If she screwed up, she would have to get the hell out of there and sprint to her car and take off before anyone came to see what had happened. That also meant that at one point she would have to come back and try again.

Not a chance, Gwen thought. She would do it right the first time.

Steadying her breath, she lay on her stomach slightly to the side of the window. She wanted to be sure that just in case Calvin turned and looked in her direction, she wouldn't be seen.

Satisfied that the boy wouldn't be able to see her, Gwen removed the gun from the pouch in her hoody, and set herself up, carefully taking aim. The boy was in her sights, a straight line forming between the end of her gun and the back of the boy's head. Gwen closed her eyes and thought of Marty, Harry, her motel room, and the two men who had raped her. With one last glance checking for any onlookers, she put her finger on the trigger.

"Forgive me, Lord," she whispered to herself. She had become a believer, it seemed.

Suddenly, a strong beam of light streamed from the right side of the house accompanied by the sound of a loud car engine. Reacting, Gwen shot up and sprinted back to the right side of the house.

In the driveway she saw a truck pulling up. The headlights turned off. Being careful not to be seen, Gwen silently stepped along the side of the house until she could see who it was. A couple of times she had to hold her breath because her breathing had become loud and fast. She needed a cigarette. This was too much.

"Shit," she mumbled and crouched down. She watched as someone she didn't recognize exited the truck and walked up the sidewalk toward the house. He had tousled, black-gray hair, and a well-muscled jaw with beard. He wore blue jeans and a plaid shirt.

The man rang the doorbell and was greeted by a woman. The boy's mother, Gwen knew.

Gwen heard Victoria shout somewhere into the house, yelling to Calvin that his uncle had just arrived. Gwen sat against the side of the house and replaced the gun into the pouch of her hoody. On her hands and knees she crawled quickly across the back lawn, stopping herself short when she saw another light go on inside the house.

How am I supposed to see in now? she asked herself. *They'll see me for sure.*

Her first inclination was to run speedily along the back of the house, glance into the rec. room and check for Calvin, then leave the yard as fast as she could. She would get in her car and drive around until the boy's uncle had left. Yeah, that would be a good plan.

One, two, three, she counted then darted across the yard. From what she was able to see, the boy had left the rec. room. While running past the rear, left side of the house, Gwen glanced into one of the windows and saw the boy with his mother and uncle in the kitchen at the table. Before she knew it, she was already jogging swiftly down Rainygravel Road, heading in the direction of her car. She heard a dull *CLUNK*. She checked the pouch in her hoody, feeling for the gun.

"Shit!" Gwen said, as a shockwave ran through her bones. The gun had slipped out of her hoody. She turned around and looked behind her. The gun was on the pavement fifteen feet away, glimmering subtly in the pale street light. She sprinted toward it, grabbed it, took a sharp one hundred-eighty degree turn, and ran back down the street.

She paused by her car and allowed her racing heart to slow down. A hot flush of sweat consumed her. She felt her jeans and hoody beginning to stick to her body. With a gulp of air, Gwen opened her car door, having left it unlocked for an easy getaway, and jumped into the driver's seat. Looking in the rearview mirror, she smiled when it appeared no one had seen her. Gwen took it as a sign that everything was somehow meant to be temporarily quiet while she accomplished the murder.

But what about the uncle coming over? she questioned.

She started the car, pulled out a cigarette, and drove further down the block. A half hour drive around the neighborhood was decided upon and then she would go back to the house and check to see if the uncle had left.

Gwen would kill the boy then.

This had to end tonight.

* * *

A Stranger Dead

While Gwen was driving, her mind wandered toward Harry. She wondered if he somehow knew that she was going to conduct the murder tonight, if he could somehow experience the killing as it occurred.

"Harry," she said aloud. A moment passed then, "Harry, can you hear me?"

She repeated the question again. A large part of her hoped that Harry would transmit his thoughts and strategies as to what to do. And, most importantly, some form of comfort. She needed to know that everything would turn out okay.

Gwen looked at the hand holding her cigarette. Her fingers were quivering. Her nerves were on the verge of burnout. Hoping that she wouldn't turn into a basket case, Gwen tossed her cigarette out the window. She put her shaking hand under her thigh.

"Harry," Gwen said again softly.

Her perceptions slowed, the humming of the car's motor, her breathing, the steady beat of her heart, all becoming clear and audible, all nearly stopping before resuming back up to speed. A profound sense of loneliness came over her. Something had happened to Harry. She didn't know if he was dead or just simply hurt, and it was that not knowing that caused her heart to sink. But she did *know* that something had happened.

Harry, are you there? Harry? she repeated in her head.

She didn't hear, or feel, a response.

"God, please make sure Harry's okay," Gwen prayed. "I don't know what's going on."

Her acknowledging God, talking to Him, signified to her that she was starting to believe again in something that she had decided was nonsense. Now, that nonsense was making sense again.

Gwen looked in the rearview mirror to see if anybody was following her. As the glare of a street lamp passed through her windows, she saw an old man sitting in the back seat of her car. He smiled at her and the next time the light glared through the windows, he was gone.

In a fit of panic, Gwen pulled the Saturn over to the side of the road, and put a hand to her eyes. It happened to her again. An image in the rearview mirror.

She cried. She cried for Harry, Marty, herself, the boy, the soon to be grieving mother, the uncle who would try to remain strong for the family.

All Gwen was—her body, her heart, her mind—grew all the more numb as each moment passed and each tear was shed. Gwen couldn't feel anything, both inside herself and out. She couldn't even feel her hand trembling beneath her thigh. Between her sniffles she would curse herself, God, Harry, Marty—everyone who had ever made her feel alone.

Because that's what she was now—alone.

Chapter Thirty-Five

Inside the kitchen of 642 Rainygravel Road, a tense situation was taking place. It started off pleasant enough with Victoria, Calvin, and Uncle Ken, sitting down calmly at the kitchen table, each having a glass of orange juice. But before any of them knew it, they were talking about Calvin's more unsettling habits and what Dr. Carol had reported back to Victoria.

"Please, Victoria. Not now," Ken had told her, acknowledging how late in the evening it was. It was nearly ten o'clock and, from experience, Ken knew that late at night was no time to start a heavy conversation.

He could also see that Victoria felt as though she had no other choice *but* to talk about it. Heavy bags had formed under her eyes and by the slight trembling of her fingers Ken knew she was smoking her ump-teenth cigarette. He sympathized with her, even more so when he noticed how thin she was getting. Before, when Victoria wore her off-yellow bathrobe, it would compliment her figure nicely. Now, she looked so small in the robe and it bunched and bagged where it used to be more full and womanly.

"This has to be done now, Ken. Please," Victoria told him sternly.

Calvin sat at the table, eyes sad, a darkness stirring deep within him. The boy knew that he was about to be the target of all of his mother's grief and that Uncle Ken would end up saying a thing or two about the way he had been acting lately.

A chill raced up Calvin's spine when he realized he had no way out of the conversation. If he got up to leave, his mother would surely say something about it and rely on Uncle Ken to tell him to sit back down.

"Calvin," Ken said, addressing the boy, "I know it's late, but your mother would like to talk about this now. She's upset, Calvin." He paused. "Now, before I go any further, know that we're not blaming you for anything. Your mother is just worried about you. So am I. We want to know what you're feeling."

Calvin relaxed a little bit at his uncle's effort to be as gentle as possible. Victoria appreciated Ken's efforts, too. It felt more reassuring when he led a conversation.

Ken continued. "Is something bothering you? We just want to help. Are you mad at me or your mom?"

The boy sat, brow knit with innocence, not answering. A part of him understood why they were so concerned about him, and another part of him thought that they were turning a molehill into a mountain.

"Nothing's bovering me," Calvin finally said.

"Do you know why you got so upset at church the other Sunday?" Ken asked.

"No," Calvin returned, uncomfortably.

His mother lit another cigarette, puffing on it as if yearning for each plume of smoke to calm her down. She wasn't upset with Calvin, only extremely concerned. More than anything in the entire world she didn't want anything to happen to him. Victoria couldn't bear to lose another loved one. She knew that if he continued down the path he was on, who knows, he might someday say something to the wrong person and get himself hurt, or even killed? Victoria always thought in worst-case scenarios—she didn't know any better.

"Okay," Ken said, "are you mad at someone else? I remember you telling me that you were having some trouble with your friends at school, that for some reason they didn't like you. Is that it?"

"No," Calvin told him. He hated this Q and A.

Victoria looked at her adopted son with an expression of concern yet odd condemnation. "Is it the old man, Calvin? Be honest with me. Have you been talking to him when I told you not to? Tell me the truth." And, boy, did she mean it.

Calvin's heart sank. He had never been good at lying to his mother. He had no choice but to tell her the truth.

"Yes," he said.

His heart broke. He didn't want to get yelled at. More importantly, he didn't want to be kept away from Sherman.

Victoria slouched in her chair. Ken eyed her. She hadn't told him much about the man who called himself Sherman Gray, save for mentioning that a strange old man had talked to Calvin on one occasion. She also said that they had played basketball together, too.

"Why?" Victoria prompted, hurt that her son would go ahead and talk to Sherman when she had deliberately told him not to.

"He's my friend," Calvin replied, feeling ashamed. He had actually fallen in love with the old man. Sherman was such a good friend to him and he was the only person in the whole wide world who understood him.

"Why did you continue seeing him after your mother had told you not to?" Ken asked.

The boy peered at his uncle. "He's my friend," he repeated.

"Has he said or done anything to you that might have affected the way you feel?"

"No!" Calvin snapped. "He actually makes me feel *wanted!*"

For a moment Ken had a mental image of an older man using Calvin for some perverse sexual purpose. He shuddered at the thought and quickly chased it away. He didn't want to have to ask Calvin if the old man had touched him anywhere he was not supposed to.

"How does he make you feel wanted, Calvin?"

The boy averted his eyes. "I don't know. He's just so nice to me. Why won't you let me be his friend? I don't say who your friends can be."

Ken sighed and leaned back in his chair. "This is different. Your mother and I are older and know some things that you don't."

Victoria took a drag off her cigarette then reached across the table, taking Calvin by the hand. "We're just trying to look out for you, Calvin. Can you promise me that you won't see Sherman anymore?"

Calvin's brow knit together in a taut, angry point. "He's not the one making me act all funny! Maybe it's you! You're not being fair!" He pulled his hand away from her with a jerk.

Victoria's eyes watered, unsure what to do or say next. The three of them sat in awkward silence for a long minute. Both Ken and Victoria knew that there would be no way to help Calvin if they couldn't find out what was wrong.

Victoria had called Dr. Carol a few hours after their meeting at the hospital to discuss Calvin a little more. She wasn't satisfied with the response he had given her.

Courteously providing elaboration on what he had told her, Dr. Carol had said that Calvin wasn't acting this way because of any outside influences. His guess was that prior to Calvin being adopted, something possibly traumatic had happened to him and now that event was slowly starting to surface itself. He had said that it wasn't uncommon for adopted children to suddenly act differently or talk differently as they start to remember something upsetting from earlier on in their life. The doctor's advice had been to give Calvin time and to watch him for any sudden mood changes. Dr. Carol had also advised Victoria not to allow herself to get too wrapped up in Calvin's trials. Victoria refuted him by saying that she loved Calvin so much and would rather endure the boy's pain for him. Dr. Carol said that that was noble, but, regardless, for both her and Calvin's sake, she should just take care of him like she always had, and eventually things would work themselves out.

Victoria was upset that he hadn't told her this when they had spoken earlier at his office.

At the kitchen table, no one had yet said a word after Calvin's statement. Victoria broke the silence.

"What do you think?" she asked, turning to Ken.

He looked at her, considering. "I think we should leave it for tonight. Remember what Dr. Carol told you?"

"What? What did he say about me?" Calvin interrupted.

"Nothing," Ken said promptly, still looking at Victoria.

Calvin got up from the table. "Can I go now?"

"Sure," his mother said and the boy left the room.

Back downstairs in the rec. room, Calvin resumed his game. The darkness that he had felt surface earlier had come back, and he could feel his breathing thicken with anger. He didn't care what his mother and uncle were saying. They were blaming him. They were telling him that it was all his fault. Somewhere inside himself he knew that if his uncle and mother kept interfering with the direction his life was taking, it would somehow cause trouble. For Calvin, life seemed to be going in the direction it was supposed to go.

On the television screen, his character, Boss Randolph, was holding the biggest gun in the game. It was a six-barreled automatic that fired a plethora of bullets all at once. Calvin liked this gun. With it, the monsters in the game didn't stand a chance against him. They could never beat him. Ever.

While he played, he took joy in the killing of the virtual monsters. Each time he ran one of them through with an onslaught of bullets, Calvin smiled as they fell to the ground, helpless, blood spurting out in all directions from their half-decimated bodies.

He was nearing the end of the level. Ten monsters were coming towards him. With tense eyes and skilled fingertips, Calvin charged toward them and emptied clip after clip of ammunition at them. His breathing quickened until his breaths became audible, more an excited panting than breathing. The monsters exploded in every direction. Blood filled the screen. More bullets, more monsters, more blood, faster and faster—

"AHHH!" Calvin screamed and threw the controller at the television. It bounced off with a loud *PLINK!*

Immediately the boy heard heavy footsteps trampling down the stairs to the rec. room. It was his mother. She looked ragged.

"What happened?" she asked.

Calvin sat on his beanbag cushion, panting, sweat streaming from his forehead.

She felt herself start to panic. "Are you all right?"

The boy stared blankly at the TV, the words "SUPER-KILLER" flashing on and off on the screen against a background of blood.

Victoria knelt down in front of him and put her hands on his shoulders. "Calvin, talk to me."

His gaze turned toward her, his eyes empty.

"Ken!" Victoria yelled in the direction of the staircase.

Ken rushed down the stairs and went directly to kneel beside Calvin. "What's wrong?"

"I don't know. Calvin, talk to me." Victoria gave Calvin a shake.

The boy still didn't respond.

"Calvin?" Ken prompted, adding a gentle shake of his own.

Without warning, the boy flailed his arms and legs, letting out a deafening scream. He scrambled out of his mother's hold and ran up the stairs. Both his mother and uncle darted after him. They heard a door slam upstairs and knew that Calvin had retreated to his bedroom.

Upon arriving at the boy's room, Ken saw that Calvin's door was shut. It was always left open except when he sleeping at night. Filled with worry, Ken reached for the door handle then turned it. When he opened the door, the room was empty.

Calvin was gone.

They frantically searched the house, both upstairs and down. They checked every niche of the house for him—behind the shower curtain, the laundry room, underneath tables and chairs—finding nothing. It wasn't until

Victoria noticed that the back door, closed, was unlocked. Calvin had run outside.

Without putting on any shoes, she and Ken ran out of the house. Ken ran down the driveway and scanned up and down the back lane, while Victoria rounded the house, checking the front yard and street.

Calvin wasn't anywhere in sight.

The backyard was checked again and the front yard one more time. Still nothing.

Ken took Victoria back inside and helped her relax on a couch in the living room.

"Do you know where he might have gone?" Ken asked her.

She bit her lip and thought for a moment. Then she remembered the Sunday of the church incident and where Ken had told her Calvin had gone.

"Fetterman Park," she said.

Chapter Thirty-Six

Gwen Reeves drove slowly past 642 Rainygravel Road. An hour had passed since she was last there, a half hour later than she had originally planned. She took notice that the big brown truck in the driveway was gone.

He must have left, she thought, obviously. *Let's get this over with.*

Like before, she parked her car a few blocks away and briskly walked toward the house, avoiding all the street lamps. And, like before, she discreetly made her way to the back of the house and looked through all the windows for the boy. Despite the fact that most of the lights were still on, all the rooms in the house were empty.

Gwen checked the windows again. Still nobody. She sat down on the damp grass, leaning against the rear of the house, feeling the moisture seep through her pants against her bottom. She got her thoughts together.

Okay, just think of your options, she started to tell herself. *While you were gone, everyone left. It's late. He's only a boy. They should be back soon. I could drive around some more and come back. Yeah, okay, I'll do that.*

As she got up she saw something out of the corner of her eye. She turned to meet it. It was the old man. The same old man that had taken her body with claim.

"Hello, Gwendolyn," he said. His voice was soothing and seductive.

Gwen was compelled to listen to him in spite of all urges to run.

"You," she rasped.

She instinctively produced her revolver and aimed it at the old man's head.

"It's been awhile, Gwen. Did you miss me?" he said with a mocking grin.

"Back off!" Gwen shouted, slowly distancing herself away from him.

He raised his hands to shoulder level in surrender, his eyes turning soft, kind. "Please, Gwen. I come in peace." He grinned again. It bothered her.

"Sadly, I'm the bearer of upsetting news," he said.

She stopped her ebbing footsteps. He continued. "I saw Harry earlier. Such a nice fellow. Did you know I knew him?"

Gwen shook her head. He had her attention. She kept the gun aimed at him for her protection.

He lowered his arms, folding them across his belly. "I'm aware of your little crusade, y'know. And I know why you're here. And I know why I'm here. And I know why Calvin is here. I will only tell you this once, Gwen. Go home."

"Sorry, Mister. If you'll excuse me…" She turned away, stopping when the old man spoke again.

"Mister? Surely we must become less formal. Call me Sherman, love. After all, we *were* intimate, now, weren't we?"

A hot pain seared Gwen's heart, pressing with heated anguish. The comment triggered a dull ache in the recovering muscles between her legs.

Sherman was glad he had hurt her. "If you think you are hurting now, dear Gwendolyn, how do you think it would feel if I told you Harry was dead? It would hurt even worse, don't you think? Though, how can it get any worse, you wonder. Well, it is true. Poor Harry Thomas is dead."

Gwen's blood curdled. Had she heard him right? Harry? Dead?

"What?" Gwen turned, demanding an answer. She re-aimed the gun at the old man.

"Harry is dead, m'dear. I had told him to tell you to stop this little hunt of yours. Rather, I told him to stop this little hunt of *his*. But he didn't, now, did he?"

Gwen thought back to the phone call when Harry had told her to come home. She now knew that the phone call hadn't been from Harry. It had been from Sherman.

Seething with rage, Gwen squeezed the trigger. A loud *BANG!* shook the quiet neighborhood. Sherman recoiled and bent over at the waist. He screamed in mock pain then just as quickly started to laugh, showing Gwen that the bullet had not harmed him. There wasn't a mark, or a bruise, or a gash, or anything indicating a wound on him, just a hole in his tweed suit jacket. Gwen stared at him wide-eyed.

Piercing the scene, lights of some of the neighboring houses flashed on, reacting to the shot.

Gwen ran out of the backyard and sprinted towards her car. She had to get away from Sherman or whatever it is that he was. How did her shot not kill him? Did she miss?

Gwen jumped into her car and peeled off the street trying to get as far away from Rainygravel Road as possible. Replacing the package of cigarettes on the passenger seat with the revolver, she pulled out a cigarette and lit it up.

"Dammit!" she exclaimed, hitting the steering wheel with the palm of her hand. She felt the shock of it all the way up to her shoulder. She had failed. Sherman had been right. It had only gotten—

From out of the back seat Sherman grabbed her, causing the car to swerve and ride up and over a curb. Gwen reached up with both hands to his forearms, trying to free herself from his grip. He wasn't letting go. The car swerved again. Gwen grabbed the steering wheel, putting the car back on course.

"I hate you, Gwen!" he snarled.

She could feel the pressure on her throat increasing. If she didn't do something quick, it wouldn't be long before she would pass out.

"Stop..." Gwen managed to wheeze. The pressure increased. A light buzz filled her ears. Black and red stars filled her vision.

The car had finally come to halt in the middle of the road. Fortunately, it was late and there wouldn't be any opposing traffic.

Fighting to loosen Sherman's grip was becoming increasingly difficult. *He didn't even flinch when I shot him.*

Her vision was gone, only red speckled blackness in front of her. Gwen pulled and pulled, trying to get Sherman's forearms off from around her neck. She had an idea but it was a long shot. She felt for the car's cigarette lighter all the while trying to focus on keeping her foot on the brake pedal.

She found the lighter, pushed it in, and counted the seconds that it took to heat up. *1, 2, 3, 4, 5, 6, 7, 8*—the buzzing in her ears was increasing and already she could feel her limbs starting to go limp—*9, 10, 11, 12*—it was over, Sherman was killing her—*13, 14*—the cigarette lighter popped out. She grabbed the lighter, summoned all her strength, and violently twisted herself around so that she did a one hundred and eighty degree turn in her seat. The turn caused Sherman's forearms to painfully scrape across her neck.

Her vision restored slightly, as if looking at the old man through a glass of murky water. She saw the expression of surprise on his face. Sherman scrambled to get his arms around her tightly again. In the quick moment that it took for him to do so, Gwen pressed the cigarette lighter into Sherman's eye. She heard a coarse, sizzling sound over the buzzing in her ears. Sherman let go one of his hands, covering his eye in reflex. He released a foul shriek. This gave Gwen enough time to lurch forward so that his other hand released her. She slammed the gearshift in PARK, and pushed open the door of the Saturn, grabbing the gun off the seat, and bolted down the street, once again concealing the weapon in her hoody.

She had to get away.

* * *

At a stop sign, Gwen put her head in between her legs, trying to catch her breath.

No more smoking after tonight, she agreed with herself. *What the hell was he?* With trembling hands she reached up to her sore neck and felt for bruises or anything that might out of place. Other than a few tender spots, she was okay. *I'll probably be bruised by morning,* she thought sadly. *More bruises…more fucking bruises!* She checked the pouch in her hoody to make sure the gun was still there. It was.

Another deep breath and she started to jog. *How am I supposed to find the kid now? He wasn't at his house. Where the hell could he be?*

She slowed her jog and closed her eyes, trying to feel the boy's presence and hoped against hopes that Sherman wasn't right behind her. Gwen prayed that whatever force had drawn her to the boy's house in the first place, would somehow guide her to him tonight. It had to be tonight. To try to kill him on another night was out of the question. She would accept no more of this crusade. No more.

She had had enough.

* * *

The boy sat quietly on the swing set, eyes downcast, forming circles in the sand with his toes. For Calvin Mandalay, becoming a prisoner to confusion had not been a choice. Going through his mind were all the words that his uncle and mother had said to him. Going through his heart was the tremendous weight of guilt and pressure to be a better child. He felt guilty for being such a burden to the two of them and felt a sudden pressure to change. The only problem was, he didn't know how. He couldn't change what he had no control over. Couldn't change because he didn't know *what* it was that he was supposed to change.

Running out of the house had been a good idea. He needed to get away from it all and he didn't care if both his mother and uncle were worried sick about him. *They'll look for me, anyway,* Calvin knew.

He got up from the swing set and walked over to where an old tire was hanging from a wooden beam by a triangle of chains. He remembered when his mother had regularly taken him to Fetterman Park, and had him sit on the tire so that she could swing him around on it. It had been one of their most favorite things to do before she felt sick more often than not, and couldn't take him to the park anymore.

Maybe Mom is right? Calvin thought to himself. *Maybe things don't get better and they only get worse? She's not better.*

Leaning back against the tire he looked up into the night sky. Only the light of a few stars could be seen poking through the layer of clouds that mapped the sky. The moon was nowhere in sight.

Calvin had always enjoyed looking up at the moon, noticing how you could almost see a reflection of the earth on its surface. To him, the moon was one gigantic mirror that watched everything that was going on. He wondered if the moon was watching him tonight from somewhere hidden behind the clouds.

It'll be all right, Calvin. A voice inside his head said. *You did the right thing by running away. You are on the right path. Don't go home tonight. Don't.*

"Who said that?" he asked himself quietly and looked around. He was alone in the park. It hadn't sounded like anyone he knew. Not even Sherman.

Where is Sherman, anyway? he wondered. The old man always seemed to have a knack of showing up every time Calvin needed him. He needed him now.

A feeling of complete innocence washed over Calvin. He felt like a baby again. More than anything, he wanted to go back home and curl up in his mother's arms, hearing her whisper reassurances to him.

He got up and dusted off some of the dirt from his pants that the tire had left on him. He started to walk home. He wanted to say that he was sorry for running away, no matter what the voice inside his head just said.

That's when he saw her.

Not making out exactly who it was, Calvin stopped in his tracks and eyed the shiny object she held in her hands. It was held toward him almost as if she were offering it to him. Upon further inspection he recognized that it was a gun. His experience at pretending to be Boss Randolph helped him with that. She wasn't offering it to him. She was aiming it at him.

"Who are you?" he asked curiously.

The person stepped closer, their image illuminated by the only lamp that dimly lit the park. Calvin recognized her. She was the same girl who had driven past him that day while he was playing basketball. The same hatred that brewed that day returned.

"I don't like you," he told her firmly.

"I know, Calvin," she said and raised the gun, aiming at the boy's head. *How did I know his name?* she wondered. It was as if her mind was suddenly flooded with reams of information about the boy.

"You were outside my house tonight, right?"

How does he know? Gwen wondered.

"What do you mean by that, Calvin?"

The boy held her gaze. "I could feel you watching me while I played my game. Why do you want to hurt me?"

"It's not me, Calvin. I promise you that. I don't even want to do this, but it has to be done. Someone is counting on me."

"Who?"

"You don't know him. Please, no more questions. I'm going to finish this now," Gwen said. She paused and took a soothing breath, calming the rapid beating of her heart. She was surprised that the boy didn't try to run away. She concluded that he was too confused to know what to do, like a deer caught in someone's headlights.

"I'm sorry, Calvin," she said and placed her finger on the trigger. It was going to be over within an instant of a moment.

Just then, a truck pulled up in front of the park, its headlights casting a glow on both Gwen and the boy. They both looked toward the truck. Calvin was relieved. The muscles in Gwen's jaw tightened.

Ken raced out of the truck with Victoria trotting quickly at his heels. Gwen shot her glance back to Calvin. He had gone from her aim and was running towards his family.

Victoria caught him and scooped the boy up in her arms and kissed the side of his head. Gwen heard her mutter something to him.

Ken stood beside them and smiled as his sister and nephew reunited. He turned his eyes to Gwen and took note as to what she was holding. Wrapping an arm around Victoria and Calvin, he started backing them away from her.

"Come on, let's go," he said, keeping his eyes fixed on Gwen. He knew it was unsafe to try to escape the eye of a weapon, but, in his spirit, he could *feel* that Gwen wasn't going to shoot him.

Gwen shifted her aim to the three of them. "Stop!"

They stopped their slow, retreating steps and looked at her.

"Give me the boy!" Gwen demanded. They didn't say anything in return.

Maybe trying to leave wasn't a good idea, thought Ken.

"Bring me, Calvin," Gwen reworded more calmly.

"What do you want?" Ken asked, standing in front of Victoria and Calvin.

"I just want Calvin. Bring him here. You don't want to test me right now." And she meant it. Everything that had happened to her had settled in, and instead of the nice and quirky girl that everyone knew back home, she was now just a walking ball of rage with no concern for anyone or anything, save for finishing the task at hand.

Ken turned to Calvin and Victoria. "Get in the truck while I try to talk us out of this."

"But—" Victoria started.

"She has a gun, Uncle Ken," Calvin said, pointing at Gwen.

"Get in the truck. Now!" Ken ordered them again.

Gwen lifted the barrel and pulled the trigger.

Victoria and Calvin gasped.

Ken was shot.

Chapter Thirty-Seven

Victoria and Calvin fell with Ken as he recoiled from the impact of the bullet. They were stunned. Neither saw Gwen approach them.

"Ken?" Victoria said, immediately panicking. "Are...are you..." She wanted to ask if he was all right, but lost track of her words.

"D-don't know..." he wheezed. His hand was covering a bloodstained blotch in the middle of his chest. "I don't"—he coughed up a sputter of blood—"know."

"Just lay still," she told him and placed her hand tenderly on his forehead.

Victoria's touch was soothing, like the way it had been when they were children and he had gotten himself hurt. Despite what Victoria thought of herself, she had the gift for comfort. The gift of a mother.

"Uncle Ken, are you okay?" Calvin asked.

"Just fine, Sport," he replied, giving Victoria a glance that said if he wasn't taken to the emergency room soon, he wouldn't be.

The small family stayed huddled together as Gwen approached them.

"I'm sorry," Gwen said. She pointed the gun at Calvin.

"Like hell you are!" Victoria retorted. She now had Ken resting in her lap. A cellular phone was in her purse in the truck. She couldn't leave Ken. She also didn't want to chance having Calvin go and get it.

"Calvin," Gwen said, drawing the boy's attention.

The boy gazed at her, tears drawing red lines on his cheeks.

About to pull the trigger, someone sprang up from out of the shadows and tackled Gwen to the ground.

It was Sherman. Somehow he had found her.

"Sherman!" Calvin exclaimed.

Victoria's eyes darted in the direction of the old man. She got a good look at the person her son so blindly loved.

"Calvin, get out of here!" Sherman shouted.

"Calvin, stay here!" Victoria yelled, giving the old man a cold glare.

The boy ran for the truck. Victoria couldn't believe that Calvin had chosen to listen to the old man instead of her.

Sherman ripped the gun from Gwen's hands. He positioned himself on top of her so that his knees pinned down her arms, prohibiting her from retaliation. Gwen glared up at him. This felt all too familiar. She flashed back to Sherman and Robin raping her. She was sick. She could see that one of Sherman's eyes was swollen, puckered with a mess of loose, burnt flesh.

From the lighter.

With a violent thrust, Gwen slammed her knees upward as hard as she could, both kneecaps plowing into Sherman's back.

"Bitch!" Sherman retorted and slapped her. He cocked the gun and placed it in Gwen's mouth.

"It's over, Gwen," he said.

From over his shoulder Sherman heard someone call his name. He looked and saw that Calvin was standing next to him. The boy placed a small hand on the arm that held the gun.

"Don't hurt her, Sherman…please," the boy begged. Killing people wasn't fun anymore. No more Boss Randolph for him. He didn't want anybody to get hurt anymore. Not now. Not ever.

"Calvin, get away from here!" The old man's voice was no longer tender, but filled with anger and desperation. "Go!"

Using this short delay to her advantage, Gwen raised both her legs again, this time wrapping them around Sherman's shoulders from behind. She twisted her head to the right so she wouldn't get shot. The barrel of the gun ripped along the inside of her mouth. She could taste the bitter, iron flavor of blood. Then, with all her might, she pushed her legs downward, causing Sherman to fall backward. Gwen scrambled to her feet and delivered a mighty kick to his head, granting her control of the weapon again.

She looked around and saw that the boy had already gone back to his mother and uncle. Gwen didn't want anyone to leave the park. Gwen fired off a round at Victoria. The boy's mother flew backward and lay on the ground.

"Mom!" Calvin shouted and rushed over to her. He was too late. Gwen had managed to squeeze off a precise shot to Victoria's head. Calvin bawled uncontrollably as he watched a smooth line of blood spurt from a hole just above his mother's left eye.

"Vicki…Calvin…" Ken gasped.

The boy didn't hear him. Instead, Calvin sat on the grass next to his mother's fallen, dead body, Ken's head still in her lap.

From behind Gwen, Sherman delivered a fierce blow to the back of her head, forcing her to fall face forward on the ground. Her head smacked the grass hard, the impact echoing throughout her skull. She rolled over, hazily seeing the old man towering over her. She shot him. The bullet didn't have an effect. Sherman scoffed at her efforts to take him down. Gwen had no idea of the power she was challenging.

"How?" Gwen said, mostly to herself, but at the same time with the subconscious intention to prompt Sherman to provide some sort of explanation.

Acknowledging this, Sherman said, "What? How can you fire a shot only for me to laugh it off, but yet you burn me with a cigarette lighter and I get hurt? Hmm—let's just say that demons hate fire, and in this world, it hurts me far more than it hurts you."

The first thought in Gwen's mind was to try to use her pocket lighter against Sherman. She then realized her foolishness. *What am I supposed to do? Wave the flame in front of me and hope he'll go away? Idiot.*

Gwen tried to get up. Sherman kicked her back down. He squatted down beside her. Gwen rolled over onto her stomach, hiding the gun. Sherman was too strong. He rolled her over, her chest upward, with minimal effort.

Pulling the gun away, Sherman saw that there were only two bullets left in the chamber. The only thing that was important tonight was that Calvin survived and that there were absolutely no witnesses left for questioning. The old man looked over to the boy and saw him huddled against his uncle and dead mother.

Suddenly a voice invaded his mind. *Give me the gun, Sherman.* He looked back at Gwen. She was struggling to her feet. Harry's power to force thoughts into other people's minds had been passed on to her. Passing on his gift was the last thing Harry had done before he died. *Gwen, what is mine is yours,* he had said.

"Very clever," Sherman said. His adversary was still fighting him, even from the grave.

Give me the gun, Gwen repeated into his mind. With a satisfying smile, the old man looked at her and pulled the trigger. Gwen fell to the ground.

"Good night, Gwen," Sherman said and walked over to where Calvin lay against his mother.

Ken appeared to be in rough shape. He had managed to bunch up the lower half of his shirt and use it to apply pressure to the wound. Calvin's eyes went back and forth from his mother's limp body to his uncle. Ken kept whispering reassurances to the boy.

Sherman came over beside Calvin and put a hand on his shoulder. "Calvin, come with me."

"No! You're a bad man!" Calvin told him and jumped up, running a few feet away. The old man took giant steps towards him and seized him by the arm.

"Next time, you listen to me!" Sherman spat.

"No!" Calvin screamed again and kicked Sherman right between the legs.

The old man fell with the boy diving right on top of him, his little fists punching Sherman in the face. Thrown off by a powerful hand, Calvin fell hard on his back against the grass. He wailed.

Leaving the boy, Sherman walked over to Ken, who lay on the grass with his eyes closed. The old man cocked the gun and prepared to ensure the death of his final witness.

Calvin looked over to his uncle. "Uncle Ken…"

Fetterman Park fell silent. Time slowed. The air turned from cool with a subtle breeze to warm and damp.

Something had happened.

The silence of the moment was interrupted by the sirens of several police cars that came to a speeding halt, forming a semi-circle around Ken's truck. From out of all four vehicles stepped out policemen with their guns poised.

"Shit!" Sherman said. He glared at Calvin, then at Gwen, then Ken, then Victoria.

The policemen slowly edged their way forward. They stopped suddenly. Their guns remained aimed at Sherman. The old man frowned at them.

"Amazing, isn't it?" came a female voice.

Gwen delivered a swift right hook to Sherman's left temple. The old man teetered backward and dropped the gun. His hand went to where she had struck him. He thought he had killer. Instead, the bullet had only grazed her shoulder.

Amazing what mind control can do, isn't it, old man? Sherman heard her say inside his head. She kicked his legs from under him, his head and back smacking the ground hard. Dazed, he realized it was she who had caused the police to stop coming forward and to only keep their aim on him.

Damn her, he told himself. Being unarmed by a single bullet was one thing. But several that would take a power he did not posses.

With the bat of an eye, Gwen motioned for two of the police officers, one male, one female, to come forward and bring Calvin to her. They complied. Calvin looked worn, his face streaked red with anguished tears, his clothes dirty with sweat and the green smudges of grass.

Gwen's lips drew taut as she looked down at Sherman. "You're not much of a demon, are you? Watch as Hell comes to an end."

The two officers held Calvin while Sherman watched in panic as Gwen prepared herself to shoot the boy. From somewhere over to the side, Ken begged for her not to do it.

Cocking the gun, Gwen looked deep into the boy's eyes. He stared back at her. She could feel his fear. *He knows he is going to die*, she knew.

"This is for the best, Calvin," she said.

Gwen pulled the trigger.

The crack of gunfire thundered throughout the night. Behind her, Gwen could hear Ken scream with a blood-choked rasp. Equally, she felt Sherman's heart yell in terror as he knew that the boy would not survive.

She was satisfied. It was finally over.

Calvin had dropped to his knees then doubled over the instant the sound burst through the air. Both the male and female officers stepped back and aimed their pistols at a shocked Sherman.

Then Gwen saw something she had never expected, something she never thought possible: tears had glazed over Sherman's eyes. His breathing was thick with anguish, with grief, with pain.

Without sympathy, Gwen told the demon to leave. Before Sherman could move, she heard a soft rustling in the grass.

Calvin was standing. There was hole in the stomach of his T-shirt with no remnants of blood. He looked at Gwen with sad eyes then at Sherman then at the surrounding officers. The boy looked dead, but a stranger kind of dead. Though he was able to stand, he appeared as if he knew that he shouldn't have been able to do so, almost as if he knew that he had just been killed.

Calvin opened his arms and was filled with a radiant beauty that could only be compared to how a child must look in their parents' eyes: perfect, pure, brilliant.

Then he spoke to Sherman. "Get up, Demon!"

Like a servant would its master, Sherman obeyed. Gwen took notice that there was something different about the boy's presence. Her body quaked as a sharp, electric tingle surged through her muscles and bones. She fell to her knees, bowing before Calvin. She tried to get up, but couldn't. Her muscles throbbed with a paralyzing energy. Around her, Gwen could sense the policemen falling to their knees, as well.

Calvin gazed up into the heavens, spreading his arms even wider. "Because my son, John, recorded: 'Then I saw another beast, coming out of the earth. He had two horns like a lamb, but he spoke like a dragon,' do I allow this child to live. It is a prophecy that will be fulfilled because I have decreed it so."

Gwen realized who it was who was actually speaking. It was not Calvin. It was as far from Calvin as it could get. She couldn't fully believe it. Wouldn't fully believe it.

God Himself had just spoken to her.

God.

Jehovah.

The Great I Am.

God.

"Demon!" Calvin addressed Sherman. "This child is now your own. Take him, teach him what you must so that My Word will come to pass. But, as punishment for your actions, I strip you of all your powers, completely void of the Morning Star's dark abilities."

Sherman wailed. His power had left him. Calvin came over to him, took his hand, and looked Sherman in the eye. The old man, lips trembling, forced a grin in return.

The Divine presence left the park before it had fully settled, and Gwen was able to stand on her feet and finally take her eyes off the grass. Muscles tired and shaky, she looked around and saw that only the policemen, Ken, and Victoria's body remained.

Calvin and Sherman were gone.

* * *

In the shadows, within the dense trees and brush that bordered Fetterman Park, someone had watched all that had just transpired. His desire to save humanity from the wrath of the Antichrist had failed. The fate of the world could not be changed.

Another opportunity to alter the future history of the earth would surely present itself in due time. His patience knew no limits. All he had was time.

There was only one option for now: return to the Purple Void…and wait.

Two weeks later…

EPILOGUE

She figured it would be the least she could do. Besides, she didn't know of any other way to bring closure to all that had happened.

Gwen, back home in Winnipeg, drove towards Eagle Park Cemetery.

On the way there, she reflected on the events of the past two weeks since she had returned home.

Excited to see her roommates, she had been disappointed when she had come home to an empty apartment. She had dropped her bag at the door, and gone into the kitchen. In a cupboard above the stove was where she kept a spare carton of cigarettes.

On the flight home, Gwen decided to quit smoking, and made disposing of all her cigarettes her first priority when she returned.

She found the cigarette carton and as she turned toward the wastebasket to throw it out, she saw a note lying on the kitchen table. Hesitantly, she lifted it off the table. It read:

Dear Gwen,

I've left. I obviously didn't turn out to be much of a friend to you after all. All I hope is that you can forgive me. I am so so sorry for what I did. If our paths ever cross again, I hope it won't be so awkward that we'll have to act like total strangers around each other.

Please don't hold anything against Marty. It was all my fault. Can you ever forgive me?

Denise

Gwen had stared at the note for a long moment before stuffing it into her back pocket. She set the cigarette carton down on the table and picked up the phone and dialed Marty's number. His mother picked up.

"Hi, Mrs. Bones. It's Gwen. Is Marty there?"

"Hold on, dear. I'll get him."

A moment later, Marty was on the line. Gwen could hear the unsteadiness in his breath. She knew he was more than just ashamed. He was genuinely scared of her. He knew it was over between them.

"Hi, Marty," she said.

Gwen read the warning on the carton to keep from crying.

"Hi," Marty returned.

"Look," she said, "I'll get right to it. I hate what you did, but right now I honestly don't care. I'm just glad to be back home. I want to forget about the past while and get back to my life. Can we just get back to the way things were and pretend none of this ever happened?"

Gwen bit her upper lip, anticipating his answer, while Marty decided with a long sigh. The truth was, he had already made up his mind as to what he would say after his confessing phone call almost two and a half weeks ago.

"I can't, Gwen," he said.

A sharp pain pierced her heart.

Marty went on. "I'm sorry. What I did wasn't fair. I turned my back on all that we stood for. I love you so much yet I still fucked up. I think we should just take some time to get our thoughts together."

"Oh," she said softly. Gwen didn't expect him to turn her away like that. Her eyes watered.

He said, "I know. I'm sorry. How about you and I see where we stand in a month or two? I know I'll still love you. I just don't want you to make a decision that you might later regret. And, if you can, do me a favor…don't get mad at Denise. It was all my fault."

"Hmph," she said, "Denise said the same thing, except that *she* took the blame."

"You talked to her?" he asked.

"No. She left a note. Don't worry about her and me. I know she's sorry. But I also know how sorry you are, Marty. I don't want us to take time off. I love you," she told him. "I don't want anymore rejection. Especially from you. Please…"

He was silent for a moment. As much as he wanted to come right over and scoop her up in his arms, he knew that he couldn't. Not now.

"Gwen, I really don't know what to say. I feel so so bad. Let's talk about it in awhile, okay? I want to be with you, but I don't know if you want to be with me."

Gwen didn't say anything, just flinched when her heart sank into her stomach.

"I'm sorry," Marty said, and hung up.

Gwen stood with the receiver to her ear for almost a full minute before setting it back down in its cradle.

Marty, she said to herself, breaking inside. Instinctively, she cracked open the carton of cigarettes and produced a fresh pack. She wasn't going to quit the habit now.

Gwen had sat at home for an entire week, barely doing anything. Her body was exhausted, especially after that night in Fetterman Park. She slept lots and ate little. And it nearly took that entire week after the park for the bruises from Sherman to fade away. The bruises from Sherman and Robin violating her still lingered but not as prominent as before. At times she would dream and relive different scenes from her time away. Her mind was just as fatigued as her body. She knew that once most of her strength returned, she would have to go see a therapist to help rid herself of the images and feelings.

Gwen had turned on the news and watched for any reports to do with gunfire in a neighborhood park in a Toronto suburb, as well.

Gwen had left her motel that final haunting night in Fetterman Park, wanting more than anything to simply get away from there and get back home. The motel owner had been pleased with the large wad of cash Gwen had used to pay for her stay. She wasn't a rich person, by any means, and had called her bank to see if she had the funds necessary to cover her stay. While speaking with a representative from the bank, she had learned of a transfer of funds into her account that had occurred just before she had left for Toronto. The man, who had worn a purple suit at the time, had claimed to be a distant relative of Gwen's when speaking with the bank teller who had aided in the deposit.

Watching the news from her apartment in Winnipeg that same night was the only time the Fetterman Park shootings and murders was mentioned. It was forgotten the next day like all the other shootings that took place throughout the country.

A call to Hans Memorial Hospital had also been made to confirm Sherman's claim about Harry's murder. Sherman had been right. Harry was dead.

"Is there any burial arrangements?" Gwen had asked Elsie.

"His body was cremated yesterday mornin', dearie," Elsie had told her. "A note he had written was found in his room. It said that if we should ever find him passed away, that we should bury him next to his wife in Eagle Park Cemetery." The receptionist paused, then added, "Such a shame, really. Though strange at times, Harry was a good fellow."

"Yes, he was," Gwen had said. "Thank you." She hung up.

After making the call, she had sat mournfully and thought about the other person who had died that night in Fetterman Park.

Poor, Victoria, Gwen thought, *that poor woman never found happiness. And Ken, did he survive?* She didn't know. She had left them there after she had mentally persuaded every cop on the scene to forget that she was ever there and to ignore any mention of her, should it ever come about. Gwen had also flashed Ken a glance that forced him to forget her as well. She persuaded the cops to call an ambulance and get Ken to an emergency room right away.

An eerie sensation shook her. It as if she were someone who had walked out of the night, leaving nothing but death in her path. She didn't know how she could move on. Hoping that Marty would be there for her gave her the strength to come home, but that quickly faded when he had told her that he needed some time away from her.

"Fuck him," she had said. *I'm sorry, Marty. I didn't mean that.*

Now, a week later, it was early evening when she arrived at the gates to Eagle Park Cemetery. She eased the car through them and drove along the graveled path, listening to her instincts to tell her which grave would be Harry's. Her power to place thoughts in the minds of others and to *feel* her way into situations was depleting rapidly. There was just enough of that ability left to help her complete this one final task.

Stopping the car when it felt *right*, Gwen got out, threw her cigarette butt on the ground, and slowly walked alongside a long row of tombstones. Near the end of the row she found the one baring the name: Harry Thomas.

From the inside of her jacket she pulled out two roses. One red and one yellow. One for love and the other for friendship. Going down on one knee she leaned them against his tombstone then stood up again.

Standing there reminded her of when she had lost her friend Sue-Ellen to cancer five years ago. In fact, it was on a similar day as this one, with a hazy overshadow of clouds across the sky. She remembered that had been the first time she had ever truly felt sad. Now sadness and loss was commonplace in her life. She looked at Harry's grave, then at Lauren's. She decided to say a few words to Lauren first.

"You would be proud of your husband, Mrs. Thomas," she said. "There are so few people in this world who spend their entire lives doing what they feel they have to do. Harry taught me a lesson about that. About being your own person, and living out a dream. I'm sorry to have never had the chance to meet you, but be assured that Harry talked about you with such love, and that every time I heard him mention your name, tears pinched my eyes. I felt sorry for him. You were the only thing in his life that he had ever loved." She thought for a moment. Then, "I wonder if you had somehow been restless these past twenty-five years, knowing that everyday your husband was being tormented. At least, now, you can finally rest in peace. The both of you."

Gwen wiped a single tear from her eye and gave a quick sniffle. She thought of Harry and remembered the first time she had seen him. A man so disheveled in appearance, wearing his pajamas to the hospital cafeteria. She remembered the way he had quietly smiled at her when he entered that room so long ago. That would be the image she would always remember him by.

Her eyes fell on his tombstone.

"Well, Harry, what can be said? It's over. I did what you asked me to do. Calvin won't bother us anymore." She had already decided on her way to the cemetery not to tell him the truth about the boy's survival and Harry's murderer getting away. She figured it would be better this way. "It's too bad what happened to you, but don't worry, I made Sherman pay for it. It's going to be okay now. It's finally over. If you think of it, say hi to Lauren for me. She's a lucky woman." Gwen paused a moment, then, "I love you, Harry."

She choked as a few more tears spilled. After wiping her eyes, Gwen thought about Calvin and Sherman.

Somewhere, somehow, they were together. And, soon, the day will come when a grownup Calvin Mandalay will lead billions of people into the eternal, fiery lake of torment called Hell. The coming rise of the Antichrist was for a purpose. His job is to prepare the earth for the day the sky would split open, for the angels to sing, for Jesus Christ to return.

With one final, heavy glance, Gwen paid her respects to Harry and his wife, and then walked away.

It started to rain.

LAST NOTE

My original plan for this story was to tell a scary tale in four or five short stories. Well, obviously, it had become much more than that. A whole hell of a lot more. In the end a manuscript of a little over than four hundred pages was birthed.

Some of this book was written on the ol' computer, and some sitting behind a small table at Gourmet Cup in Winnipeg Square, gulping back hordes of Java, smoking too many cigarettes.

Throughout it all, four special people stayed with me before, during, and after each writing session: Gwen Reeves, Harry Thomas, Calvin Mandalay, and Sherman Gray.

These very different, though commonly linked individuals, had walked with me as I traveled along the road that is *A Stranger Dead* footstep by footstep, word by word, page by page. We talked along the way, told some jokes, and shared some scary stories. Actually, I should correct myself. They had done all the talking.

I only listened.

- A.P. Fuchs
April 11, 2002
Winnipeg, Manitoba

ABOUT THE AUTHOR

A.P. Fuchs lives in Winnipeg, Manitoba.

A Stranger Dead is his first novel. Its sister novel, *For the Cause*, is tentatively planned to be released in 2003.

For more on A.P. Fuchs, or to contact the author directly, visit him on-line at http://www.apfuchs.com.

Printed in the United States
25583LVS00003B/1-30